THE NEXT-DOOR ZOO

Eleanor Watkins

Scripture Union
130 City Road, London EC1V 2NJ.

By the same author
Sam's Kind of Dog

© Eleanor Watkins 1994

First published 1994

ISBN 0 86201 831 5

British Library Cataloguing-in-Publication Data.
A catalogue record for this book is available from the
British Library.

Phototypeset by Intype, London
Printed and bound in Great Britain by Cox & Wyman
Ltd, Reading

Chapter One

Jane ran round the side of the house, across the patio and stretch of lawn to plunge into the shrubbery beyond. Even there in the cool greenness she did not pause, but made a run for the rough stone wall at the far end. Feet scrabbling for toeholds among the stones, she pulled herself up on her stomach and heaved her legs over to let herself down on the other side. She heard a tearing sound as her jeans caught on a rough edge, but she didn't care. Her feet thumped down on the soft leaf mould and she staggered a little. Regaining her balance, she plunged into the wild tangle of brambles, lilacs, flowering currant and honeysuckle that grew on the other side of the wall. Only when she was quite enclosed by leaves and branches on all sides did she fling herself down, panting, to rest.

'Ja-ane!'

Aunt Dorothy's voice sounded far away, muffled by the greenery and the high dividing wall. 'Ja-ane! Jane! Where are you?'

Jane guessed that Aunt Dorothy was standing on the patio, peering about in her short-sighted way and frowning. She didn't answer.

All day Jane had been so excited she hardly knew

3

what to do with herself. This was the day she had been waiting for and looking forward to for months. Aunt Dorothy hardly knew what to do with her. She found her niece a handful at the best of times, and Jane in this mood almost drove her to distraction. So she had worked out a programme of jobs to keep Jane busy and occupied. First she had to tidy her room and put all her toys neatly away. After that she had dusted the already spotless sitting room. Then she had sliced cucumbers and tomatoes for the salad.

'Jane!' called Aunt Dorothy again. Jane burrowed deeper into the bushes. It had taken most of the afternoon to seize the opportunity to escape from Aunt Dorothy, and she wasn't going to give up her chance for freedom now. She refused to do any more boring jobs, while all the time Aunt Dorothy did the interesting things, like making up the brand new blue crib with freshly-aired small sheets and blankets, and decorating a special cake with a tiny white stork on top and the words 'Welcome home, William' in blue icing. Jane would love to have written those icing words herself, but of course Aunt Dorothy would not hear of it — just because she'd put her finger into the blue icing and licked it, to see if it tasted different from the white. Mean old Aunt Dot!

'Jane!' called her aunt's voice once more, now very cross. 'I know you're hiding! They'll be home in half an hour, and I want you in here, washed and in your clean clothes by then. Do you hear?'

Jane heard but did not answer. She saw no reason to wash and change in the middle of the afternoon. They weren't expecting visitors. It was just Dad bringing Mum home from the hospital with her new baby brother.

4

Bang! went the patio door and Jane grinned. Aunt Dot had gone back to her polishing and preparing. She would come out when she heard the car, not before, and be there waiting for Mum and Dad and William.

At the thought of William, her heart gave a funny little jump. She had waited more than nine years for a baby brother and now that he was here she couldn't quite believe it. She had already seen him, of course, when Dad took her to the hospital. She had even held him for a moment, a warm and quite heavy bundle in a white blanket, tiny hands tightly clenched, a tuft of dark hair on top of a pink, screwed-up face with eyes closed in sleep. He breathed with little snuffling sounds and smelt of baby cream.

He was very small, but Mum and Dad said he'd soon grow. Jane felt she could hardly wait. She would teach him everything and show him all the special places she knew.

Her legs were beginning to get pins and needles, and she uncurled herself and climbed to her feet. Her mind still on William, she parted the bushes and followed the little winding path out into the garden next door. She was quite safe here. The house was empty and no one knew she often climbed the wall and came to play here.

She skirted the overgrown lawn, where the grass was so long you could hide if you sat down in it, and went across to the horse chestnut tree. It was too late in the year for the little pink candles of bloom that came in spring, but too early yet for conkers. As soon as William was old enough to be hauled over the wall she would bring him here to collect conkers, and acorns from the big old oak in the hedge. They would hide behind the lilacs and spy on the squirrels coming down to scrabble in the grass for winter stores, or watch the thrush who had used the same large stone for tapping snail shells on for years. She would show him the secret den she had burrowed out for herself, right in the middle of the rhododendrons. They would have a lot of fun, she and her brother.

The garden was long and narrow, just like their own, but seemed larger because it had been allowed to grow wild while the house was empty. A robin had built its nest in the postbox beside the front door and had hatched a clutch of ten brown-speckled eggs. The nestlings were almost ready to fly now, grown large and filling the nest to bursting point. Jane was just about to go round and look at them when again there was the sound of a door slamming. This time it wasn't Aunt Dot. It was somewhere much closer at hand. It was the front door of the empty house.

Jane retreated to the shelter of the lilacs and peeped through. She hadn't noticed before, but the back door was slightly open too, and a couple of packing cases stood just outside. There was the sound of a voice calling and another answering, and quick footsteps on stairs. Then she saw something she hadn't noticed before. A black and white football, rather battered, lay just at the edge of the long grass where it had rolled from the patio.

Someone was moving into the empty house. And they had children. Jane retreated further into the bushes, feeling rather strange inside. The wild garden wouldn't be hers any more. It wouldn't be wild either. The new people would probably mow the grass and trim the shrubs and plant cabbages and spoil everything. The garden would belong to the new children, not to her and William.

Two things happened together, while she was still trying to decide how she felt about all this. The back door opened and a girl came out, a girl as blonde as Jane herself, but taller, dressed in jeans and a Snoopy T-shirt. She hooked her thumbs into her belt loops and stood staring out at the overgrown wilderness of a garden. In a sudden panic, Jane wondered if the girl could see through the leaves to her hiding place, but a voice called from inside and the fair-haired girl turned back towards the house.

At the same time, a car drew up and stopped next door outside Jane's own house. Dad and Mum – and William! They were back!

Jane forgot the girl, forgot that she shouldn't really be here, and ran for the shrubbery, where she heaved herself up and over the wall, grazing her hand a little and turning the small rip in the knee of her jeans into a very large one.

Chapter Two

'Oh! What a big, big yawn! Is he sleepy, then?'

'Let me hold him, dear. Come to Auntie then, precious! What a big boy!'

'Oh look, he's yawning again, the little sweet! There's a clever, clever boy!'

Jane stood in the sitting room, hardly able to believe she was hearing the silly, clucking baby talk that came from her mother and Aunt Dot, while they passed William between them like a well-wrapped parcel. She looked at Dad for support. But even Dad, clutching a folded blanket and a plastic bag of disposable nappies, had a foolish, doting smile on his face as he gazed at the sleeping face of his son.

Already the room seemed full of William's possessions. His carrycot stood beside the sofa, with his travelling bag leaning against it, bulging with baby necessities. A plastic changing-mat was on the coffee table, and heaps of parcels containing presents given to Mum in hospital were piled untidily on the floor. It had hardly been worth doing all that cleaning and tidying. Aunt Dot seemed as besotted as the two parents, seated beside Mum on the sofa and gazing adoringly into William's pink, screwed-up, sleeping face.

Jane went and sat on the other side of Mum, leaning close to remind her that she was still there, too. Mum put her free arm round Jane and gave her a squeeze and a kiss.

'How are you, darling? I can't get over how *big* you look! What have you been doing for the last two days?'

Jane relaxed, leaning against Mum's shoulder. She thought she would tell Mum about the new people next door, though without mentioning that she had been over the wall into their garden. She began, 'Mum, do you know we've got new neighbours?'

But Mum was fussing with William, touching his face to see if he was too warm and unwrapping the white shawl. She said absently, 'That's nice, dear. Would you like to hold him for a moment?'

Jane knew that Mum hadn't taken in a word she had said. She found William's warm, powdery weight being deposited on her lap. He squirmed a little and she held him gingerly while Mum kept a protective arm round them both.

Aunt Dot said, 'Be careful of his head, Jane. Always support the head.'

Dad had flopped into the big armchair and was beaming proudly at his family.

Suddenly William's back arched and his legs flailed. His small red hands formed into fists and beat the air. His mouth opened wide, so wide that Jane could see the little red quivering thing at the back of his throat, and a fearful roar came from it.

'Waah! Ah-waah! Ah-Waaah!'

Jane clutched him tighter, alarmed. She hadn't expected him to cry *this* loud. His face changed from pink to red to purple, and the yells got louder. '*Waaah!*

Ah-*Waaah*!'

The three adults were galvanized into action. 'Feeding time!' said Mum, taking William back from Jane. 'What a hungry boy! He needs changing, too. Pass me a nappy, would you, darling?'

Dad began fumbling about with the disposable nappies, trying to undo the plastic wrapper. Jane could see how the bag opened but she didn't say anything. Aunt Dot leapt up and made for the kitchen, remembering the tea, the special cake and scones and sandwiches. William's howls grew louder and his kicking more furious.

Jane got up. No one, not even Aunt Dot, noticed the hole in her jeans, or her hair screwed up in an old elastic band or even her grimy face. It was as though, all of a sudden, the only thing that mattered was William.

He wasn't quite what she had expected. She hadn't thought he would be quite so helpless, or need so much attention, or have such a loud piercing cry. He howled all the time Mum was changing him, and only stopped, with a snort and a snuffle, when she began to feed him.

From the kitchen Aunt Dot called, 'Jane! Come and help me carry in the sandwiches and plates, will you?'

'I don't want to,' said Jane under her breath. No one heard. Mum and Dad were both admiringly watching William as he guzzled.

'Like a greedy little pig!' said Jane, a little louder.

'What did you say, darling?' asked Mum, without turning her head. Jane didn't answer. She got up and wandered out through the hall and into the garden, avoiding the kitchen. The big removal van was just pulling away from next door. She could hear voices and laughter, and a door slammed.

11

An apple tree grew near the adjoining fence. Jane clambered up into its branches, just far enough to see over into next door's garden. The furniture had all been taken in, but a number of large packing cases stood on the path around the porch. A boy with red hair came and rummaged about in one of them, pulled out a teapot and kettle, and disappeared inside with them. A bigger boy appeared, picked up a cricket bat and took swipes at a pretend ball with it, hitting the air at different angles. Then he bowed low as though to acknowledge applause.

'Show-off!' muttered Jane grumpily. She felt rather miserable all of a sudden. Everything had somehow fallen flat. William was no fun. The secret garden wasn't hers any more. She decided that the next-door family was a horrid one. The girl in the Snoopy T-shirt looked stuck-up, the smaller boy's hair was an awful colour, and the big boy thought himself too wonderful for words. Even the tortoiseshell cat, who had appeared on the porch and sat down to wash itself in the sun, looked fat and smug.

'Jane!' called Aunt Dot from inside. She sounded very annoyed, and Jane heard her put down the tray with a crash. She pulled her legs up under her on the branch, so that she was hidden from view among the leaves. Why should she help to carry tea things when all her family cared about was William?

She hugged her knees and pressed her hot face against the rough bark of the trunk. The tree grew Bramley apples, cookers, delicious in pies or when Mum baked them until they were transparent and golden with a little well of melted brown sugar where the core had been. Thinking of baked apples made her hungry, but

12

she wasn't going in for tea yet. Anyway, they wouldn't miss her, now that they had William to fuss over.

The next-door family seemed to be having their tea, too. Everyone had gone inside and it was quiet. The cat curled up on the path and went to sleep.

Jane began to feel really hungry. There were little Bramley apples forming on the twigs, tiny and green. She tried one, but it was so hard and sour she spat it out again. To while away the time, she picked off one or two little apples and tossed them across the wall, seeing if she could wake the fat cat. They flew wide, landing in the long grass beside the path, and the cat just flicked an ear and slept on.

Jane threw a few more apples, until one of them landed in an open packing case and there was the sound of splintering glass. She slid down the tree quickly, slipped across the patio and round to the kitchen door. There was the clink of plates and hum of voices from the sitting room. As she had thought, no one had missed her. She searched for the sandwiches and scones, but they had all been taken in, so she opened the fridge and helped herself to a hunk of cheese and a cold baked potato left over from lunch.

Chapter Three

Next day, Jane found a kitten.

They had all had rather a disturbed night. Every time Jane had drifted off into a peaceful sleep, William had woken her with his howling. Maybe it had happened only two or three times, but it seemed to her that this had gone on all night.

So in the morning they slept late, even Aunt Dot, who had got up in the middle of the night to make tea for everyone. As a result, the adults were rather tired and grumpy, and the whole household seemed at sixes and sevens.

In the afternoon, Jane had just got comfortable on the sofa to watch cartoons, lying along the seat with her legs draped over one arm, when Aunt Dot came bustling in with the vacuum cleaner.

'Oh, Jane,' she said at once. 'You can't settle down there just now. I'm all behind with the cleaning. Do go out and get some fresh air. You've been mooning about the house all day.'

Jane pulled a face at her aunt's back as she turned away to plug in the cleaner. She didn't see why Aunt Dot couldn't go home, now that Mum was back and Dad was taking a few days off work. But Aunt Dot was staying until the end of the week.

She pretended she hadn't heard. Aunt Dot came over and switched off the TV. 'It's much too loud, anyway. Your mum's trying to take a nap, now that William's gone to sleep. Do go out and play for a while.'

Jane sighed. If she stayed indoors she was in the way. If she was outside her aunt would be sure to come calling her before long. She couldn't win. She gathered herself up from the sofa and headed glumly for the door.

Hands in pockets, she mooched across to the high dividing fence, from behind which interesting sounds came. The thump of running feet, a door slamming, voices calling, laughter. The next door children seemed to be having fun. *They* didn't have to keep quiet and out from under people's feet. *They* didn't have a bossy aunt or a new baby brother who everyone fussed over as though he was the only thing that mattered.

Jane was a little surprised at her own thoughts. She had wanted a brother for ages, but now he was here everything seemed wrong. He was no fun at all. She was just as lonely as ever, or even lonelier.

She found the kitten under a redcurrant bush at the edge of the shrubbery, between the compost heap and the garden shed. He was a tiny ball of black fluff with green eyes and a little red mouth. He cowered back among the leaves and spat when she crawled under and reached out to him. Jane pulled the sleeves of her sweatshirt down over her hands and picked him up anyway. Even so, his tiny claws pierced the fabric and drew blood. Jane sat under the bush and cuddled him, stroking his tiny head until he quietened a little. His green eyes stared up at her from a small triangular face, and her heart went out to him.

Jane had pleaded for a puppy for ages, but there had always been some argument against it. She wasn't quite old enough to be sensible with one. Puppies had to be carefully handled, trained and exercised. Their needs had to be considered always. They weren't toys to be put away when one got tired of them.

'But I wouldn't get tired of it,' Jane had protested.

'Well, we'll see – perhaps a bit later,' they had said.

Maybe, just maybe, they would agree to a kitten. She would have to go about it carefully though. No use asking Aunt Dot, and Dad had gone out with a long shopping list. Mum was the person to ask.

She waited, holding the kitten curled up and asleep in her lap, until she heard William cry from indoors and knew that Mum would be awake. Aunt Dot had finished cleaning and was hanging out Babygro suits and cot sheets on the rotary washing line near the patio. Keeping to the other side of the house, Jane put the kitten into the garden shed and carefully closed the door. Then she went to find Mum.

Mum was sitting in a low chair with her feet on a stool, feeding William. That seemed to be her main occupation in life these days. An empty teacup stood at her elbow. Mum was always very thirsty when she fed William, which was only to be expected, thought Jane. The liquid that William drank had to be replaced somehow. Mum had to be topped up, like a half-empty teapot. She put her head round the door and asked, 'Would you like a glass of lemonade, Mum?'

Mum smiled. 'That's just what I would like, darling. A large glass. And put an ice-cube in.'

When Jane brought the lemonade, Mum took a long

drink and put down the glass. She put her free arm round Jane. 'Thanks, darling. That was lovely. Come and tell me what you've been doing. I've hardly seen you all day. Do you know we've got new neighbours? With children?'

It was nice to sit quietly with Mum, listening to the little snorts and gulps that William made as he drank. A light fluff of dark hair stood up on his head.

'But he'll be fair,' said Mum. 'Just like you. He's got fair eyebrows. See? And I think his eyes will be blue like yours, too.'

Mum showed her William's tiny perfect fingernails, and his little pink toes curling and uncurling. 'I know he's small, and helpless, and can't do much yet,' she said, 'but you'll be surprised how quickly he grows. By the time you start back to school in September he'll be smiling at you. You'll see.'

'Will he really?' asked Jane, and Mum nodded. Jane put her finger into William's little hand and his fingers tightened round it.

'Do you think he knows I'm his sister?' she asked.

'I'm sure he does,' said Mum.

Jane remembered the black kitten. She took back her finger and sat up straight. 'Mum, could I have a kitten?'

Mum had put William upright against her shoulder and was stroking his back to bring up his wind.

'A kitten? Well . . . no, I don't think that's a good idea. Not just at the moment. You have to be very careful with cats and babies together. Sometimes a cat will climb into a pram and sit on a baby's face. It wouldn't be safe, not until William's bigger.'

Jane's heart flopped with disappointment. She might have known! She tried again. 'But it's not a cat, not

18

really, just a teeny, tiny little black kitten! And he's all alone. I'd be very careful.'

William burped loudly and Mum said, 'There . . . what a good boy!'

If I did that I'd be sent away from the table, thought Jane. She said, 'Please, Mum, please!'

Mum said firmly. 'No, Jane. We can't take chances. And if you've found a kitten, then it belongs to someone. You must find out who and take it back. Very likely it belongs to the new people next door and has wandered across somehow. Go and ask. It would be nice to make friends with those children, wouldn't it?'

No, thought Jane. It wouldn't. They're all horrid, and it's not their cat. Theirs is a great, fat, speckled one. I wanted this one. It's not fair. Nothing's fair.

But she didn't say any of these things. Instead, she swung her feet and kicked them against the base of the sofa, thump, thump, thump.

'Jane!' Mum was beginning to sound annoyed. 'That is most irritating! And do stop sulking! Get the kitten you've found, take it round next door and ask politely if it's theirs. Go along now.'

The kitten was behind a sack of potting compost, curled up fast asleep on a piece of sacking. Jane picked him up and held his fluffy warm body against her cheek. He had quite got over being afraid of her and broke into a squeaky little purr. She carried him out into the sunlight, round to the front gate and in through the gate of the house next door.

Chapter Four

The door was answered by a brown and white spaniel, or so it seemed to Jane, though perhaps it was the boy who closely followed the dog who had actually turned the knob.

The spaniel's ears pricked with joy at the sight of the kitten, its tail wagged furiously and a big doggy grin spread across its face. But the black kitten didn't share the dog's enthusiasm at all. With a terrified meow it turned to clutch Jane with all four claws and clung like a burr to the front of her sweatshirt. The dog, not to be put off, bounded from the doorway towards Jane and tried to jump up with its forelegs against her. Jane staggered back, clutching the kitten protectively, quite overwhelmed by this welcome.

'Spam!' said the boy sternly. 'Stop that!'

He dived after the dog and grabbed it by its collar. 'Sorry,' he panted. 'He's a bit naughty with cats – ones he isn't used to.'

He gave the dog a smack on its rear and pointed sternly through the open door. The dog sat down on its behind and wagged its tail at him.

'Sorry,' said the boy again. 'He's only young, and we're trying to train him. But he's a bit slow learning.

Sorry he frightened your kitten. What's its name?'

'Oh!' said Jane, rather breathlessly, trying to dislodge the kitten's claws which were beginning to dig into her shoulder. 'I don't know. I mean . . . he's not mine, not really. I thought he might be yours. I found him in our garden.'

She waved her free hand towards her own house. The boy's brow furrowed into a frown, and then he grinned. He wasn't the big boy with the cricket bat, nor was he the red-haired one, though he looked a bit like both of them. This boy had untidy fair hair and a few freckles across his nose. He was about Jane's size.

He said, 'Oh, a stray kitten. Well, if nobody claims him you can keep him, can't you? Then he'll be yours. Get down!'

This was to the dog, who had sprung up and tried to make another dart for the kitten as soon as he saw that the boy's attention was elsewhere. The kitten yowled and spat. The boy grabbed the dog's collar and dragged it to the door, pushed it inside, closed the door and came back to Jane.

'Sorry,' he said. This seemed to be his favourite word. 'He's a bit naughtier than usual because we've only just moved.'

Jane nodded. She was relieved to find the kitten had taken its claws out of her sweatshirt – and her skin. The boy reached out to stroke it and, to her surprise, it began to purr almost at once. 'It's nice,' he said. 'I'd keep it if I were you.'

'I can't,' said Jane. 'We've got a new baby. They won't let me.'

The boy pulled a sympathetic face. 'That's a pity. Never mind, we'll keep it if you can't. Then you can

22

come and play with it every day if you like.'

'I thought you had a cat already,' said Jane, 'and what about the dog?'

'Spam? Oh, they'd soon get used to each other. He's all right with our cats. We've got three. And two rabbits. And a goat. And chickens. We used to have a monkey.'

Jane could feel her eyes growing rounder and rounder.

'You lucky thing!' she said enviously. 'I can't have anything until William's bigger, not even a puppy.'

The boy looked sympathetic again. 'Well, you can play with all of ours if you like. What's your name?'

'Jane,' said Jane. She was about to ask the boy's name, but her question was answered before she had time to ask it. An upstairs window flew open and the big boy, the one with the cricket bat, stuck his head out. 'Tim! Where's that paint brush I asked you to bring up about twenty minutes ago?'

'Sorry!' said Tim. 'I forgot. I'll bring it now.'

He began to head for the door, and then turned back to Jane. 'What are you going to do with the kitten?'

Jane hadn't thought. 'I don't know.'

'Tell you what,' said the boy, with his hand on the door knob. 'Bring him in here. We'll keep him for now. Come on.'

Jane hesitated. She wasn't sure Mum and Dad would approve of her going into strange people's houses, even if they were the people next door.

'What about Spam?' she asked doubtfully.

'Oh, I'll soon fix him! Come on. We'll find a nice basket for it. Only I'll have to take that brush for Paul first. He's painting our bedroom.'

Somehow Jane found herself following Tim into the house, still holding the kitten. He led her down the hallway into a large kitchen where the spaniel seemed to have fallen fast asleep in front of a large wood-burning stove. It opened one eye when they came in but, to Jane's great relief, took no further notice.

The room was huge, much bigger than their own small, streamlined kitchen. Sun poured in from the large window overlooking the garden. Packing cases stood about, half-unpacked, and there was a big wooden table with books and dishes and utensils piled higgledy-piggledy upon it. Something bubbled in a saucepan on the stove, and there was a meaty cooking smell mingling with a strong smell of paint. From a room beyond came the tinkling of a piano.

Then the tinkling stopped for a moment, and a girl's voice called, 'Tim! Give the stew a stir, will you?'

Almost at the same moment a roar sounded from upstairs. 'Tim! I want that paintbrush – now!'

Tim pulled a face. He picked up a wooden spoon and pushed it into Jane's free hand. 'Just stir it, could you? Won't be a minute.'

He rummaged about in a box, pulled out a paintbrush and disappeared. There was the sound of pounding feet on uncarpeted stairs, the slam of a door and voices above. The piano tinkled on. Not knowing what else to do, Jane took the lid off the saucepan and stirred the bubbling brown stew inside.

The back door opened and the red-haired boy came in, his face rather grimy looking and Wellington boots on his feet. He took off his glasses and blinked at Jane, but didn't seem surprised to see a strange girl standing there stirring stew with one hand and holding a kitten with the other.

'Have you seen my exercise book about anywhere?'

24

he asked, rummaging through a pile of books on one corner of the table. 'A red one?'

Jane shook her head, suddenly shy. The exercise book could be in any one of the boxes, tea-chests and piles of books that were waiting to be put away, she thought.

The red-haired boy looked disappointed. 'Only I've just had a good idea for the start of the next chapter of the story I'm writing. It just came to me planting lettuces.'

A thundering on the stairs announced that Tim was on his way down. He burst into the kitchen with an ancient looking cat-basket in one hand. 'This'll do for the kitten. We'll find a nice, safe, comfortable place for it.'

The red-haired boy frowned at him. 'I don't know how Dad can work with all the racket you and Paul are making.'

'He isn't working,' said Tim, 'so it doesn't matter. He's getting his study fixed up. Here, Jane, put the kitten in there.'

Jane was surprised to find that the kitten, after licking up a saucer of milk, was quite happy to settle down in the basket. Tim placed it on top of the large kitchen dresser, just in case Spam got interested again. The red-haired boy came over to the stove and peered rather vaguely into the saucepan. 'Is it nearly ready, do you think?'

'I – I don't know,' said Jane, overcome again with shyness. 'I'm only stirring it . . .'

'You can stop now,' said Tim. 'It'll be okay for a bit. Thanks.'

The red-haired boy drifted to the fridge and took out an apple and a piece of cheese. He began to eat, taking an alternate bite from each while he sat at the cluttered table and read a book at the same time. The piano player had stopped the tinkling tune and was playing a scale, up and down, over and over. Voices sounded from upstairs.

Jane thought she had better go home, though she would love to have seen the rabbits and the goat and the other animals. Had Tim really mentioned a monkey? She peeped from the window, but the only animals to be seen were the same tortoiseshell cat she had seen before, and a gingery one, basking in the sun on the warm flagstones. Where could the others be?

'I'd better go now,' she said.

'All right,' said Tim. 'Come another day, if you like. You could see how the kitten's getting on. The other animals will be here tomorrow. Julia, and Hansel and Gretel, and the hens. We only brought Spam and the cats in the car with us. Come to tea if you like. Ask your mum and dad.'

Saying goodbye to the kitten, Jane noticed a red exercise book that had slipped down between the dresser and a crate of books. She picked it up. It said 'SKY VOYAGE by Mark Willis, aged 12' on the cover in black felt-tip pen. She hesitated for a moment, then went back and offered it shyly to the red-haired boy. 'Is this the one you were looking for?'

He took it with a dazzling smile. 'Thanks! That's great! I hoped it wasn't lost, because I've done twelve chapters already and I didn't want to start all over again!'

He looked so pleased that Jane felt ashamed that she'd ever had unkind thoughts about him. He was very nice, and his hair was quite a nice shade of red, close to. He was almost as nice as Tim. She didn't know

26

about the big boy upstairs painting, or the girl playing the piano, or their mum and dad, but probably, when you got to know them, they were a very nice family altogether. She was quite glad they had come to live next door.

Chapter Five

'Chickens?' said Dad next afternoon. He raised his eyebrows and went on, 'Goats? Rabbits? Do we still live on a private housing estate, or has it turned into a small-holding or something without me noticing?'

Jane could tell that Dad was being funny, but he looked a bit put out as well. Mum, holding William, definitely had an anxious expression.

'I don't think it sounds very hygienic, all those animals just over the fence. William will be sleeping out on the patio in his pram. What about all the germs the animals might carry?'

She wrapped him a little closer in the shawl, as though to protect him. Jane imagined the germs, like hordes of little black insects with busy wings, swooping over the wall from next door and buzzing hungrily about the garden.

She said quickly, 'I expect the animals will be nice and clean. We'll hardly know they're there. We haven't heard anything of them yet, have we?'

'Well, no,' admitted Mum. 'But it does seem rather unusual to have such a menagerie in a suburban garden.'

Jane was glad she hadn't mentioned the monkey. She said, 'They just like animals, that's all. They're a very nice family. Can I go to tea with them, please? I'd like to see the kitten.'

Mum seemed to feel rather badly about not having allowed her to keep the kitten. She and Dad looked at each other, and Mum said, 'Well, I expect it'll be all right, as we're going to be neighbours. Tell Tim's mum and dad that we'll drop in and introduce ourselves in a day or two.'

Jane didn't mention that she hadn't met Tim's mum and dad herself yet. William gave a sudden yell, his little face turning red, and Mum said anxiously, 'Oh dear, he seems to have got a pain in his tummy again. Do you think we ought to call the doctor?'

While Mum and Dad were bending over William, Jane slipped out, avoiding Aunt Dot pegging out more washing. Tim hadn't said what time to come. She was sure he wouldn't mind that it was only three o'clock.

She thought it would be quicker, and much more fun, to go next door by way of the dividing wall in the shrubbery, the way she had always entered the garden. Even before she had pushed her way through the undergrowth, she became aware of great activity in the next-door garden – voices, laughter, barking and an excited cackling of chickens. Emerging from the overgrown shrubs, she found herself face to face with a large white goat, tethered to a post and stretching upwards to eat the leaves of a straggly raspberry bush. It turned to look at her with raspberry leaves dangling from its jaws, and bleated a friendly, if muffled, greeting.

Jane had never been this close to a goat before. Its coat looked very hairy and rough. It had amber-coloured eyes and a little white beard growing from its chin. It stared at her for quite a long time, but never stopped chomping the leaves. A few overripe raspberries were going down as well. It gulped and swallowed, and turned aside to find another spray of leaves.

Spam was barking excitedly and prancing round a large crate on the grass, which Jane could see held chickens. Every so often a chicken's head popped up from between the slats, cackled in alarm and disappeared again. The red-haired boy Mark was sitting on the grass beside the crate and appeared to be trying to soothe the ruffled feelings of the inmates. Tim and Paul were hammering at the fastenings of a rather ramshackle shed against the garden wall furthest away from Jane's house. As she watched, Paul flung down the hammer and said, 'There! That'll do. Now let's get them in. Tim, go and help Mark carry the crate over here.'

Jane wondered whether Tim was always the one to be ordered about by the others because he was the youngest. Maybe she'd be ordering William about in a year or two. She stepped out of the shelter of the lilacs and walked cautiously past the goat.

'Hello, Jane!' said Tim. He looked very hot and red in the face, but cheerful. 'Just in time to see the hens moving in. Shut up, Spam! You're a real pain! Would you hold him for a minute, Jane?'

Jane held on to Spam's collar while the three boys carried the crate with its cackling occupants over to the shed, opened the lid with care, caught the chickens one by one and transferred them to the shed. Almost hysterical by now, they fled squawking to the darkest corner of their new home.

'Rhode Island Reds,' said Paul, closing the door on the last one. 'They'll settle in a bit. Hens are such stupid things, always panicking and getting in a flap. Just like girls.' He grinned as he said it, and Jane knew he was teasing. He picked up his hammer and went indoors.

'We're going to make a run for them later,' said Tim. 'A big one, and a smaller one for the rabbits. Then we keep moving them round the lawn and they keep the grass short. Saves a lot of mowing.'

Jane thought that was a very clever idea. She thought it would be much nicer to have pets in runs on their own lawn, instead of the noisy mower and even noisier strimmer that Dad used so regularly.

'How's the kitten?' she asked.

'Oh fine,' said Tim. 'Still a bit nervous of Spam, so it sits on the top shelf of the dresser most of the time at the moment. But Spam's used to him now, so he'll soon be able to come down. I've called him Smut.'

A large hutch beside the hen house held rabbits, one black and one white, with floppy ears and twitchy noses.

'Hansel and Gretel,' said Tim. 'Would you like to hold one?'

Jane would. Cuddling warm, floppy Gretel, the white rabbit, she looked round the untidy garden where she had so often played her solitary games. Now it seemed filled with life and action. Animal houses at one side, a patch of newly-turned earth, with little lettuces and cabbage plants, at the other. A goat in the shrubbery, a spaniel panting at their feet, two – no, three – cats asleep on the wall, and Mark lying on his stomach scribbling in an exercise book.

She stroked Gretel's silken ears and asked, 'Are you going to make flower beds and things, and make it all neat and tidy?'

Tim grinned. 'No way! We'll plant some flowers,

p'raps – bulbs and the kinds of plants that look after themselves. But mostly we'll grow vegetables and useful things. And leave a good patch of grass for football and cricket.'

Jane sighed with relief. She couldn't have borne it if the garden had become like any other suburban garden, all trim and tidy. She said, 'I'll help, if you like.'

Then she blushed, in case Tim thought it was cheek. But he only said, 'Thanks. We all have to help, and it does take time.'

They were both sitting on the unmown grass, with a rabbit each to stroke. Mark took no notice of them at all, scribbling away with a green pen and muttering to himself. Jane wondered about Tim's parents, who never seemed to be about. 'Don't your mum and dad do any of the work?' she asked curiously.

Tim stroked Hansel's black silky ears. 'I haven't got a mum. She died when I was little. Dad has his own work to do, to make money for all of us. It takes nearly all his time, except week-ends, and even then he sometimes has to work on Saturdays, doing research. We had a home-help in our old house, and I expect we'll get one here. Only there's still a lot to do.' He rolled over and pretended to pounce on Hansel, who kicked up his legs and frisked away just out of reach.

Jane sat quite still, suddenly feeling cold in spite of the hazy sunshine. Tim's mum was dead! Some of her friends had mums and dads who were divorced, which meant that one or the other of them had gone away to live. But she had never met anyone whose mum had died. She felt her eyes grow round with horror.

'What's the matter?' asked Tim, squinting up at her. 'You look all funny. Did Gretel scratch you?'

Jane shook her head. She couldn't tell Tim that she wanted to run home to her own mum, just to make sure she was still alive and well. She looked at Tim and wondered how he could be so cheerful and freckled and ordinary when such a dreadful thing had happened to him. He rolled over again and grabbed the black rabbit. 'Come on. Let's put them back and see if tea's ready. You can stay, can't you?'

Jane pulled herself together. 'Oh, yes.'

'Good!' said Tim. 'Come on then. I'll race you. Last one to the rabbit hutch is a wally!'

Chapter Six

Someone had been working very hard in the kitchen since the day before. The boxes of books had disappeared, and there were only one or two cases of assorted kitchen utensils waiting to be unpacked. The huge table had been cleared and was covered with a bright yellow plastic tablecloth to match the yellow-striped curtains that had appeared at the window. A vase of blue lupin spikes stood on the window sill.

The black kitten was curled asleep on the top shelf of the dresser among a fine collection of blue willow-pattern plates. When Spam followed the children into the room, it opened an eye and watched warily for a moment, but soon closed it again. Spam ignored the kitten and flopped down in front of the stove.

'See,' said Tim. 'They're getting used to each other. I told you they would.'

Jane had to admit that Tim really knew about animals. She asked, 'Did you really have a monkey once?'

He nodded. 'Yes. A zoo near where we lived wanted someone to look after a baby one. He was just like a real baby, with nappies and a bottle and everything.'

Jane was sure that a baby monkey would be much more fun than a human baby. She said enviously, 'You lucky thing! What happened to it?'

'Oh, it grew up and got a bit naughty. It used to climb up the curtains and on the furniture, and throw things down – plates, and ornaments, and pictures and plants. It specially liked pulling plants to pieces and eating them! Then one day it unscrewed a lightbulb and put its finger into the socket and nearly electrocuted itself. We had to send it back to the zoo. It was always sorry when it had been naughty, and used to go and sit in a corner with a blanket over its head. It didn't mean any harm. But Dad said it had to go because it was getting to be a danger to itself and everyone around it.'

'What a shame!' Jane felt quite indignant on behalf of the poor monkey.

A door flew open and the fair-haired girl bustled in from an adjoining pantry with a breadboard full of ham sandwiches in one hand and a plate holding a huge fruit cake in the other. She looked rather pink and warm, and her fair hair escaped in little damp tendrils from her pony-tail.

She said, 'Hello, you must be Jane. The one who found the kitten? Thought so. Tea's ready. D'you like strawberry-flavoured milk shakes? Good! You're not a vegetarian, are you? Thank goodness for that, 'cos there was only ham to go in the sandwiches. Just help yourself. I expect the others'll be in, but I've got to practise.' She chattered on, asking questions and answering herself, hardly drawing breath while she mixed milkshakes at a furious pace and dumped plates on the table. Then she disappeared into the next room, and next moment there was the sound of a piano's tinkling notes.

Tim drew up a sturdy pine chair to the table for Jane and another for himself. 'Is that your sister?' asked

Jane as they sat down.

'Yes,' said Tim. 'Lisa. Have a sandwich.'

He helped himself to one and took a large bite. The tinkling turned suddenly into a bright, galloping tune that made Jane want to get up and dance. She took a sandwich instead, and said, 'She's a good piano player, isn't she?'

'Mmm,' said Tim, with his mouth full. 'She's going to be a concert pianist. But she's not a very good cook.' He wolfed down the last bite and took another sandwich. 'There's too much bread and not enough ham in these. Have a piece of cake. Paul made it. He cooks better than Lisa.'

Jane remembered watching Paul over the wall on the day they'd moved in, waving a cricket bat in a very professional way. 'Is Paul going to be a famous cricket player?' she asked.

Tim looked at her in surprise. 'No. Whatever made you think that? He's going to be a painter.'

'Oh, yes,' said Jane, remembering that Paul had been painting a bedroom upstairs the day before. She thought about the painter and decorator who had done William's nursery, and said, 'Has he been practising on your bedroom?'

'Not that kind of painter, silly,' said Tim, whose mouth was now full of cake. 'One who does pictures, I mean. An artist. That's one of Paul's over there.' He nodded towards a picture on the window seat, leaning against the sill waiting to be put up. It showed a bare winter tree with dark branches against a background of grey skies and light snow, so realistic that Jane almost shivered.

'It's lovely,' she said admiringly, and thought what a

clever family they were. 'What are you going to be?' she asked.

'A vet,' said Tim, 'of course.'

There was the sound of footsteps on the stairs, and a tall man came into the room. He looked a bit like Tim and a bit like Paul, and Jane could see at once where Mark got his red hair from, though his father's was not such a bright red and had a touch of grey in it. He wore glasses and smiled kindly at Jane. 'Hello. Who are you?'

'It's Jane, Dad,' said Tim, 'from next door. I told you about her. Remember?'

'Oh yes,' said Tim's dad, running his hand through his hair. 'Nice to meet you, Jane.' He picked up a slice of cake and devoured it at a bite, wandering over to look out of the window. Lisa's galloping tune had turned to a serious, thumpy one.

'Da da da Da, da da da Da!' hummed Tim's dad along with the tune, in a thoughtful kind of way.

'Beethoven's Ninth,' said Tim. He sucked up the last of his milkshake with a loud slurping sound.

'Must you do that?' said his dad mildly. 'Jenny will think you have no manners.'

'Jane,' said Tim. 'Are you having trouble with work, Dad?'

'I am rather,' said Tim's dad. 'A bit of a block. It's probably because of the move. I don't quite know where the plot goes next. And I have a problem with my wpc. I'll have to ring up the . . .'

He was interrupted by the sudden stop in mid-chord of Beethoven's Ninth, followed by a piercing shriek from Lisa in the next room. Tim leapt to his feet and made for the door. Jane, after a moment's hesitation, followed. Lisa had jumped up from the piano and run to the window. 'Julia!' she said. 'She's got loose! You'll have to get her back, Tim.'

Jane saw that the white-haired goat had somehow got free of its tether and had munched its way through the lilacs and gooseberry bushes until it reached the high wall between its own garden and Jane's next door. It had managed to climb, leap or scramble right onto the wall, where it now stood teetering with all four hooves close together, and peering down with interest into Jane's garden. In another moment it would leap down right into the flower border.

'Oh dear!' said Jane in horror. 'What'll Dad say?'

'Come on!' said Tim, heading for the door.

Tim's father looked not at all concerned, as though this sort of thing happened quite often in his household.

'Well, I'll leave you to it,' he said, making for the stairs again. 'I'm sure you'll manage to sort it out between you. Nice to meet you, Janet. Come again.'

He disappeared into a room at the top of the stairs. Jane followed Tim, noticing that Mark had fallen asleep with his exercise book over his face, and had noticed nothing amiss.

They approached Julia carefully, afraid that too sudden a movement would make her jump down on the other side of the wall. The goat looked at them, bleated tremulously and turned to gaze longingly at the bedding plants next door. She shifted her feet as though preparing to spring down at any minute, and Jane held her breath, hoping against hope that Aunt Dot wasn't pegging out more washing on the line.

But the goat couldn't quite make up its mind to jump, and next moment Tim had grabbed it by its trailing rope.

He gave a gentle tug and, to Jane's great relief, Julia decided to stay on her own side of the wall. She sprang down, giving Tim a gentle butt with her hard little head. Tim examined the end of the rope.

'Thought so. She's chewed it through again. We'll have to get a chain. Come on, Julia. Into the shed with you.'

The goat allowed itself to be fastened up in the garden shed which, Tim explained, was its temporary home until a proper goat shed could be built. They gave her a handful of sheep-nuts and some hay, and scratched her ears for a treat.

'She's friendly most of the time,' said Tim, 'but it's best not to turn your back on her. Specially if you happen to be bending down at the time. If you do that she thinks you're just asking to be butted. But she only means it in fun.'

Jane hoped she would remember. She didn't fancy a butt from Julia's hard bony head, whether meant in fun or otherwise.

Tim decided that they might as well feed the chickens now, so he fetched barley and filled the hens' food dishes and water container. The hens had got over their panic and had settled into their new home. They were sitting on their perches with their feathers fluffed out, cawing thoughtfully.

After doing the hens, Tim and Jane gathered fresh green dandelions, which abounded in the jungly part of the garden, and fed them to Hansel and Gretel. By the time they'd finished, the ginger and the tortoiseshell cats along with another, smokey-grey one, were winding themselves round Tim's legs and purring ingratiatingly.

'All right,' said Tim. 'I'll get you your suppers, too.

And I suppose I might as well feed Spam while I'm at it.'

Jane helped him to dish out the cat and dog food into the right bowls. The sun was going down now, and the shadows getting longer across the grass. Mark had put away his red exercise book and was watering the little plants in the vegetable bed beside the fence.

Going inside to wash her grimy hands, Jane thought that she hadn't enjoyed herself so much in ages. Aunt Dot would probably make her have a bath and wash her hair, but even that couldn't spoil such a lovely afternoon.

From the sitting-room came the soothing notes of Lisa playing a lullaby.

Chapter Seven

'Dad, what's a wpc?' asked Jane.

Dad gave a jump, and opened his eyes guiltily. He was lying full-length on the settee with his head on a cushion and a book called *The Darkest Night* by P. Grenville lying open face-down on his chest. However, Jane knew that he had been sound asleep, even though it was ten o'clock in the morning.

Dad picked up the book and turned a page, as though he'd been reading it all the time. 'Just catching up on the old library book. What did you say, pumpkin?' He gave a mighty yawn, and Jane forgave him for pretending. She knew that William had been crying in the night again.

'I said, what's a wpc?' she repeated.

'A wpc? Oh . . . a Woman Police Constable . . . a lady policeman,' said Dad, stifling another yawn. 'Why do you ask?'

'I just wondered,' said Jane, turning over this information in her mind. She had been wondering about those three initials since the day before when Tim's dad, Mr Willis, had said he worked with a wpc. A lady policeman. That must mean he was a policeman himself.

Her mind raced. Tim had said his dad worked from

43

an office at home and sometimes did research on Saturdays. Jane wasn't sure what research was, but wondered if it could mean searching for something. Clues maybe? Was Tim's dad a very high-up important policeman working on a secret case? Her heart gave a little jump of excitement.

A furious hammering sound came in through the open window. Dad groaned and closed the book, lowering his legs to the floor. He had a hunted look. 'Oh no! Can't a chap get a bit of peace anywhere? Whatever are those people next door doing?'

'I think they're building a goat pen,' said Jane, 'or it might be a chicken run.'

Maybe they would let her fetch and carry, and hold the nails, or even hammer a few in herself. She began to sidle towards the door, but her escape was cut off by Aunt Dot, coming out from the kitchen and pouncing on her.

'Ah, *there* you are! Go and get a clean dress on, because I'm going into town to do some shopping and I'll take you along to get those new sandals you need.'

'I don't need new sandals,' said Jane quickly. 'My old ones are perfectly good. They're not worn out at all.'

'Nonsense!' said Aunt Dot. 'They're far too small. The straps are beginning to cut into your feet. And you need some new school blouses for next term. It'll save your mum traipsing round the shops with the pram later, when I've gone home. Come along now. It'll keep you nicely occupied for the morning.'

Jane pulled a face at Aunt Dot behind her back, but it was no good arguing.

On the way into town she stared out of the bus window and thought of the fun she was missing. She imagined the Rhode Island hens scratching about their new run, all six of them – Rhoda, Rosie, Rita, Renée, Ria and Roberta. She recited their names under her breath, learning them by heart. The goat was called Julia, the dog Spam, the ginger cat was called Pomeroy, the smokey one Peabody, the tortoiseshell one Tibby and the new kitten Smut. The rabbits were Hansel and Gretel.

That was all the animals, so she started on the people next. Paul, the eldest, was going to be a painter and was fifteen. Lisa was fourteen and going to be a concert pianist. Mark was twelve and wrote stories, and Tim was ten and a half, and going to be a vet. Her thoughts came round again to Mr Willis. Was he really a detective? Maybe she would ask Tim. But, if his dad was working on an important mystery, he wouldn't be allowed to tell. Then again, maybe he would, because they were already friends. This thought gave her a kind of warm glow inside, despite the boring shopping trip.

'That's better, Jane,' said Aunt Dot approvingly. 'You can't imagine the difference it makes when you smile instead of scowling all the time.'

Jane's scowl had returned by the time the morning was over. She trailed round the shops after Aunt Dot, scuffing the toes of her trainers, until her Aunt said she was quite ashamed to take her into shoe shops in such footwear. She refused to take any interest in the school uniform that they picked out. She was sulky in the supermarket, even though Aunt Dot allowed her to push the trolley. She was morose over the milkshake Aunt Dot bought her while she had a coffee herself.

It was lunch time when they reached home, and all was quiet both in Jane's home and next door. But they had hardly finished their strawberry ice cream dessert when the hammering started again. Bang! Bang! Bang bang bang! William jumped in his pram and gave a startled whimper.

'Oh dear!' said Mum, looking worried. 'I hoped they'd finished that for the day. How on earth are William and I going to get our naps this afternoon?'

Dad banged down his coffee mug. 'It's really too much! All morning they've been at it, and now they start again. Don't they realize there's a young baby here? I'll have to go round!'

'I'll go,' said Jane quickly. 'They'll stop if I explain. They've probably forgotten all about William being here.'

She slipped from her chair and made for the door at once, before they could raise any objections.

She found Paul and Mark doing the hammering, knocking nails into a large, low construction of timber and wire netting, which she thought must be the chicken run because Julia was too tall to get into it. Lisa was hanging out jeans and T-shirts, socks and underwear on a washing line. She was watched with interest by Julia, tethered just out of reach.

Lisa greeted Jane with a friendly smile, shouting a little above the hammering. 'Hello! Have you come to find Tim? Thought so. He's out, but he won't be long. You can wait a bit, can't you? Good. Would you mind passing pegs to me? I have to keep the washing well out of Julia's reach, otherwise she'll eat it! Once she ate up two teacloths, a vest and half a shirt of Dad's! She had hiccups after, but that's all.'

Lisa kept up the flow of chatter all the time she was

46

pegging out garments with pegs passed by Jane. Julia watched, looking as though she would love to get her teeth into a T-shirt or a towel. The hammering stopped suddenly, and Jane remembered the reason for her visit. She said, feeling suddenly shy, 'Could you please ask them to hammer a bit quieter, because our baby has to sleep in the afternoons.'

"Course,' said Lisa. 'I didn't know you had a baby. You should have said before. I quite like babies myself. Is it quite new? Thought so. They get used to noises as they grow older.'

She picked up the washing basket and marched over to her brothers. 'Hey, you two! Shut up, can you, 'cos the baby next door can't sleep with that row going on. Well, I'm going in to practise.'

She disappeared into the house. The two boys looked at Jane, who felt very small and nervous. She wished Tim was there too. Paul pushed back his hair from his perspiring forehead. 'Sorry. Didn't know about the baby! Does it sleep *all* day?'

'Only afternoons,' said Jane quickly. 'Mornings and evenings don't matter so much.'

'We've finished the run, anyway,' said Mark. 'Just about. The goat shed's next. We can stick to mornings and evenings, can't we, Paul?'

'Course,' said the big boy. 'Tell your mum sorry from us, Jane. Can you give us a hand with this run now you're here?'

Between them they dragged the run over to the hen-house, lodged it securely against the front of it and opened the small door for the hens to come out. The hens emerged reluctantly, popping out their red-combed heads and withdrawing them hastily at first, to have a

47

nervous, cackling little conference just inside. But they came out at last, lifting their yellow feet high, and cawing long and thoughtfully, as they picked their way around the pen, pecking curiously at the grass. At last they decided that the run was a very pleasant place to be, and began to scratch and peck at the grass in earnest. One of them – Jane thought it was Rosie, but it was hard to tell – found a patch of nice dry dust and settled into it, fluffing out her feathers for a dust bath.

Paul gave an imitation of a clucking hen. 'Cl-urk, cluck cluck cluck! Isn't this a de-lightful place, my dears! Such excellent quality dust! Do join me for an invigorating bath!'

He scooped up a handful of dust and sprinkled it on to Mark's red hair. Mark let out a yell. He gathered up a handful himself and tried to stuff it down the back of Paul's T-shirt. The two of them began to scuffle on the grass.

Jane stood back, alarmed. She was half-afraid they were really fighting, except that now and then one of them let out a stifled giggle or said, 'Cl-urk cluck cluck!' in a silly voice. She had been going to ask them where Tim was, but didn't dare speak to the two wrestling figures, all threshing limbs and hard, bony elbows and knees. She edged away from them towards the house. Boys were strange creatures, especially when they were so much bigger than she was. She would go and find Lisa.

Lisa was practising the piano in the sitting-room. Jane slipped through the open door and stood quietly just inside, watching Lisa's bent blonde head and her fingers flying over the keys. She saw that there was a picture of Lisa on the wall above the piano, a painting in oils.

48

However, Lisa in the picture looked a little different to the girl at the piano, maybe because her hair was shorter and curlier. Jane wondered if Paul had painted the picture.

The music stopped suddenly and Jane jumped, because Lisa was turning to look enquiringly at her.

'Hello. Tim not back yet? He's made friends with some farmer just down the road and gone to look at his livestock. But then again, if he's hanging over some animal pen he could be hours. You never know with Tim as far as animals are concerned.'

Jane thought she had better let Lisa get back to her piano, and turned to go, but Lisa said quickly, 'You can stay if you like. Did you get tired of helping the other two?'

'They were fighting,' said Jane.

Lisa laughed. 'Don't take any notice. They only do it to make a change from writing or painting.'

Jane's eyes went back to the painting above the piano. 'Did Paul do that picture of you?'

Lisa swivelled on the stool. 'Oh, that's not me. That's my mother. I'm supposed to be just like her.'

Jane was silent. She felt again the same sick, cold feeling she'd had when Tim told her his mum had died. Lisa turned the stool again. 'She was a pianist, too, my mum. Before she had us children.' She played rapidly up and down the scale, then broke into a tune so liltingly wistful that the tears came into Jane's eyes. Lisa turned to face her again just as one overflowed and ran down her cheek. She brushed it away.

Lisa jumped up and came over to her, putting her arm round Jane. 'I'm sorry. That tune does make people cry. Please don't.'

'But your mum died!' said Jane before she could stop herself.

Lisa gave her a hug. 'I know. We all miss her, but we know she's in heaven. It's lovely there, and we'll see her again one day. That'll be the day! Everyone says I look just like my mum and I talk nonstop like she did too! We'll have some catching up to do when I see her again! Don't be sad, Jane. Listen!'

She went back to the piano and struck up the bright, galloping music that she had played the day before, the kind that made your feet want to dance. Jane dried her eyes. It was wonderful the way music could make you sad one moment and happy the next. Lisa was so clever, and kind, too. Tim was lucky to have a big sister like Lisa.

For the moment she had almost forgotten Tim but, just as she remembered him there came the sound of the back door slamming. Tim's excited voice called out, 'Mark! Paul! Lisa! Where are you?'

Next moment he appeared in the doorway, grinning from ear to ear and holding in his hands the smallest pig Jane had ever seen.

Chapter Eight

Jane had never seen such a tiny pig, small enough to be carried home tucked in the front of Tim's shirt. They took him into the kitchen.

'Pint size!' said Tim, and popped him into an old pewter pint pot that stood on the dresser. The pig fitted into it without a squeeze. Jane thought that he was adorable, a soft baby-pink colour covered with fine white hairs, and little button-eyes with long pale lashes. He blinked at them from the mug, his round snout resting on his little trotters.

'Whatever will you bring home next?' said Mark. 'You ought to put up a notice on the gate saying, "Unwanted animals taken in here"!'

Tim picked up the pig again and cuddled him.

'What are you going to do with him?' asked Jane.

'Keep him,' said Tim, 'if Dad says it's OK. He's the runt of the litter, and the farmer said he'd always get pushed away from the trough, and wouldn't do well. He's called Anthony.'

Jane giggled. 'Why Anthony?'

'Runts are always called Anthony, the farmer says. It means the smallest. Get off, Spam. This isn't a cat, and it can't live on a shelf, so you'll have to get used to it. I

51

wonder where that old feeding bottle is, the one we used to use for pet lambs.'

Jane almost said, 'We have a feeding bottle,' but she didn't think Mum would be too pleased if William's fruit-juice bottle was borrowed to feed a pig. She held Anthony while Tim rummaged about in the bottom of the dresser. He felt very warm and silky, and smelt rather pleasantly of hay. He objected strongly when they tried to feed him with a bottle of milk, digging his sharp little trotters stubbornly into her lap and, at the same time, letting out a piercing squeal. In the end, Tim had to hold him firmly wrapped in an old T-shirt to keep him still, while Jane held the bottle. Between them the milk began to go down, except for the odd dribble or splash that landed on themselves. By the time the bottle was empty, the pig was gobbling away happily, and looking around for more when they tried to take it away. They put him down on the floor, and he trotted around with a pattering of little hooves on the tiles, sniffing at everything until he came to Spam's favourite rug in front of the woodburner. There he suddenly collapsed on his side with all four legs sticking out, and went fast asleep.

'A pig?' said Dad incredulously, when Jane was telling them all about it later that evening. 'What on earth will they think of next? Goats, chickens, rabbits, and now a pig? And in the house?'

'It's only a very tiny one,' said Jane. 'This size.' She held up her hands a foot or so apart. 'He's called Anthony.'

'I don't care if he's called Hamish Macpherson,' said Dad, who had a Scottish grandfather. 'I don't think a pig in the kitchen is a healthy thing at all.'

52

'Think of it,' said Mum in a shocked tone. 'The mess and the smell, and the germs! It's just not right, with children and food about. Not right at all.'

She looked round their own sitting room, as though trying to visualize a pig in there. Jane looked round, too, at the matching cream calico, designer sofas, at the peach-coloured walls and matching peach-shaded table lamps. She couldn't imagine a pig there either, even in the streamlined, white-tiled kitchen, though Anthony seemed not at all out of place in the large homely kitchen next door with its quarry-tiled floor. Tim had explained to her that pigs were very clean animals, much easier to house-train than puppies and kittens, and were usually well-behaved in every way. Jane opened her mouth to defend Anthony's reputation, but Mum and Dad were talking to each other in hushed, disapproving tones.

'. . . really too much!' Dad was saying. 'I'll have to go round. What does the fellow think he's doing, allowing his kids to run wild and fill the place with livestock? What does he do, anyway? I never see him going to work and coming home in the evening like everyone else.'

'He doesn't,' said Jane quickly. 'He works at home, most of the time. He's a policeman. A very important one, working on a Very Important Case.'

Mum and Dad looked at her. 'Are you sure?'

Jane nodded. 'Oh yes. It's a secret, and I'm not supposed to say. But he spends all day in his office, working things out, and sometimes he goes out searching for clues.'

'Hmm,' said Dad thoughtfully, and raised an eyebrow. 'Are you sure this isn't one of your tall stories, Jane?'

'No,' said Jane indignantly, more than half-convinced that it was all quite true. She had meant to ask Tim more about his Dad, but the little pig had quite taken her mind off it. She said recklessly, 'You can ask him if you like!'

'Maybe I will,' said Dad. 'It's about time we made acquaintance with one another. A policeman, eh? He should be a responsible enough person, in that case.'

'It can't be easy, bringing up four children single-handed,' said Mum, who was beginning to think that two were quite a handful. 'I think I'd like to meet him. Maybe we'd better both go round. We could go this evening, while Dot's still here to baby-sit.'

At that moment there was a cry from William, the shrill yell that meant he had a pain in his tummy, the kind of cry that brought Mum and Dad jumping to their feet and Aunt Dot running in from the kitchen. William's face was almost purple, his hands tight-clenched into fists and his legs pumping furiously up and down.

'This is happening every night now,' said Dad helplessly.

Mum picked William up and held him against her shoulder, her face creased with worry. 'We must see the doctor – tomorrow morning, without fail, even though it is Sunday.'

'I think it must be colic,' said Aunt Dot, standing with the oven glove in her hand. 'He seems a typically colicky baby to me. But maybe you ought to get professional advice, dear.'

They had quite forgotten next door, the pig, and even Jane for the moment, and didn't notice when she helped herself to a spoonful of tomorrow's pudding and sat down to watch a TV programme they didn't approve of.

Next morning the doctor called. He didn't stay very long

and was a little tetchy because, although he was officially on call, he was expecting visitors to lunch that day. He said that William was perfectly fit and flourishing, that the tummy pains were indeed colic, and that they would probably go away by the time he was three months old. Everyone was relieved, although three months did seem rather a long time to wait.

While the doctor was still advising about feeding routines, Jane slipped into the garden, hovering about the wall between themselves and Tim's house. Everything was quiet in the garden, no shouting, not even the tinkle of Lisa's piano. She was puzzled and climbed the apple tree to take a closer look. There were the hens scratching in their run, Julia securely tethered, two of the cats basking, but no humans at all. She felt a little stab of disappointment. She had hoped to see how Anthony was doing. They all seemed to have gone out for the day.

Without Tim next door, the morning seemed to drag. Jane looked longingly over the wall from time to time, wishing she could play with the rabbits or even talk to the hens. Then she noticed Julia looking across at her with shrewd amber eyes. She saw that Julia had eaten all the long grass, nettles and other greenery within reach. She remembered the way the goat had leapt upon the wall and looked longingly down into their own herbaceous border.

Shinning up the apple tree, Jane tossed down a small unripe apple. Julia crunched it up at once and bleated hopefully for more. When she walked the length of the tether she almost reached the wall. Jane had an idea. She would give Julia a real treat, while everyone was busy indoors. Quickly she shinned down the tree and chose a French marigold from the garden bed that she thought looked rather insignificant and wouldn't be missed. She climbed the wall and hung over it, holding out the plant and calling Julia's name. The goat nickered and came at once, seizing the plant and munching it with great enjoyment. Jane felt pleased. She dropped to the ground again, and pulled up another marigold, then another.

'Jane!' called Aunt Dot from the house. 'Where are you? Lunch is ready!'

Jane slithered from the wall, noticing guiltily that quite a bare patch now showed in the border. She thought she had better rearrange the others to cover it, so she pulled up a few geraniums and begonias and replanted them.

Aunt Dot appeared round the corner. 'There you are! Are you doing some weeding? That's a good girl! Daddy'll be pleased. Lunch is ready.'

Jane jumped to her feet and dusted the soil from her hands. She had got a bit carried away with the plants, but Julia had enjoyed herself. 'Coming, Aunt Dot,' she said.

At that moment a car drew up outside the house next door, and she realized they hadn't gone out for the day after all. She could pick out all their voices in a cheerful buzz of conversation as they went into the house.

Chapter Nine

There had been talk of going out for a little drive in the car that afternoon, to celebrate the fact that William was exactly one week old today. But, by the time dinner had been eaten, the dishes washed, the kitchen cleaned, William fed and changed, a great deal of time had gone by and the grown-ups were having second thoughts. In the end, Mum and William disappeared upstairs for their usual nap, Dad sank onto the sofa with his P. Greville library book, and Aunt Dot declared her intention of getting her things together ready for packing. Now that the tummy pains had been diagnosed, Mum had got her strength back and Dad still had a few more days of his leave left, her aunt thought it was time to think about going home.

Jane was wondering if she dared ask permission to go next door, when there was a ring at the doorbell. Dad dropped his book and got up to answer it, but Aunt Dot beat him to it. Jane heard Tim's voice say politely, 'Excuse me, but please could Jane come next door to play and stay for tea?'

Aunt Dot seemed rather impressed as she relayed the message to Dad. 'Such a well-mannered boy. I think he might be a rather good influence on Jane. You'll let her go, won't you, Bob? Then perhaps you'd bring my large suitcase in from the garage.'

'Yes, Dot, if you say so,' said Dad meekly. He winked at Jane over the cover of *The Darkest Night*. 'Are you going to be a bossy elder sister, Jane?'

Not as bossy as Aunt Dot, Jane thought, but she didn't say anything. She smiled sweetly at them both and made for the door to join Tim before anyone decided to change their minds.

To save time, she and Tim dived into the shrubbery and over the wall into the jungly part of next door's garden.

'How's Anthony?' she asked rather breathlessly.

'Fine. He's started to follow me about like a puppy already. I wanted to tell you something, Jane. Something I thought of this morning in church. A really brilliant idea.'

Jane stopped to pull aside a bramble that would have got her knees if she'd walked on. 'Is that where you all were this morning? Church?'

'Yes. We always go on Sunday mornings. Don't you?'

Jane shook her head, letting the bramble fall back into place. She tried to remember if she had ever gone to church, but could only remember once or twice when she had been to a Christmas Nativity play. She said, doubtfully, 'Is church nice?'

'It's all right,' said Tim. 'The one where we lived before had a Kids Club. Here it's called Junior Church. But they're both good fun. Why don't you come next week?'

'Well . . .' Jane didn't quite know how to answer. Going to church was something that hadn't occurred to her. She remembered that Tim had been about to tell her something and asked, 'What's your brilliant idea?'

They emerged from the tangled undergrowth into the main part of the garden, where the rest of Tim's family were gathered on the large patch of grass between the animal houses and the vegetable plot. It seemed that even policemen had a day off, for Tim's dad was there, wearing shorts and sitting in a sunlounger with Spam at his feet.

'I can't tell you now, in front of the others,' said Tim in a low voice. 'It'll have to wait till we're by ourselves. Come and look at Anthony.'

Paul and Mark had set up a Swingball game, and were whacking the ball back and forth between them. Lisa lay on a blanket protected by an umbrella, hat and sunglasses, with a large bottle of sunscreen lotion by her side.

'Do you get sunburn?' she greeted Jane. 'I do, if I'm not careful. I go like a beetroot! Have some lotion, anyway. Ultraviolet rays are very bad for the skin, you know.' She turned over onto her back, and draped a cotton scarf across her face.

'We could do with some for Anthony,' said Tim, picking up the bottle. 'Pigs can get sunburnt, too.'

They found Anthony asleep in the shade of the goat house, and dabbed his pink back liberally with lotion. He squealed at the coldness, but then seemed to rather enjoy it, rubbing his back against their fingers and uttering little grunts of pleasure.

Tim's dad, Mr Willis, smiled at her from beneath his peaked hat that made him look not much older than Paul. 'It's Janet, isn't it? From next door? How's your baby brother? I'm sorry our hammering disturbed him the other day.'

59

Jane blushed. She felt that she ought to say that *she* was sorry to have disturbed an Important Policeman on a special case with such a trivial complaint. She wished she could ask how his case was coming along, but not even his own children seemed to talk about it with him. She just said, 'He's all right, thank you,' in a small voice, and didn't even think to remind him that her name was really Jane.

She and Tim had a game of Swingball when Mark and Paul stopped for a rest. They got Hansel and Gretel out for a romp on the grass, and played with the kitten Smut, trailing a last year's conker on a string through the long grass for him to pounce on. Lisa, got up and brought them all drinks of lemonade with cubes of ice clinking in the glasses. Then she went indoors to play the piano, a catchy tune that Jane hadn't heard before.

'Shine, Jesus, shine,' sang Tim. 'We had that in church this morning.'

Jane wished that she and Tim could be alone so that he could tell her about his idea. The chance didn't come until Mr Willis got up, yawned and said that he was going for a walk along the lane to stretch his legs before tea. Did anyone want to come? Mark said he would, but there was something good on TV that Paul wanted to watch. Tim would have gone, too, but Jane grabbed back of his T-shirt. 'Tell me your idea.'

Tim sat down again on the grass. 'Oh, yes. Well, it was something Mark said when I brought Anthony home yesterday, about putting up a notice saying, "Unwanted animals taken in here". This morning, I thought, why not? There must be lots more about that people don't really want, like Smut and Anthony.'

Jane's eyes began to sparkle. 'I could help you! We

60

could build houses for them, all down that wall! *And* I'd come over every morning and help feed them all, and clean the cages, and brush them. It'd almost be like having a zoo of our own, but much nicer!' A thought struck her. 'Have you asked your dad?'

'Not yet. I'm waiting until this evening after supper. He's always in a good mood on Sunday evenings, because he hasn't had to think about plots and deadlines all day. He's sure to let me.'

They went on making plans, deciding where the cats should be housed, and the puppies, birds and rabbits.

'The thing we'll have to be careful about,' said Tim, 'is making sure that animals that might get eaten – like rabbits and mice – are kept well away from things that might do the eating – like ferrets.'

Suddenly Jane shrieked. She had just caught a glimpse of Julia's greyish-white hindquarters disappearing over the wall into her own garden.

'Our flowers!' she gasped. 'Oh, Tim!'

'Blow it!' said Tim. 'She's chewed through the rope again. I forgot to get a stronger one. Come on!'

As they scrambled to their feet, Jane had guilty feelings about the tempting plants she had fed to Julia that morning from the other side of the wall. Julia had obviously got a taste for them, as they both soon discovered when they clambered onto the wall themselves. The goat was demolishing the remaining bedding plants as fast as she could, and trampling over the rest of the neat bed while she ate. She glanced up at them knowingly, but never for a moment stopped munching the geranium dangling from her jaws.

'Stop her!' groaned Jane. 'There'll be an awful row!'

They jumped down beside Julia, but the goat nimbly

sidestepped them and made for the patio, where a clothes-horse stood in the sun, laden with freshly laundered nappies, towels and cot sheets.

'Oh no!' said Tim urgently. 'We've got to stop her, quick! She eats washing!'

It was too late. Keeping just out of their reach, the goat moved daintily around the clothes-horse, grabbing first a snowy-white embroidered bib, which disappeared down her throat in a moment. Tim lunged at her, but she dodged, stretched her neck and seized a towel, which she began to chew. Jane stood frozen in horror as the towel disappeared, inch by inch, into the energetically munching jaws. Then she came to life and snatched at the towel, tugging desperately. Reluctant to give up her prize, Julia clamped her teeth firmly round the other end and held on. At the same time, Tim clutched at Julia's back legs. Seeing him coming from the corner of her eye, Julia again sidestepped neatly, without releasing her grip on the towel. Between them the clothes-horse, with the whole load of washing, toppled over into the dust.

There was no sign of life from the house. Jane fervently hoped that not just Mum and William, but Dad and Aunt Dot too, were enjoying a Sunday afternoon nap. Tim grabbed the frayed end of the tether and Jane managed to pull what remained of the towel away from Julia's champing jaws. It had a large jagged piece ripped from one corner. She picked up the clothes-horse and threw the other things higgledy-piggledy onto it, dusty and disarranged as they were. She bundled up the torn towel.

'Come on, let's get out of here. They won't miss the bib, and I'll hide this somewhere. Come on, quick before someone comes.'

They hauled on the tether and dragged the unwilling Julia out of the gate and back to the safety of her own garden.

Chapter Ten

Jane breathed a sigh of relief when they reached Tim's garden in safety. She pushed Julia into the dim confines of her shed. The goat was reluctant to be penned up in the middle of the day, and pushed her nose against the wire-netting window, bleating pathetically. 'It's your own fault!' said Tim, more cross than Jane had ever seen him before. 'I've a good mind to make you go without your supper tonight.'

Mr Willis and Mark were not back yet from their walk. The sound of the piano and the TV set meant that the others were occupied indoors and were not likely to be looking out of the window. Jane took the lid off Tim's dustbin and stuffed the torn towel inside, pushing it well down under two or three baked bean cans. They had got away with it.

She grinned at Tim. 'That was lucky! Dad would have been round complaining if he'd seen, and they'd have stopped me playing with you. And your dad might not have let you keep any more animals.'

Tim looked uncomfortable shuffling his already scuffed trainers through the gravel. 'But they *will* know. They'll see that everything's been on the ground and the towel's missing. They're bound to ask.'

'Don't worry,' said Jane. 'I won't tell on Julia. They know I was over here with you. Maybe they'll think the wind blew the clothes horse over.'

'There isn't any wind,' said Tim, 'and the wind wouldn't have picked everything up again, would it? And what about the flowerbeds?'

Jane grew impatient. 'They didn't see us. That's all that matters. If they ask, I'll think of something to say. I wish you'd stop worrying. Let's get some felt-tip pens and make a notice to stick on your gate.'

'We haven't asked Dad yet,' said Tim.

'Well, it doesn't matter. It'll be all ready for when we *do* ask. What's the matter with you? You're no fun any more.'

Tim didn't answer, but got out his collection of felt-tipped pens and rummaged about in some old painting materials of Paul's to find a large sheet of strong, white drawing paper. They sat at the kitchen table and, after much discussion, between them designed a colourful poster with little pictures of dogs, cats and rabbits all round the outside. In the middle a notice said in large bold red letters, 'Home For Unwanted Pets. Animals, birds and reptiles taken in. Excellent ackommodation. Small fee.'

At this point Tim suddenly threw down his red pen and said, 'Look, it's no good. I can't do this.'

Jane was puzzled, not knowing whether he meant he couldn't finish the poster or couldn't charge a fee. She said, 'Let me finish it, then. But I think we'll have to charge money, or how will we buy food for the animals?'

'No, I don't mean that,' said Tim in a funny kind of voice. He jumped up and stuffed the poster under a pile of magazines on the window-seat. Then he ran out of the door. Following him, Jane was surprised and dismayed to find him rummaging in the dustbin. He pulled out the torn towel, now more the worse for wear than ever. 'Tim! What are you doing?' she cried.

Her amazement grew as he made for her house, taking no notice of her protests. She hung back round the corner of her house, while he marched up to the door and knocked.

Her father opened the door and she heard him say in surprise, 'Hello! Where's Jane? Everything all right?'

Tim said in a desperate voice, 'Please, I'm very sorry but our goat got free and climbed over the wall. She's eaten some of your plants, and a bib, and half of this towel, and knocked over all the washing. I'm very sorry and I'll save up to buy a new bib and towel.'

Jane took a quick peep and saw her father take the torn and dirty towel with a very strange look on his face. He looked across at the trodden flowerbed and back at Tim's downcast face and said, 'Well, she *has* made a bit of a mess, hasn't she? I don't think a garden is the best place to keep a goat, you know, but accidents do happen. I wouldn't mind betting our Jane had something to do with it, too. Tell you what, you rake over my flower bed and tidy it for me, and we'll say no more about it this time.'

'Oh, thank you, sir!'

'Don't let it happen again, mind! By the way, where *is* that girl of mine?'

Jane shrank back around the corner and slipped into the shrubbery, hearing with relief Tim say that she was in his garden and none of it had been her fault at all. Now that Tim had got off so lightly there was no harm in keeping herself in the clear. By the time Tim came back she was sitting by the rabbit run and feeding Hansel and Gretel with dandelion leaves through the mesh.

Tim flopped down on the grass beside her. She could see that he was mightily relieved. He said, 'That's all right, then. Your dad wasn't anything like as cross as I thought he'd be. Thank goodness!' He lay down and fanned his hot face with a large dock leaf.

Jane was silent, pulling up tufts of grass. She was rather surprised herself that Dad hadn't been crosser, especially about the destruction of his neatly-kept flowerbed. And Tim hadn't involved her at all – not that he knew, of course, that she had tempted Julia across the wall with the French marigolds in the first place. She wasn't going to tell him either, despite the strange guilty feeling that still flickered somewhere inside.

She said, 'I don't know why you had to go and own up. They would never have guessed. They wouldn't have missed a bib. William's got dozens.' She added, 'You're silly,' under her breath, but didn't quite dare to say it aloud.

Tim stopped fanning himself, but didn't say anything. Jane looked down at his freckled face, furrowed with a slight frown. 'They'd never have known,' she repeated.

'We knew,' said Tim quietly, and sat up. 'I didn't want to tell either, only . . .'

'Only what?'

'Only it's wrong to cover things up and tell lies when you're in trouble.'

'Who says?'

'My dad, for one.'

'Well, so does mine, but I still do sometimes. Everybody does.'

'It's not just Dad,' said Tim slowly, 'it's Jesus, too.'

Jane was so astonished that her mouth fell open. Jesus? Baby Jesus in the Nativity plays? Whatever could it have to do with him? He wasn't even real.

She said, 'I don't know what you mean. Baby Jesus is only someone in a story . . . isn't he?'

'No,' said Tim, 'he isn't. And he's not just *Baby* Jesus. He's God's Son.'

Jane didn't know who God was either. Suddenly she had the feeling that compared with Tim she knew nothing at all. The feeling somehow made her cross. She wanted to thump Tim, even though he was bigger than her and more than a year older. She wondered if he would thump her back. Dad *would* be cross with him if he did that, but that might put an end to her coming over to play.

All the same, she felt so mad at him that she couldn't help doing something. She reached out and gave him a push, so that he fell over. Next moment she wished she hadn't, because Tim struggled up and pushed her back, and it was her turn to topple over. She looked up at him in surprise and saw that his face was redder than ever.

Next moment he had grabbed her by the arm and was yanking her up again. 'Sorry,' he mumbled.

Jane was sorry, too. Tim was the best friend she had ever had, and she didn't want to quarrel with him. She didn't know why she felt so nasty.

She said, 'Let's be friends. Can we get the rabbits out?'

'All right,' said Tim gruffly. They played with Hansel and Gretel until it was time for tea.

Everyone had tea together round the big kitchen table. Jane was glad that she and Tim were friends again, but when she thought of Julia and the garden, the strange feeling of guilt came back. Tim hadn't got into serious trouble, and neither had she, though the whole thing was her fault. However, the one who was really suffering was Julia, locked up in a dark shed with the prospect of no supper ahead of her.

Jane didn't know whether Tim intended to give Julia her supper or not. While the others washed up and cleared the table, she wandered out into the garden and looked in through the goat-shed window. Julia jumped up and ran forward, her eyes pleading. Jane couldn't bear the thought that she might get nothing to eat until breakfast. She found a couple of fruit gums in her jeans pocket and gave them to Julia. Then she found half a bag of squashed crisps in the other pocket and offered them, too. Julia gobbled them down eagerly and then ate up the packet. She bleated gratefully, and Jane began to feel a lot better.

While she waited for Tim to come out and feed the other animals, Jane amused herself by breaking off branches and stems from the nearby shrubs and bushes. She pushed them through the wire-netting door where they were seized at once by the goat's eager jaws. Julia chewed and swallowed everything she was offered – stems, leaves, berries, even the prickles on the raspberry and gooseberry bushes. By the time Tim appeared from the kitchen door with a bucket of chicken feed, Julia had eaten enough greenery to make *two* suppers, and Jane's conscience was quite clear again.

Chapter Eleven

The first thing Jane saw next morning, poking her head round the back door, was Tim busily raking and smoothing over the soil in the disturbed flowerbed. The sun hadn't come out yet, and it looked as though it might rain later.

'Hello,' she said, running out in pyjamas and bare feet. 'You're up early.'

'I wanted to get it done before it rained,' said Tim. He straightened up and looked at his work. 'I have, almost. I brought a few more marigolds to fill up the bare spots. It looked quite nice, doesn't it?'

Jane agreed. 'I'll go and get dressed, and then I'll come over and see Anthony.' She pulled a face. 'I have to stay here for the rest of the day. Aunt Dot's going home tomorrow, but Aunt Pauline, Uncle Terry and my cousins, and Aunt Cathy are all coming over today before she leaves. I know Mum will make me play with the little kids.'

'That's tough,' said Tim sympathetically. 'Come and help me feed the animals while you have the chance.'

Jane fed the rabbits with dandelions while Tim went to fetch sheep-nuts for Julia's breakfast and corn for the chickens. A funny sound between a gasp and a yell when he went into the goat shed brought her running to the door.

'What's the matter?'

Tim was peering inside, his face white and eyes wide. 'It's Julia! I think she's dead!'

Jane's heart began to race in a way that made her feel sick. She strained her eyes to see into the gloom. The goat lay on her side in her bed of clean straw, her legs sticking out in front and her neck stretched out. As they watched in horrified silence they saw her eyes open and roll a little, and she gave a feeble moaning bleat.

Tim came to life himself. 'She's not dead, but she's dreadfully ill. Let's have a look.'

Suddenly he was all vet, bending over Julia, opening her mouth and prodding at her body. 'Her stomach's all hard and swollen. She's breathing really fast and frothing a bit at the mouth. She's in dreadful pain. It must be something she's eaten.'

Jane could hear the way Julia was breathing in fast little grunts. Her own mouth was dry and her eyes were smarting with tears. It was dreadful to see the goat lying there, helpless and in pain, so ill that she might die. She gulped down a sob, and followed Tim out of the shed.

'Now, what did she have to eat yesterday,' said Tim, thinking aloud. 'Was there anything different from usual?'

Jane remembered the bedding plants in her father's border. She said in a wobbly voice, 'What about the flowers from our garden? Or the bib, or the towel? Could it be those that made her ill?' Suddenly she remembered the things she had fed to Julia later in the day, and added in a burst of misery, 'I gave her some sweets – fruit gums – and some crisps. She ate the bag too!' A

72

tear slid down her cheek.

Tim shook his head. 'No, none of those things would hurt her. She's eaten things like that before. What about the green stuff you were giving her? Was there anything poisonous in it? Try and remember.'

Jane knew that Tim wasn't really blaming her, just trying to get to the bottom of things. She said miserably, 'I don't know. It was just . . . leaves and things.'

'Show me,' said Tim. 'Show me all the bushes you got them from.'

Jane tried hard to remember, showing him the gooseberry and raspberry leaves, and the flowering currant, lilac and forsythia she had fed Julia with. Tim shook his head, muttering, 'No, that's not it,' to everything, until Jane pointed out a shrub near the wall with shiny, dark green leaves. 'That's it!' he yelled. 'That's rhododendron and it's poisonous! Deadly! Didn't you know?'

Jane shook her head dumbly. She had picked some of the shiny leaves for Julia and the goat had gobbled them down like everything else. They were deadly poison!

She stood and stared at Tim for a moment, and then burst into horrified tears. 'Oh, Tim! Oh, Tim! Will she die?'

Tim was in control again. 'I'll phone Mr Thomas. He's the vet. He'll know what to do. Stop crying, Jane. It was stupid, but you didn't do it on purpose.'

Jane's tears flowed on as she peered at poor Julia through the window while Tim was indoors phoning. She started to wail even louder when he came back with the news that Mr Thomas said he would call later, but he was afraid not much could be done.

Tim began to lose patience with her. 'Oh, shut up,

Jane! If you want to do something useful you can help me give her a dose of castor oil. Mr Thomas said it might help, though it's a long shot.'

Poor Julia was so far gone that she could not be persuaded to sit up for them to administer a dose of castor oil. In the end, Tim held up her head and opened her mouth while Jane poured in the dose. It was a messy business. At first Julia could not, or would not, swallow, and the sticky oil ran out down her tufty beard and all over Jane's hands and jeans. At last she made a sound that was a kind of half-choke and half-gulp, and some of the oil went down.

'Give her some more,' said Tim, panting with the effort of holding up the goat's head. 'I'm not quite sure of the dose, and we've wasted a lot of time already.'

In the end they used up almost half a bottle, which seemed an awful lot. They laid Julia's head down in the straw, and she gave a faint sigh and stretched out her neck again.

'Oh, she looks awful!' said Jane. 'I'm sure she's going to die.'

'Now don't you start again,' said Tim, wiping some of the oil off his hands. 'We'll pray, and see what happens. You had better get some of that oil off yourself. Wash your face while you're at it, or you'll be in for a telling-off again.'

Jane remembered her aunts, uncles and cousins, and the special lunch and tea, and having to be on her best behaviour. She probably wouldn't be able to come next door all day, or know how Julia was, or what the vet said.

She was right. The expected shower of rain arrived at

74

the same time as the visitors, which meant that playing in the garden was out. Jane had to take Kate and Sally, aged five and three, into her bedroom and entertain them while the adults talked. This turned out to mean that they amused themselves by pulling all her books off the shelves, sorting through the contents of her toy-box, and removing the doors, windows and chimney, as well as the furniture, from her dolls' house. At lunch time Aunt Pauline remarked on Jane's peaky looks, and at tea time Aunt Cathy recommended a good iron tonic. It was a tremendous relief when they all piled into the car and were waved off. Even Mum, Dad and Aunt Dot seemed relieved. They had another cup of tea together in the debris of the last meal, and then set to clearing up and seeing to William. It was easy for Jane to slip away.

Heart in her mouth, she climbed the wall and pushed through the damp and dripping jungle, past the lilacs and fruit bushes and the fateful rhododendron, and out into the clear space. The garden smelt of fresh damp earth after the morning's shower. No one was about. The hopeful clucking from the hen run, and the three cats waiting expectantly on the patio wall, showed that the animals had not yet been fed. It was a dull evening, and lights were on in the house, upstairs in Mr Willis's study and the boys' bedroom, and downstairs in the kitchen and sitting room. The tinkling of Lisa's piano sounded faintly, and someone was playing a lively pop cassette.

The door of the goat shed stood slightly ajar, as they had left it that morning. Feeling lonely and scared, Jane tiptoed across the damp grass and peeped inside. Her heart thumped. She dreaded what she would see. A sick goat, lying there in dreadful pain? A dead one?

There was nothing there. The shed was quite empty. Jane went inside to make sure, but Julia was gone. Just a large flattened space in the straw which showed where she had lain, and an unused food dish.

Choking sobs rose again in Jane's throat. She guessed what had happened. The castor oil had not worked, neither had the vet's treatments. Julia had died, and had been taken away. She had died because of the things Jane had done. She stumbled outside almost blinded by tears. Tim and the animals were the best thing that had ever happened to her, and now everything was spoilt.

She didn't hear the sudden rustling from the damp greenery behind her. The next moment two things happened at once. The kitchen door flew open and Tim came out, carrying chicken feed, Spam bounding beside him. He saw Jane and gave a shout of warning, 'Jane! Watch out!' At the same moment there was a rush and a pounding of hooves from somewhere behind, followed by a butt on the bottom from something hard and forceful. She sprawled forward onto the muddy grass

All the breath was knocked out of her. She wanted to cry or to laugh, she wasn't quite sure which. She had no breath to do either. She raised her head from the mud to see a rough-coated goat, very much alive and fully recovered, glaring at her with beady amber eyes, daring her to get up and turn her back to get butted again.

'Julia!' said Jane weakly. She wondered if the extra dose of castor oil had done the trick. Whatever it was, it had worked. Still sprawling on the muddy ground, Jane began to giggle breathlessly. Tim came over and gave her a pull to help her struggle up. Then they both laughed, holding on to each other and spluttering help-lessly, while Spam pranced around them and Julia snorted and stamped her hooves.

'I won't do it again,' she said when they paused for breath. 'I promise. I won't give her anything without asking first.'

'All right,' said Tim.

That was all he said. No calling her a stupid girl, no mention of speaking to parents, or not coming to play with the animals again. She felt very humble and wished there was something she could do to show him how grateful she was.

Then she remembered the half-finished poster. It would be a nice surprise if she finished it and put it up for him. While Tim was feeding the animals, she went indoors and rooted among the comics and magazines on the window seat until she found it. Mark was sitting at one end of the big table, his red head bent over an exercise book. She sat down opposite him.

'Do you mind if I use the felt pens?' she asked politely.

'Mmm,' said Mark vaguely, which she interpreted as yes, though she wasn't sure whether he had really heard her or not. Sometimes, when he was staring right at her, chewing his pen, he wasn't really seeing her at all. His mind was somewhere far away, lost in an adventure in space. She collected the pens together as quietly as she could so as not to disturb the workings of his story.

Jane took the red pen and wrote 'Aply within' at the bottom of the sheet. She filled in the remaining space with a few more little animal pictures, and the poster was finished. She found a blob of *Blutack* in Tim's pencil case, carried the poster downstairs, out the front door, and stuck it firmly to the front gatepost.

Chapter Twelve

Jane was up bright and early next morning, to find the
sun shining from a bright and cloudless sky. She jumped
out of bed at once, remembering the events of yesterday
and especially the joyful relief of knowing that all was
well again with Julia. There were stirrings in the upstairs
rooms, but so far no one else had appeared downstairs.
Jane didn't wait for breakfast. She let herself out of the
back door, hoping that Mum and Dad wouldn't mind if
she paid another early morning visit to Tim's house.

Tim was already out and about among the animal
pens, feeding, watering and cleaning. Jane helped by
fetching and carrying, relieved to find that Julia looked
as well as she ever had, snorting truculently and lowering
her hard little head when they filled her food dish. Jane
kept a respectful distance.

'I think she'd like to butt me again,' she said ruefully.

Tim grinned. 'I wish you could have seen your face!
But never mind. Let's go in and feed Anthony.'

Taking milk from the fridge, they were surprised to
hear a hum of voices from the dining room.

'Funny,' said Tim. 'Dad's got a visitor already.'

They peeped through the slightly open door, to see a
woman sitting opposite Tim's dad at the big table. Evi-

dently he had been making a cup of tea for her, for she took a sip and replaced the cup on the saucer.

'Now,' said Mr Willis. 'Shall we discuss this a little, Mrs Barrett?'

Jane thought he looked every inch a policeman, leaning forward with his forearms on the table and looking intently at the woman, though his tone was quite gentle and kind. Mrs Barrett was elderly and quite plump. She sat squarely on the dining chair with her handbag firmly planted on her lap, and her hands on her handbag. Jane noticed that a sad-looking, golden cocker spaniel was lying beside her chair with his nose on his paws.

'Who is it?' she whispered to Tim. 'Has something happened?'

'I don't know,' Tim whispered back. 'If we're quiet while we're feeding Anthony, we might hear something.'

But nothing could be heard for a while because of Anthony, jumping up with his little front trotters against their shins and squealing impatiently for his breakfast.

'Just a little pet pig,' she heard Tim's dad explaining to the visitor. It was not until Anthony was gulping down his bottle as Jane held him on a small stool that they were able to hear more.

'It's all down to the cost of living,' Mrs Barrett was saying in rather a tearful voice. 'Everything's so dear these days, and the price of dog food is a disgrace. I only have my pension, you see, I didn't want to have to do this, but there seemed no other way. And then when I saw your advert . . .'

Mr Willis made a sympathetic sound. He said, 'I do understand, Mrs Barrett. I'm sure we can work something out. When did you see the advert?'

'Just last evening, when I was taking poor old Sandy

out for his walk,' said Mrs Barrett. 'I thought, that might be a real godsend for us, that might. I'll go round first thing in the morning. So here I am.'

Jane gave a little jump of surprise, and the teat fell out of Anthony's mouth. She put it back quickly, before he could squeal again. At first she had thought that Mrs Barrett had been caught doing something wrong and was being interviewed by Mr Willis. Now she saw that, in fact, Mrs Barrett had come in reply to the poster she had stuck on the gatepost. Tim was looking puzzled. She remembered she had forgotten to tell him that she had put the poster up. She wanted to explain to him, but first she wanted to hear what was going on next door. Was Sandy to be their first animal guest?

'Well, you're my first reply,' said Mr Willis. 'Would you like to see round the house, and meet whichever of my children are around? Some of them are up and about, I think.'

Mrs Barrett seemed to hesitate. 'Well . . . I don't know as I'll need to do that. I would like to see the kennels, though . . . you know, where the animals are kept. Just to satisfy myself that everything's right and proper. Not that it wouldn't be, but I'm sure you'll understand I want to be quite clear in my own mind that everything's in order and that.'

'The animal pens?' Mr Willis sounded surprised. 'Well, of course, if you'd like to. I'll take you out there as soon as you've finished your tea.' He cleared his throat. 'Now, about payment . . .'

'I'm afraid I can't afford much,' said Mrs Barrett quickly. 'I was just going to ask about that. I do hope you don't charge a large fee, because I've only my pension, as I said. If it costs more than Sandy's food then I

81

might as well carry on as I am . . .'

She began to sound tearful again. Mr Willis made sympathetic noises, though Jane had a feeling that he was somehow puzzled. She felt rather puzzled herself. There were things about the conversation that she didn't understand at all.

Anthony finished his bottle, and Jane put him down on the floor. Tim was leaning against the draining board and looking at her strangely. 'Come out here a minute,' he said.

Jane followed him into the garden, wondering if he was going to tell her off for listening. He had been listening himself, and he couldn't pretend he hadn't.

'Look here, what did you do with that poster?' he demanded.

'I stuck it on your front gate. That's what the lady has come about. It's all right. Your dad doesn't seem to mind.'

'That's what's so funny,' said Tim. 'I forgot to ask him if it was all right. He can't have seen it yet, 'cos he's still in bare feet. I saw them under the table. He hasn't been out. He doesn't know anything about it '

They looked at each other blankly. A hum of voices rose and fell from the dining room, just out of earshot. Something was being discussed, but what? Were they going to get into yet more trouble?

It seemed sensible to keep out of the way for a bit, until Mrs Barrett had left and Tim's dad went off upstairs to his study. They retreated to the cool leafy depths of the jungle at the bottom of Tim's garden, followed by Anthony, who began to root about the soft damp leaf mould like a proper little pig. Neither Tim nor Jane had had breakfast yet, so they found a blackcurrant bush with berries that were ripe and gathered a handful each.

A familiar voice sounded from over the wall. 'Jane! Ja-ane! Where are you? Breakfast's ready!'

Jane groaned. 'Aunt Dot! I'll have to go. She's going home today and we're all going to the station to see her off.' She popped a handful of blackcurrants into her mouth and made for the stone wall.

They all went to see Aunt Dot off on the train, even William in his blue carrycot. When it came to the point, Jane found she was quite sorry to see her go. Aunt Dot gave her a little black china dog and a big hug.

'I'll miss you, Jane. I've enjoyed taking care of my little brother and his family. You take good care of yours now.'

'I will, Aunt Dot,' said Jane.

On the way home from the station, Dad stopped at the newsagents for his paper. When he came out of the shop, Jane saw to her surprise that Tim was with him.

'Look who I've found,' said Dad. 'My young jobbing gardener. Budge up Jane, and we'll give him a lift home.'

He bought them each an iced lolly. Jane could see that Tim looked rather bursting with something or other. She wondered if he had found out anything about Mrs Barrett's visit. She didn't ask until they got out of the car at her gate.

Tim took a white card out of his pocket and showed it to her. It said, 'Widower seeks household help for busy family of four children and assorted pets,' and Tim's address and telephone number.

'Dad sent me down to the newsagent to take this out of the window,' he said, 'because we're fixed up now. He won't let us take in animals, I'm afraid, but Mrs Barrett is going to be our new household help.'

Chapter Thirteen

'Dad, who's Jesus?' asked Jane.

Dad had a butcher's striped apron round his middle and was cleaning down the worktops in the kitchen. If anything, he was even more fussy round the house than Aunt Dot, and *that* was saying something. Jane had never seen the kitchen so white and clean and sparkling, with everything exactly in its place.

He didn't answer for a moment, frowning a little as he put away the cleaning liquid and peeled off the rubber gloves. Then he turned to face Jane. 'What did you say, pumpkin?'

'I said, who is Jesus?'

Dad pulled out one of the white, metal-and-wicker kitchen chairs and sat down. He and Jane faced each other across the gleaming white expanse of the table top. Dad and Mum always tried to answer Jane's questions in a balanced and fair way, and she could see he was searching very hard for words that she would understand. She propped her chin on her hands and waited.

'Jesus,' said Dad. 'Well, Jesus was a very good man, a prophet and a teacher, who lived in Israel about two thousand years ago and went about doing good to everyone he met.'

Jane was disappointed at this description, which sounded so ordinary. There must be more to it than that. She asked, 'What else was he? Wasn't he special?'

Dad looked uncomfortable and seemed to be struggling for words. He said, 'He was supposed to have claimed to be the Son of God, so the leaders of the country were angry and put him to death.'

'So he's dead now?' asked Jane, a little puzzled. Tim always talked about Jesus as though he was alive here and now. How that could be if he'd lived two thousand years ago? She couldn't understand.

'The story goes,' said Dad, 'that he was resurrected – that is, he became alive again and proved that he was God's son. But of course,' he added quickly, 'you must realize that the Christian faith is only one of many. There have been lots of prophets and people who claimed to be holy men – Mohammed, for instance, and Buddha. You're a bit young to be thinking about all this, pumpkin. When you're older you'll be able to understand more easily about the different world religions and make up your own mind about them.'

Jane was feeling more confused all the time. She wasn't interested in Mohammed or Buddha or world religions, whatever they were.

Dad said, 'Have these questions been prompted by next door?'

Jane nodded. Dad looked a little grim. He said, 'I hope they're not turning out to be a family of weirdos or religious cranks. I really will have to go round and find out for myself. Have a good talk and see what makes them tick.'

Jane had heard him say this so many times before

that she scarcely took any notice any more. Her mind went off on a slightly different tack.

'Dad, why don't we go to church?'

Again Dad looked uncomfortable and a little embarrassed, but he always tried to be honest with Jane. He said, 'I don't know, really. I did go as a boy – to Sunday School, too – but you kind of get involved with other things in your teens. It's important to do well at school, for example, and pass exams. Then there's college or university, and starting out in a career. Responsibilities like a wife and family come along, and the need of a nice home to live in. I have to work hard, you know, to pay the bills. Money doesn't grow on trees.'

Jane looked at him. Why did grown-ups sometimes say such silly things? She said, 'I wish I could go to church. Couldn't I go with Tim?'

Dad frowned a little. 'If you *want* to go, I think it would be better if I took you,' he said firmly. 'Then I can see what's what. One has to be careful. There are some very strange cults about these days.'

'What's a cult?'

Dad's frown deepened into real furrows. Jane could see that he was going to do his best to explain. Then a whimper from above suddenly turned into a wail. Dad jumped up.

'Half past four already. I've only just finished clearing up after lunch and it's tea time!' He filled the kettle at the sink. 'Look, pumpkin, we'll have to finish this talk another time.'

Jane had the feeling that he was relieved. He hadn't really answered her questions about Jesus. She wandered out into the garden. She hadn't seen Tim all day. She and Dad had driven to the supermarket that

87

morning to do the big weekly groceries shop, which was even larger than usual because of the bulky packs of disposable nappies and extra detergent that had to be piled into the trolley. She had felt a twinge of guilt when Dad went to the textiles department and bought a large new bath towel. Dad hadn't said anything except, 'Do you think this aqua colour matches the bathroom, or is it a bit pale?' Mum and Dad were quite fussy about getting colours properly matched, though Jane couldn't see that it mattered much.

She was looking across at the newly-restored flower-bed when she heard her name called in a hiss from the edge of the shrubbery. There was Tim, half-way up a gnarled plum tree and looking across the wall. 'Can you come over?'

Jane didn't need asking twice, and plunged into the shrubbery. Tim was accompanied by Anthony, Spam, and two of the cats – Jane thought they were Pomeroy and Peabody – who liked to go for a walk with him, though they always pretended to be quite independent.

'What happened?' asked Jane, who had been wondering all day about the notice on the front gate.

Tim pulled a rueful face. 'Dad made me take the notice down. He said we've got enough of a menagerie without adding to it. Anyway, it's illegal to advertise like that, he said, without proper permission.'

'Oh dear.' Jane's heart flipped with disappointment. A boarding kennel of assorted livestock would have been such fun. But if a parent said something was not allowed then that was it, especially if that parent happened to be a policeman.

She said, 'Did you get into trouble?'

'I got a bit of a telling-off, that's all. Dad's okay, really.'

Jane didn't ask if her own part in the affair had been discussed. Somehow she felt sure Tim wouldn't have told tales on her if he could help it.

She said, 'What about the woman with the dog?'

Tim brightened. 'Mrs Barrett? Oh, she's already started work. With the wages Dad pays, she'll be able to keep her dog and not get rid of him. Dad says she can bring him to work with her – one more won't make much difference. She's great. We had cottage pie and gooseberry crumble for lunch, and she did all the washing up! She's made gingerbread for tea. Dad says she's an answer to prayer.'

'How do you mean?'

'Well, we needed someone to help. So we prayed to Jesus about it, and then put that card in the window, we got an answer almost straight away.'

There he was, talking about Jesus again, almost as though he lived in the house with them and helped them with ordinary things. Dad seemed to think that people like that were a bit odd. Tim with his freckles, untidy hair and grimy face didn't seem odd at all, just nice.

Jane sighed and thought, If Jesus is real he probably likes nice people like Tim and answers prayers for them. He wouldn't like me. I'm not very nice sometimes. I tell fibs, and I nearly poisoned poor Julia. I don't even like my little brother much, and I gave Aunt Dot an awful lot of trouble. He wouldn't like me, so he wouldn't answer my prayers. But then, Dad doesn't think he's real anyway. So I don't care.

She didn't say any of those things, but picked up Anthony and rubbed her face against the soft bristles on his pink back. He squeaked in a friendly way and tried to nibble at her nose. She sighed, wishing once again that she could have a pet of her own.

'Can you stay?' asked Tim hopefully. 'Paul said he'd get me started on building a little pen for Anthony, now that he's finished decorating.'

Jane sighed again. 'I can't. I'm not supposed to be here. Mum and Dad will be having tea in a minute. Then I've got to have a bath and change, because more boring old visitors are coming to see William.'

'Tomorrow then,' said Tim. 'I've got to go too. Mrs Barrett made a pile of scones as well as the gingerbread. Cheerio.'

Jane watched him disappear into the jungle with his following cats, dog and little pig. She didn't go back straight away, but stayed for a moment leaning against the cool rough stones of the wall, her eyes closed. Then she climbed dejectedly back into her own garden.

William was in the pram on the patio, lying awake after his nap. She stopped to peep in at him, lifting the fine mesh of the insect net that protected him. She thought that he looked much nicer when he wasn't crying, pleasantly pink instead of crimson, and quite pretty. His little fists curled and uncurled, and he seemed to be watching the patterns cast by the apple tree onto the hood of the pram.

A hum of voices mingled with the clinking of crockery showed that Mum and Dad were having a discussion about something as they got tea ready. Jane's ears pricked as she heard her own name mentioned. She went in very quietly hoping to hear more, but by then the microwave was humming and drowning out the conversation.

'Ah, Jane,' said Mum as she appeared in the doorway.

'There you are. Come on in. We've got something we want to tell you.'

Jane stiffened, half-expecting that either her part in the episode of Julia, or the Unwanted Animals advert had somehow come to their attention. She prepared for a telling-off. Then she saw that both her parents were smiling. Mum put out an arm to give her a hug.

'We've been thinking,' said Dad. 'We feel you've perhaps been a bit neglected this past week or so, since William arrived. He's been getting all the attention, and that's why you seem to be round next door as often as not.'

Jane blinked at him. He couldn't be going to stop her going to play with Tim, could he? That would be dreadful.

But Dad went on, 'We know you've been wanting a puppy for a long time. Mum and I have talked it over, and we think now might be as good a time as any to get one. We'll start looking round for one tomorrow, if you like.'

Chapter Fourteen

Jane found it difficult to sleep that night for excitement. She could scarcely believe her luck. At last, at long last, she was going to get a puppy of her very own.

She was awake early next morning. up and dressed before Dad, Mum or William had stirred, hardly able to wait until they set off. The evening before, Dad had searched the 'Livestock/Pets' section of the local paper and drawn a ring round any adverts for puppies that seemed hopeful.

Just before she had dropped off to sleep the night before a new idea had occurred to her. She mentioned it to Dad now when he got up, almost before he reached the bottom stair.

'Please, Dad, could Tim come with us to choose the puppy? He's going to be a vet, and he knows all about dogs.'

Despite his doubts about the family next door, Dad rather liked Tim. 'Yes, I don't see why not,' he said, rubbing a hand over his unshaven jaw. 'Go and ask him while I get breakfast going.' He yawned and picked up the kettle.

Jane arrived breathlessly in the next-door kitchen to find Mrs Barrett already in residence, scrambling a saucepanful of eggs, while the smells of grilling bacon and toast filled the air. Her spaniel lay nose on paws in front of the stove, sharing the warmth with Anthony. Mrs Barrett was comfortably plump and her eyes twinkled.

'I only hope,' she said to Jane with a smile, 'that this nice bit of bacon didn't come from one of that little chap's relatives. It does seem a bit tactless, grilling rashers with him in the room, but I daresay he don't realize the implications. Are you looking for Tim?'

Jane nodded, feeling a shock at the idea of bacon actually having come from some poor pig. She comforted herself with the thought that Tim would never let Anthony end up as rashers in a frying pan.

Tim was almost as excited as she was to hear of the puppy hunt. He got ready in record time and came round with her to wait for Dad.

Their first call was on a lady called Miss Blake who was advertising basset hound puppies for sale. 'Two litters, ready now,' said the advert in the paper. Even before they rang the bell, they could faintly hear little yips and whines coming from inside. The bell's ring was greeted by an excited clamour of shrill barking. The door was answered by a thin, bespectacled lady and about sixteen small basset hounds, milling in a black and brown sea around her feet. She peered at them shortsightedly, while the puppies spilled out and clustered around their feet in a mass of wet noses and wagging tails. Dad explained about the advert and, somehow or other, the lady ushered them all in and led the way to her sitting-room.

'Now,' she said, 'As you see, there are two litters to choose from. Flossie had nine and Gipsy seven, and they've reared every one, the clever girls!'

94

Flossie and Gipsy, the two mothers, were cosily ensconced in armchairs by the fireplace, looking rather smug. They obviously considered that their puppy-rearing was now complete, however, and both nipped at their offspring if they tried to jump and scramble too near. Miss Blake seemed to have taken over as mother of the sixteen puppies, and kept saying things like, 'Down, Freddie!' or 'Not now, Bootsie' or 'Bunty dear, do stop that', although as far as Jane could see all the pups looked exactly the same. She, Dad and Tim sat in a row on the sofa, with a mass of little basset hounds tumbling over their feet, licking at their ankles and nibbling their shoelaces. Miss Blake didn't disturb the two mothers, but pulled up a hard-backed chair for herself.

'As you can see, they're fit and healthy,' she said proudly. 'All inoculated and wormed up to date. Lovely temperaments, bassets. So friendly. You couldn't do better for a pet. Are you looking for a male or a female puppy?'

Jane hadn't thought, but Dad said hastily, surveying the milling small dogs, 'A male, I think. We don't intend to breed from it.'

Jane thought that they were all quite beautiful. She picked up one warm, wriggling body after another and cuddled it, admiring its floppy velvety ears and tiny black-leather nose, feeling its sharp little teeth on her fingers.

But Tim said, 'Basset hounds are pack animals, really. One might be a bit lonely on its own.'

Jane thought Miss Blake looked rather crossly at Tim.

Dad said, 'Of course, we don't intend to decide here and now. We have several other litters to look at.'

'Oh, but Dad . . .' began Jane. No puppy could be more adorable than these. Dad got to his feet and said firmly, 'We'll let you know what we decide. Thank you very much for showing us the puppies, Miss Blake. Come along, children.'

Flossie yawned and Gipsy closed her eyes as they left the room, but the sea of puppies escorted them to the door and would have followed them down the path if Miss Blake had not scooped them back in wriggling armfuls.

'Phew!' said Dad, starting the car engine. 'Now I know how it feels to be mobbed. I think you're right about them being pack animals, Tim.'

'But they were lovely!' wailed Jane. 'I'd have loved one of them!'

'Wait until we've seen the others,' advised Dad, putting the car into gear.

Jane mourned the basset hounds all the way to the next place, but she cheered up when she saw the pups that were for sale there. Four collie-cross pups on a farm, curled up in a nest of soft hay in an outhouse with an amiable mother called Nan.

'Real bargains, these,' said the farmer, 'They're cross-breds, so I won't be charging much. A real pretty cross, too.'

The pups were certainly pretty, with collie's ears and noses. But instead of their mother's black and white colouring they had pretty, reddish-brown markings on white coats, little brown noses and brown eyes. They smelt sweetly of hay and made snuffly little noises when Jane touched them. The one she picked up fell asleep on her lap, on its plump back with its little paws in the air.

'Oh, Dad,' said Jane. 'Can I have this one? Please! This is the one I want.'

The farmer had moved away just out of earshot, and was raking up some loose hay. 'What do you think, Tim?' asked Dad.

'Well . . .' Tim looked at Jane and hesitated for a moment. Then he said, 'They're nice, but I think they've got a bit of springer spaniel in their breed. That's not very good crossed with a collie sheepdog. They have a hunting instinct, you see, and they might chase sheep and things when they get bigger.'

'Oh dear,' said Dad. 'We don't want that, do we? Especially with a menagerie like you've got next door. Maybe we'd better give these a miss.'

Jane was furious with Tim. She stroked the plump sleeping puppy and glared at him. He was putting Dad off every puppy they saw. Why was he being so mean? Especially when he had fourteen pets of his own at home, not counting Mrs Barrett's Sandy.

Dad was already saying his farewells to the farmer. 'That's something I wouldn't have thought of,' he said to Tim as they climbed back into the car. 'I'm glad Jane had the idea of bringing you along.'

'I wish I hadn't!' muttered Jane.

She aimed a kick at Tim's ankle. He moved it away in time, but looked uncomfortable. Dad didn't see the kick, but he looked at their two glum faces in the driving mirror and grinned. 'Cheer up! There's one more place left on the list. Maybe this time we'll find your perfect dog, Jane.'

The third lot of puppies were spaniels, a kind of black and grey mixture, with plump cuddly bodies, large paws and the beginnings of floppy ears. There were five in the litter and they belonged to a couple who kept kennels. 'Now then, Tim,' said Dad with a grin. 'What breed do you call these?'

'Blue roan cocker,' said Tim promptly, and grinned back at Dad. Jane glared at them both. She was still cross, and pretended not to be interested in the puppies at all, standing stiffly with her arms folded. Tim would only go and say something to put Dad off!

Dad picked up one of the puppies and held it out to her. She took it and felt her annoyance begin to melt at the feel of its wriggly warm weight and a little pink tongue licking her bare arm. She put it down and it waddled after her on short legs, making little playful runs at her ankles. When she stopped, it stopped too, sat down on its plump behind and looked at her with its head on one side and one ear cocked, wondering what she was going to do next. It was no use. Try as she might, she couldn't help falling in love with it.

She looked at Dad and Tim to see if they were going to raise objections, but they were both smiling. All Tim had to say was, 'Cocker spaniels make really nice pets. They're so good-natured.'

'Well, Jane?' asked Dad, raising an eyebrow. 'Will he do, do you think?'

'Oh yes, Dad!' Jane picked up the puppy again and held him against her cheek. He squeaked a bit and tried to turn his head to lick her face. She saw that he had a little round patch of white under his chin among the black and grey.

'Patch,' she said. 'I'll call him Patch.'

And suddenly she knew that Patch was the exact dog she had been looking for all along.

Chapter Fifteen

Within twenty-four hours it seemed that Patch and Jane had always belonged together. In just one day she felt she had learned to know him so well, the little whining noise he made when he thought he had lost her, the way he suddenly fell asleep when he was tired, sometimes right in the middle of a game, even the thoughtful look that came over his face when he was just about to make a puddle on the floor.

She mentioned this feeling to Mum.

'It's just the same with babies,' said Mum. 'You can read all the baby books you like, listen to all the advice, but two days with your own baby tells you more about him than weeks and months of reading can.'

All that first day, Jane looked after her new baby while Mum looked after William. It was quite hard work. Mum and Dad made it quite plain that she was to be responsible for him all by herself. So she fed him and bedded him down, brushed him and played with him, and wiped up all the puddles he made. She began to see why Mum often felt tired since William had come.

In the afternoon, Dad sent her and Patch round to see Tim, so that he could get on with cooking the supper without them under his feet. Jane and Tim sat on the patio steps with Patch between them, lying where he had suddenly fallen asleep on Jane's cardigan. He made snuffly sounds, like William did when he slept, and now and then a twitchy movement. Most of the animals, except the hens and Julia, had come up and sniffed inquisitively at him, with Jane hovering protectively nearby. They seemed to have accepted him into their garden, though one of the cats had looked rather cross when Patch tried a nip at its tail. Smut had been quite happy to have a game of chase with Patch, which ended when Smut raced up the plum tree and Patch fell asleep.

At the end of the long patch of grass where it joined the jungly part of the garden, Mark and Paul were busy with a new construction of bricks and metal.

'A barbecue,' said Tim. 'We're making a nice big one, big enough to cook chops and sausages and burgers all at once. We're going to have a barbecue party for my birthday next week, if the weather's still fine.'

Jane wondered if she was going to be asked. She couldn't help remembering how horrid she had been to Tim the day before. He had been right, of course. None of the other pups would have done at all. Patch was the only dog for her, the best puppy in the world. She leant forward so that her hair swung down and covered her face.

'You can come too, if you like,' said Tim. 'You and Patch. That'll make twenty-three, with all the animals, and p'raps Mrs Barrett and Sandy.'

Jane felt a little bubble of happiness rise inside. She said quickly, 'I'm sorry I tried to kick you yesterday, in the car.'

Tim grinned. 'That's okay. You missed anyway. If you hadn't, I'd probably have kicked you back.'

'You wouldn't,' said Jane. 'You're nicer than me.'

Tim looked rather red and embarrassed. 'Don't be daft! You're quite nice as well – for a girl.'

'I'm not!'

'You are!'

'I'm not!'

'You are!'

They might have kept up this ridiculous argument for a long time if a masculine voice behind them had not suddenly said, 'Hello, hello, what's all this about then?'

Jane jumped. It was Tim's dad, wearing an ordinary shirt and jeans, but sounding so much like a policeman that for a moment she felt quite alarmed. However, he was only joking, and sat down a couple of steps above them.

'Have you finished work, Dad?' asked Tim. He still looked rather red, and Jane knew that he wanted to change the subject.

'For today,' said Mr Willis, 'and the whole thing by the week-end, I hope. Then I won't think about tackling anything else until you go back to school in September.'

'Brill!' said Tim. 'I hate it when you have to work in the holidays.'

'I don't like it much myself, but it couldn't be helped this time. Never mind, we'll have fun for the rest of the holidays, I promise. Is this your new pup, Jane? Nice little chap, isn't he?'

He tickled Patch, who yawned and stretched in his sleep. Then he turned back to the two of them and said, 'You haven't told me yet what the argument was about.'

Normally Jane was a little shy of Tim's dad, but suddenly she found herself blurting out, 'I was saying I'm not as nice as Tim.'

'Oh shut up!' said Tim. 'Let's go and have a game of cricket.'

'No, wait a minute,' said Mr Willis. 'What do you mean, Jane? Let's get to the bottom of this.'

He gave them both a look that made Jane glad they weren't criminals being arrested by him. He had a sort of look in his eye, kind but direct, that made you feel it would be quite useless to try to pull the wool over his eyes. She said in a small voice, 'I'm not like Tim. I do lots of bad things. I tell fibs and make up stories, and sometimes I'm unkind.'

These things had never bothered her before, but all of a sudden they seemed to matter very much indeed. The little bubble of happiness burst and was replaced by a tide of misery. She put her head down on her knees and sobbed.

Mr Willis reached down and put a large strong arm round her shoulders.

'Hey, hey! It's not as bad as all that!'

'It is! Yesterday I *kicked* him! And he hadn't done anything wrong! He was only helping p-p-pick a p-p . . .' Another sob rose up and burst. Mr Willis gave her shoulder a comforting squeeze. Tim moved up so that his father could sit between them, carefully shifting the sleeping pup, cardigan and all, to one side.

'I wish I could c-come good, like Tim.'

'I never looked on Tim as such a model of goodness,' said Mr Willis with a smile in his voice, 'but he's not a bad old sort, I suppose.' He gave Tim a gentle punch with his free fist, then turned to Jane again.

'Listen, Jane, don't cry. Let me tell you something.'

Jane's head came up and she listened.

'It isn't that Tim's any more good than anyone else,

in himself. The difference is that he's had Jesus in his life since he was quite little. It's Jesus who makes him the kind of person he is.' He paused for a moment and went on, 'You know about Jesus, don't you, Jane?'

Jane hesitated. 'Well, only a bit. That he was a good man and a prof-prof . . .'

'A prophet? Yes, but much more than that. He's God's own Son, and died to take the punishment for all the bad things we do. Then he became alive again, so that *we* can all live for *ever*.'

'He's alive now?'

'Yes, and we can talk to him any time. That's what we call praying. You can tell him about all the bad things that worry you and ask him to make you good. Would you like to?'

'Yes.'

So Mr Willis said a prayer. Though Jane couldn't afterwards quite remember the words, she somehow knew that, just as Jesus helped Tim, maybe he would help her now, too. Mr Willis gave her his large white handkerchief to dry her streaky, tear-stained face, and she found that the horrid, miserable feeling had gone away. She thought Mr Willis was a very nice policeman, almost as nice as her dad, and couldn't imagine why she had ever been shy of him.

Spam came over and sniffed at Patch, who woke up with a start and rolled down onto the next step, and they all had to comfort him, too.

Chapter Sixteen

By the time Tim's birthday came, everything seemed more or less to have settled into a routine. Dad was back at work, William's colic was giving less trouble, and one night he actually managed to sleep right through. During the day, Mum took care of William, and Jane took care of Patch. She was trying hard to house-train him because she was tired of clearing up puddles from the floor, but it was a slow job. Things were much better when they could be out of doors all day. Then puddles didn't matter.

In other ways Jane was very proud of Patch's progress. Already he knew his name, came straight away when he was called, except when something interesting took his attention on the way, and he knew very definitely that he belonged to Jane. When they were in Tim's garden with the other animals she was very proud when Patch trotted at her heels, instead of following Lisa or one of the boys.

The barbecue was finished in good time for the birthday. It was an impressive affair of brick walls with a pan, made by Paul, of metal and wire mesh, a long metal fork for turning the meat and a brick bench for the cook to sit on. The boys had made a picnic table of wooden planking, and a couple of wooden benches. Mrs Barrett had been busy making trifles, sausage rolls, and an elaborate birthday cake decorated with blue icing, farmyard animals and a little man in a white coat who was supposed to be a vet.

The day before the birthday, Mum took Jane into town to buy a present for Tim. It was Mum's first real trip to the shops with William, and it took quite a lot of planning. William had to be fed, winded and changed before they left, and they had to take everything they would need with them on the pram shopping tray. Jane badly wanted to take Patch, too, but Mum drew the line at that. He had to be left behind in the kitchen, with Jane's old sweater and a hot water bottle in his basket for company. Even so, he ran to the door after them and Jane could hear him whimpering as they left the house. Tears came into her eyes and she felt like a traitor.

She chose a trendy black-and-green sweatshirt for Tim, and a birthday card with a dog and kitten that looked rather like Spam and Smut on the front. Shopping with a baby was slow and tiring work. Mum kept meeting people that she knew, and they all peered in under the pram canopy and made clucking noises, saying things like 'Is he good?' or 'Isn't he like his Dad (or Mum or sister)?' Jane felt hot, sticky and bored. She wished she could get home to play with Patch. She tried not to complain, and held William on her lap while Mum went into a changing cubicle in the big department store to try on a new dress.

It was late afternoon when they returned home. William was fretful. Mum said she was getting a headache and that she thought there was thunder in the air.

She was rather put out to find a lot of small puddles on the kitchen floor. Patch had also chewed the oven glove and the back of one of Jane's slippers, but he was so pleased to see them, with wrigglings, tail waggings and little joyful yaps, that she forgave him everything.

Preparations for the birthday barbecue began in earnest the next day. Mr Willis took the day off especially. All morning Jane could hear him and the children busy in the garden, with much laughter and talk, and coming and going between the indoors and outdoors. She wrote out her card, wrapped Tim's present in green shiny paper and played with Patch in the garden, until Tim's untidy head appeared over the wall. He called across, 'Jane! You don't have to wait until four o'clock, you know. Why don't you and Patch come across now?' Jane needed no second invitation.

'Take your parka, dear,' said her mother. 'It still seems thundery to me and you don't want to get caught in a shower.'

Jane arrived next door with present, card, and bundled-up waterproof under one arm, and a wriggling Patch under the other. She put Patch down with relief and handed the parcel to Tim who opened it at once and said that it was just the sweatshirt he would have chosen himself. He tried it on straightaway, then took it off again, as it was a hot and sticky day. He put the card with a row of others, that had been slung over a length of string stretched between the forsythia and a plum tree, well out of range of Julia's busily chewing jaws. A cluster of bright balloons were tied to the lilac bush, and a yellow plastic cloth covered the picnic table. The barbecue was already lit with twigs and newspaper and charcoal, and a plume of blue smoke rose from it. Mark was busily fanning the charcoal with a pair of bellows.

'You have to light it ages before you start to cook,' said Tim. 'The charcoal has to die down to a hot bed of ash.'

Jane's dad had a small portable barbecue that they sometimes used on summer evenings, but it wasn't nearly as much fun as this huge brick and metal affair. In the kitchen, a lot of sausages, chops and burgers were thawing from the freezer. Mrs Barrett and Lisa were chopping potatoes and onions, and mixing salads.

'Do you want a job, Jane?' asked Lisa, and went on without waiting for an answer, 'You can put mayonnaise on these potatoes and onions if you like. Here's a bowl. Then there are all those baps to be cut in half, and then you can mix a couple of jugs of orange juice and lemonade, if you don't mind.'

Jane didn't mind at all. Doing things here was so much more fun than boring jobs at home, especially when there were interesting diversions like a dog or cat waiting to steal a sausage, or a pig getting underfoot and squealing when he was trodden on. She sat at the table, enveloped in a large spare pinafore of Mrs Barrett's, with Patch lying at her feet, keeping close because he was still a little nervous of so many other people and animals. Jane felt proud of the fact that she and Patch belonged together and that they both knew it.

Everyone kept glancing at the sky and hoping it would stay dry until the barbecue was safely over. Mrs Barrett said that she felt a thunderstorm in her bones, though it was very warm and Jane couldn't imagine why everyone thought it might rain.

At four o'clock Paul and Mr Willis, in large aprons

and armed with long-handled forks, began the serious business of cooking. Chops and burgers sizzled over the charcoal, dripping down fat which sent up bright spurts of flame, and a mouthwatering smell of barbecued meat rose into the air.

Salads, bread and sauces were arranged on the yellow cloth, with the birthday cake in all its glory at the far end. Biting into her first, slightly charred and smokey-tasting beefburger marked with black lines from the wire mesh, Jane thought she had never tasted anything so delicious. It was a lovely way to have a party, with no worries about mess and crumbs, and an assortment of animals ready and waiting to clear up anything going spare. Jane noticed that there was something for everyone – chop bones and bits of overcooked sausage for the dogs and cats, crumbs and odd bits of salad for the chickens, lettuce leaves for the rabbits. As for Anthony and Julia, they were a real pair of dustbins, gobbling up everything they could get hold of and looking around for more.

Later, when the cake and lemonade had been served and no one could eat any more, they piled the debris with some dry sticks on the barbecue and watched the flames leap high. Lisa brought her guitar from the house and they sat on the grass, grimy and smokey-smelling and sang songs – 'Sing hosanna', 'The colours of the day', and 'Shine, Jesus, shine', which Jane thought was her very favourite one of all.

They were singing so lustily that the only ones who noticed the first rumble of thunder were the animals. Spam and Sandy pricked their ears nervously, and Patch came scrambling up Jane's legs to reach her lap. The cats one by one took themselves off to the house. Julia rolled her eyes nervously, but she kept on chewing at a spray of raspberry complete with berries which she had managed to reach unnoticed.

The second rumble, nearer and louder, was heard by everyone. Lisa stopped her guitar-playing in mid-chord. Mr Willis looked up at the sky where ominous purple-grey clouds rolled across to blot out the sunshine. He got to his feet.

'I'm afraid it's going to rain. Good thing the party's nearly over. Everyone give a hand and let's get all of this stuff indoors.'

There was a sudden burst of activity, with people rushing to pick up and carry in food, dishes and other belongings. Lisa ran to deposit her precious guitar indoors out of danger of the strings getting wet, while Tim's first thought were for the animals who might be frightened by thunder. Jane ran to rescue Tim's line of birthday cards. A moment later, a huge crack of thunder sounded overhead and the first drops of rain began to fall.

Chapter Seventeen

The rain gathered speed. There was a great hustle and bustle of hands trying to grab things from the big table, of feet running indoors and back for more, and bodies colliding on the way. After a moment Mrs Barrett sensibly said that there was no point in everyone getting soaked and they might as well carry everything at once. So she, Mr Willis and Paul bundled everything together in the middle of the yellow plastic tablecloth, took the four corners in their hands and carried it all into the house.

The glowing charcoal ash in the barbecue hissed, spluttered, turned grey and died. The balloons came loose in a sudden gust of wind and sailed up in a bright bobbing bunch of colour. Jane tried to grab their strings, but they were already too high, flying up and away above the roofs in the wind and the rain.

'Jane!' yelled Tim from the patio. 'Never mind! Let them go! Come on in. You're getting soaked!'

All the animals were safely under cover, and the humans gathered in the kitchen, damp and breathless, laughing at the sudden end to the birthday barbecue. Mrs Barret threaded her way between various cats and dogs to reach the kettle and put it on for some hot chocolate all round. It suddenly became quite dark, so someone switched on the lights. Outside the rain lashed the windows, but the big kitchen with its wood stove was warm and cosy.

'Well,' said Mr Willis, 'that's what I call timing! I think I'll pop upstairs now and finish that last bit of checking out I have to do.'

He disappeared towards the stairs. Everyone else suddenly felt hungry again, and they began to sort out edibles from the remains of the party.

Jane looked round for Patch and couldn't find him. There were Spam and Sandy crowding close to the stove with Anthony somewhere between them, protesting shrilly at being squashed. The cats were having a good wash, putting their damp fur in order and pretending they had never been alarmed at all. But she couldn't see her own precious puppy. She began to search behind the chairs, under the sideboard and in the corners, anywhere a frightened little pup might seek refuge.

'What are you doing?' asked Tim, with his mouth full of birthday cake.

'It's Patch,' said Jane, with the tears not far away. 'I can't find him. Where did he go? Did anyone see?'

No one had noticed where Patch went when the panic started.

'I don't think he came in at all,' said Jane in a wobbly voice. 'I think he's still out there in the garden, all alone and frightened. And I forgot all about him!'

She made a dash for the door but Lisa grabbed her. 'You can't go out in this. Wait until it stops a bit. He's probably run under one of the animal pens, out of the rain.'

Already the rain seemed to be slackening, and the

thunder had stopped crashing overhead and retreated to a distance. Jane grabbed her waterproof and made another dash for the door. She began to run about the wet grass, calling Patch's name, bending to peer under the chicken run, the rabbit hutch and the goat shed.

She was joined by Tim, Paul and Mark, sensibly dressed in waterproofs and Wellingtons. Together they combed the garden, even searching through the wet shrubs of the jungle, with drips going down their necks and wet undergrowth slapping against their knees. There was no sign of the small puppy.

Tears were trickling down Jane's face in earnest now, mingling with the raindrops. 'It's all my fault! I forgot all about him! How could I?'

Then she saw that the front gate, leading to the lane, was slightly open. She let out a shriek.

'Oh! The gate's open! He's gone! Now he's really lost!'

Before anyone could stop her she ran out into the lane, and began to search the wet verges and fences, peering into the gardens of the neighbouring houses. The rain had almost stopped by now, but the grass and foliage were sodden and trees sent showers of droplets cascading over her as she passed. She felt her feet squelch in her wet socks and shoes. Her jeans clung damply to her legs. No one else was about, though abandoned deckchairs, garden umbrellas and tricycles showed signs of sudden flight when the storm had come.

There was the sound of running footsteps, and Tim came charging down the lane after her, his hair sticking out at all angles. 'Hey! Where are you off to? Wait for me!'

Jane hunched her shoulders and walked on stub-

113

bornly, looking at gates to see if they were closed or open enough to let a small dog through.

'I've got to find him,' she said miserably.

'But you can't just go wandering off on your own.'

'I *can*.'

'You're not allowed to.'

'I don't care.'

'You'll get into another row.'

'I don't care.'

Tim let out a long sigh and fell into step beside her. They turned the corner into the next road.

'You're being silly. You can't just go on and on. They'll be out looking for *us* next.'

'Well, you can go home if you like.'

They had emerged from their own housing estate into a much busier road leading to the shopping centre, where cars were speeding past through the puddles.

'Look here,' said Tim. 'If he's come this far, someone will have seen him by now. Maybe picked him up and taken him home with them, or to the police station.'

A dreadful thought came into Jane's mind. If Patch had come this far he would be in dreadful danger from the passing traffic. Maybe, already, he had run out into the road under the wheels of a passing car . . .

Suddenly she couldn't bear to look any longer for fear of what she might see. She covered her face with her hands and burst into tears, standing on the wet pavement.

'Come on,' said Tim. 'Let's go home and see what the others think is best. It's still raining a little and it's starting to get dark. You're sopping wet.' He hesitated for a moment and then said, 'I've been praying like mad, so he'll be all right, don't worry.'

114

'You can't have,' said Jane, tearful but still argumentative. 'You haven't had time.'

'I just prayed running along the lane,' said Tim. 'You can do it anywhere. I'll pray all the way back. We both can.'

Back in the warm kitchen, Mrs Barrett tried to comfort her with hot chocolate while the others got torches and dry coats. Then Paul and Mark set off to search, while Lisa said she would phone round the neighbours and ask them to keep a lookout for a blue roan cocker spaniel pup. Hearing her describe Patch over the phone made Jane's tears flow again, and Mrs Barrett put a comforting arm round her. 'They'll find him, never you fret, love. If all else fails, we can notify the police.'

Jane sat up straight. The police! Why hadn't anyone remembered that they had a policeman right here in the house, and a very important one too! He'd know exactly how to find a lost person. Policemen always did, even if that person happened to be just a small puppy. She would go and ask him at once. She slipped out of Mrs Barrett's embrace and made for the stairs. Tim was putting out the cat and dog food, and looked up in surprise.

'Where are you going now?'

But she was already half-way up the stairs, pounding along to the door that entered Mr Willis's study. She turned the handle without bothering to knock. Mr Willis was sitting at a big desk under a tilted anglepoise lamp, his glasses on, a big word processor switched on in front of him and papers spread out all over the desk. He turned to look at her in mild surprise. His own children were strictly forbidden to barge in like this, and they usually obeyed. He peered over his glasses at her damp and distressed face. 'What's all this?'

'Patch is lost!' said Jane in a breathless gasp. 'He's got out through the gate. You've got to find him! Please, please!'

She ran right up to him and clutched his arm. Still a little bemused, Mr Willis got up. 'All right, all right. Now calm down! I'll come.'

He took off his glasses and laid them on the desk.

Tim's jaw dropped when he saw his father and Jane descending the stairs hand in hand. Mr Willis said, 'You'd better get some dry things of Lisa's to change into. You look like a drowned rat. And don't worry! I'll find him.'

Somehow, Jane had every confidence that he would.

Chapter Eighteen

With Mr Willis on the job, a great weight seemed to lift from Jane's mind. He must be a very clever policeman because hadn't he told her and Tim that he had just finished working on a long, difficult case and had been able to solve it? He would surely be able to track down and find a lost cocker spaniel pup.

With all this settled in her mind, Jane was quite happy to do as she was told. She took a good hot bath and changed into dry clothes, as Mrs Barrett insisted she should.

'We can't send you home like a drowned rat, now can we?' she said, adding bubble bath to the hot water.

Jane was left alone to soak herself in the pink bubbles, feeling quite worn out from all the excitement. Such a lot had happened in the last few weeks that it was difficult to take everything in – William, and Tim and his family, and all the animals, and her own lovely Patch. She repeated again the prayer she had said all the way back up the lane, in time with her wet plodding footsteps. 'Please, Jesus, let him come back safe. Please, Jesus, let him come back safe.'

She dried herself on the big striped bath towel waiting for her. Then, wrapped in the towel, she padded along to Lisa's bedroom to find the clothes laid out for her – a red tracksuit, long outgrown by Lisa, and green woolly socks. Sitting on the edge of Lisa's bed to pull them on, she found herself yawning again and again. The bed looked soft and inviting, covered by a plump pink eiderdown. Jane yawned again and thought that Lisa wouldn't mind if she crawled under the eiderdown and rested for a few moments. Within seconds she was fast asleep.

She slept deeply, worn out by excitement. She didn't stir when Lisa tiptoed in to look at her, nor did she hear the busy hum of voices downstairs, the opening and closing of doors, the ring of the doorbell and Spam's answering bark, the quiet opening of the bedroom door and a small plump body being deposited on the bed beside her. She only stirred when a warm pink tongue licked her face, and something warm and wriggling snuggled under the covers with her.

'Patch!' said Jane. 'Patch! You're back!'

She hugged him joyfully, smelling his damp puppy smell and hearing the happy little whimpers he made to show he was glad to be safely back with her. Then they both fell fast asleep again.

When Jane woke again, it was quite dark. Someone had been in to draw the curtains and switch on the bedside light. Patch was still sleeping, his puppy whiskers quivering with every breath. But when Jane kissed him he woke up at once, ready for a game. He began tugging at a corner of the pink eiderdown and growling puppy growls. A tiny rip appeared in the eiderdown and a small feather came out. Patch pounced on it and began to play. Jane thought she had better get up before any more damage was done. She sat up and slid to the floor, taking Patch firmly under one arm.

Upstairs and downstairs, the house seemed full of people, animals, talk and music. A burst of pop music came from behind Paul's bedroom door as she passed by. From the sitting-room the soft notes of Lisa playing Brahms' Lullaby drifted up. A buzz of conversation came to her ears as she softly descended the stairs in her stockinged feet. To her surprise she recognized her father's voice, and then her mother's, mingled with Mr Willis's deep tones. They must have decided to come round at last for their long-planned visit.

A sudden uneasy feeling came that she might be in trouble again. She had run off into the busy street, which she was definitely not allowed to do. However, stopping at the half-open door she saw that the adults seemed to be in the best of moods and on the best of terms. They were sitting around the kitchen table drinking coffee and chatting away like old friends. Mrs Barrett and Sandy had gone home, and the soft murmur of voices from the sitting-room showed that Mark and Tim were watching TV there. No one noticed Jane for a moment. She put down the wriggling Patch, who trotted unnoticed to the hearth to join Spam and two cats.

'It's really made me think,' her dad was saying, holding a large, red coffee mug in both hands. 'I mean, we naturally want all the best things for our kids – a good home, security, the best education, health, holidays and so on. We find the best schools we can afford, teach them manners, keep their dental appointments, check up on what they're reading and watching on TV. But Jane's questions these last couple of weeks have really made me think. Is there something more, something

119

we've neglected, maybe?'

He cleared his throat, sounding a little embarrassed.

Mum broke in, 'We feel, Bob and I, that there's maybe something we're missing out on – spiritual values perhaps. Do you know what we mean?'

Mr Willis nodded. 'Yes, yes, I do.'

Dad cleared his throat again. 'You see, Mike, there's so much odd teaching in the world today that we don't quite know what to believe ourselves, let alone teach our children. But Sue and I feel they ought to be taught something. Don't you agree?'

Mr Willis nodded, but didn't say anything. He seemed quite content to let Dad do the talking. Dad went on, 'You take your children to church, don't you, Mike? Jane's been pestering me to go too, and I've promised to take her. Would you mind if we went along with you?'

'Not at all,' said Mr Willis, 'not at all.'

Jane caught her breath in a little gasp. They would be going to church with Tim and his family! Now she could learn to sing the songs that Lisa played on her guitar. Perhaps she would go to the Junior Church with Tim, and learn more about Jesus. He had answered her prayers for Patch. That must surely mean he cared for her just as much as he cared for Tim.

Mum heard the sharp little intake of breath and turned her head. 'Jane, darling, you're awake!' She held out an arm. Jane ran over and perched on Mum's knee, feeling suddenly shy again. 'Were you pleased to find Patch was back?'

Jane nodded, and then suddenly found her voice. 'Where did you find him, Mr Willis?'

Mr Willis grinned across at her. 'Well, I tried to put myself in his place, work out where I'd go if I was a little

120

pup frightened by my first thunderstorm. I thought I'd run into the first safe dark place I came to. And I was right. That's exactly what he had done.'

'Where was that?'

'The big drainpipe just opposite our front gate, left over from when they did the drains. He must have rushed straight out of the gate, across the lane and into the pipe. He was right at the back, shivering all over, but very pleased to see me and be rescued.'

Jane nodded again, thinking how cleverly Mr Willis had worked it all out.

'Aren't you going to say, "thank you, Mr Willis"?' prompted Dad.

Jane didn't feel shy any more. She jumped off Mum's lap and ran round to where Mr Willis sat and threw her arms around his neck in a choking hug. 'Thank you, Mr Willis,' she said. 'It was so clever of you. I think you're the best policeman in the whole world!'

Chapter Nineteen

Jane thought that Mr Willis was looking at her rather oddly as she let go her stranglehold of his neck. 'What did you say, Jane?'

'I said, thank you, Mr Willis, it was clever of you and you're the best policeman in the whole world,' she repeated in a small voice.

She was overcome with shyness again, and moved round the table to take refuge against the knees of her own dad. She wondered whether Mr Willis was cross with her, but he didn't look cross, just puzzled.

'Did you think that I was a policeman?'

Jane's eyes grew round. She nodded speechlessly. She saw that Dad and Mum looked surprised too. Dad cleared his throat, and said, 'She did. In fact, we all did. Aren't you a policeman, then?'

Mr Willis shook his head. Then, suddenly he roared with laughter, throwing back his head and tipping his chair back on two legs until it was in imminent danger of falling backwards. Jane felt herself beginning to grin in an uncertain kind of way, although she had no idea what the joke was.

'Well,' said Mr Willis, still spluttering a little. 'I don't know how you got that impression, but I assure you it's not the case.'

Jane couldn't quite remember why she had thought so either. There had been so many small hints of a job, a plot, a search – or was it re-search? The idea had just grown and grown, and eventually been taken for granted. Tim and the others had never *said* that their father was a policeman. But if not, what was he? What was the important work that he did up there in his study, with his books and papers, phone and computer?

As though echoing her own thoughts, Dad asked, 'Might I ask what your work is then, Mike?'

Mr Willis brought the chair down on all four legs again, and got to his feet. He went over to the bookcase under the window and took out three or four paperbacks, rather tatty and dog-eared. He put them on the table in front of Dad. Jane spelled out the titles, in big red letters on the covers – *Mountain Fire, Midnight Journey, Winter Harvest* – and there was *The Darkest Night*, the book that Dad had just returned to the library. All of them were by P. Grenville.

Dad's eyes lit up with interest. 'Ah, one of my favourite writers, P. Grenville. Tells a good gripping yarn without any unneccesary violence, but really makes you think. I can see you're one of his fans too. Although I don't quite understand what . . .' He stopped suddenly in the middle of a sentence and Jane could see that he had gone rather pale. He pointed a finger at the books and then at Mr Willis. 'You – you don't mean that you . . .'

Mr Willis nodded and roared with laughter again, slapping his thigh. 'A policeman! I'm sorry, but I just can't get over it.'

Dad seemed quite taken aback, and Jane joggled his

arm, puzzled. 'What is it, Dad?'

'Well,' said Dad. 'It seems we have a best-selling author for our new next-door neighbour. None other than P. Grenville himself. Well I never! What do you think of that, Jane?'

'I don't understand,' said Jane. 'Mr *Willis* is our next-door neighbour, not P. Grenville. What do you mean? You can't be P. Grenville, because you're Mr Willis.'

She glared accusingly across the table.

'I'm afraid I'm both,' said Tim's dad apologetically. 'P. Grenville is my pen name. I hope you're not too disappointed.'

Jane didn't really know whether she was disappointed or not, but she was certainly confused. Mr Willis wasn't a policeman at all. Maybe he wasn't even Mr Willis at all, if he was P. Grenville too. Maybe Tim wasn't Tim Willis, but Tim Grenville, but it didn't really matter. She picked up one of the books and opened a page. It was full of long, grown-up words that she couldn't understand much.

'Tell me,' said Dad, leaning forward with great interest. 'That scene in *Mountain Fire*, with the helicopter making a forced landing in the desert. Have you piloted a helicopter yourself in those conditions? It's so realistic. However do you manage it?'

Then they were deep in technical discussion, talking about things that were far above her head. Jane looked at Mum and saw that she was pink-cheeked and excited. Mr Willis was obviously someone quite important, even though he wasn't a policeman.

'Jane,' said Mum. 'Could you please go and take a peep at William? I put him in the dining room in the pram.'

Jane closed the dining-room door behind her. It was cool and quiet there, with a dimmer light on. William's pram was parked under the window. Jane perched on the window seat and looked down at him. He was awake and, wonder of wonders, he wasn't crying. Instead, he had crammed one of his thumbs into his mouth and was making contented slurping, sucking noises. His eyes were open and looked navy blue in the dim light. She saw that the dark fluff covering his head was getting thin and patchy, giving way to a cap of short, smooth, golden hairs which were growing underneath. Mum had been right. He was going to be as blond as she was herself.

Jane leaned closer and whispered, 'William!' To her surprise he turned his head towards her, still sucking hard on his thumb, and gazed up towards her face.

'Hello, William,' said Jane softly. 'This is me. Jane. I'm your big sister.' William sucked noisily, his eyes on her face. Jane felt that she was bursting with things she wanted to tell him. She said, as though he could understand everything, 'Do you know what, William? Tim's dad has turned out to be P. Grenville, the man who wrote those books Dad's always reading. He's not a policeman at all. But he found Patch when he ran away and got lost. Patch is my puppy. You can play with him when you're bigger, if you're very careful. P'raps Tim will let you play with Anthony, too. Anthony's a little pig, all greedy and pink, like you.'

She paused for breath, and went on, 'You're much nicer when you're not crying all the time. You're quite nice really.'

William gazed unblinkingly, sucking on his thumb. Then, all of a sudden, he took his thumb out and smiled, a wide toothless smile that seemed to go right across

126

his face. Jane felt breathless, as though someone had squeezed her hard around the middle. William had smiled, his very first smile! And he'd smiled at *her*.

She held her breath, in case the smile turned into one of those awful grimaces that meant there was a '*Waah-ahh-ahh*!' to follow, but he just put his thumb back into his mouth and went on sucking.

'Jane!' called Mum from the kitchen. 'Everything okay?'

Jane tucked the cot sheet in around William and tip-toed to the door. Mum and Dad and Mr Willis/P. Gren-ville had moved their chairs to sit comfortably around the stove, with their coffee mugs freshly filled. They were talking and laughing as though they'd known each other for years. Mum had kicked off her sandals and Dad had his feet on the fender.

'William asleep?' asked Mum.

'No,' said Jane, 'but he's okay.'

'Good,' said Mum. 'Why don't you go and watch TV for half an hour or so with the others while we finish our coffee?'

Jane half-opened her mouth to tell her mother that William had smiled at her, but she changed her mind. Mum had told her that babies couldn't smile properly until five or six weeks old, and William was barely three weeks. Until then, Mum said, it was just a touch of wind or maybe wishful thinking. She and Dad might think she was making up stories again. She wasn't, because it really had happened. He had really smiled.

She thought of picking up Patch and taking him with her, but he looked so cosy that she left him where he was, flopped in a heap with his feet against Anthony's tummy and his head tucked under Spam's chin. She headed for the sitting-room door. It had been an interesting sort of day, and wasn't quite over yet. In fact it looked like being quite a late night.

She decided she wouldn't tell Tim that William had smiled at her, even though he was her very best friend. There were some secrets you only shared with your brother.

WHAT TO DO WHEN
LIFE
SUCKS

For Jillie with our love.
Margaret and Dr Claire

Random House Australia Pty Ltd
20 Alfred Street, Milsons Point NSW 2061
http://www.randomhouse.com.au

Sydney New York Toronto
London Auckland Johannesburg
and agencies throughout the world

First published in 2001
Copyright © Margaret Clark and Dr Claire Fox 2001

National Library of Australia
Cataloguing-in-Publication Data

Clark, M. D. (Margaret Dianne) 1943- .
What to do when life sucks.

ISBN 1 740 51753 9.
1. Teenagers – Life skills guides. 2. Young
adults – Life skills guides. 3. Life skills – Handbooks, manuels, etc.
I. Fox, Claire. II. Title.

158.10835

Cover photograph by Getty Images.
Cover design by Gayna Murphy, Greendot Design.
Photograph of Margaret Clark by Reece Scannell.
Photograph of Dr Claire Fox by her husband.
Typeset by Asset Typesetting Pty Ltd in 10.5/14 Garamond.
Printed by Griffin Press Pty Ltd, Adelaide.

WHAT TO DO WHEN
LIFE
SUCKS

Margaret Clark
& Dr Claire Fox

RANDOM HOUSE AUSTRALIA

This book represents educational material as a reference only and is not intended to substitute for an individual's medical and/or psychological treatment. For individual advice regarding your physical and emotional health you should consult your own doctor. The authors and the publisher disclaim any liability arising directly or indirectly from the use of this book.

Contents

Introduction

Some of you are going to feel pretty good about yourselves generally, and will read this book knowing that you can learn a number of things to help make your life better. Others of you are going to be feeling really bad and upset. Even if you feel like you're at the bottom of a great big hole, alone in the darkness, we'll help to show you that there is a way out from that darkness to a better place.

Some of the problems that are discussed in this book you might recognise, and some you mightn't, but we all have problems at some time or other. Life sucks sometimes. But it doesn't need to, because there are things you can do to influence what happens in your life.

Here're some of the problems that young people face:

Siobhan didn't want to wake up and face another day. She wanted to burrow down under the bedclothes and stay there. Her life really sucked. Siobhan lived with her mum — her parents had divorced six months ago. Her mum had a new boyfriend, Paul, who was a total jerk and spent a lot of time telling Siobhan what to do. School was just gross, and her best friend Lana had moved interstate two months ago. Siobhan felt very alone and unhappy. She dragged herself out of bed ...

How many of you are in Siobhan's situation? From the emails Margaret gets there are hundreds of young people in the same predicament.

Mike made his way down the school corridor on his way to his maths class. He'd been feeling sort of depressed for the past couple of months, but he wasn't really sure why. He felt sad and miserable a lot of the time, and he'd never told anyone but at night sometimes in bed he just started crying. It was like someone had died — the same sort of feeling — except that no one he knew had died recently.

Mike comes from a well-off family. His dad frequently tells Mike how lucky he is to have all the opportunities he's got, like going to a really good school, travelling overseas for holidays and living in a big house with a swimming pool. Mike's dad is a doctor who often works late and on weekends. Everyone expects that Mike will follow in his dad's footsteps and become a doctor too. He does really well in science and maths. But Mike feels sort of grey and empty inside. He's not sure whether he even wants to be a doctor. He doesn't know what he wants to be. Sometimes he wonders if he'd be better off dead ...

Mike's idea of wishing he was dead doesn't really solve anything. It doesn't allow him to take control of his life and have a good one!

Jessica looked at the bathroom scales in despair.

She hadn't lost a single gram. She'd tried so hard last week, and some days she'd only eaten an apple and nothing else. Why wasn't the fat dropping off? 'You're a fat cow,' she told herself, grabbing at her thighs.

Tomorrow the summer swimming lessons started at school. She couldn't let anyone see her in bathers! She'd have to pretend to be sick, or skip school. Jessica felt panicky and desperate. Without really understanding why, she went out into the kitchen and took a packet of chocolate biscuits from the cupboard. She scurried into her bedroom, shut the door and sat on her bed, cramming the biscuits into her mouth, crying as she ate ...

Life can be difficult for all of us, and being a teenager can at times be really difficult. It's confusing. Sometimes you feel like a child and want protection and help from your parents, and other times you want to be grown up and independent and wish your parents would just get off your case.

There is lots of pressure to do well at school and get a good job. Your parents may be on your back about your homework and your grades. Your body is changing and growing up and doing strange things. You have new hormones zipping around in your bloodstream.

You switch on the television and watch your favourite programs and all the women are skinny and gorgeous, the men are handsome, no one has acne, no one gets their period all over their pyjamas or has a wet dream all on the sheets, all their clothes are beautiful. Just like in real life. Yeah, sure.

Margaret receives lots of letters and emails from teenagers with troubles. Unfortunately, there isn't a course at school called 'Life and How To Do It'. Margaret often jokes that we would be better off being born with instructions taped to our navels. Margaret is an author and was a drug and alcohol counsellor. Dr Claire is a medical doctor. We decided to write this book to help you feel better about yourself and your life. Also, as two human beings we've had our ups and downs ourselves and we hope we've learnt some things along the way we can also share with you.

Some problems are fairly straightforward to deal with but others are more tricky, so it can take some time and a fair bit of help to untangle certain situations and find a way out. So hang in there and don't ever give up because there is always be a way forward, even if it doesn't feel like it now.

The extracts from emails, letters and people's stories are based on real life incidents, but to protect the people and their anonymity, all names, places, dates, times plus some of the details have been changed.

Dr Claire and Margaret

1 Body Image

Dr Claire,
The girls in my class are all so pretty and I feel
like an ugly lump. I have fat thighs, my bum is
huge, and I have freckles all over me. I can't
tan, I just burn. The boys in my class tell me
to 'move your fat arse'. I don't have much
money for clothes, make-up and hair. I feel like
a real freak.
Sheridan, age 16

Dear Sheridan,
I'm sure all the girls in your class aren't pretty,
only maybe one or two. The others are making
the most of their assets and downplaying their
imperfections. You don't mention your face, hair,
eyes, teeth, nose, neck, arms, legs, breasts,
stomach, hands or toes. You've focused on two
areas, fat thighs and huge bum. Look around
you. Most females have fat thighs and big bums,
except for the breed of female who has long thin
legs and is built like a boy in the hips. If you
really have thunder-thighs and a bum like a
working bullock, then you can do some spot
exercises to tone them down a bit. Be realistic,
though. If you are naturally pear-shaped
— which is a healthy shape for females to be

1

— you're not going to end up with skinny legs and a thin butt. Also, at 16 your body is still developing and changing, and you may find things change shape as you get older.

If you have pale skin, use a fake tan if you want that tanned look. The new ones aren't brown and streaky when you apply them. Margaret's tried one and she tells me it's good. Personally, I'd go with the pale look. Those girls who are tanning themselves out in the sun are doing themselves no favours. The sun damages your skin, leaves you at risk for skin cancers and ages your skin faster. A tan is really your body's way of frantically trying to produce more melanin to ward off damage from the sun. Every time you get a tan it's a sign that you have damaged your skin. So really, thank goodness you can't tan because you'll stay out of the sun and end up with better skin. Also, many people — including me — think freckles can look really attractive and cute, so try not to get hung up about them. Get some advice on some simple make-up to put on your face if you feel you must blend in the freckles.

Try to focus on your good points and make the most of them. A new hairstyle can do wonders. You don't need to spend a fortune on streaks and colours — regular shampooing and brushing plus a healthy diet of vegies, fruit, raw nuts, bread, cereals, meat/chicken/fish/tofu/beans/lentils and low-fat dairy products, and drinking lots of water plus a regular exercise program will give your skin a natural healthy glow and make your hair nice and glossy and make you feel fit and well and good about yourself regardless of a little thigh and bum pudge.

And what about the rest of you? Your intelligence, your personality, your studies, your hobbies and interests, your causes and your passions in life, these are the things you truly need to focus on rather than bum and thighs. If it's any consolation, when I was in school some boys snuck up behind me while I was sitting on a bench and measured my bum with a ruler, then took great delight in telling the whole class and taunting me. Think of these comments as just some verbal farting these boys are doing. See the verbal farts just waft up into the air and vanish, they don't even touch you. Of course, if you're feeling strong, you could try a smart reply, like 'move your tiny dick'. But that is optional.

Dr Claire

Our society is obsessed with looks, especially the way women look. It pays to think about history here. We still live in a patriarchal society, where men retain most of the power and control in our society. Just look at the smaller number of women than men in parliament, and how few women are the heads of industry and organisations.

There is still an emphasis on how women look rather than what they do. Newspaper reports comment on what female politicians and sportswomen look like and what they wear and how they do their hair. They don't usually bother to comment on what the male politicians or sportsmen are wearing. With women, we still tend to look first at how she looks, then at what she does.

We can tend to take it for granted now that women can work in decent jobs, do any course they want at university, have their own money and buy cars, apartments, investments, whatever they want. But a lot of these changes are only relatively recent in our society.

Did you know that equal pay for equal work laws only came about in the early 1970's. In the 1950's for example, a man and a woman could be doing exactly the same work, but the woman would get paid less, and this was legal! Margaret's Aunt Dorothy spent years working in a bank getting paid less than the men when she was doing exactly the same work! And women in certain occupations, like working for the Government in the Public Service, were forced to resign if they got married. Education was considered to be 'wasted' on women, because it was thought that women would not work outside the home once they were married. So a family might pay to send their sons to university, but not their daughters! And further back in history women didn't inherit from their families, it was all left to the sons!

So, women have been in an economically vulnerable position in society, as they did not have the same opportunities to get an education, to get a decent job and to make money. So, if you wanted some financial security, you'd better get married, and if you wanted to get married you'd better look good to attract a husband!

Throughout history, standards of beauty have changed. Currently, female models are tall and thin — very thin. But if you look back you'll see that the rotund, chubby and curvy figure was once considered gorgeous, which is reflected in the paintings of women. Look at the famous paintings of women in an art book. You'll see very curvy and cuddly women painted there.

Marilyn Monroe was considered one of the sexiest women in the world. By today's crazy standards she would be considered 'chubby'. Also, statistics kept on the winners of the Miss America contest show that over the decades the women have become thinner. Those women who won the Miss America contest back in the 1950s would be considered too fat today, and yet at the time they were considered the epitome of American beauty. Much of the pressure to look a certain way simply reflects what's in vogue at the time. Emaciated is in now in models, but that doesn't make it right or good. And did you know research shows men actually prefer girls and women with a bit of flesh on them, rather than the skeletal beings pictured in magazines and on telly? There has been research conducted where men and boys were shown pictures of real women

versus skinny models, and guess what, they prefer the
real women with real bodies!

Girls compare their bodies to the 'ideal' shapes they
see in the media all around them, on television, in films,
in magazines. But the stupid thing is that heaps of the
photos we see are 'touched up' — that is, they are
altered to make the models' bodies and skin and hair
look more perfect. So the photos are not even real
images of the models, let alone real images of ordinary
people. And the models themselves do some pretty
crazy things to themselves, like trying to starve
themselves to the current waif-like look. Models can
really suffer and feel awful from having to starve
themselves. Recently we read an interview with Christy
Turlington, a supermodel, who has given up modelling
because of the bad effects on her health.

Did you know that the commonest size of women's
clothing sold in Australia is size 16? So the models we
see in the media have very little to do with the reality
of the size and shape of Australian women.

Girls learn to dislike their bodies, having been
bombarded with unrealistic images of thinness since
childhood. They learn that 'fat is bad' and they try to rid
their bodies of what they see as loathsome fat. And girls
can end up hating their bodies, which when you think
about it is very serious, because to hate your body is
really to hate yourself.

Dear Margaret,
I'm fat and ugly. When I sit on the toilet my
thighs look like tree trunks. I'm only 11 and

already I feel like a huge ugly blimp. Can I get plastic surgery to make my thighs thin?
Miranda, age 11

Dear Miranda,
You're lucky that your thighs only look like tree trunks when you sit on the toilet. Mine look like a whole forest! Sitting on the toilet and looking at one's legs doesn't give a true picture of how they really look, believe me. Try standing and looking in a mirror.

When you are older, like eighteen, you can probably get surgery, but by then hopefully you'll have decided that this is a dumb idea. If you're truly too fat, cut down on junk food that is high in sugar or fat, eat more fruit and vegies instead, drink water instead of fizzy sugary drinks, and walk/ride a bike more. Learn to love your body and yourself, and focus on your good points, rather than on your imperfections, okay? And I'll let you into a secret. Boys prefer curvier women! True.
Margaret

Because of guilt and shame about their bodies, most girls are constantly on the defensive about this. Almost all teenage girls at some time worry about their weight, go on diets, and feel guilty when they eat. Instead of valuing and loving their bodies, they are at war with them. Females are usually curvy, because our hormones give us a different shape from men, and our bodies are naturally designed to have a slightly higher fat content than males. The female pelvis is constructed so our hips are wider than a male's. That's Mother Nature's clever way of helping a woman out if she decides to have a baby in the future because there is a wider space inside the pelvis compared to a man's to allow for the baby to be born. This is not to say you have to have a baby one day, but that it's there if you need it.

Some people who are psychologists and other people who write about women's issues in our society say that this pressure on girls and women to be thin is an anti-female thing, because the pressure to be unnaturally skinny is going against the normal female curvy shape. Also, some say that the pressure on girls to be so thin is almost like girls are getting the message that they don't have the right to exist, that they should just shrink away and not take up space and form and have substance and ideas and opinions of their own. Certainly there are a whole lot of girls out there whose time and energy is taken up with worrying about how to get skinny, whereas that energy could be put to more productive uses like hobbies or working for a cause or working on furthering their studies or their job opportunities. These are very interesting ideas you might like to think about, and maybe discuss with your friends.

We focus on being skinny even when we are children these days. A research study found that young children select pictures of slim people compared to bigger people when asked to identify good-looking people. But who says skinny is good? Where does it come from? Not the medical profession, they are protesting at the pressure on teenagers to be ridiculously thin. And not from God, because there is no commandment to be very skinny. So have a think about where all this pressure is coming from.

There is an enormous multi-billion dollar weight loss industry that revolves around body image: diet books and magazines, TV programs, exercise equipment, videos, diet products and diet foods, weight loss pills and potions, weight loss organisations, plastic surgery. Also, cosmetics, skin-care, make-up and hair care products are another huge billion dollar industry. By presenting us with ads where the models look skinny and totally beautiful, the companies that make these products persuade us to go out and spend our dollars.

And while men and boys have been spared a lot of pressure and emphasis on appearance, now advertisers are cottoning on that there is still half the human race to persuade into using skin care and hair care products, and even make-up. Boys are starting to feel much more pressure about their appearance too these days. You can support a friend by admiring their good features — eyes, hair, body.

What can I do in the face of all the hype about body image?

Here are a few suggestions:

1   Realise the undeniable truth that people's bodies come in all sorts of heights, weights, shapes and sizes. Have you seen that saying they had up at The Body Shop, that there are billions of women in the world but only a handful of supermodels?

2   Be on the alert for examples of 'lookism', that is where people are judged on the basis of their looks alone. Watch for it on TV programs, such as *Ally McBeal* and *Friends*, where all the female actors are so skinny they look like they need a decent meal. Check out the pictures in magazines of models who are so skinny they look like they'd blow over on a windy day. Question what is so supposedly fantastic about being super-skinny? Who says skinny is perfect? Some movie stars and models starve themselves to these unnatural shapes. They can end up passing out and getting sick or using drugs to maintain unnatural thinness, having liposuction and operations to the point where they look like walking skeletons. Notice how their heads seem to be too big for their bodies. When you actually analyse this, they look like aliens. Which, in a way, they are, because they're chopping and changing their natural human form.

3   Be supportive of your own and your friends' positive body image. Remind yourself and them

about all the great things about your bodies and your looks. If your friend is groaning that her bum is too big, remind her that her bum is only a fraction of her total body, and what about her gorgeous eyes and great hair and cute nose. Try to be positive and supportive, rather than critical.

4 Aim to have a fit, healthy body, nourished with good food and nutrition. Learn to care for your body with love and respect, rather than punish it with self-hating attitudes. If your natural shape is curvy and soft, or you are a solid build or tall or short or a bigger size, accept that you are you. Being a bit overweight can be healthy if you're fit and you exercise. Being underweight can be healthy if you're born with a tiny frame and you eat decent meals and you exercise moderately but aren't madly over-exercising.

Being overweight, overeating and unfit is bad news, because you're not giving your body the best chance to be fit and healthy and perform at its best, plus you're not going to feel as well as you would if you were exercising regularly and eating in a more nutritious way.

Being underweight and half-starved is bad news, because you are depriving your body of essential fuel and nutrients, and your body will be going into overdrive trying to keep everything going on insufficient fuel and will be screwing up its metabolic functions as it tries desperately to soldier on without adequate food.

5 If you are overweight such that you feel it is
   unhealthy for you, realise that a 'diet' is unlikely
   to help you. A 'diet' is something that you go on
   then go off. Then you have the yoyo syndrome
   where you lose weight but then put it all back
   plus some more, because your body's
   metabolism has gone haywire from the dieting.
   Research has shown that the only people who
   lose weight and keep it off are those who
   continue to practise a healthy eating plan after
   they've lost the excess weight. What can help you
   to be a more healthy weight is to develop an
   eating plan that is more healthy than what you're
   used to and that you can live with long term.
   Often it's not so much that you need to learn to
   eat less but that you need to learn to eat more
   healthy-type foods that are less laden with sugar,
   fats and bad hydrogenated oils, and stop eating
   unhealthy foods. Also, putting some type of
   exercise into your life is essential to have a
   healthy body and healthy mind. Exercise includes
   a wide range of things from walking your dog,
   riding your bike instead of Dad giving you a lift in
   the car, roller-blading (don't break anything!),
   going for a swim, through to organised sports
   and gym programs. Think of the change as an
   overhaul to be more healthy rather than to
   'be thin'.
6 If you feel you need help because you are
   overweight then a good place to start is your local

doctor or a qualified dietician. They can tell you if you are in fact overweight and then help with advice. If you feel your eating is really out of control you may have a problem with compulsive overeating. This can be more tricky to deal with than simply trying a new eating plan. There may be underlying psychological issues. You may want to get some counselling to help you deal with this and perhaps join a support group such as Overeaters Anonymous.

7   Some people find that certain foods trigger them off to binge or overeat. For example, if they eat sugary things they feel like they just can't stop. Or it might be other things, like cheese or peanuts, or something else. We don't know why particular foods seem to act as 'trigger' foods to overeat. It may be a problem of the body being sensitive to that type of food. Some people find they just have to eliminate certain foods from their food plan. The point is that there are lots of different foods out there you may never even have heard of but that are great to eat. Sometimes a look in your local health food shop or the health section of your supermarket may reveal foods you'd never even considered before. Also there are lots of different fruits and vegetables you may never have tried. Dr Claire now has tofu, soy milk, sprouted legumes, natural yoghurt, sunflower seeds, puffed millet cereal, rice cakes, pumpkin seeds, olive and

soybean oil and all sorts of other things she'd
never even heard of once. Finding new healthy
things to eat can be quite an adventure.

How can I look good on a budget?

Dear Margaret,
I'm getting depressed because our family
hasn't got much money and I can't afford
to buy all the designer gear that my friends
have got. I look like pauper city when I
go out. It's making me lose confidence in
myself. What can I do? How can I make my
budget stretch so I don't look like a Vin
Bin reject?
Zoe, age 16

Dear Zoe,
You can look like a million dollars in a
green plastic garbage bag if you have *it*.
What is *it*? Well, *it* is the ability to look good
in whatever you wear, and it doesn't involve
designer gear and expensive brands. It involves
developing your own personal style. Dare to
be different and wear your clothes with
aplomb. Visit op shops and rifle through the
retro racks. When I was fourteen I had
the same predicament as you, so I took sewing
classes. That's another option. And then, of
course, there's the Seconds shops where big
names are marked down cheaply. You don't

need hundreds of outfits. A couple of pairs of good jeans or pants, a few tops and you're organised.
Margaret

Here are some tips:

1 Clothes, and accessories like belts and jewellery, can often be found in op shops and second-hand clothing shops. Now, before you turn up your nose at this idea be assured both Margaret and Dr Claire have dressed themselves from these types of shops (and still do!) and you can get some very nice stuff at a fraction of the new price. You might have to try a few of these shops, and you may have to go through some junk before you hit on some good stuff, but it can be fun and you can have some good finds. Shops where second-hand clothes are sold on consignment for their previous owners often have some fantastic things. Your local Yellow Pages should have listings for Second Hand or Recycle Clothes shops and Op shops.

2 Other good places for both boys' and girls' clothes are samples and seconds shops and warehouse outlets. Most cities have some of these. You can get clothes and shoes at many dollars off the normal retail price. Don't forget you can also get sports clothes and equipment too.

3 A good haircut can make anybody look better. Ring around different salons for prices of haircuts

as they vary a lot. Some salons give a discount for students, or a family discount if Mum, Dad and the kids all go to the one place. Hairdressing schools often run salons where the students will do your hair — both girls and boys — for a much cheaper price than a normal salon. Look in your Yellow Pages under Hairdressing Schools.

4 Basic grooming tips include looking clean. That includes hair and fingernails. Lank, greasy hair isn't going to make you feel good about yourself.

5 For girls, make-up can be a big cost factor if you decide you want to use it. You can go to any large department store and make an appointment with the cosmetic consultants who sell the products. (You might want to take your mum with you. But then again ...) The beautician will make up your face and write down what she's used. You can smile, say thanks very much, that you'd like to think it over or see how your face reacts to the cosmetics and then walk off without buying any of the stuff. You can try several different company's consultants for different looks. Then you can pick out what you like. Usually you can find the same make-up cheaper in a discount cosmetics store. Also, cheap cosmetics can look just as good as highly priced cosmetics. Check in your supermarket or big variety store like Target or K-Mart. (Margaret uses Maybelline. That is, when she bothers wearing make-up.)

6   Acne advice can be got from your local pharmacy,
    where the staff will be able to show you a range
    of products. If the advice doesn't help or you feel
    your acne is bad, head off to your doctor for
    some help.

7   Clean teeth and fresh-smelling breath are
    important. The best teeth cleaning comes from
    using an electronic toothbrush, because it gives
    your teeth and gums the best going over. If you
    can't afford an electronic toothbrush, regular use
    of an ordinary toothbrush is the next best thing.
    Dental floss is good for the health of your teeth
    and gums. If your teeth need dental attention and
    you and your family are short of money, ring
    around different dental surgeries before you go
    to find out what they charge for a check-up or
    a filling, because the prices can vary a lot. Your
    school may have access to a school dental
    service, and large cities usually have dental
    hospitals that provide lower priced care. Your
    local community health centre may also be able
    to provide dental care. Try to look after your teeth.
    If you feel you need braces (orthodontics) but
    your family can't afford them, again try the
    suggestions above for cheaper rates. Remember
    too that these days a lot of things can be done for
    adults' teeth, so if you have to wait until you can
    pay for it yourself don't despair. There can be a lot
    of hype about having the 'perfect smile'. Try to
    focus instead on having healthy teeth rather than

perfect teeth. (A tip for girls: red lipstick makes your teeth look whiter.)

8 For basic skin care you need something to clean your skin and a moisturiser. Check your local supermarket. You don't have to use expensive products. Health food companies often make nice skin products with fewer chemicals, so try the health food section at your supermarket. (Margaret uses soap and water, no creams, and has done so all her life. What you use depends on your skin type and what feels right for you.)

9 Take care in the sun. We know that exposure to the sun's rays damages the skin. Australia has one of the highest rates of skin cancer in the world. Also, baking your skin in the sun leads to ageing of the skin and wrinkles so you can end up looking like a wrinkled prune when you are still a relatively young adult. So remember to use sunscreen, wear a hat and sunglasses, seek out shade, stay out of the sun during the hottest hours of the day, and best of all, cover up. Those new solar suits you can wear to go swimming but which cover up your skin and protect it from the sun's biting rays are fantastic. (Margaret has used fake tan when she's gone to a party or the beach, not wanting to look like a white rice pudding.) But the day will come when pale is here to stay, and those with real tans will be looked upon as poor misguided losers.

Body image and boys

Dr Claire,

I am so worried I am going out of my mind, and I am very embarrassed and can't talk to anyone about it. I have a very small penis. The boys at school have called me 'stumpy' because they see me when we're getting changed for swimming. I am totally off my head with worry. I've heard you can get plastic surgery to make your penis longer. Where can I go for this and how much does it cost? Would I have to tell my parents? Please help me.

Dave, age 13

Dear Dave,

First some facts. For most boys their penis starts to grow in length and width during puberty about a year before he reaches his peak rate of height growth, so for most boys we're talking about 12 to 13 that the penis starts to develop into its adult size. But, this is just an average, and development can start earlier or later. So, with you your penis probably still has some growing to do. The penis usually reaches its final size between around 14–16 years, but sometimes it will be later than this.

Next, penises come in different sizes, especially when they're soft or flaccid. It's true, some are smaller than others. But, the interesting thing is that when the penis is erect, the size differences between men tends to even out, so the average length of most erect penises is around 15 centimetres, although some will be bigger and some will be smaller.

Also, especially for the penis when it is in a soft or flaccid state, lots of things can affect size, like if you're cold, or nervous, this can make the penis shrink a bit, whereas when you're warm and relaxed it looks bigger.

There are other variations between penises apart from size that are also completely normal. The glans or head of the penis may look wider or narrower than the shaft. The shape of the glans can vary. The flaccid (soft) penis can hang straight down, or to the left or the right. The erect penis can stick straight out, or to the left or the right. The angle at which the erect penis sticks out from the body can vary.

During my career I have seen a gazillion penises, and I can assure you they come in all sizes. You cannot tell from looking at a man with his clothes on what size his penis will be. I've seen very tall men, very muscular and macho sportsmen who have very very small penises, and I have seen short, flabby, unfit looking men who have very large penises. Even the penises of the rich and famous come in all sizes.

Men get more hung up about penis size than women do. How good a man is as a lover has nothing to do with the size of his penis. There are men with big penises, who are lousy at sex, and men with small penises, who have their women begging for more. It has more to do with how you learn to use what you've got, and what you do to stimulate your partner with your other body parts including touching with your hands and kissing. The most sensitive nerve endings in the woman are in the clitoris and around the entrance of the vagina, and just inside the vagina. This is where the action is, not at some deep place way inside the vagina, where in fact the vagina is not very sensitive. And the most sensitive part of the penis is the skin around the glans (the head) of the penis (at the end of the penis), and even with a small penis these bits will easily make it into the vagina and get stimulated.

It is true that there is plastic surgery available that will make the penis appear longer. However, like all surgery, it has potential risks. This sort of surgery that is done for cosmetic reasons is expensive. You are not a candidate for plastic surgery because your body has not finished its natural growing. Hopefully, men will realize that penises naturally vary a lot in size and shape, and we won't have a stampede of men running off to get unnecessary surgery.

So, for now, you'll need to be patient and let mother nature finish her work. If you would feel re-assured by having a doctor look at your penis, then you can go along to a general practitioner or family doctor and get them to reassure you. Doctors are used to dealing with these sorts of concerns and worries about penises, so you don't need to feel embarrassed. When you make an appointment you can ask for either a male or female doctor, whatever you're most comfortable with.

What to do about locker room teasing is a tough one. Can you disappear into one of the toilet cubicles whilst you are getting changed? Either that or learn to laugh it off. Usually people zero on our insecurities, so if you can stop worrying about it, your peers will sense that they're not getting too far with their teasing and will move onto their next victim. Good luck with it all, Dr Claire

There are many myths (untrue sayings) about penis size. Let's have a look at some of these:

1 Men who are tall or a big build have bigger penises.
   WRONG — tall men can have short penises and big muscular men can have small penises and small, short or skinny men can have large penises.

2 Big thumbs, or big hands, or big feet or big ears mean you will have a big penis.
   WRONG — the size of you penis has nothing to do with the size of any other part of you. You cannot look at these bits of a man's body and predict his penis size.

3   A penis that is shorter than usual when soft or
    flaccid has a shorter than average size when erect.
    WRONG — size when soft does not have much to
    do with size when erect. When erect, most
    penises end up around the same size.
4   Men with big penises are more masculine, manly
    or macho.
    WRONG — penis size has nothing to do how
    masculine or manly a man is, has nothing to do
    with bravery or courage or physical strength.
5   Men with big penises make more sperm and can
    make babies more easily.
    WRONG — size of penis has nothing to do with
    how much sperm a man produces nor the quality
    of the sperm, (and neither does the size of the
    testicles or balls).
6   If a penis is small, it won't 'fit' into the vagina
    during sexual intercourse.
    WRONG — the vagina is like a balloon with no air
    in it, the sides of the vagina lie up against each
    other, and so even when a smaller sized penis is
    inserted it will still be a nice snug fit. Conversely,
    the vagina can expand to fit a larger sized penis.
7   Big penises mean more sex drive, more erections,
    erections that last longer.
    WRONG — penis size has nothing to do with sex
    drive or erections. A man with a smaller-sized
    penis can have a high sex drive, and heaps of
    long lasting erections. Size has nothing to do with
    these things.

8 Women enjoy sex more with big penises.
   WRONG — how much a woman enjoys sex with a
   man is going to depend more on the skills he has
   as a lover using what he's got to stimulate her,
   and also on the emotional feelings between her
   and her partner as well.

An excellent book dealing with changes to a boy's body
during puberty is *What's Happening To My Body?
Book For Boys* by Lynda Madaras, Newmarket Press,
2000.

Dr Claire,
I am teased at school because I am short and
skinny and don't have much muscles. I get
called 'weed' and 'shorty'. It's got so I hate to
go to school. Also, I am no good at sports like
football or soccer, I just get picked on and
bashed up. I hate sports days, I usually wag
school when sport's on. Could I have something
wrong with me? What can I do to get taller and
get muscles? Are there drugs I can take? I've
heard you can get stuff at the gym? How will I
get a girlfriend?
Travis, age 14

Dear Travis,
Most boys reach their adult height by around
seventeen or eighteen years and some keep
growing later than this, so you most likely still

have some growing to do. However, as you know
people come in all different shapes and sizes,
and some people are short and some people are
tall. At this stage you don't know how tall you're
going to end up, but maybe you are not going to
be as tall as some of your peers. Rarely, some
people have hormonal abnormalities that means
they don't develop and need specialist treatment,
but I stress this is rare. Have you started to
grow at all? Do you have other development of
puberty occurring, like your penis and testes
growing, pubic or armpit or facial hair sprouting
etc? If so, you know that your male hormones
such as testosterone and other androgens (male
hormones) are kicking in. You don't say how tall
you are. If you are really freaking out about all
this then a trip to your local doctor for re-
assurance may ease your fears. It is most likely
that either puberty is happening a bit later for
you, or that you will be a shorter build.

Unfortunately, for no logical reason, there can
be some prejudice in society against shorter
men. However, how tall or muscular you are in
your body shape has not much to do with how
masculine or manly you are. You can be very
physically fit without being ultra muscular. I go
to a gym and I see the fittest men there are not
the big muscle bound guys but actually the
shorter, wiry build thinner guys are the fittest
people I see there.

It's not easy I know but accepting your body

height and build is very important, rather than
longing for something that is not going to be.
Regardless of your height or your body build,
you can make the most of what you've got. I
would recommend to you going along to your
local gym and enquiring about getting a
personal program from a qualified instructor
for appropriate weights training and
aerobic fitness as well (like treadmill or
stepper). It is important you get correct
instruction on how to do exercises with weights.
If you don't lift the weights properly it is
possible to damage yourself, especially when
your body is still growing. It is much more
effective to lift lower-sized weights in the
correct way rather than heave around heavy
weights with incorrect technique. It is
possible for anyone to improve their muscle
strength and definition, and by getting to know
the body you've got and working with it you
will learn to be proud of your body and you will
improve your self confidence. Also, you will
improve your posture and the physical image
you project.

It is okay not to like or be much good at
footy or soccer. There are a heap more sports
you might like to consider, everything from
table-tennis to swimming to horse-riding.
Seriously think about learning a martial art, like
Aikido, Judo, Karate, Tai Kwon Do or similar.
Especially for boys who feel they are a bit

physically 'under-developed' and who get picked on, learning a martial art can have a profound effect on your self-image and how you perceive your body. Another plus of learning a martial art is knowing that you could, if you had to, lay out flat one of these boys who is calling you shorty. And believe me, you will project a more confident, self assertive aura, and they will back off.

In terms of girls, most women are shorter than men are, and there are plenty of girls who would feel swamped and intimidated by tall men. What makes a person most attractive is that they project a sense of self-confidence and self-worth, and a happy sense of who they are. This is what draws people to other people. Girls will be attracted to the you that is self-assured and happy with himself. How you treat girls, what you say to them, being respectful and sensitive, being fun to be with and do things with, these are the attributes that will bring the girls.

With regards to drugs, yes you are right some people take drugs called steroids to build up muscle. These steroids are called anabolic steroids. There is a black market that exists in these, often centred around gyms because some body-builders get into taking steroids. The steroids on the black market are often veterinary steroids, designed to be used on animals. These are dangerous drugs with umpteen side effects, and you can make a major

mess of yourself by taking these drugs. They
can screw you up physically and psychologically.
Stay well away from these drugs.
Dr Claire

Dr Claire,
I am out of my mind with worry about my acne.
I have really gross pimples all over my face, and
on my back and shoulders. It is really, really,
ugly with big red lumps as well as big pimples.
I have tried heaps of stuff from the chemist,
nothing helps. I am called 'pus face' and 'zit
head' and worse at school. I am so self-conscious
I don't want to go to school, and especially I
don't want to have to do anything that involves
people looking at me, like having to stand out
the front of the class or something. I can feel
people looking at me on the bus. We had a school
social but I didn't go. What girl would want
anything to do with me covered in pimples?
It's getting so I don't want to leave the house.
My mother is studying naturopathy, and she's
had me on zinc and herbs and stuff for months,
but it's not helping. Mum says she doesn't want
me to take drugs from a doctor because she's
heard they're dangerous. Please, please help me.
Steve, age 15

Dear Steve,
I'm sorry to hear you are going through hell
with your acne. It is very obvious to me that

your acne is having a very drastic effect on
you and your self-confidence at the moment.
You need specialist help. Look, I've got
nothing against naturopathy, but it sounds
like you've given that a go and it hasn't
worked. You need to tell Mum you are
desperate to get help for you acne. Go to
you local doctor and get a referral to a skin
specialist (dermatologist). There are very
effective drugs available to help acne these
days. All drugs have potential side effects,
even herbs and naturopathic drugs can have
side effects. And, it is true some of the drugs
used to treat acne can have some uncommonly
nasty side effects, but by seeing a specialist
you will be prescribed the medications in the
correct dose by an experienced professional
who will monitor you for any adverse effects.
The damage that is being done to your self-
esteem and self-development by your acne is
more likely to cause you trouble than potential
side effects of treatment. Mum might like to go
with you to the specialist to help put her fears
at rest.
Best of luck, Dr Claire

Acne can be a real curse. It is most common in puberty,
and in boys, but occurs in both sexes and can occur in
adults as well as teens. About three-quarters of teens
will get acne to some degree.

The hormonal changes of puberty stimulate the sebaceous (sounds like seb-**ay**-shus) glands within the hair follicles (pores) in the skin. Simply, these glands produce more oil and substances than can exit the follicle, and they build up. As the follicle gets plugged up it can make a whitehead, or a blackhead when the plug oxidises to a darker colour. The walls of the follicle can rupture, the area gets inflamed and red, and bacteria that normally live harmlessly on the surface of the skin can get into these plugged follicles and white blood cells gather in the area and cause pus. If these areas are deeper in the skin, they can form cysts, which are the red lumpy things that don't have the obvious white stuff coming out of them like an ordinary pimple. Having these cysts means you have a more severe from of acne, called cystic acne. With severe acne you can get little tracks or pathways under the skin connecting the pimples and cysts, spreading the acne across your skin.

We now know that the tendency to get acne runs in families. It has nothing to do with not being clean, and current medical opinion is that diet has nothing to do with acne.

Acne is a problem not only because it is unsightly and causes problems with your self-image and self-esteem and social confidence and can be physically painful, but also it can leave nasty scars on your skin. So, what can be done?

How to treat acne:

1 Keep your face clean. Use a mild soap or a mild acne facewash twice a day.

2 Keep your hair off your face. Oily hair lying on your face just brings more oil onto your skin.

3 Don't pick, squeeze or scratch your pimples — you can damage the skin causing scarring and spread infection to other parts of your face

4 Identify and avoid anything that aggravates your pimples. Some oily cosmetics, and even some acne creams, can make the acne worse in some people.

5 For mild acne, application of treatment available from your chemist can do the trick: there are a variety of ointments containing things that help dry up the oil and peel the acne skin off, like benzoyl peroxide, sulfur, salicylic acid and tretinoin cream. Ask your chemist for advice.

6 For more severe acne and for any acne not helped by these over-the-counter treatments, take a trip to your local doctor. There are medications your doctor can give you a prescription for:
   — antibiotics can help by controlling the bacteria that get in the follicles. These can be tablets that you take, and there are also antibiotic creams that can be applied to the skin
   — synthetic vitamin A compounds. These come in tablet form and ointment form. The tablet form is usually used for severe acne and is called Roaccutane. It is very effective for severe

acne. You will need to see a skin specialist
(dermatologist) to get this prescribed. Your
general practitioner will give you a referral to
the dermatologist. Usually treatment is for
around 4–6 months, with improvement within
first few months. Roaccutane can cause side
effects, like causing dry skin, dry lips, dry eyes,
which can be treated with cream or drops
suggested by your dermatologist. There is a
small risk of more serious side effects, such as
severe depression, so it is important you are
being monitored by your doctor. For girls, it is
crucial not to get pregnant while taking these
medicines, because it can cause damage to the
developing foetus. The medication does not
affect your reproductive system nor any babies
you might have in the future once you've
stopped taking the medication.

7   To treat scarring due to acne, there is
dermabrasion (which removes top layers of skin,
a bit like giving your skin a sandpapering),
chemical skin peels, removal or drainage of cysts,
which can be carried out by doctors such as
dermatologists and plastic surgeons. If you need
to have these treatments make sure you have an
experienced doctor doing it, to decrease risk of
any complications.

For severe acne seeing a skin specialist (dermatologist)
is a good idea so you can get specialised, individualised

advice and follow-up. These doctors spend years studying skin problems, and can give you the latest up-to-date treatment for your acne.

A good website with info on acne and other skin problems, from warts to athlete's foot, is www.dermcoll.asn.au, which is the website for the Australian Dermatologists association.

Dr Claire,

I have a very serious and urgent problem, and I am worried sick about it. I am a 13-year-old boy and I have started to grow breasts. What is happening to me? Could I have breast cancer? I have heard there are men who have penises and breasts, like freaks. Am I growing into one of these? I am getting teased at school. I am wearing big loose shirts to hide the problem, and we are supposed to be all going to swimming once a week but I am wagging school and getting into trouble for not turning up. I can't tell anyone or they'll know I'm a freak. I am so desperate.
Brandon, age 13

Dear Brandon,

I have some very good news for you. No, you are not turning into a freak. It is not uncommon for boys to get some breast swelling at puberty, in fact over half of all boys will get some swelling of their breasts at this time. Sometimes there can also be a bit of tenderness or discomfort in that part of your body too. The swelling is due to the hormonal changes occurring in your body, and is merely your body's normal reaction to some of the new hormones getting going in your body. It will settle down, but it can take months to about a year to do so. It is just that you are unfortunate enough to have got a bit more swelling than some of the other boys, so it is more noticeable.

If you feel you want someone to examine your chest and further put your mind at ease, a trip to your local family doctor would be a good idea. Your doctor will have seen plenty of teen males with this problem, and can help to further reassure you nothing is wrong.

Your problem is really what to do whilst waiting for it to go away. Some boys have surgery to remove the swelling, but then you're stuck with two scars on your chest for the rest of your life.

Now that you know that you are not a freak, could you talk about it to Mum or Dad? They may be able to speak to the school and get you excused from swimming. Big loose shirts sound like a good idea. Being teased can be very painful I know, so doing what you can to avoid the other boys seeing you getting changed and so on is a good idea.

Breast cancer is much rarer in men than in women, and not something that you need to worry about at your age. As for the men with the penis and the breasts, possibly you are referring to men who are trans-sexual or trans-gender. These are men who feel that they are

really women who have been born into a man's
body. They live as women, wearing women's
clothes and make-up and so on, and they feel
they are women trapped in a male body. They
can get special medical help to have plastic
surgery to change their bodies. They can take
hormones to make their breasts grow, so when
they do that if they haven't yet had their plastic
surgery to remove their penis and create a
vagina for them, then yes for a while they would
have breasts and a penis.
Dr Claire

Dear Margaret,
Do you know of any other boys with problems
with their voice? I am finding my voice cracks
and goes squeaky, and I sound like Donald Duck.
It is really embarrassing, like I rang up this girl
to ask her out and I said, 'Hi, it's Jorge' in a
normal voice, but then when I said 'We're having
a barbecue at the beach tomorrow, would you
like to come?' it came out all squeaky like I was
a real dork. She said no, she had something else
on, but I think why would she want to go out
with me and my squeaky voice. I've heard gay
men have squeaky, hi-pitched voices. What can
I do?
Jorge, age 15

Dear Jorge,
Your voice box and vocal cords (which make

your voice) also grow and change as you develop
into a man. Your vocal cords get longer and
thicker as you go through puberty, and your
voice drops. Now, for some boys this happens
suddenly, their voice 'breaks', and they have
their new, deeper voice. But for some boys it's
a bit of an on and off thing for a while. So, they
can be talking in their normal voice, then their
voice will sort of crack or get squeaky. You are
not the only one to have this, it is common. And
unfortunately, when you are nervous or excited,
like asking a girl out on a date or standing out
the front of the class or something, it happens
and you feel like a dork. But, it's just Mother
Nature tuning up your vocal cords, and your
voice will settle down with no more of these
squeaks.

You can explain if it happens, like 'Oh, there
goes my voice box again. I'm still growing into
my deep, grown man's voice'. Maybe the girl you
asked out had something else on. Often people
need more than a day's notice to go out. Why
don't you give her another try? And it is
nothing to do with being gay. Tone and pitch of
voice varies from man to man, regardless of
whether they are gay or straight. There are
plenty of gay men with deep voices, and there
are straight men who have lighter, higher
pitched voices.
Margaret

2 Self-esteem

Dr Claire,
My mother says I have low self-esteem. When I ask her what she means, she says I don't seem to think much of myself, and I'm too shy and awkward. She's very flamboyant and outgoing, but I just can't be like her.
Angie, age 16

Dear Angie,
Your mum is probably trying to help you in her own way, but I doubt what she's saying is help-ing your self-esteem. It could be she has difficulty understanding and accepting that you two are different from each other. Not everyone can be flamboyant and outgoing. Imagine how horrible the world would be if we were all like that. It would be a nightmare. Angie, focus on your talents, skills and good points. Often, being awkward (and I guess Mum could mean clumsy or gawky, all arms and legs like a young foal, or she might mean you seem tongue-tied and stumbling for words when you have to talk to people) is part of being a teenager, and you'll develop more poise in time. Being shy is an attractive trait if it's not too extreme. Shy people are usually good listeners. Did you know

that a lot of famous actors, dancers, scientists, writers and celebrities were shy as children or were 'awkward' adolescents?

You might want to think about things that would improve your self-confidence in dealing with other people, like learning public speaking or doing a course on assertion. There are also books and courses on how to improve your conversation abilities. There are books on etiquette that tell you things like how to introduce people to each other and other social bits and pieces. You don't have to do any of these things if you don't want to. These are just suggestions if you decide you want to improve some of your social skills. Try to have a talk with Mum or write her a letter and tell her how you are different from her, and it is upsetting you to be pressured into being something you're not. Accept yourself as you are, and be proud and confident that you are *who* you are and not a clone of your mother.

Dr Claire

What is self-esteem?

Self-esteem means that you 'esteem yourself', which means that you care for yourself, you hold yourself in high regard, you like yourself. This is not always easy or straightforward, so let's look at this more closely.

What does it mean when a person truly cares for himself or herself? We know that when people say,

'Oh, he really loves himself' they can mean it as a put down. What they're really trying to say is that he's conceited or arrogant. To truly care for yourself has nothing to do with being arrogant or conceited. In fact, caring for yourself is essential in order for you to have any chance of a good life.

Where does self-esteem come from?

Many teenagers (and adults) believe they can't like themselves because they haven't accomplished enough to deserve feeling good about who they are. They think that in order to value themselves they first have to do more: such as lose weight, get A's at school, get a boyfriend or a girlfriend, be chosen for the sports team, get accepted into university, get a job and so on.

Self-esteem can really only come from the inside, from inner acceptance and approval of yourself. If you get hooked into only liking yourself when you've achieved a certain goal, then ultimately the rewards and achievements will not be enough. Many high achievers remain on a treadmill, driven to do more because no matter how much they achieve, underneath they really don't like themselves all that much.

Many of you may think it would be really good to be like Margaret, a famous author known all around the country. However, Margaret will tell you she too has had to find self-esteem that comes from within, and is not dependent on outside recognition and approval.

We need to approve of ourselves for who we are,

and we need to CARE for ourselves. Care, Accept, Respect, and Encourage.

Care

To care for yourself means to nurture yourself. Often we learn how to care for our bodies as we grow up — for example, have a shower, brush our teeth, wear deodorant, put stuff on our zits. How many of us know how to care for ourselves emotionally? Do we even know what that means? Many of us long for love, appreciation and approval from others. Did you know you can learn to give love, appreciation and approval to yourself?

Acceptance

This does not mean that we simply throw up our hands and say, 'This is just the way I am' and don't think we can change anything about ourselves. We need to accept and appreciate ourselves for who we are, even as we strive to improve ourselves and our lives.

Jenny's Story

Jenny is 15 kilograms overweight. She doesn't accept herself as she is but tells herself she's a failure, a fat pig, hopeless, a real loser. Jenny is tall and a rather large-framed person. Although Jenny may not like being 15 kilograms overweight, she will be more likely to lose the weight when she says to herself 'I accept, care for, and nurture myself just as I am. I am a good person. I am 15 kilograms above the weight I would like to be.

I'm finding it difficult to lose the weight. I'm going to get myself some help to lose this weight and get to a more healthy size for me, but I'm never going to be a size 8 and a skeleton on legs, and that's that.'

Acceptance means that you stop beating up on yourself. To be human is to be imperfect. We all have failings. We all sometimes say and do things we wish later we hadn't; we all make mistakes and muck things up. We all make fools of ourselves in front of others, whether it's falling over or passing wind or spilling something or making a mess of a talk we had to give. We all wish there were certain things we could do better, or that we could be more like somebody else. Welcome to the human race ...

Dear Margaret,
I have to go to a new school this year and the summer uniform is anklet socks. Arrgghh. Everyone will see my white, hairy, mosquito-scabby legs.
Renee, age 14

Dear Renee,
Okay, your problem can be solved. White legs? Fake tan them, or start a new white legs fashion. Hairy? Shave them or start a new plaited-hairy-legs-with-ribbons fashion. Scabby? Stop scratching your mosquito bites. Or start a scabby fashion. Arrggh, no. But you see what I'm driving at, don't you? You can either accept that this is how your legs look and leave them

alone, or you accept this is how your legs look but decide you want to improve them. Either you rock up to school with white, hairy scabby legs and forget about them, or fix them.
Margaret

When you look at other people you only see their outsides. You don't see what's going on in their heads. Other people look like they've got their act together. If you had special X-ray vision and could look inside other people's minds, you'd find they too struggled with self-doubts, self put-downs, anxieties, worries, doubts, fears and depression. Imagine you got on a bus full of people and could see inside everyone's minds. You'd be blown over by all the thoughts inside people's heads. Imagine the bus filled with 'I'm too fat', 'I hope I don't stuff up the talk I'm giving at school today', 'I'm so stupid, how could I forget to bring my diary', 'I'll never pass the exam', 'He'll never want to go out with me', 'Man, I feel down today' ... The negative thoughts would be so loud and overwhelming that you'd have to get off the bus quick smart.

Another thing you can do to remind yourself that people tend not to have it all together and often need help to sort themselves out is to open up the Yellow Pages. Look under counsellors, psychologists, therapists, marriage guidance. See those pages of psychologists and counsellors, do you think they're all making a living seeing one person a month each? Nope. They're flat out helping people deal with their problems and improve their self-esteem. Then there are doctors and psychiatrists who don't even advertise in the phone book. One girl who emailed Margaret with her problems told us she's waiting three months to see a psychiatrist because they're so busy she can't get an appointment before then! So we *know* everybody else doesn't have it all together!

Respect

Do you feel taken for granted and underrated? Do you wish you were appreciated and valued? Do you feel irritated when you've been put down or treated like you're not important? Are you always trying to please people so you'll get the recognition you long for? If so, then you know how much you want respect from other people. But what about respect for yourself? Do you treat yourself with respect and dignity? Do you value yourself?

Dear Margaret,
I've got a problem. I've started cutting myself, mainly on my arms. Mum's sent me to the school counsellor and I've got to go through all this psychological bullshit, like, 'I see you are feeling mad at the world' and stuff. Margaret, I'll tell you a secret. The reason I'm doing this is because I want to hurt myself. I deserve to be hurt.
Laura, age 14

Dear Laura,
No one deserves to be hurt. And I mean, *no one*.
There's no way you could be that awful a
person. I think you need professional help.
Margaret

Dear Margaret,
I hate myself because I've done stuff with my
brother and grandpa that I didn't want to do. I
tried to tell Mum but she said I was over-
dramatising the situation and she wouldn't listen.
    Nowadays I do these things with boys if
they'll give me presents, like this boy bought me
$30 of Red Earth for letting him have sex with
me. The other girls call me a slut for stealing
their guys. Shows they're not giving out, huh.
Plus the teachers think I'm feral and pick on
me. Like, I have the reputation for being a
smart-arse. I can't help it. Like this teacher said,
'Do you want time out?' and I said, 'Let me get
back to you on that one' and of course I copped
time out. Margaret, I know I'm just dirt and
trash, and like I said, I want to be hurt.
Laura

Dear Laura,
Look, you've had some bad things happen.
You're not alone. I get a lot of emails from
girls who've been sexually abused by men
— fathers, stepfathers, grandfathers, uncles,
brothers. The important thing is that it wasn't

your fault at all. The shame you feel really
belongs to Grandpa. It was totally Grandpa's
fault because he was an adult and you were a
child. Not all men are like this: there's some
decent ones out there, so try not to judge them
all the same way or view them as sexual
gift/money trees. Your brother and grandpa
committed criminal acts. It doesn't matter if it
was years ago, it is still affecting you. You've
lost your sense of dignity. I think you really
need to talk this over with a counsellor (not the
one at school, seeing you don't get on with her)
— try a youth worker who can then get you in
to see a rape or sexual assault counsellor, or
you can look up sexual assault or rape
counselling services in your phone book (usually
listed up the front in the Community Services
section) and ring them yourself. These
counsellors will be very experienced in dealing
with the effects of sexual assault. Also, you
might find some good books on healing sexual
assault, such as *The Courage To Heal*, by Ellen
Bass and Laura Davis. You'll find stories from
other girls and women who have been abused
and the book talks about all sorts of things.
Try your library. Your innocence was abused as
well as your body. That's why you're hurting
so much inside, in your soul and your spirit,
and it's deep, deep, deep. Because you were
abused as a child you had no chance for
your self-respect to develop. You've had so much

pain as a child, emotional and physical, that
even now pain feels like it should still be a part
of your life. So, even now boys treat you like a
sexual object, and you feel so bad about yourself
you believe you deserve to hurt yourself. Once
you let it come out, and it's started because
you've told me, then you'll feel better, a clean,
decent worthy person. Because you are, Laura.
Hang in there and write back. Oh, and try and
control your backchat to the teachers. Count to
ten quietly to yourself before you say anything,
okay? Try it!
Margaret

Laura's story makes a person wonder how she's
managed to cope. Once she starts to like herself, she
won't want to hurt herself any more, and her self-
loathing will gradually be replaced by self-liking and
self-respect, if she seeks help, although the scars of this
stuff will always be there. Laura can, with help, heal her
soul and her spirit and begin to understand she was a
victim, that she learnt to believe she was bad because of
what happened to her, and that she can gradually begin
to develop self-esteem and self-respect and move on in
her life.

Crystal's Story
Crystal is sixteen and she has sex with her boyfriend
Greg who is eighteen. Crystal doesn't really like having
sex with Greg, he's rough and makes her do things she

SELF-ESTEEM

doesn't really want to do. She does them because she thinks he loves her. When he drops her off at home she feels used and dirty inside. Greg doesn't seem interested in talking to her or in doing things like seeing a movie or going for a walk. Crystal feels used and dirty because she's not treating her body or herself with respect.

We helped Crystal to see that what she and Greg had was not really love. When people care for you and respect you, they don't treat you roughly and make you do things you don't want to do. Crystal learnt to value and respect herself, and she broke off with Greg, which was hard at first because she was pretty lonely.

Now Crystal's going out with Toby. They do things together like walking on the beach, going for a cappuccino, seeing a movie. They talk a lot and laugh together. Now Crystal finds when she has sex with Toby she feels happy and safe. Toby doesn't want Crystal to do anything she's not happy and comfortable to do, because he cares for her. Crystal likes the fact that she respects herself, and when she comes home from seeing Toby she feels good about herself.

Troy's Story
Troy, age thirteen, comes from a family that is not well off. Troy's Dad has been sick and off work for months now, and Troy's mum works packing frozen chicken pieces into boxes, which doesn't pay much money. Troy had a job on a paper round using his dad's old bike. Warren and Dean live in the same street as Troy, but they have new mountain bikes and their families

have much more money than Troy's. Warren and Dean called Troy's bike a shitheap and called Troy a loser. Troy used to get really upset and feel awful inside. He was mad at his dad for being sick and mad at his mum for not having a better job.

Troy ended up in trouble for shoplifting a Nike T-shirt. He was sent to a counsellor who helped Troy to see that he was actually making a very good go of a difficult situation, by doing his paper round and other odd jobs to help with family finances. Troy learnt to respect himself for trying hard during tough times for his family.

When we respect ourselves we don't go around telling ourselves we are no good. We don't constantly criticise ourselves.

Let's look at some of the negative things we say to ourselves:

- I hate the way I look.
- I'll never be able to learn this.
- I'm dumb.
- Everyone else handles things well, I'm always messing things up.
- I should have done a lot better.
- I don't deserve to get this good thing.
- I'm not good enough.

By treating yourself with such a lack of respect and seeing yourself with such low regard, all you can end up feeling is dejected, depressed and hopeless. These sorts of thoughts lead you to a dead end, where positive feelings and actions seem very difficult.

By saying these sorts of thoughts to yourself you are attacking yourself. You are not going to feel confident, buoyed up and ready to go out and meet the world.

Now, imagine instead you say to yourself:

- Okay, so I'm not as gorgeous as I'd like to be, but I have great eyes and a winning smile and I like my hair cut like this. I like the way I look.
- I've been having a hard time learning this because it's difficult homework and I'm getting anxious about it. Everyone else is probably finding it difficult too. I'm going to calm down and go over it again, then I'll get it.
- I am not always messing things up. Okay, I've messed up something today but there are lots and lots of things I do well.
- I made a mistake but so does everybody. It's part of learning and growing up.
- I am a good person and I deserve to be happy.

Do you see the difference between being down on yourself versus valuing and respecting yourself?

Encouragement

We all need encouragement to become our best, to fulfil our potential and to go out into the world ready to try new and exciting things. You probably can't remember when you learnt to walk as a baby. A baby learns to walk by taking a step, falling down, getting up again, taking a few more steps, falling down again, getting up again, falling down again and so on until eventually the baby is doing more walking than falling and then ultimately walks around with just an occasional fall. Now, what if the baby fell down and said, 'That's it, I've fallen down, I'm a no-hoper, I'm a failure, I'll never learn to walk. Other babies learn to walk so easily. I'm just dumb.' Imagine the baby didn't get up and try again, just kept talking about failure. Hey, we'd end up with a lot of 70 kilogram twenty-year-olds who still couldn't walk!

Think about that baby learning to walk when you have something new to learn or do. Imagine yourself encouraging the baby to keep going, keep trying. Now do the same thing for yourself.

You can be your own cheer squad. If you employed a cheer squad for a footy team and they turned up and stood on the sidelines yelling out things like 'You're a big bunch of losers. Ya big failures. You're so bad. You're worthless.' What would you do? Would you employ that cheer squad again to help the team? Of course not, you'd sack them immediately, tell them to get out and don't come back, probably complain about them to the Cheer Squad Association!

So when you have your own cheer squad in your head imagine them yelling out good things, positive things, things that encourage and support you, like 'You *can* do this.' 'Go for it.' 'One, two, three, four who do you think I barrack for? Me!'

Some of you are going to find it easier than others to CARE for yourself. The sad truth is that some of our parents and teachers don't have good self-esteem themselves, and so don't teach their children and

students ways to have good self-esteem. For example,
Johnny is four years old. He's just dropped his lunch on
the floor. His mother has gone spare. She yells at him,
'Johnny, you're a bad boy, you're a messy pig' and she
slaps him. Now, let's put Johnny in a time machine and
grow him instantly to age twenty-five. Johnny can now
say to his mother, 'I'm sorry I dropped the dish, Mum.
But gee, that doesn't make me a bad person, nor does it
make me a messy pig. I just had an accident with the
bowl. You know, you sound really strung out. I've
noticed you looking miserable lately and you and Dad
have been fighting and arguing. I reckon you are yelling
at me and slapping me because you are feeling really
stressed. Have you thought of going to counselling to
sort out your problems?'

But, of course, little Johnny, being only four years
old, simply absorbs everything his mother says to him
like a sponge. He's not old enough to sort out that it's
not him who's bad, rather it's his mum taking out her
stress on him. However, Johnny believes it: 'I am bad'.
If Johnny is told over and over again that he's a bad boy
as he is growing up, what does he grow up believing
about himself? You got it: 'I am bad.'

Unfortunately, most parents don't get any lessons in
how to bring up children, so they do the best job they
know how. But a lot of parents don't know how to
bring up a child to have good self-esteem. Many parents
and teachers don't make the distinction between a
child *doing* a bad thing and *being* a bad child. Think of
the difference in Mum yelling at Johnny, 'Johnny, you are

a bad boy' versus 'Johnny, that was a bad thing to do.'

There will be some, maybe many of you, who've grown up in homes where you've been constantly told you're no good, been put down, yelled at and abused. There will be those of you who have been physically and sexually abused. It's no surprise then that you've learnt to feel really bad about yourself, and you may believe you are truly a bad person, that your essence, your inner self, is bad and tainted and shameful.

All of you can begin to CARE for yourselves. Some of you will need help from a supportive person, maybe a relative, a counsellor, a teacher, a youth worker, a doctor to help you find your way through the muck of bad thoughts and feelings you have about yourself. That's okay.

As you grow up, other people will come and go in your life. The one steady and constant thing will be that you are with you from start to finish. Learn to hold your own hand as you go through life. Learn to truly CARE: care for, accept, respect and encourage yourself. Believe in yourself.

Dear Margaret,
I have this problem and I get upset about it a lot. It doesn't seem much to my family but it is to me. I really want to be an actor. I've tried so hard to do this but I can't make it by myself. Everything seems to come to a dead end and no one will help me. I've had singing lessons for three years and I know I'm very good. I'd prefer to be an actor rather than a singer. I'm only 13

but I can't wait any longer. How do I get on
stage or on TV?
Alice, age 13

Dear Alice,
You need an acting agent. It will cost money to
join, but you can find some reputable ones in the
Yellow Pages. You can't get acting jobs without
an Actor's Equity permit, and an agent can help
you get one. When you approach your parents
about this, make sure you pick an agent that
doesn't involve driving for hours. Point out that
the money they're forking out for singing
lessons will not be wasted if you can get a TV
commercial or a paying job. Believe in yourself
and your abilities. Best of luck.
Margaret

Exercises you don't need runners for: here are some
things you can do to build your self-esteem
1   Make a list of five things you like about yourself.
    It could be anything at all that you like about
    yourself, such as, I'm good with animals, I have a
    good sense of humour, I'm a good friend, I have
    nice teeth, my toenails are nice, I always take my
    library books back on time, I'm a good surfer, I
    remember words to songs easily, I look really
    good in my blue T-shirt, I'm honest, I'm a caring
    person, I'm creative, I tell good jokes, I swear
    really well — whatever you like about yourself.
    Now, keep this list of five things you like about

you next to your bed and read it every night before you go to sleep. Every two weeks write down five new things you really like about yourself.

2   Make a list of five things that you can do that show you respect yourself. Some examples are I look after my body well, I don't have sex with anyone unless I really want to, I don't let people put me down and I'm learning to be more assertive (we'll talk more about this later in the book), I get my school assignments in on time, I don't talk down to myself in my head, I speak up in class if I have a question or have an idea to contribute, I tell myself that I like me, I praise myself for trying to learn new things. Every month write down five more ways you've found to respect yourself. Be on the lookout for things you can do and that you can say to yourself that increase your self-respect.

3   Make a list of ten things you really like to do (make sure they're good for you), and every week make sure you do at least two of these things. Examples include soaking in the bath with nice smelly bath bubbles, watching my favourite TV show, patting my dog or cat, massaging my feet, playing my favourite computer games, watching a video, playing basketball, riding my bike with my friends, listening to my favourite CDs, going window shopping, reading my favourite books, buying a magazine, going to the local pool for a

swim and then sitting in the spa, going for a walk with my dog, kicking a football with friends, buying myself a cappuccino.

You can't buy self-esteem in a shop, and no one else can really give it to you except yourself.

Actively try to improve and increase your self-esteem. A solid sense of your own self-worth and self-respect will help you enormously to deal with life's hassles. You need time out to enjoy the things you like and to feel good.

3 Eating Disorders

Dr Claire,
I saw something on TV about this girl who does
the same things as me, and they said she has an
eating disorder. I think I must have this too.
Like, I starve myself and don't eat much for a
day or so and then I pig out big time. I'll sneak
food into my room so no one can see me and eat
whole packets of biscuits at one go. I can eat a
whole tub of ice-cream at the same time. If I'm
at a shopping centre I'll buy a whole lot of food
then go into the toilets and eat it where no one
can see me. Afterwards I feel bloated, sick and
fat and I hate myself. I try to stop but I can't.
Every day I'd wake up and think 'today I'm not
going to overeat', and I might be okay that day,
but then I'll bust out the next. I just feel driven
to eat all this stuff. On other days I try to eat
hardly anything, to make up for all the eating.
But I am putting on weight. I feel so ashamed
about this pigging out that I want to die. Please
help me.
Beckie, age 15

Dear Beckie,
It does sound from what you say that you could
have an eating disorder. Sometimes you can

start overeating in response to difficult feelings and personal problems. However, the overeating and the starving and your worry about this behaviour can start to take on a life of its own, and it feels increasingly like it's beyond your control. So then you end up with two problems, the overeating behaviour and all that goes along with that including feeling out of control about it and self-hatred, and also whatever the original issues were in the first place that started you overeating. Sometimes it also seems that eating disorders start when we first start interfering with our body's appetite and metabolic control mechanisms by severely trying to diet which then backfires as we end up over-eating, almost like the body's over-reacting to the dieting. Anyway, I think you need to get yourself some help with all of this, Beckie. Start by going to your doctor and telling him or her you want a referral to someone who is experienced in helping teens with eating disorders. It may also be helpful to join a self-help group to go along with your individual therapy, as this can help to lessen the feelings of shame and isolation and offer you valuable support.
Dr Claire

What is an eating disorder?

An eating disorder is an illness where the way in which the person thinks about food and their body, and the way they eat, becomes seriously disturbed. The person has trouble with either over-eating or under-eating. The underlying reasons why the person does this can be quite complicated. There are different types of eating disorders including anorexia nervosa, bulimia and compulsive overeating.

What is anorexia nervosa?

This is an illness where a person suffers a drastic weight loss from dieting. The way the person views their body, that is their body image, becomes very disturbed. For example, they may look in the mirror and see their body as being fat and to their mind disgusting, when actually they are extremely underweight. An intense fear of becoming fat takes over their life. They become obsessed with avoiding food and eating, and often try to cover up how much weight they've lost and how little they're eating. Often it is family or friends who see the person becoming extremely thin and not eating, but when they point this out, the person often strongly denies there is a problem.

The person with anorexia is terrified of becoming fat. Although it may seem that they have no appetite for food, some recovered anorexics recount how they suffered terribly with feelings of hunger, but their terror of eating was the over-whelming force in their life. They can view those who are trying to help them, like parents or friends pleading with them to eat, as 'the enemy' who is trying to force them to eat.

Anorexia is a very serious illness, which can lead to severe problems in both physical and psychological health, and can lead to death. It can affect both teenage girls and boys, although is more common in teenage girls. The term anorexia nervosa was coined in the 1870's, but the illness has become more common since the 1970's and 1980's.

Why someone develops anorexia can be complex. Often the sufferer lacks a sense of who they really are, and they feel they have little real control over their life, and they discover food is an area where they can start to exert rigid control. But, what starts out as a feeling that they are in control of their under-eating can quickly spiral out of control so their whole existence becomes focused around not eating.

Physically, their body becomes extremely undernourished. For girls, their periods are affected and sometimes stop. Outwardly, they start to look emaciated and unwell. They can get a covering of fine downy hair over the body, called lanugo. Inwardly, the body is in a state of emergency, desperately trying to find the fuel to keep itself going. The brain can't function properly when it is starved, and so the anorexic person's thinking becomes disturbed from both physical and psychological reasons. The body will chew up its own fat supplies first, then will turn to its muscles and start breaking them down to use as fuel. Vital organs such as your heart, kidneys and liver are affected, and if the starvation continues these organs eventually give up. Once a person drops below a critical weight, it becomes a medical emergency to get them to eat, because they are on the verge of literally starving to death.

Treatment is usually aimed at the physical and the psychological aspects. Physically, the anorexic has to start to eat again and put weight on. If the illness is severe and the person is severely underweight, often hospitalisation is required, and if the person will not eat voluntarily, then they may have to be force-fed via a feeding tube. However, getting nutrition into the body and getting some weight back on is only part of the answer, because if the underlying issues are not addressed then the person will leave hospital and start starving themselves again.

Anorexics need to recover not only their weight, but their sense of self-worth, and learn a way to live and deal with their emotions and the issues in their lives without resorting to starving themselves. This can take some time in psychotherapy, and there may be relapses with weight loss on the way to recovery.

Leona's Story

I am writing to you Margaret because I want you to warn girls about the dangers of anorexia. I am 18, and I first started battling anorexia when I was 13. I was always a good student at school, and also good at sport, but looking back I see I was a perfectionist. I never thought I was good enough. I was a bit chubby and it worried me, and girls at school were talking about their diets, so I thought I would diet too. At first it was good because I lost weight and people gave me compliments and I looked good. But I kept going, and then my parents started

freaking out that I was getting too thin. I
couldn't see it, when I looked in the mirror I still
thought I was chubby. I would tell Mum I'd
already eaten, or I'd push the food around my
plate, and even put food into my pockets from
my plate so they'd think I was eating. I felt good
that I could control my food so well, when other
girls had trouble sticking to their diets.

Eventually, Mum took me to a doctor, who
sent me to see this psychiatrist who was useless.
I cheated when I went to get weighed. I would
drink a whole lot of water so my bladder was
bursting before I had to weigh in, and I sewed
lead sinkers you use for fishing into the hems of
my clothes and in my pockets. I got so thin I
was put in a hospital, and I was so scared of
being in hospital that I started eating just so I
could get out of there, and once I reached target
weight I was allowed home.

Once I got out of hospital I felt so depressed,
like I was a disgusting, ugly fat blob, and I felt
that the only thing I could control, my eating,
had been taken away from me. For a while I was
out of control with my eating, just eating on big
binges. I was totally terrified I'd end up fat. I
took an overdose of pills and ended back in
hospital. Once I got out of there I started
starving myself again. I couldn't cope with
school, I left school and was at home. Most of
my friends didn't understand why I just couldn't
start eating. Most of them got sick of being

around me, and I was very lonely. I had my dog Goldie, and I think having her to love me helped save my life.

I was sent to see a different doctor, and I am doing better now though I still have a battle to eat. I am having therapy and learning how to make choices in my life that I want, not just what I think other people want me to do. My doctor and I have jointly agreed on the weight I should be, and I know if I get a certain weight below that I'll have to go into hospital. Also, I have come to see that I was afraid of a lot of things, and I am going to a group where we discuss about growing up and stuff like that. I am taking one subject at night school, and hope to be doing another subject next semester.

Please, please Margaret tell girls to be very careful if they decide to start dieting, and to get help if they start to get obsessed about losing weight.
Leona, age 18

Dear Leona,
Thank you so much for writing to me and telling me about what happened to you.
I get many emails from girls worried about their weight and telling me about their diets.
We need to be reminded as to how serious this can end up if someone develops anorexia.

I'm very glad to hear things are going better for you. Stick with your psychotherapy and your group. Be proud of the efforts you are making to regain your health and get your life back together.

Leona's story is a gruelling reminder of what the illness of anorexia can do to your life. The next letter from Leisa rings warning bells that if she continues on as she's been doing, she could find herself in serious trouble.

Dear Margaret,
I worry about my fat thighs and my bulging stomach. I weigh 52 kilograms but I want to get thinner, down to about 48 or 45 would be okay. I know that to lose weight I have to eat less and move more. I jog 6 Ks before school, I don't eat breakfast because it makes me feel sick, and I drink lots of water during the day. I have an apple at lunch time. Sometimes I bust out and have a Mud Puddle from the canteen because we're collecting the sticks and trying to win the competition. I guess that's no excuse. Then dinner, I don't eat the meat or gravy or any fattening stuff Mum serves up. But I can't get rid of more kilos. Everyone says I'm too skinny and that I'm getting anorexic. But I look in the mirror and all I see is fat!
Leisa, age 13

Dear Leisa,

You don't say how tall you are. If you're a dwarf then that weight is okay, but if you're average height or taller, 52 kilograms is too thin. If you don't already have anorexia, then you're on the road to it, fast. You're not eating enough. You need cereal, fruit and toast with milk or juice for breakfast. If you can't eat that, try making a banana smoothie. Breakfast is the most important meal of the day. Without fuel in your tummy you can't operate properly. You can't drive a car without petrol, you can't work your mind and body without food. Take (or buy) a salad sandwich and fruit for lunch. Then eat a decent meal at night. You'll find that you won't get fat if you keep up your running. You'll be healthy and fit. If you can't do this, and you keep loosing weight, you'll end up hospitalised and force-fed, a ghastly experience. Body image is over-exaggerated through the media. It's fashionable for female movie stars look like Chuppa Chups on legs, with big heads and thin bodies, and I can understand that's what you want to achieve. But it's abnormal, not the 'real' world, and very unhealthy. They do it with pills and operations. So, forget the walking Chuppa Chup look, and aim for a healthy, fit, body, okay? If you find you can't do this and you're still starving yourself, you need to seek help. Your doctor can recommend a specialist.

Margaret

What is bulimia nervosa?

This is the most common eating disorder. The person
has episodes of binge eating, often in secret, where they
eat a whole lot of stuff at once, like whole cakes and
packets of biscuits and a whole tub of ice-cream. This
may be followed by self-induced vomiting. They may
also fast (not eating anything) or else severely under-eat
for a while, like maybe a day or two, before having
another binge. Some people may binge every day,
sometimes many times a day. They may also undertake
excessive exercising (trying to work off the calories),
and may try to lose weight by using laxatives or
fluid tablets.

This is also a serious illness that needs attention.
People with bulimia often feel very bad and guilty
about themselves and their over-eating, and feel that
they have lost control over their eating. They often feel
very deeply distressed about their eating problem.

Dr Claire,
I go on eating binges where I eat a whole lot of
stuff, like whole packets of biscuits and a whole
cake and bread and so much stuff in one go that
you wouldn't believe. Then I make myself vomit.
I am very careful to hide all this so my family
don't know, like after I've been sick in the toilet
I clean it all with disinfectant so there's no smell
or anything. It's got so I'm doing this at least
once a day, more on the weekends. If I'm out I'll
go into the toilets like in a shopping mall and

overeat then vomit. I've tried so hard to stop,
but I just end up doing it again. I know I'm weak
willed, otherwise I could just stop it. I make
plans of what I'm going to eat for the week,
healthy meals that I plan out, but I can't even
make it through one day without bingeing. I am
feeling totally desperate, often I just wish I was
dead. I'm either bingeing and throwing up, or
planning my next binge, or trying not to binge.
I feel like people will know what I'm doing. Like
when I go into a shop to buy a whole lot of food,
I pretend to the shop staff I'm buying it for a
party or a group of people, so they won't know
I'm eating it all by myself. I steal money from
home so I can buy all the food. I hide food in my
room. I've thrown food out into the bin, then
gone out later at night and retrieved it from the
bin and eaten it. I cannot go on living like this.
Andrea, age 16

Dear Andrea,
You may have an eating disorder called bulimia.
This is an illness, it is nothing to do with being
weak-willed. What starts off as something you
feel you have control over can quickly spiral into
a nightmare where you feel like you've lost
control over your eating and vomiting.

You already know you can't go on like this
because you are feeling so much despair living
like this. Also, bulimia can cause severe
problems with your physical health. Like you

can wreck your teeth because of the acid coming up from your stomach, which erodes the enamel on your teeth. Also the constant vomiting can cause damage to the lining of your oesophagus (gullet), and you can become seriously deficient in essential minerals like potassium.

You need to get yourself some help. You are not alone, there are many other sufferers out there. I know it is hard for you not to feel ashamed, but it really is an illness and you don't need to be ashamed. You must reach out for help. Go to your local doctor and ask for a referral to someone who specialises in treating eating disorders. Treatment usually covers several things. Having a healthy plan of eating is part of that, but you also need to look at the issues that may be underlying the illness. Sometimes an eating disorder develops because of difficult feelings and issues in your life.

You might also find you get good help and support from going to a self-help group. This can especially help with feelings of shame and isolation, because you find out you're not the only one, and you can learn helpful things from others' experiences and what they've found helpful. There is Overeaters Anonymous, and also the Anorexia and Bulimia Foundation may be helpful.

Best of luck, Dr Claire

What causes anorexia or bulimia?

People can develop eating disorders for many different reasons. Society's emphasis on being slim, especially if you are a girl, creates a pressure for many girls that they have to be thin. Also many boys are now starting to feel the pressure to have the 'perfect body'. Many teenage girls worry about their weight and are constantly trying to diet and lose weight. For some girls this worry about weight and food becomes an obsession and an illness, and starts to take over their life. Sadly, this is happening at a younger age, where Margaret gets letters from ten-year-old girls thinking they are too fat.

These illnesses are serious, because they can physically harm the body, but also they wreak psychological havoc in people's lives. You can't have a good, healthy life and grow up into a healthy adult with a good sense of self-worth and self-esteem when your life constricts to the point where food and eating issues become your whole life.

For some teens, eating food is used by them to help deal with difficult and painful feelings, like anger, insecurity, loneliness and fear. Some teens find growing up feels very scary, with all the physical and emotional changes that go with it. When they feel that they can't control their lives and what's happening to them, then they may try instead to try to control their food intake and weight to extreme degrees.

Having anorexia or bulimia can be a very painful and desperate way to live. Denying that anything is wrong is often part of the illness.

How can I get help for an eating disorder?

A good place to start is your local family doctor, who will be able to refer you for special help.

Treating an eating disorder usually involves having counselling or talk therapy with a person especially trained to help in this area. Attending a support group with other people who have an eating disorder can also be very helpful. Sometimes medication is prescribed, and sometimes a person will need special help in a hospital.

Some self-help associations for eating disorders include the Anorexia and Bulimia Foundation, and also Overeaters Anonymous, (www.overeatersanonymous.org) which is like Alcoholics Anonymous but for food. There is an Eating Disorder hotline in Sydney: (02) 94124499 or the Australian Psychologist Society can give advice where to go on toll free 1800 333497.

4 Dealing with Feelings

Dear Margaret,
I get so pissed off with things. It sort of builds
and builds and I just get so mad I want to
explode, especially after a day at school. I come
home past this place where there's an old fence
and I kick the shit out of it.
Jason, age 15

Dear Jason,
I think you need to get some help in sorting out
your feelings of anger and frustration. Like,
kicking the fence is a release, but what if you
start kicking the walls at home? And then you
graduate to kicking animals? And people? Do
you see what I mean? Kicking the fence isn't
getting to the bottom of the problem and solving
how you feel. There are counsellors who
specialise in anger management and can teach
you how to get your feelings out in a more
useful way. Your school counsellor should be able
to do this or suggest someone else who can.
Margaret

What are feelings?

Feelings come in all shapes and sizes: little feelings that are okay to deal with, like *I'm irritated*, to great big feelings that can knock you over, like *I'm feeling rage*! There are many words and many ways to describe feelings. They are of course the stuff of great books, great movies, great songs and also a great life! They can make us double up with laughter, or can wrench at our hearts in sadness and grief. Feelings are how we experience our lives.

How do I know what I am feeling?

We can narrow things down so that we can consider four basic feelings: we can be sad, happy, angry or scared. And we can have more than one feeling at once. Let's say you're coming out of a shop only to find someone in the middle of trying to cut off your bike chain so they can steal your bike. You feel angry because the person is trying to steal your bike, but you may feel scared at the same time, because you don't know what they might do if you confront them.

Sometimes we can experience our feelings in a very physical way. When you are scared you might notice your mouth goes dry, your armpits go wet and you feel 'butterflies' in the tummy. When you are angry you might feel your muscles tense, your jaw clench and your tummy feels tight. When you are happy you might notice your body feels sort of light and energetic, whereas when you are sad you might feel that your muscles are heavy, your eyes are watery or crying, and you have a heavy feeling in your tummy.

Be on the lookout for what your body experiences when you have certain feelings. It can help you get to know yourself and how you react, because sometimes it's not easy to work out just what it is that you are feeling.

What's the difference between a thought and a feeling?

Thoughts are the things you say to yourself in your head, or what you think in your head. They are what we tell ourselves about things. Our actions are what we end up doing. So you might feel scared about an exam, then you have the thought 'Heck, I'd better do some study', then you have the action of getting out your books and sitting down and studying. So you can see that feelings, thoughts and actions are actually three different things.

Sometimes it seems the thoughts come before the feelings, like I might think 'Oh hell, I just know I'm going to fail the exam!' and then I notice that I am feeling scared. Some psychologists believe that the thoughts come first and these thoughts then trigger off certain feelings. Why, you might be thinking, does it matter which comes first? The answer is, as you will see later, that by changing the way you think about certain things you can change the way you feel about them. At other times it seems that certain feelings just come along and there they are. That's okay.

If you feel lost about what you are feeling, you might find it helpful to:

1   Tune in to how your body is feeling What things can you describe?
2   See if the feeling fits one of our four basic categories of sad, happy, angry or scared.

The good news is that you can learn to control feelings that can be harmful to yourself and others, by how you react.

Sally's Story

It's me again. I just wanted to tell you that being with Danny is so amazing. He's just one cute, sweet guy, so different from Aaron. Actually Aaron rang me on Tuesday and started abusing me over the phone, saying I was a bitch and a whore and all these things. My immediate reaction was to blow my top at him, but I remembered what you said, and I sat there calmly and quietly till he'd finished. Then I told him that our relationship was in the past, that I had a new boyfriend and that I am enjoying life. I told him that I hope he has a happy life, told him to have a nice night and I hung up. I was amazed at how calm and rational I was.

Also in court yesterday with the knowledge that my father and his girlfriend would be there, I sat calmly with my little sister clinging to me although some of the strain must have showed on my face because Mum told me to relax. But I kept my cool the whole time and didn't yell at the magistrate like last time. The case was in favour of Mum and we can keep the car and some money.

Also on the way home I stopped in to see if my older brother was at his last-known address. I was all set for major disappointment, because he never stays in one place for too long, but he was there! That was a mega power trip because I haven't seen or heard from him in five years! We talked for a while and I got his email and everything. He said he's going to send me something for my birthday. I remember what you've told me about expectations, so I won't feel too disappointed if he forgets. His intentions are good, and that's what counts.

There's this crazy lady across the road from us, and we found out last night that she sits and watches and knows everything, from numberplates of our visitors and who's visiting. And she's putting in a petition to get us kicked out of this street. Mum was told that she has eight households worth of signatures. Apparently she says we must be dealing drugs, which is crap. We get a lot of visitors because we have a big family. My mother said she was going to go over there and punch her, but I said she wasn't worth going to jail over, so Mum calmed down. See? I'm even teaching my family not to react and snot people in the nose!

Arrgh, today I woke with a cold which is bumming me out. Danny comes back from Perth

today and I want to give him a big kiss. Hope he
doesn't get a cold! Everything is so great in life.
Just shows that with a little self-confidence, self-
respect and determination, and controlling my
temper, I can achieve a lot. Thanks for helping
me so much.
Sally, age 15.

What is anger?

When you feel anger you might notice your muscles go
tight, your jaw clenches, your tummy feels tight, you
might feel a rush of energy rise up inside you, your face
might go red, your eyes are glaring, your fists clench,
your voice gets louder … Anger is a feeling that lots of
people have trouble dealing with. In our minds we tend
to link together anger and violence, although they are
really two different things. Most people would agree
violence is bad, and unfortunately in our society many
people think anger is a 'bad' feeling and one they
shouldn't have. People can feel guilty about having the
feeling of anger. Anger is a normal, healthy emotion, part
of being a human. Being angry is not the same as being
violent. You can feel angry, you can tell someone you
feel angry, but you will not be violent unless you make
the choice to act upon your anger in a violent way.

Dear Margaret,
Um, does it piss you off when you get like ten
million emails all with problems? I don't know
how you can keep it up. I'd end up deleting them
all but that's me, an impatient cow. Well, I'm

writing to ask you something. I had this really
big blowout with this girl in school in year 8
called Bree, and I'll be in year 10 this year and
she still won't let it go! She's the head of the in
group. I've had to have all this mediation
organised by the school and it makes everything
worse, but my parents don't seem to understand
no matter how much I tell them. I try to avoid
her at all costs but I have this so-called friend
who tries to drag me near Bree because she
wants to be cool by association, so I walk off
when she does this. I don't want to be near
Bree. She's trouble, and I'm sort of scared of
her. Belinda (the friend) tells me not to be
scared, but she doesn't know the half of it. It's
getting me depressed and angry and frustrated.
It's like I have nowhere to go and I can't talk
to people for days. I'm not sure what I'm meant
to do. I'd kill myself only I'm a wuss and too
scared. I sound like a psycho, and sorry to load
all this on you, but I've heard you're non-
judgmental and stuff and you don't make a huge
deal of things, so please write back if you get
the time.
Zara, age 15

Dear Zara,
Yes, if this happened in Year 8 it should be over
by now. But some people hang onto feelings for
life, and that makes them end up bitter and
twisted. You have some options. You could:

1 Keep going to mediation (except that you don't feel that it's worked too well, so that mightn't be a good option).

2 Get some personal counselling from a youth worker or someone not connected to the school, so that you can learn to release your feelings of fear and frustration. And, I think, also feelings of powerlessness, because that's what's making you feel so bad about yourself. You see, you're starting to lose your confidence, and you need to get it back, then you won't feel depressed and feel like killing yourself.

3 This friend Belinda might be trying to be helpful, but by dragging you near Bree she's compounding the problem. Tell her firmly not to do this. Tell her that if she wants to be friends with Bree, fine, but you don't want to, because you have a personality clash. Then leave it at that.

4 Your parents can't understand your feelings unless you tell them. They still mightn't understand that you've tried to get over it, tried to have a friendly stance with Bree, and she scares you and you aren't coping. They need to know that this incident has grown to gigantic proportions in your head and it's affecting your confidence, so you want to see a counsellor away from school.

As we go through life, we find people whom we really like and people whom we don't. You don't

have to *like* everyone, but you *do* have to try and get along with them, especially in situations like sports teams, school and the work place. So when you go to see a counsellor, look on this as not only learning to deal with Bree and your fear of her, but also that these discussions will help you deal in the future with other Bree-type people whom you'll probably meet as you go through your life.
Margaret

Are certain feelings right or wrong?

Feelings aren't really ever 'good' or 'bad', they are just there. Labelling and judging your feelings as being good or bad or right or wrong, and being guilty about certain feelings like anger, often doesn't help much. What matters is how you talk to yourself about your feelings, and what you do with them in your actions. It is not wrong to be angry, nor is not wrong to have thoughts and fantasies that are very angry. But it is wrong to take those thoughts and fantasies and act them out in reality by being violent.

For example, you might feel so angry at someone that you imagine doing something violent to them, like hitting them. This is okay, as long as you don't then act out the feeling by going and doing something violent to them. There is a very big difference between thoughts and fantasies and actually going and doing violence in the real world. Many of us have at times felt so angry at someone we might think 'I could kill you for doing that'. However, that does not mean we are really going to kill someone.

Anger is a normal, healthy human emotion. It is a healthy emotion because it can serve as your warning signal that something is not right. Often we feel angry when someone or something is infringing on our rights as an individual. Anger can protect us from being manipulated or down-trodden. It can fire us up to deal with certain injustices in society, and try to help and protect the weak, ill, animals and the environment.

Dr Claire,
I have really angry and violent fantasies. Usually I'm smashing things and people up and really hurting them, and I'm torturing them too. I think about it all in great detail. I have wondered what it would be like to really act out these fantasies.
Rob, age 14

Dear Rob,
If you find yourself starting to dwell on angry fantasies and getting off on the violence of it all it would be a good thing for you to talk about this to a trained professional person like your doctor, a psychologist, or a counsellor or a youth worker. Sometimes people need special help to deal with their anger and their violent fantasies. Open your mouth and talk about it with someone who can help you. You can say something like 'I'm having lots of angry and violent thoughts

and it's bothering me', or 'I'm having lots of angry thoughts and I worry I'll be violent'. You may need special help to sort all of this out without you resorting to violence, which can totally stuff up your life by getting you in trouble with the police, going to jail and so on.
Dr Claire

Learning to handle feelings of anger appropriately is one of the most important things we can do in our lives. Sometimes people let their anger simmer away under the surface and they never let it out. This is almost as bad as letting it erupt and get out of control. It's good to get the anger out, but there are ways of doing it that won't harm objects, animals or other people.

Dr Claire,
I just get so angry about everything. Like, my family drives me crazy and school is just the ultimate downer. Last night I really lost it and I broke a heap of plates and cups. I threw them down on the floor, I mean I really hurled them down as hard as I could. I felt better at the time when I broke them, but afterwards I felt stupid for doing it. I had to clean it all up and Mum went right off at me. Now I have to buy replacement dishes out of my pocket money.
Marella, age 12

Dear Marella,
You've actually learnt a valuable lesson out of
this. It felt good when you were hurling the
dishes and smashing them, but then the
consequences of that weren't worth it. Like, you
had to clean up the mess and now you have to
pay to replace the dishes, and you probably felt
embarrassed at what you'd done once your
temper had subsided. There are other ways of
getting rid of your anger, and that's learning to
get it out of your system, not by smashing
things, but by talking it through with someone.
Dr Claire

What can I do when I feel really angry?

Sometimes you can feel really angry about something
that has happened, and other times it seems like angry
feelings just come out of nowhere. There are lots of
things you can do with anger even when your anger
feels overwhelming. Although there may be times when
you feel 'out of control' with your anger, in fact your
actions are *always* under your control. Unhealthy ways
to deal with anger include physically hurting other
people or animals or yourself, or damaging other
people's, society's or your own possessions. All of these
things are not a good idea because you can get into
trouble with other people and the police, and also they
are not very effective ways to deal with anger.

But you don't have to walk around fuming and

feeling like you're going to explode. You can use
the following suggestions to help you feel a whole
lot better:

1 Get physical. No, don't go and beat someone up
   — that's violence and is not helpful to you. But if
   you go for a run, go for a swim, work out with
   weights, do an aerobics session, even a really
   brisk walk can help angry feelings to settle down.
   Then, when you're feeling more settled, you can
   think about what your anger means. Is there
   something you need to say to someone? Do you
   need to speak up for yourself about something?
   Is there something you can do about what you
   felt angry about?

2 Have an anger session. You can get rid of the
   angry energy in a healthy way.

   • Rip up old newspapers and old phone books.
     This is a really great way to release anger, and
     you can even talk out loud as you do it. For
     example, 'I hate you, Janey, for stealing my
     boyfriend (rip, rip). I hate your guts (rip, rip).'
     You can end up surrounded by lots of ripped
     up paper and feeling a whole lot better. It's
     best to do this in private where you can clear
     up the mess before Mum or Dad see it.

   • Drawing. You can draw out your anger with
     colours, shapes, squiggles, pictures of what
     you'd like to do to certain people, or
     sometimes by just putting angry colours on
     the page — red, black, whatever you think

angry colours are for you. You can also write angry words on the page, even swearwords, and again you can talk out loud as you do it. You can use felt tip pens, crayons or pastels or paint. At the end you can either throw it away or keep it, and maybe you'd like to show it to someone else and talk about it.

- A bash session. No, not heading off down the street and finding someone to bash up. You hold a bash session for yourself by hitting a pile of old pillows or cushions, maybe putting some pillows on your bed so they are at the right height for you to bash. You can use a newspaper rolled lengthwise with sticky tape around it to make a bat, or you can buy a light plastic toy baseball bat at a toy store. Then, position yourself bat in hand and hit the pillows. It often helps too if you talk or yell out loud at the same time. For example, 'I hate you Janey for stealing my boyfriend (bash, bash). You are a real bitch (bash, bash).' You get the idea. You might want to put on some loud music, and if you have understanding parents you can tell them what you're doing. 'I'm going to my room to get out some of my angry feelings by hitting pillows.' You'll be amazed at how much better you can feel after a good bash session.

- An anger dance. Put on music and express your anger using your body. For example, you can really stomp down on the floor, or punch at the air, or pretend to chop up the air. You can find your own rhythm and movement to express your anger. You can make noise and sounds or say words if you want to. Maybe you can even make up a song: 'I hate you, Janey, you're such a bitch, I never knew you were such a witch.'

- Buy a punching bag or borrow one (sometimes relatives have an old one lying about) or you can make one (a sack filled with foam beads or similar). Hang it up somewhere, maybe in a shed or garage, and get stuck into punching it. Wear gloves to protect your hands.

3 Write an angry letter to the person or thing you are angry at. This can be a really good thing to do. No, you are *not* going to send it. The idea is that you write down all the stuff you want to say in the letter. The benefit is that you get it out of you and onto the paper, and the very action of doing this can help you relieve your angry feelings. Once you've written it down you can take the next step if you like of imagining the person or thing you are really mad at as being there with you, maybe sitting in a chair opposite you. You can then read your letter out loud. Then rip the letter into tiny shreds and throw it away in the bin.

What else can I do with my anger?

Often with anger, once you get the angry energy out of you and are feeling calmer you can think about what you are angry about. Importantly, you can ask yourself if there is anything you can do about whatever is making you angry. Here are some suggestions of things you can do:

- Can you talk to the person you feel angry with? Maybe you need to tell them what you feel angry about. Maybe they are doing something to you and you want them to stop it. (See the chapter on being assertive.)

- If it's a problem at school can you talk to your teacher or another teacher or even the principal of your school?

- Is the situation something you can discuss with your mum or dad or a friend? Perhaps they will have some good ideas about how to deal with the situation.

- Sometimes there are things that make us angry but we can't change the situation. For example, maybe your mum and dad are getting divorced. You can't change the fact they are getting divorced but you feel angry about it. Maybe you can talk to them about how you feel. Writing down your thoughts can help a lot. If it's something you think you're going to feel angry at for a while, you might like to keep a journal or a diary where you can write down your angry feelings (and any other feelings) every day.

Dear Margaret,
There's this girl at school who is a real bitch
and she called me a slut and a skanky hoe and
other stuff I can't tell you. So I got into a fight
with her and pulled out handfuls of her hair,
and like scratched her face because I was so
mad, and the duty teacher came and hauled me
off. Now there's a disco I want to go to, but she's
spread it around if I go there she'll get her
brother and his mates to kick my head in.
Lexie, age 15

Dear Lexie,
Anger begets anger. In other words, you attacked
her and now she's getting her payback. There
are lots of options. You could:
1 Call her bluff, go to the disco, and you might
   or might not get your head kicked in.
2 Arrange to meet her in school with a bunch
   of friends nearby, tell her you're sorry that
   you lost your temper, but she'd really upset
   you calling you those names, and say, 'Look,
   this fight is really juvenile. Let's just forget it
   and get on with our lives.' This might work,
   or she might say, 'Forget it. I'd rather see you
   with your head kicked in.'
3 Get some mutual friends to mediate between
   you two.
4 Don't go to the disco and avoid going where
   she is (but long-term this could get tedious).
5 Learn karate.

6 Learn to ignore people when they call you
   names and then they won't do it. True.
   They only do it if they get a reaction.
Me? I'd go to the disco, stay near my friends,
make sure my parents took me there and collected me, I wouldn't go outside during the disco,
and I'd take my friends to the toilet with me
when I went. And if she taunted me or called me
names or threatened me, I'd ignore her.
Good luck.
Margaret

Dr Claire,
I am really mad at my sister Effie because she
kept borrowing my stuff without asking me. I go
off my head and yell at her but it makes no
difference. Mum comes in and goes spacko at
me, and sticks up for Effie.
Stavroula, age 13

Dear Stavroula,
I think you need to tell your sister how upset
you get when she borrows your stuff without
asking you. Why don't you write her a letter and
explain calmly how much it irritates you, and
that you're happy to lend her some stuff if she
asks you? Let's face it, why keep getting angry
when there is a simple solution?
Dr Claire

Is it good to yell at people when you get angry?

When you get really mad and yell at people, often all they hear is the noise of you yelling, they don't properly take in the words you are saying. Because they are being yelled at, they may feel hurt, then they'll get self-defensive and may start yelling back. What you've got then is a fight, and neither person is really listening to the other one any more.

If you're feeling angry at someone, it is usually much more effective to approach them when you're feeling *calm*. Doing one of the anger sessions on pages 82–84 may help to clear some of the angry energy out of your body. Then you can think clearly about what it is that is bugging you and what you really want to say.

When Stavroula sat down and wrote about why she felt so mad at Effie for taking her things, she sent me a copy and this is what it looked like. 'Effie takes my stuff. She doesn't ask me! She wears it. Okay, she gives it back and she doesn't damage it. It's the fact that she doesn't ask me! I feel invaded when she just rummages through my cupboard without asking!'

Once Stavroula worked out that it wasn't so much that Effie wore her stuff, but that she *didn't* ask, then she was able to go up to Effie and say calmly, 'Effie, I need to talk to you about something. When you take my stuff without asking me I feel angry that you don't ask. Most times I'd be happy to lend you things, but you need to ask me, otherwise I feel angry and I end up yelling at you.' When Effie

heard Stavroula say this to her calmly, she realised
how bothered her sister was and she agreed to ask in
the future.

Your message to the other person is usually received
much better when you talk to them calmly and directly,
rather than yelling at them. Also, it often helps you
before you go to talk to someone you are angry with to
write down just what you are angry with. Break it down
into small stages so you can find just what it is you are
really angry at, then you can focus on that when you
talk to the person.

Dear Margaret,
Today I was in the classroom finishing some
drawing at recess, and this teacher came in and
yelled at us to get out, and I said, 'Just a
minute' so I could finish the drawing and before
I knew it she'd grabbed the bag and the drawing
and thrown them on the ground outside the
room. Just as well there wasn't something
breakable in the bag. How can they let her be
a teacher when she has such a bad temper?
Cindy, age 14

Dear Cindy,
I guess one thing to learn is that adults have
breaking points too, although I must admit that I
don't think this teacher handled things very well
at the time. Who knows how many other things
had got up her nose, and you were the final
straw that broke the camel's back, so to speak.

Obviously you knew you weren't supposed to be
in the room at recess. If I were you, I'd go to
her and apologise for breaking the rule. She
might then apologise for losing her temper, or
she may not. Two wrongs don't make a right,
and at least if you say you're sorry for breaking
the rule, you've done the right thing.
Margaret

What about when anger goes inside and stays there?

Dr Claire,
When I get mad at someone at first I feel angry,
but then it kinda goes away but I feel really
tired and all gummed up inside, like I just don't
care any more.
Andy, age 16

Dear Andy,
What you are doing is turning your anger
inward, and it's making you feel weighed down
because you're not letting it out. The problem is
that it stays there, and more anger mounts up
and up like an anger bank until, one day, you
may explode big time. You know what happens
sometimes when a crazed gunman shoots people
in the street and stuff, and everyone says 'But
he was such a nice, quiet man'. They didn't
know that years of inward anger and other
unresolved stuff had made him a walking time
bomb. Now I'm not suggesting for one minute

that you're going to do this, but I'm hoping you can see by this extreme example what I'm getting at. Or it could be you'll sort of limp through life feeling tired and miserable, and maybe all that stored up anger inside your body will make you physically unwell. You need to find a more healthy way to deal with your anger, such as talking about it to someone or writing or drawing about it, so that it doesn't just go inside you and stay there. Also, learning some assertion skills might help you a whole heap too. Good luck.

Dr Claire

When you are angry there are three things you can do with your anger:

1   You can deal with your angry energy with one of our suggestions on pages 82–84, and then see if there is something you can do to change the situation, like talking to someone about what is making you angry.

2   You can turn your anger outwards in an unhealthy way, such as blowing up and yelling or screaming at someone, being violent and physically abusive, generally exploding and having a big temper tantrum.

3   You can turn your anger inwards in an unhealthy way. Anger can be turned back inside so that it sits there, making you feel heavy and tired and sluggish and depressed. You might even forget what you were angry about in the first place.

If you always turn your anger in towards yourself, you can end up feeling very tired and depleted. You may end up being very sulky and miserable, and like you can't be bothered with anything. Unfortunately, anger turned inwards tends not to go away, but festers inside you and can really interfere with feeling good about yourself and your ability to take CARE of yourself and enjoy your life.

If you know you turn your anger inwards try some of our anger suggestions on pages 82–84. You might want to start with something not very physical at first, like writing or drawing your anger. It can be very difficult to bash cushions and get your anger out when it is so gummed up and jammed up inside you. Janice, age sixteen, when confronted by a pile of cushions and told to hit them with a bat by her counsellor was only able to poke gently at the cushions with her finger. It took her quite a few practice sessions to be able to finally start bashing the cushions with the bat. So you might find that you need to just gently prod at your anger and try bit by bit to get some of it out from where you've stored that anger inside you.

What is passive anger?

Dear Margaret,
When my sister and I have a fight, I always win. But then she'll do something sneaky as a payback. Like, she 'accidentally' tipped a vase of flowers on my bed. She 'accidentally' spilt coffee all over my homework. When I've told her she's

trying to pay me back, she denies it. Mum
thinks I'm being paranoid. Am I?
Megan, age 12

Dear Megan,
No, you're not being paranoid. Your sister is
getting back at you because, in your words, you
always win the fight. If you let her win a few,
then she'll stop the paybacks. She needs to vent
her anger in a healthy way too, and right now
she feels powerless. What she is doing is not a
good way to deal with her frustration, so
encourage her to say what she's really thinking
and feeling, and don't howl her down or have
the last word. Give it a go.
Margaret

Megan's sister's behaviour is an example of what's
called 'passive anger', which means that you get back at
people in sneaky and underhand ways. You may not
even realise that you're doing it. For example, you might
promise to do something for someone and then
conveniently 'forget' to do it. You might promise to pick
up milk and bread on your way home from school, but
you always seem to forget it. You might promise to
make your mum some biscuits to take to her tennis
club, but then you burn them. You might promise to
practise footy with your little brother but you forget to
show up at the right time.

   You might say yes to going out to a picnic you really

didn't want to go to, and then on the day you get a
rotten headache and can't go. You might promise to
take out the garbage and you take it out but don't put
the lid on properly so it blows all over the front lawn.
Do you get the idea? We're not saying you're
deliberately mucking things up. When your anger is
leaking out of you things like this can just seem to
happen to you.

Why can't I express my anger in a healthy way?

You may have grown up in a household where you
were not permitted to express your anger in a healthy
way. Your parents may have told you that you were
'bad' for feeling angry, and that you should feel guilty.
Maybe they became really mad at you if you got angry,
maybe they really yelled at you or even hit you
when you were angry, so now when you feel angry
you feel really scared.

Maybe you grew up in a family in which people
don't express their anger in healthy ways. For example,
when your mum and dad are angry they don't say
anything, just hold it all in and go silent, or maybe feel
unwell and have to go and lie down. Maybe Dad yells
and carries on when he's angry, and Mum gets passive
anger, like she accidentally burns a hole in his favourite
shirt while ironing. Because anger can be a pretty scary
feeling for a lot of people, not all mums and dads know
how to handle anger in a healthy way, and so they can't
teach you to handle your anger in a healthy way either.

Girls are often taught as they grow up that they shouldn't feel angry or express anger because it is not 'ladylike' or its 'unfeminine'. This can lead to girls just getting walked all over and being unable to speak up for themselves, while deep down they may be seething with anger. Anger is a normal human emotion. Girls need to learn that anger is an okay emotion, and learn assertion skills to be able to express their anger appropriately and speak up for themselves.

Boys and men may grow up with the message that it is macho to get angry and yell and even to be violent. The task for them is to learn to express anger in a more appropriate way, otherwise their anger can lead them into trouble and alienate them from people. Some of you will have grown up in homes where Dad is violent, yelling, hitting and breaking things. You can see that this causes a lot of problems in the marriage and for the children growing up in the family. There are better and more effective ways for boys and men to deal with their anger.

Try to think about what you do with your anger. Be on the lookout for when you feel angry and see what you do with it. Notice how your body feels when you get angry. What do you do? Do you explode and yell, or do you turn it inwards and end up feeling low and yuk and like you can't be bothered ? Do you tell other people when you get angry at them, or do you pretend you're not angry with them, only to get back at them later by doing something sneaky. Look around you and watch what other people do with their anger.

You can learn to handle your anger in a more healthy way that is more helpful for yourself. Anger is a normal, healthy part of being a human. Learn to use your anger in a way that is helpful to you, rather than harmful.

When is it okay to get really aggro?

We just wanted to remind you that if someone is threatening your physical or sexual safety, then you let rip with everything you've got. If you can get away, then run flat out until you reach safety. If you can't get away, then yell, scream, swear, hit, kick, whatever you need to do to ensure your own safety. Don't worry about making a fool of yourself in public place — if you are under threat then yell loudly to attract attention and fight back. Use your commonsense, though. If someone has a knife and wants your wallet or your new runners then just hand them over, don't get yourself killed or injured over a material possession. But if someone is threatening to sexually or physically assault you then trust your instincts and fight for your personal safety if you can't get away from them.

Learning self-defence techniques is a very valuable thing to do. It can teach you how to avoid potentially dangerous situations and what to do if your safety is threatened. Your local gym, YMCA, YWCA or school may offer courses, or look in the Yellow Pages for a self-defence course. Learning self-defence techniques is also a good way to increase your self-esteem. Anything you can do to improve your physical safety is worthwhile learning.

My anger is causing me a lot of problems

If your anger is causing you a lot of hassles and you are having trouble dealing with it then consider getting some expert training in how to deal with your anger by going to see a counsellor or psychologist. Having individual help in learning anger management skills could help your life a lot. People get coaching for sport and with schoolwork, and you can get coaching to help you with things like anger too.

What is sadness?

Dear Margaret,

My dog Buffy was run over and we rushed her to the vet, but she had to be put to sleep. I feel really awful, I really miss her. My brother says I should get a grip on myself, because she was just a dog. I cry at night and sometimes during the day. Why did this have to happen?

Emily, age 14

Dear Emily,

The death of a loved one, whether it's a person or a pet, is always sad. Life is sometimes hard and we don't know why sad things have to happen, except that it teaches us to appreciate the happy times, and to appreciate people and pets while they are with us. Give yourself time to grieve. I had a pet cemetery when I was a child, and my animal friends that died were

buried there. If Buffy was buried or cremated
by the vet, you could still make a little
monument to her in your backyard and put
some flowers there. Remember that Buffy had
a good life with you. Sometimes people
recommend getting another pet straight away.
I think give yourself a bit of time to get over
Buffy first. Another dog cannot replace Buffy,
but it will have its own special loving little
personality too. Loving pets and taking care of
them teaches us to be responsible and loving
human beings.
Margaret

Feeling sad is another normal, healthy emotion.
If you feel sad about something that happens,
then you just feel sad. It's not right or wrong,
good or bad, it's a feeling called sadness. It is
normal and natural for Emily to feel upset when
her dog Buffy died. It is normal and natural to cry
when you feel sad.

   If you feel sad about something then acknowledge it
to yourself. Say to yourself, 'I feel really sad about that.'
If you try to pretend you don't feel sad, then usually it
doesn't just vanish. The sad energy will eventually come
out somewhere — maybe you'll burst into tears when
you don't expect to, maybe you'll get a headache or feel
worn out or exhausted.

   Sadness is another normal human emotion that you
can learn to deal with more effectively.

Dr Claire,
My best friend Alex was killed in a car accident.
How can I ever accept that he is dead?
Jason, age 12

Dear Jason,
I'm sorry that you had to lose your friend at
such an early age. Sometimes we search for
answers and there are none. You are still in
shock, but gradually you will learn to accept
that Jason is dead and he won't be coming back.
But give yourself time to grieve. There is no set
time. For some people it can take months, for
others years, and some people never quite get
over it. It's like a black hole that slowly starts to
fuse together until finally there's just a grey
patch. Jason will always be in your memories,
but he wouldn't want you to grieve forever. He'd
want you to make new friends and get on with
your life. If things are still really gloomy for you
after a while, it might help to get some grief
counselling.
Dr Claire

There is a book with the title *When Bad Things
Happen to Good People*. Unfortunately, this title is true,
sometimes bad things do happen to good people. One
of the many things you begin to understand as you go
through your life is that life can be very unpredictable,
and things can happen that you never dreamt could or

would happen to you. Have you heard of the expression 'Shit happens'? Well, it's true, sometimes shit really does happen, and it can happen to *you*.

Life can at times seem very unfair. Bad things happen for which there seems to be no reason. People who are very religious may believe that whatever happens is God's will: this belief gives them comfort and helps them cope. Other spiritual people may believe that whatever happens is part of some bigger plan for the universe. If you don't hold these beliefs then you just have to accept that there is often no apparent reason for why bad things happen, it is simply part of the unpredictable nature of life where things don't always make sense. We don't know why some things happen, they just do.

Often when something bad happens to us our first feeling is one of shock and disbelief. How can this awful thing be true? We may feel like we're in a nightmare, from which we must surely wake up. We think, it can't be true that our best friend Alex was killed in a car accident. It can't be! But it is. Disbelief is a normal and natural reaction to unexpected bad news. It's as if the mind says 'Oh no, it's just too much, I can't take this in' and goes into a kind of emotional shock state, and we might feel numb and like we can't feel any feelings at all. Gradually this state wears off over a few days or weeks as the reality of what has happened starts to sink in.

It is quite normal to feel angry when something bad happens. How dare life do this to me? You can even feel angry at the person who died, for dying and leaving you feeling so sad and lonely. People then often feel guilty for feeling angry at the person who has died, but research shows anger is a quite common feeling for people when someone close to them dies. It is not bad or wrong to feel this way. People can feel anger at the person for doing something that appears to have led to their death, like 'why did he get in the car when he must have known the driver had been drinking?' or 'I told my dad if he didn't stop smoking he'd have a heart attack'. People don't always do what is the most sensible thing to do.

People commonly have a mixture of sad and angry feelings when something bad happens, like when someone dies, your parents get divorced, or your boyfriend or girlfriend dumps you for someone else.

What can I do when I feel really sad?

The first thing is to say to yourself, 'I am really sad about this.' Don't try to pretend to yourself that you are not sad. Here are some things that can help:

1 You can write about your feelings. It might be just single words, or sentences, or you might write a poem. Putting your sadness out on paper can be really helpful.

2 You can write a letter to the person who has left you or died or hurt you. Again, this is a letter that you don't send. You pour out all your feelings of sadness into the letter. Then you imagine the person sitting opposite you, and you read out

your letter to them. Keep some tissues handy as you're likely to cry.

3 Have a good cry. Give yourself some time and space to let go and let it all come out. If there's someone like your mum or dad or someone else to comfort you while you cry then that can be helpful. However, you can cry and hug your teddy bear or hug your pillow. Often you will find that after what Grandma would call 'a good cry' you'll find yourself feeling a bit better, a bit more peaceful.

4 Open your mouth and talk about your feelings. Talk to a friend, your parents, another trusted person. You can say, 'Gee I feel really sad about what's happened. It's really upset me.'

5 You can express your feelings with music or song or dance. In the same way you can create an anger dance, you can create a dance for your sad feelings. The dance doesn't have to have elaborate steps, you can just move your body and arms around to the music to express your sadness. Maybe you could write a song about how you feel.

6 Drawings and art can help you to express your sadness. You can draw or paint anything you like. It might be a scene, or a symbol, or just colours and shapes. You can keep it to yourself or you might like to show it to someone and talk about it.

7   You can make a collage. Cut out pictures from old
    magazines and cards that mean something to
    you. You can also use pieces of fabric, ribbon,
    anything you like. Get a big piece of paper and
    paste your pictures and objects on it so that you
    create something that means a lot to you.

Courtney made a collage after her friend Robin's
death. She got a photo of Robin and pasted it in the
middle of the page, then she cut out pictures from
magazines of things that represented Robin. There
were pictures of horses because Robin loved
horses, there were pictures of beautiful scenes of
the beach because Robin liked the beach. She put
flowers, stickers, ribbon and glitter, and the whole
thing looked very good when she'd finished it.
Making the collage helped Courtney with her feelings
of sadness.

Matt's Story
My best friend Thomas died when a tractor
rolled over on him and I felt, like, blown away.
I felt awful inside. I had this painful feeling in
my throat, and I was in a real bad mood for
weeks. I felt all choked up, but I couldn't cry.
My dad said why didn't I write a letter to
Thomas, telling him how much I missed him,
how sad I was that I'd lost my best mate, and
how angry I felt that he'd died. So I did. Then
my dad took me to Thomas's grave where I read

out my letter to Thomas. I buried it at the side
of his grave and then finally I cried.
Matt, age 13

When they are growing up boys are often given
the message that they shouldn't cry, that only
cry-babies and girls cry. You know, 'Be a man, don't
cry'. This is not a helpful message for boys — they
need to be able to cry too. There is research to show
that men's inability to cry and express their sad feelings
to others can make it harder for them to cope with
grief and loss.

Crying helps us to express our very human feelings
of sadness and grief. Our tears are a part of what makes
us human. Never be ashamed of crying, it is part of the
very essence of your humanity.

What other things can I do when I am sad?

When something bad or painful has happened to you
and you are feeling sad and miserable, it is a time in
your life when you must treat yourself with lots of
understanding, and you really have to CARE for yourself.
Here are some things to do to help you feel better:

1 Do something with water. Have a nice hot shower
  or bath, maybe use some nice smelling bath or
  shower gel. Go to your local pool and have a
  swim, a sauna and a spa.
2 Spend some time with a pet. Cuddling and
  playing with a dog or a cat or any other pet can
  help you feel a lot better.

3 Get outside into nature. Look at the sky and the clouds, look at the trees and the grass and the flowers. Go to the beach and watch the waves roll in.

4 Don't be afraid to go out and do something you enjoy, like seeing a movie or going out with friends. Especially after someone we know has died, we might feel guilty at going out and enjoying ourselves. We think 'How can we be happy when our friend has died? What a horrible person we must be!'

The truth is, even when something really bad happens and we feel totally miserable, the rest of the world does go on. Of course, initially you're not going to feel like you want to be going out and enjoying yourself, and that's okay. But later on, and maybe that will take you hours, days or weeks depending on what happened, even though you still feel sad, you can continue on with the rest of your life. You can still go out, you can still laugh at a joke if you feel up to it.

Imagine you're up in the sky in a spaceship and you can see everything that is going on in the world at any given second. What you'd see is a great big mixture of very good and very bad things, and lots of in-between things. If you could see what was going on in the world in any one second you'd see in that same instant people dying and people being born, people being told they've got cancer and other people being told they're cured, people in court getting a divorce, other people in

church getting married, people hugging, people
fighting, people being dumped by their girlfriend or
boyfriend, people being told they're loved, people being
told they've been sacked, other people being told
they've got a job … At any one instant on Earth there is
a whole mish-mash of good and bad things happening
at once. And in your life there can be good and bad
things happening at the same time. So when you're
feeling sad and miserable, allow yourself, when you can,
to have good moments when you can feel good too.

What is fear?

You guessed it, fear is another normal human emotion,
unpleasant as it often feels.

How do we know when we are afraid? Often we feel
it physically in our body — our gut churns, our mouth
feels dry, our palms and armpits get sweaty, we may
have a sense of dread, our thoughts can run along the
lines of 'I'll never cope', 'I'll fail', 'Something bad will
happen to me'.

Dear Margaret,
I'm a dancer. I do serious ballet and I want to be
a pro, but I'm frightened that if I stake
everything on this, it mightn't work out. What if
I'm not good enough? I'm in the Aussie Ballet
School so I'm an okay dancer, but the
competition's so fierce. My instructors say I've
got what it takes, I have talent, but I know I'm
sort of holding back. Sorry if this sounds dumb,
but part of me wants to be a prima ballerina

and part of me is really scared that I'll injure myself, or fall over on stage in front of a huge audience, or I'll be thirty and a hacked-out dancer with nothing else left, stuff like that. Sometimes I'll get a spurt of inspiration when I'm dancing, and other times it feels like hard work that I don't enjoy. Can you help me decide whether I should really be a ballerina or not?
Tamara, age 16

Dear Tamara,
Only you can decide if you want to be a prima ballerina, and it *is* hard work, but then again, if you have so much talent, and you must have if you made it into the Australian Ballet School, then I think you should stick at it for, say, a year, and then see how you feel. Many of your fears are holding you back, and they'll probably never happen. Look, if you were a shop assistant or a teacher or a cab driver or whatever, daily fears would be encountered too. Life is about risks. I'd go for it. But *you* have to be happy in what you do, and only you can decide that.
Margaret

What's this thing I've heard of called 'flight or fight'?
Our response to something fearful triggers off what psychologists call the 'fight or flight' response. When we

are scared, our brain communicates this to the rest of our body by triggering the release of certain hormones, such as adrenaline. This hormone in particular causes our heart to race and our breathing to speed up.

If you think back to primitive times you can understand how this 'fight or flight' response developed. Imagine you are a cave man or cave woman out for a walk. Lo and behold, you come across a fearsome tiger, ready to pounce on you and eat you. Instantly you are afraid, your body starts to pour out adrenaline into your bloodstream. Your heart rate and breathing rate increases, you take in more oxygen, blood gets directed towards your muscles to help maximise your strength and energy. Why? Because you'll either have to fight the tiger, or you'll have to take flight — that is, run like hell to get out of there. Either way, the adrenaline has helped your body prepare to either fight or take flight.

In modern-day life there are many things that can make us afraid, but we cannot usually physically fight or physically run away. You don't have to see a tiger to have these fear responses. A scary thought can make your body feel the same types of scary feelings and the adrenaline is still released. Our heart rate increases, our breathing increases, our mouth goes dry and we notice these things and we feel very uncomfortable in our bodies.

Does everyone get frightened?

Everybody gets frightened, whether they admit it or not. Unfortunately, those of us with a poor self-image or self-esteem may experience more fear than those with a good self-image or self-esteem. Why is this?

If you have a poor self-image and lack confidence you are more likely to talk to yourself in your head in ways that end up making you feel scared. For example, 'I'll fail the test, I'm not good enough', 'How can I go on the school camp? No one will talk to me and they'll all laugh at me', 'I couldn't go on the plane from Melbourne to Sydney, what if I get lost at the airport', 'How can I ring up and ask her out? She wouldn't want to go on a date with a nerd like me'.

Can you see how these sorts of negative and self put-downs can make fear worse? Why would you want to go out, or try something new, or travel somewhere by yourself if all you can see in your mind is a disaster waiting to happen?

Dear Margaret,
There's this boy, Adrian, and he's just so cute. I really like him. I'd like to ask him to take me to the school disco, but what if he laughs at me? What if he says no? I could ask my friend to ask him out for me. I'm just so scared he'll say no though, and then I'll look like an idiot in front of my friends. Please write back.
Marie-Anne, age 12

Dear Marie-Anne,
What you are feeling is normal. Most people are scared of being rejected and this is what you are fearing. Well, as we go through life we get

acceptances and rejections, so now's a good time to start learning how to cope. Ask Adrian to go to the disco. If he says no there could be lots of reasons, like he doesn't want a girlfriend, he already has one, he likes someone else, he likes you but he's too embarrassed to take you to a disco in front of his mates, he doesn't like you ... You'll never know what is in someone else's head, so if he says no, then, okay, ask someone else. Fear of rejection keeps us from having potentially good friendships, and later in life, going for jobs, studying and doing all sorts of interesting stuff. So, Marie-Anne, if he does say no, learn to accept it as part of life without freaking out, okay?
Margaret

No one likes being rejected. Ever. But it's a feeling that we need to learn to deal with. For every no there are two or three yes's. So, focus on the wins and not on the losses.

What is catastrophising?

Catastrophising is a style of thinking. It means that when confronted with something new we have to do, we think of all the things that could go wrong, until we're so scared we might not be able to do the new thing we wanted to do. That is, we turn the whole thing into a big catastrophe before we've even started!

Jana's Story

Jana was travelling by plane from Melbourne to Sydney for the first time. She was thinking, 'What if I get to the airport and I can't find which gateway for my plane? What if I can't find where to put my suitcase in? What if I end up on the wrong plane and it takes off and I'm stuck in the wrong plane? How would I get back home? Maybe I'll get airsick and throw up. What if my clothes are covered in vomit, or I throw up on the person next to me and they get really angry at me and everyone on the plane is looking at me? Maybe there'll be something wrong with the plane. What if it crashes? I'll be hurtling towards the ground at hundreds of kilometres per hour, the cabin filled with smoke, everyone screaming. Maybe I wouldn't even die instantly, maybe I'd be squashed under tonnes of metal and be in agony with my leg cut off knowing I was dying, slowly, before help could get to me …'

Would you be surprised if Jana decided to ring up and cancel her trip? She's turned the whole event into a terrible catastrophe and she hasn't even left the house.

Now, let's take Jana and have her think some different thoughts about her upcoming trip. Try this: 'I bet when I get to the airport there'll be big, clear signs and it will be really easy to find where to go. The people at the check-in will be friendly and helpful. I'll get a good seat where I've got a great view out the window. It will be a beautiful, sunny day. Hey, it will probably be one of those new planes I saw on the TV, they're very safe. I'm going to put on the headphones and listen to some great music as we fly and I'm going to be able to look down on the clouds from above. I wonder how many shapes I can make out in the clouds? Yes, this is going to be great!'

You can see how this different way of thinking would have Jana feeling excited, rather than terrified, which is what happened with how she was thinking before. Naturally, she's still going to feel a bit anxious even though she's excited, because it is a new experience for her to fly on a plane to Sydney.

Catastrophising can be a very easy habit to fall into, especially if you have an active imagination and can imagine all sorts of horrendous things that might happen to you. What you tell yourself can enormously influence how you end up feeling about something, and how scared you feel.

Are there going to be times when I feel frightened?

Of course! There are times when all of us feel scared. Any time we have to do something we've never done, go somewhere different, learn something new, meet new people it's natural to feel a bit scared or anxious. Any time we have to give a talk in public, take an exam, start a new job, we're going to feel anxious. We realise we're going to feel anxious or scared, and we know that we'll feel a bit churned up for a while, but it will pass eventually.

How can I help myself when I'm frightened?

You can help yourself when you have something to do and you know it is scary by first of all accepting you're going to feel a bit scared and a bit yuk. You know when you're waiting outside the room to go in for an exam or an interview you're going to feel anxious. Remind yourself that this is perfectly normal under the circumstances. If your body feels strange, like sweaty palms and a dry mouth or your heart is pounding, remember about the adrenaline and know this is just your body feeling scared, which is perfectly normal and natural during a scary situation. The feeling will pass.

You can help yourself by talking to yourself in your head with supportive words. For example, 'I expect to feel scared before an exam. I'm going to go in there and do my best. I can remain calm and answer the questions even though I'm scared', or 'I expect to feel scared before a job interview, everyone else will be feeling nervous too, and the interviewers know people are nervous. I'm going to go in there and give it my best shot.'

By talking to yourself in a reassuring and calming way, you can be of great help to yourself. Don't tell yourself, 'I shouldn't be frightened.' Much better to accept that you're feeling scared and to talk to yourself in a supportive, calming manner. Phrases to use include 'I can remain calm', 'Everything will be all right', 'I can do this even though I feel frightened', 'I know I'm frightened now but I can get through this calmly'.

Once you've got through the exam or the interview or whatever it was, pat yourself on the back and congratulate yourself. Say to yourself, 'I'm really proud of myself. I got through that and I was pretty scared to start with.' Next time you have to do a similar scary thing, remember the last time you got through an exam or an interview, and remind yourself that you have the ability to do the same again.

With some things like speaking in public or giving a talk or a presentation, you might find the more you do it the more confident you become and the less scared you feel. Many things get easier in life with practice and become less scary. However, there are some things that always tend to make us feel scared, and that's okay. Some actors and singers have given many many performances, but they can still feel scared each time they go out on stage. They know they're going to feel that way and they accept it, even though it doesn't feel good at the time. They know once they get out there and get started the feelings of fear will start to settle down.

Dr Claire,
I've just had this horrible experience and I hope you can help me. I was in the tram when suddenly I felt totally weird, like I was not there. I couldn't breathe, I felt tingly around my mouth and in my hands, my heart was racing, and I broke out in a sweat. All I could think of was getting off the tram. I got off at the next stop and then I started to feel better. The whole

thing was really terrifying. I know this sounds
stupid, but I thought I was going to die. I went to
see my doctor and she checked me over and she
said I'd had a panic attack. I don't understand,
I was just sitting on the tram when it started,
it wasn't like there was something to be in a
panic about.
Amelia, age 17

Dear Amelia,
It does sound like you've had a panic attack.
This is an attack of severe panic feelings that
usually comes on suddenly and builds up quickly
so that you feel the peak of the panic attack in
seconds to minutes. You described most of the
symptoms. Often there is a strong sense of
fright and dread. Usually the heart races,
breathing may feel tight, you have tingly feelings
in the hands and feet and around the mouth,
and you might break out in a sweat. You might
feel you are losing control, going crazy or dying.
The attack often lasts for minutes, and then goes
away, leaving you feeling very shaken up. Many
people experience this briefly at some stage of
their lives. Amelia, if it happens again, breathe
slowly and say to yourself, 'This is just my body
having a panic, I am safe, I will not die and this
will pass', and allow your body to have its awful
panic feelings because it will stop and you won't
die. Try to stay on the tram or wherever you
are rather than getting off the tram if you have

a panic attack. When you start running from the panic attacks by getting off the tram or leaving the shop or wherever they occur, then you can get caught in a vicious cycle where the more you try to avoid having a panic attack the worse it gets. It is better not to run away from them but to live through them, because this will help them go away. You may never get a panic attack again, but then again you might, but you will know what it is next time. If it starts to become a big problem for you, go back to your doctor who can refer you to learn relaxation and other techniques to help.
Dr Claire

Actually, panic attacks are thought to be a fairly common experience, with up to one in three people experiencing a panic attack at some time.

What is a panic disorder?

When someone starts having frequent panic attacks and becomes very worried about having panic attacks, then they may have what is called a panic disorder. In this situation the person starts to be very afraid that they are going to have another attack. They may fear that the next attack will kill them or drive them over the edge to insanity. (It won't.) The person might start avoiding those places where panic attacks have occurred. For example, they might start to avoid going on buses or to supermarkets or shopping malls. In some cases the person ends up confined to their house and cannot go outside because they are so terrified of having another panic attack. So having a panic disorder can end up being a very serious thing that can interfere a great deal in a person's life and cause them a lot of suffering.

What causes a panic disorder?

A panic disorder can be thought of being due to a mixture of physical, psychological and social factors. On the physical side it's as if the body goes into overdrive and pours out heaps of adrenaline that makes the person have those awful body feelings. On the psychological side the person may not know how to say calming thoughts inside their head that could help them to get through the panic attacks when they come. Also sometimes panic attacks can come at a time of stress in someone's life, and the person might need help to sort out those stresses. Often times, however, a panic disorder can seem to come just out of the blue.

What sort of treatments are available for panic disorder?

There is good treatment available for people who suffer from panic disorder. This can include therapy, which helps the person to learn about panic attacks and to understand that although they feel like they're going to die in fact they aren't going to die from the panic attack. The therapy helps the person to understand where the symptoms come from in their bodies. For example, the tingly feeling and the far away feeling can come because the breathing rate has sped up and because of that the level of carbon dioxide in the bloodstream drops to lower than normal. A simple thing like low carbon dioxide level in your blood can make you feel really awful. It is not dangerous, just makes you feel really terrible. One of the things people can learn to do when they feel a panic attack coming on is to slow their breathing rate down so the carbon dioxide level doesn't drop.

People can also be taught relaxation and breathing techniques that help. And in a gradual way, they can learn how to go back to the places and activities they avoid for fear of bringing on another panic attack. There are also certain medications that a doctor can prescribe to help with panic.

So, fear ranges from the normal everyday fear that we all get right through to where the fear is right out of balance, like in panic disorder. By talking to yourself in your head in a calming and reassuring way, and knowing that certain bodily feelings are a normal part of feeling fear, you can help yourself get through those times in your life when you are scared.

We once heard a Special Air Services soldier being interviewed. As you probably know, the SAS are highly skilled soldiers, often considered the elite of the armed forces. This man was talking about parachuting out of planes during his missions. The interviewer asked him if he got scared. The soldier replied, 'Of course I get scared, every time I jump. And the day I stop feeling scared will be the day I know I have to quit doing it.

My fear helps me check all the details and helps to keep me alive.'

Fear is not always easy to experience because it can be so uncomfortable and we just want it to go away. Remind yourself that your fear is a normal part of being human, and that you can help yourself get through it by talking to yourself in a supportive way.

5 Loneliness

'I'm so lonely I could die.'

That's the final line of Elvis Presley's song 'Heartbreak Hotel', written in the 1950s. Being alone and being lonely are two different things. You can be alone and perfectly happy with your own company. You can be alone and feel lonely. You can be among a mass of strangers and feel lonely. You can be among friends and feel lonely.

Feeling lonely is an uncomfortable feeling that most of us don't like. We often try to escape from it, but we can't run away from loneliness: we take it with us like a shell on our backs.

Everyone feels lonely at some time or other. Often it's the feeling that we want genuine contact with others, but we feel stuck on our own and unable to reach out. There are a lot of things you can do to make friends and interact with people.

If we're surrounded by family and friends but feel loneliness inside, sometime it's because we feel alone with difficult and painful thoughts and feelings that we think we can't talk to anyone about. Or maybe something bad happened to us and we feel we can't tell anyone. But there is nothing so bad we can't talk about it. If you really feel you can't talk to anyone you know about these things, then ring one of the crisis telephone lines and talk to them about it. Talking about it will truly help to relieve this type of loneliness, which can be a very bleak feeling.

And remember different personality types react differently. Some people like a lot of time to themselves and are happy to spend time on their own without feeling lonely. Other people hate spending time on their own, and feel best when they are interacting with others.

Dear Margaret,
I'm so lonely. I don't seem to fit in at my new school. There's the popular group, the creative group, the nerd group and then the leftovers. I don't even fit in with the leftovers. I don't really have any good friends. On weekends I just mope around a lot by myself. My parents are always making uncool suggestions like why don't I join a tennis club or the local church youth group. I went to one of their meetings and it was boring. And I hate tennis. I don't know what to do. I wish I could go back to my old school again but it's on the other side of the country. I wish we'd never moved here.
Georgie, age 15

Dear Georgie,
One of the biggest stresses in life when you're a teenager is moving away from your friends. Many of us have experienced loneliness at times of change, like moving or going to a different school. You don't say how long you've been in

your new school, and you don't say whether you had lots of friends before, or if you were always a bit of a loner. So I'm going to assume you haven't been in your new school for long. To make a friend, you need to look relaxed and cheerful, not desperate and needy, because that will frighten most people off. It helps to have good hygiene, clean hair, no bad breath, etc. Then look around, find someone else who is alone, and approach them. Sit down and make a few comments about the weather, the timetable, the swimming carnival that's coming up, stuff like that. If the person's reading a book, apologise for interrupting and then say you're interested in that book and has the author written other books? Obviously the school library's a good place to do this.

The idea is to make conversation, no matter how dumb you think the topic is. If you get a rebuff, move on to someone else. Set yourself a goal: 'Today I will approach two people and strike up a conversation. Tomorrow, four people.' Practise. You'll find it gets easier. You might think that trivial conversation about stuff like the weather and books is a waste of time, but that's what is called a social lubricant. It oils the wheels towards a potential good friendship.

Look for opportunities to make friends. Accept an invitation that in the past you might have turned down.

Joining clubs in or out of school is a good way

to meet people with like interests. So is the
internet, but you have to be careful that some
weirdo doesn't latch onto you. So if you use chat
channels, treat it as a way of brushing up on
conversational skills to use in face-to-face
contacts. Hope this helps.
Margaret

Loneliness is a problem lots of people battle with. There
are several things you can do to help with loneliness.

Find an activity you enjoy that involves other people.

Of course there are the usual sporting groups such as
tennis, netball, basketball, softball and baseball, football
and soccer, swimming, athletics, gymnastics and so on.
But remember there are other sporting activities like
the martial arts — karate, judo, tae kwon do, kung-fu,
jujitsu and others. The martial arts can be marvellous
physical exercise and they can also improve your self-
esteem and confidence. If you like being outdoors try
a bushwalking or walking club, learn horse riding or
sailing, or join the Rover Scouts or the Sea Scouts.
You could learn canoeing or rock-climbing. You could
join a dog obedience club if you have a dog, and there
are also groups where your dog can enter fun games
like fly-ball. Yoga or tai chi are wonderful things to
learn, again giving you physical exercise but also
fantastic for relaxing you as well.

If you're more an indoors person there are chess

clubs, scrabble clubs and computer clubs and reading groups. Local libraries have information about groups and hobby classes. Many towns and cities have a Council of Adult Education or similar, which run all sorts of classes and groups. The local YMCA or YWCA may run classes and groups. You could learn a craft, from pottery to leadlighting designs to calligraphy. What about taking some drama lessons, or joining a young person's drama group? You could learn to play a musical instrument and then join a musical group or band. Do you like writing? You could take classes on creative writing, or join a young people's writing group. Maybe you could write a school newsletter with some other students?

Another good thing to consider is getting involved in volunteer work. All sorts of organisations are looking for volunteers. You can volunteer to work with humans or with animals. Animal shelters and animal aid organisations use volunteers to help with all sorts of tasks, from helping clean out cages to raising funds to taking dogs out for walks. You meet other people who like animals too and care about them. You could also work with an organisation concerned with the environment.

Look in the Yellow Pages under Clubs and Organisations for good ideas. The point is that there are lots of activities and clubs you can join that you might not even have thought of, and while you are participating in the activities you will meet and talk to people.

Many places will let you come along and have a look first to see if you'd like it. Obviously, things like taking lessons can involve paying fees, but volunteer work is free.

Think about what friendship means to you

Many people have only one or two really close friends but know many people on a more superficial level. Some people are more quiet and shy than others and hate parties and things like that, whereas others are more outwardly social and love going to parties and seem to have heaps of friends. It doesn't mean one sort of person is better than the other, just that people come in different varieties and types.

Dr Claire,
Can I get pills that can stop me feeling lonely? One of my classmates takes antidepressants, and I thought they could help me. I get bored easily. There's nothing to do and I have no friends.
Ryan, age 14

Dear Ryan,
Sorry to disappoint you but there are no pills to stop loneliness. Antidepressants are used to treat the illness of depression, so maybe your classmate has had troubles in that area. I think you need some friends and interests so you don't feel lonely and bored. Do you play sport? How about martial arts? Or are you interested

in art? Theatre? Computers? Reading?
Birdwatching? The trick is to join a club that
caters for your interests. This then gives you a
venue to meet people, and you have something
to talk about, and also something to be
interested in. Don't worry if you try something
and it doesn't work out, try something else.
Maybe you would be passionate about a cause,
like helping stray or abused animals at an
animal shelter, or helping to save the
environment by volunteering at an environment
group, or helping make sandwiches at a
homeless shelter. Maybe you are a budding
entrepreneur and can think up ways to make
money and meet people, like dog-walking or car
washing or lawn mowing. Brainstorm with a
piece of paper and write down anything and
everything you could be interested in. Then see
what practical steps you can take to get
something happening for yourself.
Dr Claire

It's often said that to have a good friend you have to be
a good friend. Think about how you behave in your
friendships. Do you show your care and concern for
others by listening to them? Do you avoid getting
involved in gossip and backstabbing your friends?

Dear Margaret,
I want to ask you something. Why do most of
my school friends hate me when I am nice? I

don't know why, but one of my friends Alana
told me that a lot of people don't like me. I
admit I can be a bitch, but I'm not that bad.
There's this girl Ivana and I know she hates me
because she says I stole her best friend, when I
didn't. I told her to lengthen her school dress
because it was too short and now she hates me
even more. I feel lonely and unwanted. Then
Alana said she'd call me on Monday after school
and she didn't. She often does this, or makes
arrangements then breaks them. I am almost in
tears writing this.
Chelsea, age 12

Dear Chelsea,
This sounds really messy. Do you know why?
It's because you are embroiled in gossip and
bitchiness. You've stated, 'Why do a lot of my
friends hate me when I'm nice?' Obviously you
think you're nice, and obviously they think
you're not — well, not all the time. You've
admitted you can be a bitch. So, I suggest you
drop the bitchy behaviour even if someone is
doing it to you. Don't backstab people, don't
gossip about them, and if you feel that you must
tell a girl that she should lengthen her skirt, do
it in a way that makes it your opinion and a
suggestion, so that the person can do it or not
do it. It's her choice about the length of her
skirt, whether you like it or not. Re Alana not
following through, tell her calmly that this is

annoying and you'd like her to phone if she
says she's going to, or at least apologise if
she couldn't. Alana sounds a bit bitchy too.
I think you both could be more loyal and
trustworthy, and kind to each other and
the other girls. Everyone should stop
the bitchy behaviour, okay?
Margaret

If you make an arrangement with a friend do you keep
to it, or at least ring them up and let them know if you
can't make it? Do you try to communicate openly with
your friends, and use your assertion skills to let them
know when something is bothering you?

Sometimes it's hard to take the first step, especially
if you're a bit shy. Just because we like someone and
would like to be friends with them does not necessarily
mean they want to be friends with us. Now, you don't
have to get in a total state if that happens to you, like
feel it's the end of the world because someone rejected
you. It's just part of the ebb and flow of human life,
sometimes you click with someone and they just don't
click with you back. Sometimes it can happen the other
way around that someone really takes a liking to you
but you don't really like them. Then you have to use
your assertion skills to tell the person, 'I'm sorry, but I
just don't feel that a friendship with you is what I want.'

Chatting on the internet

Of course the internet can be a great place to chat, either emailing friends you know from school or a club, or to chat to new people on the net. However, it is also very good to have face-to-face contact with friends, which is why joining a group with a common interest is good because you can meet and talk to people. Of course you know you have to take sensible precautions when you chat to people on the web. Unfortunately, there are weirdos out there who pretend to be fifteen-year-old girls or boys when in fact they're fifty-year-old perverts. Always be careful about what identifying information you give about yourself — don't give out your address and phone number to people you don't know. We don't recommend meeting people you don't know that you've met on the net: it can be dangerous. But, if you're determined to do so, then tell your parents if you are thinking of meeting anyone from the net. If you do arrange to meet someone make it in a public place like at McDonald's or similar where there will be lots of people around, and you should take someone with you like a parent or older relative. If the person you are meeting from the net is a genuine person they will be quite happy with this sort of arrangement, because they will understand it is sensible from a safety point of view. It would be a good idea for them to turn up with their parent. Never agree to meet someone from the net on your own or in an isolated place, like going to their house or meeting them in a motel or having them pick you up in a car. Away from other people and on your own you are vulnerable. You could think you're meeting another nice teen and they turn out to be a total psychopath. This has happened, so we're not just being paranoid. Always meet in a public place and take someone older with you.

6 Communication and Assertion

Dear Margaret,

My best friend Chelsea and I have this problem. We go to an all-girl school and we don't get much chance to meet guys. We're both 16 and we've never had boyfriends. Everyone else keeps trotting out their boyfriends and we're starting to feel abnormal. We're not exactly ugly, but we're just not good at talking to boys. Chelsea goes bright red and I get the giggles. Boys probably think we're weird. Please give us some advice about what to do.

Megan

Dear Megan,

In your photograph you both looked pretty, but for a second opinion I showed your photo (not your letter) to my neighbour's son, aged 18. He said that you're both total babes. So I guess that means you're eye-candy to most males. I am assuming that you haven't got bad breath, body odour or any other put-offs. However, you seem to have a communication problem. First thing to remember is that guys are just people too. They are usually feeling a bit unsure around girls, even if they are acting macho and cool. So with that in mind, don't worry if you blush and giggle from shyness in the initial stages. Most guys find that cute. Guys like to talk about sport and their hobbies, so to get a conversation rolling, ask about these things and let them talk. All you have to do is listen, look interested, smile and ask a few questions.

If you're always stuck together like Tweedledee and Tweedledum this can be daunting to guys, so I suggest that you split up and circulate. Also if you appear desperate to grab one for a boyfriend, this will scare them off. Be friendly, cool, casual and interested in them as human beings and not as potential permanent relationships, okay? Best of luck. Bye from Margaret

What is communication?

We give and receive messages to each other by the process of communication. The way we communicate with others is important because that's how we let people know who we are, what we believe in, what our values are, how we feel and what we want or need.

Most of our communication occurs without speaking

About 65 per cent of the messages we send out to other people are non-verbal. We look at people's body language when they are talking to us. If someone is angry they may be standing up very straight, eyes glaring, face red. If someone is sad they may be hunched over and looking miserable. Even if they said they were all right, you probably wouldn't believe them.

When our words say one thing and our body language says something different

When this happens it can get mighty confusing. Maybe you've seen it yourself. Your friend says they're feeling okay but they look upset. This can lead to misunderstandings — which bit do you believe, their words or their body language?

Try to match up your words with your body language. Many girls are brought up to believe that it is not 'nice' or 'ladylike' to express anger. They smile or giggle nervously when they are trying to say something about how angry or upset they are. If you want to be taken seriously it is important to look serious when you are saying something about being angry or upset.

Dear Margaret,
I find it hard to make friends with other girls. I go up to different groups and try to join in the conversations but then they seem to drift away from me. I'm starting to think they're jealous of me or something. I do part-time modelling and I know I'm good-looking. I am also good at sport and top of my class in most subjects. I tend to flirt a lot with the guys, and at the moment I

am having trouble deciding between three guys.
One is going with this really plain-looking girl,
and I know he likes me better. I think I am a
fun person even though some of the girls keep
telling me to shut up and get off myself. Deep
down I'm not as confident as they think, but I
still believe I'd make a great friend if they'd
give me a chance.
Kim, age 14

Dear Kim,
Well, you seem to have it all — brains and
beauty, great conversationalist, good at sport.
But no girlfriends. Maybe you are so busy telling
everyone how successful you are that you're not
stopping to listen to their stories. Sometimes
talking about oneself all the time is a cover-up
for deep insecurities, which we all have at some
stage of our lives. Try listening more to the
other girls and see how you go. You won't win
any popularity contests with other girls if you
nick their crushes, either. So maybe slow down
with the flirting. How about making a big effort
to listen more and talk less and see what
happens? Good luck.
Margaret

What is good listening?

Speaking to people both with our words and our body
language is only part of communication, the other big

part is listening. Many of us don't know how to listen
very well. How we hear the other person often depends
on what is going on in our own lives and the thoughts
we have in our mind at the time. Let's say you're talking
to your friend Adam about your holiday when you went
to a national park and went bushwalking with your
family. Let's say Adam is worrying about something his
girlfriend said to him and is actually thinking about that
in his head. How much do you think Adam is really
going to be hearing about your holiday?

Think about when people are talking to us. How
often are we thinking of what we want to say next, our
minds racing ahead, maybe we want to jump in and
interrupt, maybe we're off in our head on a daydream?
Often it takes some effort to really listen.

Dr Claire,
I've started high school and I hate it because it's
an all-girls' school and I never wanted to go
there in the first place. Before I went there I
didn't have any problems, but now my life is
shit. My parents forced me to go there and they
say they want the best for me, and they expect
me to get good grades. It is a high pressure
school where they're all brainy, and getting
really good marks is expected. I know I just
don't belong there. I want to be a gardener when
I grow up or maybe have a flower shop. My
parents think I should go to university but I
don't want to. I'm not smart enough for this
school, and when I do badly, Dad yells at me and

says I should be doing a lot better and that I'm
not trying hard enough and I am wasting his
hard-earned money. Because I'm not smart the
teachers either get impatient with me or just
forget about me. I hate my school and my family
and my friends, except a few from my old
school, and they don't go to my new school. Once
I got so upset I cut my wrists with a knife but
then I told my one friend who noticed that the
cat scratched me. My family didn't notice.
Sometimes I get these weird panic attacks at
school, and sometimes I wake up crying because
I have to go to this school and try to be someone
I'm not, like the perfect daughter. I can't
communicate with my parents. They don't listen,
they just say 'Don't start with that again Yvette'
and then I get upset and just go in my room.
Please help me. How can I get them to see I
don't want to go there?
Yvette

Dear Yvette,
It's important that you sit down quietly with
your parents and tell them how you are feeling.
Obviously they think they are giving you the
best education, but you are feeling under
tremendous pressure to be this perfect student
and daughter and to be someone you're not. It
sounds like you just don't fit in at this school,
and that it is making you miserable. I think that
you need to communicate all this to them. If you

can't talk to them, then write it all down and
give it to them as a letter. But try not to be
overly emotional when you talk to them or write
the letter, just calmly state the facts. Remember,
they mightn't have learned the art of good
listening, so state your case simply and don't get
side-tracked into arguments. Use the broken-
record technique and keep repeating what you
want. This means you have to know what you
want (the alternatives to this school and some
ideas about what your talents are which can
help you decide your school program) and have
suggestions ready to help solve the problem. It
sounds to me that you might be better off at a
school where there is more emphasis on creative
things rather than academic stuff. However, even
if you want to run a flower shop remember you
need to learn maths and computers or else how
are you going to keep track of the money? And
please don't cut your wrists. As you've found,
this doesn't solve anything. Talking this out will
do more good, believe me. If you can't get
anywhere by talking to Mum and Dad, then
try the school counsellor, one of the teachers
at school, an older trusted relative, or even
your local doctor. It's important you sort all this
out by communicating through talking or writing
about how you feel to others, rather than
taking out your frustrations on your body by
hurting yourself.
Dr Claire

Some tips to being a better listener

1 Try to give the person your attention. Look at them. We've all had the experience of trying to talk to someone who's glued to the TV or got their nose in a magazine or is gazing out the window.

2 Try active listening. No, this does not mean doing star-jumps while you're listening, it means that you use methods to show the other person you really are listening.

- Try reflecting back what you've heard. Let's say your friend has been talking to you about what a hard time her mum has been giving her over her homework. What you do is summarise what she's been saying and you say it back to her, not word for word but the general guts of what she's said to you. You could say, 'Sounds like your mum has been giving you a really hard time with your homework.' Then she can say 'yes' and she might go on to explain a bit more, but she'll know you've really listened to her. This reflecting back method can work really well when you're dealing with someone who's very upset and you don't know quite what to say. You just say, 'Sounds like you're really upset' or 'Sounds like that was really hurtful for you'.

- Try asking a question or asking for more details. Like, 'In what ways does your mum get on your back about your homework?' or 'Can you tell me more about that?'

- Check that you've understood what they're saying. You could say, 'I'm not sure I've got this right, are you saying your mum is giving you a really hard time when you don't do your homework?' or 'Can I check that I've heard you right, your mum is really giving you a hard time when you don't do your homework?'
- Listen to the body language as well. Maybe a friend is saying that they feel fine, but they look upset to you. You can say, 'You're telling me you're okay, but gee you look like you're upset to me. Do you want to talk about it or is there anything I can help you with?' Your friend may then decide to open up and tell you what the matter is. Or maybe they don't want to talk about it, in which case you'll have to back off and let them be. Checking out the body language and the general vibe you are picking up from the conversation can be a really helpful thing to do. You can say, 'I'm picking up that something else may be going on here, is there something you want to say or is there a problem you want to discuss?' When you bring it out into the open the person may tell you what is really on their mind. Of course they may not want to, but at least you have given them the chance.

Learning to listen well to other people is really important. Think how good it makes you feel when you know someone has really listened to you. A lot of communication problems can be solved by good listening techniques.

One barrier to good communication is not feeling confident to state what you feel and what you want. But you can learn to be assertive.

What is assertion?

Dr Claire,
My sister, who's 15, went to something called Assertion Class. She was always rather quiet and withdrawn. Now it's like Jekyll and Hyde, and she's turned into a verbal monster. She keeps telling us all what to do, even Mum and Dad, speaking loudly and bossing us around, and getting really aggressive if we don't do what she wants. She says things like, 'It's my right to do this or that.' What about my rights? I share a room with her and if she doesn't stop being such a bossy cow I'll end up hitting her over the head with her assertion book. I think this assertion stuff sucks.
Suzi, age 13

Dear Suzi,
It is a fantastic idea for people to go to assertion classes, because they learn how to stand up for themselves and say what they feel and need and want. People who are passive and let others take over their lives are often unhappy and have poor self-esteem. However, people who do

assertion classes need to learn that they are not going to necessarily get what they want all the time. When people learn a new skill they often go overboard with the power of it. That's what your sister is doing. She has this powerful new tool and she's wielding it, but she's swung the pendulum from being passive and unassertive right over to the other side and is being aggressive. Assertion is not about telling other people what they should be doing with their lives or bossing them about. You'd be doing her a favour if you quietly sit down with her and point out that there is a huge difference between being aggressive and bossy, and being assertive. They would have taught her this in her class, but she hasn't yet got the message. Sounds like she'd better read the book again. Assertive people don't need to shout and be aggressive. They can quietly and firmly state what they feel and what they want.

And other people can quietly and firmly agree with this or disagree with this. Assertion class doesn't give anyone a licence to be aggressive!
Dr Claire

Lots of people think being assertive means being snappy, snarly and aggressive. Nothing could be further from the truth. Assertion means that you use clear and direct communication to express your feeling, thoughts, needs and wants in a straightforward manner. It means you talk to other people in a way that maintains your dignity and their dignity. And it means if you have anger or other strong feelings you express these in a direct manner, but also in a way that takes into account other people's rights as well. Behaving in an assertive way helps you build your self-esteem and confidence. It will help you to feel that you can take charge of yourself and your life.

What are some tips to help me be assertive?

1   Use 'I' language. That means that instead of starting off your statements with 'You always ...' or 'You never ...' you begin instead with 'I think' or 'I feel', or 'I notice that ...' People tend to hear statements that start with 'You' as being accusing, and they can get their back up and be on the defensive before you've got another word out. Here are some examples:

-   Instead of 'You are always late when we go out, I'm fed up with you!' try 'I feel really let down when you repeatedly arrive late when we go out. I either worry that something has happened to you or think you don't want to go. Can you please be on time in the future, or at least ring and let me know if you are late?'

-   Instead of 'You are such a bitch, you haven't spoken to me all day' try 'I feel put-out that you haven't spoken to me all day. Is there something wrong?'

- Instead of 'You always sit with John in art class now, rather than me. What's the matter, do you think you're too good for me?' try 'I notice that you sit with John in art class now rather than with me. I'd still like to sit with you. Is there a problem we should talk about?'
- Instead of 'You don't give me enough pocket money, you're so mean, everyone else has more money to spend than I do' try 'I feel awkward mixing with my friends because they get a bigger allowance and have more money to spend when we're out. I feel really self-conscious about it. Is there any way I can have an increase in my allowance?'

2 Try not to blame or judge the other person, as this tends to make people defensive and they will stop listening to what you say. Rather, give your own views and express your own thoughts and feelings.

3 Keep your body language consistent with what you are saying: stand tall, look the person in the eyes, or if you can't look at their eyes look at their nose. Avoid aggressive gestures such as pointing with your finger, standing over the other person, putting your hands on your hips, making a fist. On the other hand, don't send a mixed message when you are angry or upset by smiling or giggling because you won't be taken as seriously as you want to be. Don't use passive and unassertive body language like being hunched

over and staring at the ground and talking in such a quiet voice no one can hear you. Stand up straight, talk so people can hear you and look at people. You have a right to be here and have your own feelings, thoughts and opinions.

4 Learn to say 'No'. Many of us have a hard time saying no to requests from friends and family. We end up agreeing to do something we don't want to do, mainly because we are scared they won't like us or might get angry with us if we say no. We can end up feeling really resentful and angry at the other person, all the time going along with what they wanted us to do.

Dr Claire,

I am totally in love with this guy Matt, but I'm only 14 and I don't want to have sex yet. We've been going out for four weeks now, and he's getting more insistent. Like, the other day he slid his hand down the front of my jeans. I pulled it out and I said 'No' and then I burst into tears. He said he was sorry, but then ten minutes later he did it again. If I don't have sex with him, he'll probably dump me. He's really good-looking and there's heaps of girls ready to grab him. I just don't know what to do.

Meg

Dear Meg,

Matt needs to be reminded that 'No' means 'No'.
Unfortunately, some boys learn incorrect
messages about how to treat girls. Maybe he
thinks it is 'manly' to try to touch you sexually
when you've said no — it isn't manly, it's abuse.
Or maybe he just doesn't think girls have the
same rights as boys. Maybe he believes how you
feel about your body and your feelings are not
as important as his feelings. Clearly this is
rubbish. You need to be assertive and tell him
that you will dump him if he keeps trying to
maul you, and that you are definitely not going
to have sex with him at this point in time. This
might shock him into behaving himself. You
might try talking to him about all this and
explain to him what I've just been talking
about. You see, he's not respecting you as a
person if he keeps trying to feel you up when
you've expressly said no. But this is where you
need to set boundaries when you pash. I think
that if you do have sex with him, he'll dump
you fairly soon after it anyway, so be assertive,
state what you want, and take control of what
happens. If sex is the most important thing
to him then he'll go off with another girl and
you can heave a sigh of relief that you got
rid of him.

You might actually find that you're happier
going out with someone who doesn't try to grope
you, and with whom you can relax and talk and

have a good time with. There are plenty of
decent guys out there who wouldn't just shove
their hand down your pants. Both girls and boys
should ask whether the other person wants to
be sexual. Ask 'Would you like to be sexual with
me?' 'Can I touch you sexually?' 'How far do
you want to go?' And if the other person says
no then you back off. Don't just start groping.
If you have a friendship with a boy first, then
you're on a better footing to discuss with each
other how far you want to go if you both
decide you want to be sexual with each other.
It might be ages, even years before you feel
you want to have sex. That is just fine.
It's your body and your feelings, so don't
you have sex until you are happy that you
want to. And if you eventually do decide to
have sex because you feel ready, and not just
because he wants to, don't forget to use a
condom, will you?
Dr Claire

The best way to learn to say 'No' is to practise.
Get some lines you can use like, 'No, I don't want
to' or 'No, I'd rather not do that' or 'No, I prefer
not to do that' or 'No, that doesn't suit me'. It
might sound stupid but if you stand in front of the
mirror and look at yourself while you practise
saying 'No' it can really help you get used to
being able to say it.

Dear Margaret,

There's these girls who I'm now friends with after my best friend moved to another town. I've only been friends with them for two weeks. They want me to go to this party and I'm not allowed to go. One of them said, 'Sleep over at my place and your parents won't even know.' But I'm scared because there'll be older guys and some of them take drugs. I don't want to go, but I don't want to say no because they'll think I'm a loser and not cool. This is the in group, and if I say no they mightn't want me in their group. I feel real stupid. How can I say no?

Elena, age 15

Hi Elena,

I think you need to just say a straight no! Tell them you hope they have a great time, but you're not going. You don't need to give a reason. Just repeat, 'No, I'm not going' no matter what excuses they bring up. It's called the broken record technique. Eventually, they'll give up pestering you. Hopefully, they'll respect you for being assertive. If not, you don't need them as friends because there will be other issues like this one that crop up, and eventually you'll have to say no or get into trouble with your parents and maybe even the law. So, practise saying a calm, firm no!

Margaret

Another good thing to say if you get caught on the spot is, 'I need some time to think about that, I'll get back to you', or 'I'll have to check what I'm doing that night, I'll let you know.' That is, if you feel a bit flustered and don't know whether to say yes or no to a request or invitation, sometimes you can get around it by giving yourself a bit of time away from the pressure of the other person standing there or being on the phone. Then you can think more calmly about what you really want to do and how you will tell them.

It's important to learn to be assertive, because you're going to need this skill all through your life if you want to feel happy and confident and valued. Remember too that if you have the right to say no to other people, then they also have the right to say no to you. So if a friend says no, they don't want to do something or go somewhere or whatever, you don't have to fall in a rejected heap. In the ebb and flow of life there will be times you say no, and times someone else says no.

Saying no with a long excuse is sometimes not the best way to do it. Let's say you say no to a friend's invitation out by saying you're already going out that night when you're not. Then they might say, 'Oh, well I'll come with you when you go out. Where are you going?' And then you're trying to concoct some lie. Often it is better to be straightforward and say, 'Actually, I've planned a quiet night at home', rather than make up an elaborate story.

5 Learn to apologise when you need to, but don't go around saying 'I'm sorry' all the time. Many of us, especially girls and women, are brought up to be constantly apologising for ourselves. You have a right to be here, to have opinions, to ask for things, to say no. Many of us are so used to saying 'I'm sorry' we say it even when someone else bumps into us! Keep a look out for phrases like, 'I'm sorry to bother you but ...' Learn to make requests of others without starting off with 'I'm sorry'.

6 Learn to deal with compliments. Compliments are easy, just say, 'Thank you.' How many of us when someone gives us a compliment such as 'I like your shirt', say, 'Oh, this old thing, I've had it for years.' Or someone says, 'I like your haircut,' and you say, 'It's too short.' Just learn to say 'thank you'. People like to feel their compliments are accepted, not thrown back in their face.

7 Learn to handle criticism. When other people criticise you, don't just fly off the handle at them. On the other hand, don't immediately think that they must be right. Take a deep slow breath, in and out quietly, remain calm and think about what they've said. Sometimes the old standby of counting to ten in your head can help. If you feel like you're going to explode, or you're going to start crying, give yourself some time out. You can

say, 'I need some time out, I'll talk about this later,' and then leave the room. Don't storm out, just make a quick exit. Then go for a walk around the block while you calm down. When you're calmer, you can respond to the criticism.

Often a good tactic is to ask for more information. For example, you can say, 'Can you tell me more about why you think I'm a lazy slob?' Then you can get behind the labelling to what is going on for the other person. You can then either agree, 'Yes, I can see that you would think I've been sloppy in tidying up my room. Actually, I've been distracted by an exam next week, I'll clean it up when I get a moment.' Or you can disagree, 'No, I don't agree with you, that's not how it is for me,' or 'No, I don't see it that way.'

If you can remain calm when you are being criticised then you will have learnt a very good skill. Sometimes criticism can be a gift, because it can help you see something about yourself that you hadn't considered before. Also, arguments often start when someone criticises someone else and that person immediately gets angry and bites back, and then each person starts snapping at the other and off they go with an escalating argument.

How can I learn more about being assertive?

There are many books, tapes and videos on how to be assertive. Your local library and school library may stock

these, or you could find them at any large bookshop.
Going to a class on assertion can be a marvellous thing,
because then you get to practise being assertive with
each other. Often the instructor gets you to role-play
pretend situations, like you have to return something to
a shop for a refund, or you have to tell someone you
don't want to go out with them.

Remember, we often find it easier to be assertive
in some situations than in others. For example, you
might have no trouble returning a faulty item to a store
for a refund, but you might find it really hard to say no
to a friend.

What are the opposites to being assertive?

The opposites are aggressive behaviour, passive
behaviour and indirect behaviour.

- Aggressive behaviour includes yelling, swearing,
  verbal put-downs, name calling, threatening people,
  violence and intimidation. Usually the person being
  aggressive may think they are getting their own way,
  but the other person feels trampled on. In the short
  term, aggressive behaviour may seem to get you
  what you want, but in the long term it damages
  relationships, and you will lose the trust and
  cooperation of those people you are aggressive with.

  You will not be having genuine interactions with
  anyone, and you won't learn to grow and mature as a
  person. You're liable to end up feeling quite lonely
  inside, because no one will want to get truly close to

you because they will feel afraid of your aggression. They will not be free to tell you how they really think or feel. Also, sometimes after you've blown up at someone and yelled and screamed you can feel guilty afterwards. You might have said things you later regret. You might even apologise, but the damage has been done.

Sometimes people go through their lives acting out being really aggressive and tough when in reality they are scared to let people get close to them. Their aggressive behaviour keeps everyone at a distance.

If you have friends who are aggressive towards you, maybe you need to think very carefully about whether you really want to be friends with these people. If you've grown up in a family with aggression in it you might end up being friends with aggressive people because that is what you're used to. But hey, there are people out there who will treat you with more respect. None of us needs to get stuck in a relationship with a violent or aggressive person. There is a better way.

- Passive behaviour has typically been more common in girls and women because of the way in which they are brought up, but boys and men can struggle with this too. You are being passive when you don't express your opinions or feelings and when you let your own needs be overlooked. You may allow others to control you and make decisions for you. When you feel angry and upset you may say nothing, just smile sweetly. You try to be nice all the time and have a hard time saying no. You may often end up doing things you don't really want to because it's so hard for you to say no. Underneath you may feel resentful and put upon.

- Indirect behaviour means instead of being direct about your feelings you might agree to do something like go out with someone and then on the night you 'forget' or you ring up and say you're sick. Someone might ask you to do something for them and you forget, or you do it but you muck it up. We talked a bit about this in the anger section. Indirect behaviour also includes things like going silent and refusing to talk, walking out of a room and slamming a door and so on, instead of being assertive and direct about your feeling of anger or being upset. Your actions leave other people guessing about your feelings, and you don't get your true thoughts and feelings out in the open. Try to learn to be assertive with what you say, rather than being indirect in what you do.

The numbers game

Dr Claire,

I can't communicate with my family. I come home from school and I'm tired and worried about my schoolwork because I'm in Year 12 and if anyone says anything to me I just feel my fuse snap and I'm liable to yell at them to leave me alone or whatever and go into my room and slam the door. My sister is a total bitch and thinks she's so good because she got into law at

university and she harps on at me that if I want
to get good marks like she did I'll have to study
harder. My father has a high-powered job
managing a big firm and he often comes home
having a stress fit and starts yelling at us. My
mother is a teacher but she is also studying to
do a PhD in education, and she is always
running around at full speed doing a thousand
things. We are all hyper and stressed and just
end up yelling at each other. If you ask anyone
how they are they just start snapping and
snarling and yelling. Have you got any ideas
about anything I can do to improve things?
Sharon, age 17

Dear Sharon,
Your whole family sounds stressed out. A simple
thing that can help with communication in
stressful situations is to play the numbers game.
What happens is you think about how you're
feeling and you rate yourself on a scale of 1 to
4. 1 means you're okay, happy to talk to people,
interact. 4 means you're feeling stressed to the
eyeballs and you don't feel like talking to anyone
and if anyone pesters you to talk you're liable to
blow up at them. 4 means you need time on
your own to settle down. 2 and 3 are in
between. So, when you come home from school
you simply announce that you're a 1 or a 3 or a
4 or whatever depending how you feel and this
gives people a guide about whether to steer clear

of you and give you some space, or whether you'd be happy to talk about your day. Often when we're feeling really stressed and someone wants to talk to us it can be very difficult to calmly state that you don't feel like talking now. Often what happens is we snap or snarl or pick a fight when all we really need is some distance. It sounds like your dad is a 4 most nights he comes through the door. Tell your family what you're doing and give it a go. The rest of them might want to try it too.

I developed this numbers system to use when I was getting stressed out and tired from working long hours in hospitals and spending most of the rest of my time studying. It might sound silly but it changed my life drastically at the time, because I stopped snapping and snarling and had a lot less arguments at home. Also, when I realised that just about every night I was coming home rating myself as a 4, it dawned on me that I had to work on calming myself and trying some relaxation strategies on the way home so I didn't walk through the door ready to bite the head off anyone who spoke to me. Gradually I was more often rating myself a 1 or a 2, although I still had my 4 days! Give it a go.

Dr Claire

7 Sex Hassles

Dr Claire,

I was 16 and I went out with my boyfriend Steve to a party. I'd had a few drinks but I wasn't drunk or anything. On the way home to my place he pulled the car into a park. We started kissing but then he wanted to go further but I said I didn't want to. He kept trying to take my underpants off and I said 'No, I don't want to' but he didn't listen. It really hurt and I was screaming and crying all the way through it. Afterwards he drove me home like nothing had happened. Next thing I heard he was going out with someone else. I never told anyone what happened. I still feel awful and I don't want to go out with anyone. I still get nightmares, and it makes me scared to be alone with a guy. I've been out with one guy since and I was just so on edge all the time.

Cathy, age 17

Dear Cathy,

What happened to you is called date rape. When he forced himself on you after you had said 'No', this is rape, and it is a criminal offence. After being raped feelings of being betrayed, invaded, degraded, having flash-backs of what happened,

feeling confused, feeling ashamed, all of these
things are normal under the circumstances.
You need to look up in the phone book under
Sexual Assault Centres or Rape Crisis or Rape
Counselling Centres (these services are usually
listed in the community help section at the front
of the phone book) and get some counselling.
Usually, you will be able to talk initially with a
counsellor on the phone, then make an
appointment to see them. They could also
discuss whether you want to make a report
to the police, not that you have to if you don't
want to. Many date-rapes go unreported to the
police, as they can be difficult to prove, and
sometimes girls believe they were at fault
because they'd gone with a guy to his place or
they'd had a bit much to drink. If someone
rapes you after you've said 'No', it is not your
fault, it is his crime. No means no, whether
you're in his car, in his apartment, you've been
drinking, you were wearing sexy clothes, you'd
started some sexual stuff but then decided no,
or whatever. If the police start getting multiple
reports about the same guy, it may make it
easier for them to do something. Guys who date
rape are likely to do it to other girls too. Also,
you might want to go to your local library or big
bookshop and look at some of the books about
recovering from rape, and about rape in society.
You are not alone. Of course you are going to
feel scared around guys for a while, but

gradually you'll find you'll settle down. I'm so
sorry this happened to you. Get yourself to
counselling, okay?
Dr Claire

What is date rape?

Date rape or acquaintance rape is when a girl is raped
by someone she knows. Boys can be date raped too.
A boy can be date raped by a woman, but statistically
it is much more common that men rape women. A gay
(homosexual) boy or man is also vulnerable to date
rape by another boy or man. Since date rape more
commonly involves girls, we'll talk about it from the
girl's viewpoint. It can be someone she's recently met,
or it can be someone she's known for a while, even a
boyfriend. Sometimes alcohol and drugs are involved,
in that the girl may have been drinking alcohol or using
drugs or she may have been given drinks 'spiked' with
extra alcohol or drugs by a boy in order to get her
affected by the alcohol or drugs so she won't be able to
resist him when he rapes her. Also, some of these drugs
make the girl feel like she can't remember what
happened, so the boy thinks he will be able to get away
with it because she won't have a clear memory of what
he did to her.

Dear Margaret,
My friend Sara and I went to a disco with a
bunch of girls, and while she was dancing,
someone put a drug in her drink. She went
all numb and floppy and weird and we had to

take her to accident and emergency. What
was this drug?
Emma, age 17

Dear Emma,
When I went to dances about a hundred years
ago, my mother always said, 'Never leave your
drink in case someone puts a Mickey Finn in it.'
A Mickey Finn was the name for knock-out
drops. The Mickey Finn has now been
superseded by designer drugs and sedatives.
Rohypnol has been one of the drugs most
commonly used to put in drinks. The
manufacturers of this drug have been talking
about putting a blue dye in with the drug so it
would turn your drink blue and you'd know your
drink had been got at. However, there are other
drugs that can be used. The idea is that the girl
will be too woozy and out-of-it to refuse sex, and
she will have memory gaps and confused
recollection for what happened. The moral of the
story is, never leave your drink unattended,
even for a second.
Margaret

What sort of drugs are used for date rape?

Throughout history alcohol and other drugs have been
used to affect women (and sometimes men) for the
purposes of sexually assaulting them. There are today a

lot of drugs that can be used for this purpose, and they come in all different types including pills, liquids and powders that can be put in a drink and given to an unsuspecting person. Street names of some of these drugs you should be aware of include Liquid Ecstasy, Liquid X, Grievous Bodily Harm, Easy Lay, Special K and Roeys. There are a whole stack of these drugs that can be used for these purposes.

Some suggested rules for safe partying

1 Don't leave your drinks unattended at parties or bars, someone may slip something into your drink while you are away from the table.
2 Do not accept drinks from someone you do not know well and trust. The best thing is to get drinks that come in cans or bottles and open them yourself, or get your drink directly from the bartender.
3 At parties, don't accept open container drinks from anyone. If you want to avoid a scene take the drink but don't drink it.
4 Be alert to the behaviour of friends and ask them to watch out for you also. Anyone who acts extremely drunk after having only a small amount to drink may be in danger of having been drugged.
5 If you or a friend feel dizzy, confused or have other strange symptoms after drinking a drink, get to a safe place immediately by asking for help

from the staff, calling a friend or family member or the police. If you think you have been drugged you can go straight to a hospital emergency department for help.

What do these date rape drugs do to you?

People will react differently to drugs depending on their sensitivity to the particular drug. You might feel dizzy, confused like you can't think properly, you lose your sense of judgement, you could go numb, and you may feel uninhibited and want to do things you wouldn't normally think were a good idea. You may feel drowsy and sleepy, and like you are in a dream. You might have trouble with walking. Your memory can be messed up. Depending on the drug and whether you have other drugs or alcohol in your system you might get more serious effects like problems with your breathing and your heart.

Why would a boy want to rape a girl he went out on a date with?

Of course most boys would be horrified at the idea of raping anyone. However, unfortunately in our society some boys and men end up with ideas about sex that disregard the girl's feelings. Some boys and men grow up thinking that girls and women are not equal to them, that girls and women are really second-class citizens and that what the boy wants to do is more important than how the girl feels or what the girl wants. Also, films and pornography may give the incorrect message to boys that women may mean 'yes' to sex when they say 'no'. Pornography portrays women as being willing to accommodate whatever the man wants to do, and some pornography involves violence and force against women, like scenes of rape and violence. Pornography often does not actually depict women as real human beings with their own needs and feelings, and able to say 'no' to sex if they don't feel like it. We think that women need to speak up about 'hard' pornography, because it is degrading to women in particular, and if it involves children or teenage girls/boys, then it's disgusting, because they've been coerced and abused by adults.

Dear Margaret,
I was typing in my address on the computer so I could check my mail and this thing came up, www.hooters. So I thought 'What the hell' because I've never been to that site and my parents don't seem to use the internet much when I'm around. I pressed enter and was so shocked that I started to shake. It was a porn site with all these women with big tits, so I got out. Then I was thinking about my dad, because sometimes when I come out of my room late at night he quickly gets out of whatever he's doing on the computer when Mum's at work. So I typed in www.b and suddenly up comes the site bigboobs.com and as I kept going to the saved websites and there were about 30 I saw that

Dad went to bigtits, teenagekids, peeinggirls. I was so stunned. Margaret, what does this mean? That my dad doesn't love my mum any more? That he's just not getting it from her? What sort of sick creep is he?

Anyway, I was wondering what you thought about this, because I'm worried that Mum and Dad will get divorced or something. Plus when I look at Dad I feel like throwing up.
Phoebe, age 13

Dear Phoebe,
I'm sorry that you had to find out that your dad's been having a bit of a perv at rudie-nudies and stuff on the internet. Many men like looking at big tits, and they are often curious about porn stuff, but it doesn't necessarily mean they are going to divorce their wives and go after the big tits. I'm sure your father still loves your mother and they have a happy sex life.

However, I think your father is betraying his family by doing this at home, while Mum's out working and you're in your room.

Some options:

Option 1   Keep quiet about it, which means he'll keep doing it.

Option 2   Write him a message on the computer so you know he's been sprung bad, then see what he does.

Option 3   Take away the computer cable, and
               when he asks why, tell him.

Option 4   Talk to him quietly about what
               you've found he's been doing, and
               point out that you are shocked and
               that you feel it's not appropriate
               for him to be doing this on the
               family computer in your family
               home. I think option 4 sounds the
               most sensible.

If you go for option 4, he'll be really worried that
you'll tell Mum. So, tell him it won't go further if
he immediately stops looking at porn sites,
because you believe it's degrading to both your
mother, you, and any other females on the planet.
Margaret

'Some guys just want to have sex'

Some boys mistakenly believe it is 'manly' to force sex
on a woman when she does not want it. A study at a
university in California that asked teens about
acceptable behaviour found 54 per cent of teens felt it
was okay to force sex if a woman had at first said yes to
sex and then changed her mind, 39 per cent felt it was
okay to force sex if he spent a lot of money on her, and
36 per cent felt it was okay to force sex if he is so
turned on he feels he can't stop.

It is sad to think that some boys think this way,
because, under any circumstances, to force sex on a
woman when she says no is rape.

Boys can get some very confusing messages from our society about what it means to be 'manly', and unfortunately some of the wrong messages they can get is that sex is the man's right and he should not be denied. Sex is never anybody's right over another person. Sex should be between two people who freely agree to have sex with each other because they want to, not because they're forced too.

What can a girl do to reduce the chances of date rape?

The more a girl knows about date rape, the more likely she can avoid being put in a situation where it can occur.

1 Don't give mixed messages: when mixing with other boys and girls, and in a dating situation, be clear about saying what you mean. Say 'yes' when you mean yes and 'no' when you mean no. Speak up for yourself on a date, whether it's about which movie to see or where to go to eat. When you show you mean what you say, you show that you are not just going along with whatever the boy wants to do.

2 Know your sexual limits: it is your body, and no one has the right to force you to do anything you do not want to do. You can say 'get your hands off me' or 'don't touch me' or 'if you don't stop now I'm leaving'. Stopping sexual activity you don't want doesn't mean you are frigid or not a real woman. It means you know how to protect the limits you have set for yourself.

3 Trust your gut instincts: if you feel you are being pressured into sex, if a situation starts to feel bad or wrong or you start to feel nervous about what's happening, confront him immediately or leave the situation immediately. Speak up loudly, leave, go for help.

4 Be independent on dates: Mum always used to say have enough money for a taxi home, and she was right. Pay your own way on dates and always have money with you so you can get yourself home independently if you need to. Also, it is a good idea to have change for a phone and a phone card for public phones so you can ring home or ring the police in an emergency. If you have a mobile phone take it with you.

5 Alcohol and drugs: if you want to be in control of your body and your life, you can't afford to get drunk or drugged because you will be in no state to speak up for yourself or look after yourself.

6 Avoid being vulnerable: avoid isolated and lonely places especially early on in the dating situation or relationship when you are just getting to know him. Do not go into his house or invite him into yours when no one is home. Do not go for walks or drives to out-of-the-way places. Go where there are other people, where you feel comfortable and safe, like out to a movie or out for coffee or out to eat or for a walk in an area where you know there will be a lot of other people around.

Whilst you don't want to end up paranoid, it pays to take sensible precautions to try to keep yourself as safe as possible.

Now, by listing these sorts of precautions we are not suggesting that if you didn't do these and you got raped it was your fault. When someone gets raped people can tend to blame the victim, saying 'Oh, she shouldn't have got in the car with him' or 'Well, she was wearing a skimpy dress, what do you expect?' The bottom line is that rape is a crime, and the fault lies with the person who does the raping. No woman asks to get raped.

What can boys do to prevent themselves being in a situation where they are accused of rape?

As we've already said, most boys would be appalled at the idea of rape. However, some boys as we've pointed out do think that forcing sex on a girl is okay in certain circumstances, so you can see with thoughts like these they could end up raping a girl and maybe not even understand that what they did was criminal.

So, here are some things to help clarify the situation for boys:

1 No means No: Men or boys who are accused of rape use excuses like 'She asked for it because she was wearing a skimpy dress', or 'She was flirting with me and I'd paid a lot of money to take her on a date', or 'She was teasing me, leading me on, and she said no just at the last minute just so I wouldn't think she was easy.' The bottom line

is that when a girl or woman says no, there is never a reason to force yourself on her. Even if she says no right at the last minute, you should stop the sexual activity and sort out clearly what is going on. There will always be other opportunities for sex with other girls, and if you are feeling very turned on you can go into another room or move right away from her and privately masturbate yourself. This is a lot better than forcing sex on a girl, which not only will cause damage to her psychologically, but could see you charged with rape, a criminal offence.

2 Stop and ask: If you have any doubts about what the girl or woman wants, stop and ask. Clarify what she wants. Are you really listening to her, or just listening to what you want?

3 Responsibility: It is not true that if a boy gets very sexually excited he 'can't control himself'. Sexual excitement does not justify forced sex. Your sexual actions are always under your control.

Dr Claire,
All my friends say they are having sex, so I feel like I should too. But I don't know whether I really want to or not. What do you think I should do? My friends are going to think I am like weird or something if I don't have sex.
Emma, age 15

Dear Emma,
It's your body, not theirs. It's not pleasant
having sex for the sake of it with some uncaring
person, either. Having sex with just anyone just
so you can say you've had sex is likely to be a
fairly miserable experience where you grit your
teeth and wish it was over! You are the one who
should decide when you want to have sex and
with whom. And I can guarantee that some of
these girls haven't gone all the way. They're just
big-noting. I think sex is too important a thing
to take lightly, so don't feel that you have to do
it, okay? It should be an experience where you
feel safe, comfortable, happy, respected and
cared for, and where you respect and care for
the other person. And when you do eventually
decide to have sex, and that could be years
away, make sure that you use contraception.
Dr Claire

As a teen, you can decide whether you want to be sexually active or not. There is absolutely nothing wrong in
deciding you want to wait until you're older, or in a stable
committed relationship, or wait until you are married if
you want to. Your decision might also be influenced by
things like the family you come from and what their
views are. Maybe you belong to a particular religion that
has views on sex. Maybe you just don't feel ready, which
is perfectly okay. You can always have sex later on in the
future, but once you've had sex you can't 'unhave it.'

Whether or not to have sex is a very personal decision. It's not a decision to base on what your friends are doing or say they're doing. Don't forget that what your friends say they are doing and what they are actually doing might be two different things. Sometimes people talk about all the sex things they're doing when in truth they're not doing much at all, they just want to 'big-note' themselves.

If you decide you want to be sexually active, then you need to act responsibly to look after yourself and others.

Dear Margaret,
My best friend Marnie had sex with this fantastic guy Rowan, and she thought like he was her boyfriend, then she found out that he'd been bragging at school about how he'd scored with her and about what they'd done together, and like the next week he was off with Jo, who's a real slut. Marnie is really devastated. Why did he do this? He'd told her he loved her and everything.
Jane, age 15

Dear Jane,
Unfortunately, some males will tell a female they love her even if they don't, so she'll be a willing sexual partner. It's devious, it's underhand, it's pathetic, but some boys do this, then boast to their mates. It's so they'll look like stud muffins. And it's also because underneath they see girls

as second-class citizens and not as important as
themselves, so they think it's okay to lie to her
and manipulate her, with zero thought for her
feelings. Whereas the poor girl ends up being
labelled a slut. Not fair? Of course not. Why
should a boy who screws around be considered a
'hero' and a girl who screws around get labelled
a slut? It is a put-down of women's sexuality.
That's why it's a good idea not to have sex with
some smooth-talking guy unless you like one-
night stands and sleeping around and you don't
care what others might think of you, or you
truly believe the person is sincere and you've
been going out together for quite a while. I
always recommend letting a firm friendship
develop first before having sex. I'm sorry that
Marnie is devastated, but Rowan is weak in
character and untrustworthy, so she's better off
without him.
Margaret

Many young men feel pressured to be sexually active
to 'prove' their manhood, and to feel they are
accepted by their peer group. For some young men sex
becomes an issue of performance, the more times and
the more girls the better in their eyes. They might 'keep
score' of how many girls they've had sex with.
Unfortunately, a double standard still exists in our
society such that the boy who 'sleeps around' may be
thought of as a 'stud', but the girl who sleeps around is

thought of as a 'slut'. You can see how unfair and discriminatory that is.

In the heat of the moment, young men may say what they think a girl wants to hear, and that may include things like 'I love you' or 'you're special'. For many young women, what they are yearning for is to feel loved and special, to have a 'relationship', to have a boyfriend. For the young man the pressing need for him may be to have sex. He may not be thinking along the same lines as she is, and so you can see that the two of them can have sex but it can mean quite different things to each of them.

Afterwards, she can think he is going to be her steady boyfriend, while he may want to go off and try sex with a different girl.

Girls may say 'yes' to sex because they fear rejection or they are afraid the boy will get angry with them if they say 'no'. Some girls are brought up in a way where they haven't learnt to be assertive or how to be clear about what they want and don't want.

Dr Claire,
I've been going out with Luke for five months.
He's now pestering me all the time to have sex.
But I think I'm too young. I really want to wait
for at least a year, but he says he's not going to
wait that long. He's implying that if I don't come
across, he'll dump me. What should I do?
Kate, age 15

Dear Kate,
He's trying to emotionally blackmail you into
having sex. If you don't want to, and feel that
it's not right for you yet, then don't. Having sex
when you're not really ready for it is likely to be
a) unpleasant and b) you won't feel good about
yourself afterwards. If he dumps you for
someone who's ready, willing and able, you can
see it was the sex, and not you the person, which
was the most important thing to him. I get many
tales from young girls who give in then get
dumped, and the story spread around about the
guy's sexual conquest. So stick with your
principles. Better to be dumped than devastated.
Dr Claire

Of course, sex works best when both participants are
clear to themselves and each other about what they
want, and are both happy participants in sex. Sex
should be a safe, happy experience between two
people who are having sex with each other because
they want to.

Be aware that movies and TV often portray sex in
unrealistic ways, like two people who've just met leap
into bed and have fantastic, earth-shattering sex the first
time they do it with each other. In reality, good sex can
take some time for two people to work out who likes
what and when, and you often need a good sense of
humour about it all for when things don't quite go like
you'd imagined.

Being a teenager and dealing with sex is a bit like being given a very powerful car. If you take the powerful car out of the garage, you need to act responsibly otherwise you can crash and hurt yourself and others. The 'crashes' of sex are things like pregnancy, sexually transmitted diseases including HIV, broken relationships, and hurt and injured feelings.

Dr Claire,
I had sex with this girl at a party. She's known as sleeping around with a lot of different guys. Then a few days later I had a burning sensation when I peed and I was really worried that I'd caught something. But it all went away so I didn't worry anymore. Then I read I could still have a disease in my system. Is this possible?
Toby, age 16

Dear Toby,
It is likely you caught a sexually transmitted disease and yes, it can still be in your system, so go straight to a doctor and definitely do not have sex with anyone else until you've finished taking your treatment in case you pass it on to that person. And in future if you're going to have casual sex I strongly advise you to use a condom.
Good luck. Dr Claire

Toby had in fact caught a sexually transmitted disease.
Even though the symptoms went away, he still had the
infection in his body and could pass it on to other
sexual partners. Also, he and any partners he gives it to
could end up in the future with permanent damage to
their reproductive organs unless it is properly treated.
He needs to go to see a doctor and ask him or her to
test him for STD. Treatments are usually simple and
involve taking antibiotics prescribed by a doctor.

What are STD's?

These are sexually transmitted diseases. They are passed
on from one person to another during sexual activity,
which can be genital sex, or oral or anal sex.

STD's are usually caused by germs like bacteria or
viruses. These germs are very clever because they have
found a great way to spread themselves around. STD's
have existed throughout history, and it is very
interesting because before there were effective
treatments, they did great damage. Unfortunately,
untreated syphilis sent people mad in its late stages.
It has been said syphilis (an STD) changed the course of
history, because some of the kings and leaders of the
time were mad with syphilis and that it affected the
decisions they made, like going to war!

There are heaps of different types of STD's, just like
there are heaps of different germs that can cause
infections in other parts of your body. Some of the more
common ones are herpes, genital warts, chlamydia,
gonorrhoea, and of course there is Human

Immunodeficiency Virus (HIV). There are also strains of hepatitis that can be passed on sexually, such as hepatitis B. The only STD you can currently get a vaccine against is hepatitis B, and if you are going to be having casual sex with different partners it is a good idea to get vaccinated for this.

How would I know if I had an STD?

Anyone who is having sex is at risk of getting an STD. People who are STD free and have sex with one other STD free partner and are in a monogomous relationship, that is they don't have sex with anyone else, are at a lower risk than people who have casual sex with different partners. The more people you have sex with, the more likely you'll end up having sex with someone carrying an STD infection in their body.

Some STD's cause symptoms, like:

— Discharge from the vagina, penis or anus
— Pain or burning when having a wee
— Blisters, sores, warts, rashes, or swelling in the genital area like the vulva, vagina or penis or testicles, mouth or anus
— Pains in the abdomen (women) or testicles (men)
— Flu-like symptoms including fever, headache, aching muscles or swollen glands

However, the tricky thing about these STD germs is that some of them cause no symptoms at all, which is pretty clever of them if you think about it, because it means they can continue to be spread around because the person won't know they've got it and won't take treatment for it. For example, chlamydia (sounds like kla-**mid**-eea) is one of the STD's that can cause no symptoms. A girl for instance can have chlamydia and not find out about it until years later when she finds she can't have a baby because of damage done to her reproductive system by the chlamydia.

Other STD's have symptoms for just a short while and then clear up, but the disease is still being carried around in the person's body and can still be spread by sex.

Dr Claire,
Help. I think I've got an STD. What should I do?
Brad, age 17

Dear Brad,
Don't freak out. Go to your doctor or an STD clinic and get a test. Then you'll know if you have or not. If so, you can get treatment.
Dr Claire

If you think you might have an STD, don't panic! Make an appointment with your local doctor, a medical clinic, STD clinic or Family Planning Clinic. All capital cities and many smaller cities will have special sexual health clinics. Look in the phone book. If you can't find where to go you can ring up the emergency department of your local hospital and ask them where you can go for STD testing. At sexual health clinics you often don't even have to give your name, often they just use a number. Don't ignore it, it is better to get treatment so you have peace of mind and look after your health. Also you don't want to spread the STD around.

Doctors have to keep your medical information private and confidential.

Dr Claire,
I feel so ashamed. I'm really itchy in my pubic hair and there's tiny spots of blood, just specks, not like a period, in my knickers. I think I caught something called crabs when I had sex with this guy at a party. I feel so dirty and unclean. I never want to have sex again.
Lucy, age 16

Dear Lucy,
There's no need to feel ashamed. You are not dirty, you have just caught an infection. Crabs is another name for pubic lice. Lice have been around the human race for eons. Go to your doctor who will examine you to make sure that you have pubic lice and not something else, like an allergy. The lice are easily treatable, okay? It wasn't your fault. However, use this experience to think carefully about whether you want to be having sex casually at parties. Use condoms, they won't stop pubic lice because they live on the pubic hairs, but they will help prevent other potentially more serious diseases.
Dr Claire

There is no need to feel ashamed or guilty or even embarrassed. The doctor you see will have seen thousands of patients, and will have seen so many penises and vaginas it will be all routine for him or her. The doctor you see will have treated heaps of other people with STD's, and should treat you with dignity and courtesy. Remember STD's have been around since the dawn of time, and you are just one of millions of people in the world who have caught an STD. People from all walks of life, from sporting stars to politicians to doctors to movie stars have gotten STD's.

What will the doctor do?

The doctor will talk with you and examine you. He or she will give you some tests.

If you need treatment, your doctor will discuss this with you. You may need to take antibiotics.

Can't I just take some left over antibiotics from when I had an ear infection?

There are many different types of antibiotics, and you have to have the right antibiotic for the right bug. Antibiotics for an ear infection may be totally useless against the STD you've got. You need to see your doctor so they can prescribe the correct antibiotic for you. Make sure you take the antibiotic prescribed for you in the proper dose and at the proper times, that way it will be absorbed into your body at the right amount to kill off the STD. Finish all the antibiotics you are given. If you get a reaction to the antibiotic or they make you feel sick, ring up the clinic and tell them and they will be able to arrange a different type for you.

It is no good taking a couple of the tablets, missing a few days, taking a few more then missing some more, they won't work for you unless you take them properly.

Dr Claire,
My doctor said I've got herpes. The doctor gave me a booklet, but, like, how bad is herpes?
Linda, age 18

Dear Linda,
Herpes can be annoying because you can get repeated attacks of it. It lives quietly in your body until it decides to make another appearance and cause symptoms again, like tingling, redness, then little blisters that break out on your genitals. Sometimes a person can have one attack of herpes and that's it. Other people will get recurrent attacks as the pesky little virus decides to remind you it's still there. It won't kill you, but it can be painful and a nuisance during an outbreak. There are some very effective medications to help with herpes these days. Read your booklet and talk with your doctor about what is available. Keeping your immune system (your body's own natural virus fighting system) healthy by eating well, exercising, not getting over-tired or over-stressed can help your body fight the virus. You also need to know that you can pass herpes onto

other people, especially during an outbreak when lots of the virus is being shed from the affected area, so you should not have sex during an outbreak, and use a condom at other times because it is possible to shed and spread the virus even when there are no symptoms. I know it can seem overwhelming to find out you've got herpes, but try to keep some perspective by realising that it is a common infection and there are many people in the community who have herpes and it doesn't have to become an overwhelming problem in your life.
Dr Claire

It is important if you have something like herpes that you understand about it fully. Read all the information like pamphlets you are given and go back to your doctor or to a sexual health clinic if there are things you don't understand or are worried about.

Many STD's can be easily treated by a doctor. Other STD's are more serious. HIV is a very serious disease that can potentially kill you. As yet, there is no cure for HIV.

Dr Claire,
Ugh, I got warts on my genitals, and had to have them frozen off by my doctor. Will they come back?
Gina, age 16

Dear Gina,
This is a common virus. They can recur, so you want to go back to your doctor for regular check-ups. Ask them how often they think you should go along. Trouble is, they can be hard to see yourself unless you're a contortionist and can get your eyes down there for a decent look, or you try to do tricky things with a mirror. They can grow inside the vagina as well, so that's where your doctor can look where you can't. If any more occur, the doctor can freeze them off for you again. It's best to get onto them early. It would seem that for many people the body's own immune system clears the virus out of your system eventually. There are a lot of different strains of the wart virus. Some of them are associated with development of cancer of the cervix (the cervix is the neck of the uterus or womb). Now, there is no need to panic, it doesn't mean you are going to get cancer. It just means you'll need regular PAP smear tests to ensure that cancerous cells don't develop. If they did develop, they can be easily treated when picked up early.
Dr Claire

Genital warts are pretty common. A recent research in Canada showed 1 in 5 girls aged 19-24 had infection with human papilloma virus, which is the wart virus. Unfortunately, certain strains or types of this virus are associated with causing cancer of the cervix, which is the neck of the womb in women. Also, you can carry the virus without necessarily having visible warts on your genitals.

This does not mean people with genital warts should freak out. The warts themselves can be treated by your doctor who will freeze them off for you, for both girls and boys. However, the girls need to go to the doctor for regular Pap tests, which involves taking a small scrape of cells from the cervix and looking at them under the microscope to see if there's cancer developing. When detected early, cancer of the cervix can be treated. All sexually active girls should go for a regular Pap test every year.

What's a Pap test?

This is where a girl goes to the doctor. You lie down on the examining table, or some clinics have a special chair you lie in, which then tilts flat. You spread your legs open, and the doctor passes an instrument called a speculum into the vagina, which helps to spread the walls of the vagina open so the doctor can see the cervix, the neck of the womb. The doctor will then pass a small brush or spatula (like a skinny icy-pole stick) into the cervix and twirl it around to get a little scraping of cells. The doctor then spreads the scrapings onto a special microscope slide and the slide gets sent off to the laboratory to be looked at.

That sounds awful

Although most girls could probably think of things they'd rather do, the test only takes a few minutes. Sometimes the speculum instrument can feel a bit uncomfortable, especially because some girls find it a bit difficult to relax the vaginal muscles in this situation. The actual scraping of the cervix doesn't hurt. If you've had a Pap test and it was uncomfortable for you, tell the doctor the next time you go for one. Speculums come in different sizes, a smaller one might be more comfortable for you, or the doctor may be able to adjust their technique to make it feel better.

How do I avoid getting an STD? If I'm on the pill won't that stop it?

The only 100 per cent guaranteed way not to get an STD is not to have sex! However, if you are having sex, then there are certainly things you can do to help prevent getting an STD, but be aware that even condoms can't give you 100% protection against an STD.

1 Contraceptives other than the condom don't protect you effectively against STD's. Things such as the pill, lubricants, diaphragms do NOT protect against STD's. Some spermicidal products can kill some STD's, but they do not give as good protection as condoms. If you want to use spermicidal products you should use them with condoms.

2 Having a bath or washing the genitals before or after sex does NOT protect against STD's.

3 Having only oral or anal sex does NOT protect
   against STD's.

The following will help to prevent getting an STD
1 Try not to have casual sex with lots of different
   partners, because you are more likely to catch an
   STD.
2 USE CONDOMS: these won't 100 per cent stop
   you from getting an STD, but they are the best
   protection if you are going to have sex.

Dr Claire,
How do I use a condom properly? I don't want
to look like I don't know what I'm doing when I
put one on. Like, in school we all practised on a
zuccini, but my penis isn't quite the same shape.
Steven, age 15

Dear Steven,
Maybe you could practice in the sanctity of your
own bedroom. When you buy a box of condoms
there is usually an instruction leaflet inside the
box complete with diagrams. Your penis should
be erect when you do it. Carefully pull the edge
on the tip of your penis and roll it down gently
right to the base. There should be a little area at
the end of the condom so there is some space
for your ejaculated semen to collect, so if there
isn't, pull gently on the end of the condom to
make some space. Then you're ready.

Lubrication, such as water-based jelly such as KY, can make it easier for both you and your partner, so smear some on the condom when it's on your penis. Don't use non-water based lubricants like petroleum jelly (Vaseline) as they can damage the condom. When withdrawing your penis, you should leave the condom on and hold it around the base with your fingers. Remove the condom only when safely out of the vagina, tie it and dispose of it thoughtfully (which doesn't mean flinging it into the bushes or out the car window.)
Dr Claire

If you don't use condoms properly, they won't work for you.

1   Buy good quality condoms and use them before their expiry date. In Australia, the box should say they conform to Australian Standard.

2   Store condoms in a cool, dry place. Don't keep them in the glove box of the car, they'll get too hot. Don't keep them in your wallet, wear and tear from coins and plastic cards can damage them.

3   Carefully remove the condom from the packet and put it on the penis as soon as the penis is erect (hard). Don't unroll the condom when you get it out of the packet and then try to put it on. Put it on the penis in the rolled-up form in which it comes out of the packet, then unroll it down the penis right to the base. You can practise

putting a condom on an appropriately-shaped object like a carrot or a zucchini. This will give you a good laugh but you can also see how to do it. Of course, boys can practise on themselves.

4 Don't wait until the penis is just about to enter the vagina to put the condom on, the drops of fluid that can come out of the penis right at the start of getting sexually excited can spread infection (and also cause pregnancy).

5 Carry the condoms with you. Girls can keep them in their handbags, boys can keep them in their pockets when they're going out.

6 If your partner doesn't want to use a condom, you can say something like, 'I'd like us to use a condom, since either of us could have an infection and not know it. To take care of both of us this is what I want to do. I care about you, and I care about me.'

7 You can buy condoms at pharmacies, supermarkets and from vending machines, which are often situated in toilets at pubs or clubs.

8 Only use proper lubricant with the condoms, like KY-Jelly. Don't use petroleum jelly which can damage the condom.

Dr Claire,
If I carry a condom around with me people will think I'm a slut.
Tina, age 16

Dear Tina,
You don't wear it around your neck on a string
so the whole world can see it, you carry it in
your bag. And you don't need to tell anyone
you've got it unless you're about to have sex,
okay? So who's going to think you're a slut
unless you tell the whole world you're ready,
willing and able? Being prepared is just plain
common sense.
Dr Claire

There is very interesting research that shows that girls
won't carry condoms around with them because they
worry that if the boy or someone else sees the
condoms, they'll think the girls are sluts. The girls get
involved sexually with the boys, but they sort of think
to themselves that they just got swept along in the heat
of the moment rather than that they planned to have
sex. Because of the double standard in society where
sexually active girls can be labelled sluts while sexually
active boys can be labelled studs, you can see why girls
who enjoy sex and want to have sex can end up
pretending to themselves and others that sex just sort
of happened. However, this is a put-down of female
sexuality, and not owning the fact that girls can be
interested in sex and enjoy sexual activity and want to
have sex.

Girls of the 21st century should know how to look
after themselves. They know they are just as entitled to
be sexually active and enjoy sex as boys. They also

know that part of caring for themselves is to take their own condoms with them, so they will always be protected during sex. This is part of having good self-esteem, and looking after your health. Girls, if you're sexually active, carry your own condoms around with pride. If you're embarrassed to be seen with them, put them in a little cosmetic purse in your bag.

If a boy says anything negative to you about having your own condoms, look him straight in the eye and say 'I care about my sexual health, and you should too!'

So, you can see from this chapter that the decision to have sex is a serious one that you need to give thought to. And if you decide you are going to be sexually active then you have a responsibility to both yourself and your sexual partner to behave in a way that is considerate and respectful. And be prepared to protect both of you against STD's by using condoms properly.

Sex Hassles and Boys

Boys can have problems too as their bodies grow and mature. Damien told us how embarrassed he was by his body seeming to have a mind of its own. So if you've ever had an unwanted erection, read on …

Dear Margaret,
Is it normal to have erections happening all the time? They happen even when I'm not touching myself or thinking about sex. Like even standing on the bus and the swaying motion of the bus brings it on. And I had to stand out the front of

the class giving a talk and I had a huge hard-
on, and I was so embarrassed. Am I over-sexed
or something?
Damien, age 16

Dear Damien,
Don't worry, Damien, at your age this is all
normal, even if it is embarrassing at times.
What you are getting is spontaneous or
involuntary erections. It's just that your body
has heaps of male hormones floating around at
the moment, and this can make your penis go
hard for no obvious reason. You know that if
you are touching yourself or having a sexy
thought or fantasy that will bring on an
erection, but these other ones for no apparent
reason are quite normal. They are more of a
nuisance for some boys than others.

Here are my hints to cope with a penis that
seems to have a mind of its own:
1 Shift your bag, book or folder to the front of
   you to cover up. This is a good one for the
   school bus. Many a man has hidden an
   erection in this way.
2 Wear long shirts that hang out over your
   pants.
3 Sit down if you are standing up so it will be
   less noticeable.
4 Put your hand in your pockets. You can either
   shift your penis to the side, or just having
   your hands in your pockets will stretch the

material around your crotch so the erection is
not so obvious.

5 Think about something else and wait for it to
go away.

6 Pick your bathers carefully, something loose
like board shorts might be better than
Speedos.

Many men can tell some stories of how their
erections caused them to be embarrassed
when they were a teenager. Keep a sense of
humour, and remember it is all perfectly natural
and okay.

Margaret

For boys who are shy there can be a lot of worry about
how are they going to meet a girl, and they worry the
girls might expect them to act like the know all about
sex when they don't!

Dear Margaret,

Why do girls go for the jerks? There are total
creeps at my all-boy school who are talking all
the time about their girlfriends and all the sex
stuff they do. I have been brought up by my
mum and dad to respect women, not just see
them as sex objects. I am desperate to have a
girlfriend, but not just for sex. I want someone
I can talk to and do stuff with, like go out and
stuff. I am fairly shy and sensitive, not as
obviously in-your-face macho as a lot of the boys
at school. I've never had sex, and I worry at my

age this makes me a total retard. Also, I am
worried if I go out with a girl she's going to
expect me to know what to do with sex stuff,
and I'm really worried I wouldn't know what to
do or I did it all wrong or something and she'll
laugh at me. I have thought I should go and
see a prostitute, but maybe she'd laugh at me
too, and I know it is expensive, and I don't
really want to have sex with someone for
money anyway.
Steve, age 17

Dear Steve,
It's a good thing I'm not running a dating
service. I get heaps of letters from girls telling
me they wish they could find sensitive boys who
want to talk with them and do things with them
and not just see them as sex objects. So don't
worry, girls are going to go mad about you once
they find you.

There used to be a song called 'Why do girls
dig jerks'. Sometimes it seems like that, but I
think what happens is the ultra-confident in-
your-face macho guys can have pretty thick
skins and they just get out there and ask heaps
of girls to go out, and a certain percentage of
girls are going to say yes.

So, it's really about getting yourself into
situations where you can meet some girls. At an
all-boy school, this can be tricky. This means you
need to look at clubs and groups outside school

that are going to have some girls in them, like
sporting groups, everything from tennis to
bushwalking to martial arts, Rover Scouts,
special interest groups from astronomy to
community service to chess and drama groups.
Youth hostels run weekend trips away to do
things like horseriding and walking. Churches
often have young people's social groups. The
trick is to find something you're interested
in but where you meet girls, so it becomes
a natural thing that you talk to the girls
about whatever the activity is, and then it's
sort of natural that you go out together for a
coffee or whatever.

With regards to the sex bit, first make sure
you're educated about sex, what anatomy is
involved and a bit about sexual technique. Your
local library or big bookshop should have some
good books. You don't need to learn 400
different sex positions, the basics will do but in
particular to be a good lover you need to know
what stuff will turn a girl on, like how to touch
her breasts and her clitoris so she feels
sexually excited.

The other thing is that it's not like you ask a
girl out and then have to leap into bed with her.
First you can hold hands, later progress to some
kissing and cuddling. Hopefully, you've built up a
bit of a friendship first, so if you decide you
want to have sex together, you can talk about it.
It has been said that the most important sex

organ is between your ears, that is your brain.
Talking to each other about what is happening is
crucial for good sex. Silently groping and poking
and hoping you're doing the right thing is bound
to be a flop if you don't give each other a bit of
feedback about what feels good and what each
of you likes.

Also, don't worry that you haven't had sex
yet. Heaps of boys haven't done much at your
age. Believe me, a lot of the sex talk will be
made up. No one at school has to know you're
a virgin. Tell a few white lies to the boys if you
have to. But when the time comes for you to
have sex with a girl, tell her you haven't had
sex before. If she's sexually experienced she'll
be delighted to help you out, and if it's her first
time then you can explore and learn together,
plus she'll appreciate your honesty. Good luck.
Margaret

A new problem that has arisen since the internet has
become widely used is people getting hooked on
internet porn sites. Her Evan tells us how he feels
internet porn sites are taking over his life.

Dear Dr Claire,
This may sound crazy but I think I am addicted
to sex. I spend heaps of time looking at the
internet porn sites. Like, I come home from
school and I have study to do, and I say to
myself that I'm going to do it, but then I end up

looking at porn sites for hours. Also, I feel like I'm masturbating all the time, and I mean all the time. I do it so much I get sore. Even at school I will excuse myself to go to the toilet, but it's so I can masturbate. I used to play basketball on a team, but I gave it up so I would have more time to look at porn sites and masturbate. At weekends I spend most of my time in my room looking at porn and masturbating, or having sexual fantasies. My parents think I am in my room studying. I don't want to go away on holidays because I can't take my computer with me. My grades have slipped, and I think I will fail school this year. But when I get worried I don't settle down and study, I feel driven to look at more sex stuff. I feel like I can't stop, and I feel ashamed that I can't stop. Evan, age 17

Dear Evan,
Although it can be normal for teen males to think about sex very frequently and masturbate frequently, it seems you've gone beyond this to where you feel the sex is in charge of you, rather than you being in charge of the sex. People can become what's called obsessive and compulsive about sex. The obsession is when you start to think and fantasise about sex in a way that feels like it's taking over your life, and where you feel like you can't stop it. The compulsive aspect is where you feel driven to

act out sex-related behaviours, like masturbating excessively and looking at porn sites, and that you feel that you can't stop it. The key to knowing it's gone beyond normal is that it is interfering with the rest of your life, like your studies, and you've given up your basketball, and you shut yourself away on the weekends and don't want to go on holidays. So, yes, you can consider it to be like an addiction, because it is starting to take over your life and you feel you are losing control over it.

If you've tried to control it yourself and you can't, then it's time for some professional help. You need to find a counsellor who has experience dealing with compulsive behaviour, who understands what you are talking about and doesn't brush you off by telling you it's normal teen behaviour. Basically, I think you'll need help to set some boundaries or limits around your behaviour, and have a look at what any underlying issues might be. You might need help from your parents to find a counsellor. Do you think you could talk to your dad about what is happening? If that doesn't seem possible, your local community health clinic or your family doctor may be able to refer you to someone. It is important that you get help before it mucks up your life, like you fail at school and so on.

There are some good books written on compulsive sexual behaviour you might be interested to have a look. Dr Patrick Carnes has written several books on this topic, including *In The Shadows of The Net — Breaking Free of Compulsive Online Sexual Behaviour* Patrick Carnes, David Delmonico, Elizabeth Griffin, Hazelden 2001. You will find sections on compulsive masturbation and porn use.

You are not alone with this problem. In fact there are several organisations for people who feel they are sexually addicted, including Sexaholics Anonymous and Sex Addicts Anonymous. Maybe you could have a look at their websites.

Dr Claire

8 Being Gay

Young people often feel confused about their sexuality.

Dear Margaret,
I don't know whether I'm a lesbian or not. I go
to an all-girl school, and when I look at girls
getting undressed and stuff, I want to touch
them. Do other girls feel like this? I don't want
to be gay because my family will freak out. In
fact, I don't think I want to even keep living if
I have to be a lesbian. Do lesbians know from
the start that they're lesbian? Like, do I have
a choice of being one or not? Sometimes I think
I'd like to get with boys too. But not as much
as I want to get with girls.
Karla, age 14

Dear Karla,
If you're confused it means you're still sorting
out your sexuality. Girls can be attracted to
other girls in a sexual way and not necessarily
be gay. What you are feeling and experiencing
happens to lots of girls. Try not to give yourself
a label until you go out with both guys and girls.
Then if guys repulse you sexually and girls
attract you sexually, then, okay, you're probably
gay. Gay people usually don't deliberately choose

to be that way, they just are! And if you go against what nature has intended you can be unhappy, same as if you try to force yourself to be gay and you're really heterosexual. Give yourself time. If it turns out that you prefer sex with girls then eventually you'll tell your parents, and no doubt they'll also eventually be accepting of this.
Margaret

What does being gay mean?

Being gay means that a person's sexual orientation is toward people of the same sex, so a man is sexually attracted to another man, and a woman is sexually attracted to another woman. Men who become sexually involved with other men are called homosexual, and women who become sexually involved with other women are called lesbian. The word heterosexual applies to people who are sexually involved with people of the opposite sex — men with women, women with men. The word 'straight' is often applied to heterosexual people. So, if someone says John is gay and Peter is straight, they are saying John is homosexual and Peter is heterosexual.

People, especially teens, can get very hung up about who is gay and who is straight, and whether they themselves are gay or straight.

Dear Margaret,
I am a 14-year-old girl and I hope you don't mind me asking your advice. I think I might be

a lesbian. I mean, I like guys and all but I seem to find better qualities and things I like about girls more than guys. All my friends are in love with male celebrities and my all-time fave rave, the one I stick on my wall, is Drew Barrymore. One of my friends even accused me of being a lesbian a few days ago. I have no idea whether I am a lesbian, or straight, or bisexual, or what! I've read in magazines that this is a phase but I don't think it is.

Sarah

Dear Sarah,

What you are feeling is normal. I had pin-ups of women on my wall when I was 14 and I wasn't a lesbian. On the other hand, maybe you will find out that you prefer women as sexual partners to men. Try not to label your sexuality at the moment and just cruise along and enjoy life. Time will give you the answer.

Margaret

It pays to remember that as you go through life you will meet people of the same and different sexual orientation to yourself, and this is just one aspect of a person's personality. Our society is geared very much to a heterosexual view of the world, so gay people can often feel isolated and discriminated against.

Discovering that you are gay can be a big shock, and although the public view is more accepting, being gay

can be tough. Some people find out early in life that
they are gay, whereas some people don't accept they
are gay until much later.

Dr Claire,
My friend's dad has left them to go and live
with another man. How can a man be married
and have children and then decide he is gay?
James, age 15

Dear James,
This man has probably been gay all along and
has fought against it for years. No doubt the
pressure of living a lie has become too much for
him. It won't have been an easy decision to walk
away from his family. Your friend may feel that
his father does not love him anymore, or that
his dad can't be a real dad anymore because he
his gay. His dad can still be loving and caring,
being gay does not mean you can't be a good
dad. All the love and caring he has for your
friend, and all the good times they've had
together will not be wiped out by him being gay.
Nor does it mean because your friend's dad is
gay that he will be gay. Meantime, your mate
needs your friendship and support, okay James?
Dr Claire

There are people who are really gay yet feel so much
societal and personal pressure to be heterosexual that
they try to deny to themselves and others they are gay.

They try to maintain a heterosexual lifestyle, even getting married and having children. Then, later, they find they can't go on living a lie and start to be open about their homosexuality. As you can imagine, this can cause a lot of heartache for all involved. Because being gay creates problems within families and communities. What is important is to remember that we only have one life and we need to live it in the way that makes us happy and fulfilled.

What if I fall in love with someone who is gay and I'm not?

Dear Margaret,

I've been best friends with a boy called Jon for four years. I'm 18 and he's 19. He was friends with my boyfriend Charlie with whom I've broken up. Jon is bisexual and going through some doubts about whether he's attracted to girls at all. In fact he's just about decided that he's gay. The only thing is, I think I'm in love with him. And I'm terrified to tell him in case he really is gay and in case it wrecks the great friendship we have.

Lauren

Dear Lauren,

One mistake that many people make is in trying to 'change' someone who is gay (or bi) into someone who is heterosexual. Could you share him sexually with another man? And do you love him or are you *in* love with him?

There's a big difference. In other words, do
you want to have sex with him or do you
want a monogamous long-term relationship that
involves sex? He sounds confused, so pressure
from you is probably going to make him even
more confused. You can tell him how you feel,
but be prepared for a rejection at best or an
unhappy insecure relationship at worst. He
needs time to sort out his sexuality. If you are
a true friend I suggest that you give him some
space. He might decide that he prefers girls after
all. Then again, he might find that he prefers
guys. So for the moment I think it would be a
good idea for you to stay a staunch friend and
see what happens.
Margaret

Often when hormones are firing up, sexual
feelings become confused. Suddenly someone you
simply regarded as a friend or mate becomes
someone sexually interesting. Or sometimes you
react physically (and sexually) and can't understand
what's going on.

Dr Claire,
I hope you can help me. I was having a shower
after a swim and when I saw Matt turn around,
I suddenly thought he looked — well, I just
wanted to touch him. And I started getting this
huge erection. It was really embarrassing. But
worse, I'm worried that I must be gay. The other

guys won't want anything to do with me if I am, will they?
Brad, age 16

Dear Brad,
Well, it's hard to say on this one experience whether you're gay or not. We can get turned on by members of the same sex and not be gay. Some people who are gay say that from the time they were very young, even five or six, they 'felt different'. Other people don't figure out they're gay until they are teenagers or adults. So I suggest you don't panic. Just take your time, and regard this as an experience that may not actually mean all that much. However, if over time you keep feeling sexual attractions for guys and not girls, then you would start to know that you were gay.

It is common for teens to get a crush on someone of the same sex, and having sexual experiences with someone of the same sex as a youngster or a teen does not necessarily mean you are gay. For many people, teen years are a time of exploration, and there are plenty of heterosexual people who have had sexual experiences with same sex people, especially when they were growing up, but then as they get older they realise that they really are heterosexual and not gay.

Our sexual identity develops over time. You don't have to label yourself as gay or straight

today. Eventually you will find that you are
drawn mostly to men or to women, and
you'll know.

You are correct that some of the boys would
want nothing to do with you if they found out
you were gay, not because there's something
wrong with you but because there is still
prejudice against gay people in our society. It
can be a tough road finding out that you are
gay. If all this is bothering you a lot then you
need to find someone to talk to, like a counsellor
or trusted older person. But don't worry and
stew about whether you are gay because of this
one experience with Matt.
Dr Claire

Why are some people gay?

No one knows exactly why some people are gay and
others are straight. Most experts believe genetics and
biology have a lot to do with it, and that people may
simply be 'born gay'.

How many people in the world are gay?

Up to 10 per cent of the population is estimated to
be gay.

Dr Claire,
I thought all gay men are effeminate and act
like girls. My friend David is a top footballer.
Like, he works out, he's got a great body and he

looks really male, but he tells me he is gay.
How can this be true?
Jeremy, age 16

Dear Jeremy,
Gay people, like straight people, exist in all
kinds of ways. Gay people are represented
throughout society in all types of professions
and sports, even in areas which are
stereotypically considered macho. There are gay
top athletes and sportsmen, gay soldiers, gay
policemen, gay firefighters. There are gay men
throughout all areas of employment, including
doctors, politicians, lawyers, judges, teachers,
builders, engineers — every job you can think of.
Some gay men are more out in the open about
their gay lifestyle than others are. For those gay
men who are more demonstrative of their
gayness, you might meet them and think, 'Oh,
this person is gay'. However, there will be many
people you will interact with on a day-to-day
basis and you wouldn't have a clue that they
were gay. Just as heterosexual people come in
all different types, so do gay people.
Dr Claire

Are gay people different from everybody else?

The only thing that makes gay people different is their
sexual preference. Other than that, they're exactly the

same as everybody else. They work many different jobs, they want to have friends and love in their lives, they are sons and daughters and involved in family life, they have plans for the future, they do lots of regular things and have the usual worries and hassles like everybody else does. Some gay people choose to live with their chosen partner in a long-term relationship, others choose to stay single. And just as some straight people are really nice and some are total creeps and criminals, the same with gay people. Being gay is just one aspect of a person's personality.

Dear Margaret,
Why are some people so against gays? My best friend Tom is gay, and he's been bashed up twice. It isn't fair! I really want to help him and so do a bunch of my friends, but we really don't know what to do.
Jennifer, age 15

Dear Jennifer,
Unfortunately and sadly, there are still people who are very prejudiced against gay people. Some people believe gays are abnormal. Some people hold strong religious views that homosexuality is wrong. But many churches are now developing more welcoming attitudes to gay people.

People often fear what they don't understand, and hate what they fear. And maybe they are scared that they themselves are gay, so they use

this fear as anger against anyone who is gay.
Unfortunately, there will always be people who
want to physically or verbally beat up anyone
who is different from them. Keep offering your
friend your caring and support.
Margaret

Attitudes are slowly changing as more gay people stand
up and say 'I'm gay and I'm proud'. They are also
changing because other people are saying 'These gay
people are my friends, or my children, or my brothers
and sisters, and I'm proud of them'.

Dear Margaret,
I'm gay. Definitely. I've known this for some
time. I like girls as buddies but that's all. I feel
so alone. Who can I talk to? I can't tell my
parents, they would throw me out, especially
my dad
Travis, age 16

Dear Travis,
It's not so easy to discover that you are gay, is
it? Parents think about their children growing
up and getting married and having
grandchildren. Most parents forget that their
child may be gay. You have choices. You can
either tell them now, in which case they'll
probably panic and send you to a shrink. Or the
ultimate — they'll throw you out. But if you
have a good relationship with your parents, I

doubt that they'll do that. Or keep it to yourself until you're older and then tell them. That's what a lot of gays tend to do. But first, I'd seek outside help from people more experienced in this than I am. There are gay counselling groups you can phone for advice. Be careful to choose a proper gay counselling service, as some dodgy-looking phone-in lines could be fronts for older men seeking younger guys. Your local community health centre should be able to recommend one.
Margaret

If you are are like Travis, living at home and dependent on your parents, then you might have to think very carefully about whether you tell them you are gay. If your parents have open and tolerant attitudes about gay people, then obviously it's going to be easier to tell them. If, like Travis, you think that telling them would cause a major upset and you might get thrown out on the street, then maybe it is better not to tell them until you are in a stronger position.

For instance, you might have to wait until you are older and have moved away from home. Or perhaps there is another supportive relative you know who would back you up and give you practical support like taking you in if you are thrown out of home. Some people never tell their parents they are gay.

If you can't talk to your parents then try to find someone else to confide in so that you are not totally

alone in coming to terms with being gay. The person
may be a trusted friend, a friend's parent, a trusted
relative, a teacher, a school counsellor. If you don't think
you can talk to anyone you know, then you can ring a
service like a kid's helpline, or you can ring a gay helpline, which would be listed in the Community Services
section usually up the front of your phone book. Or
contact your local community health centre.

The organisation PFLAG (Parents and Friends of
Lesbian and Gays) has a very helpful website at
www.plflag.org, with sensible information for parents
and friends of gays. Founded in 1981, PFLAG promotes
the health and wellbeing of gay and lesbian people,
and their families and friends.

Dear Dr Claire,
My brother Ewan was gay. He told me, but he
never told Mum and Dad. He committed suicide
last year. Do you think that could be because he
was gay? I feel guilty because if I'd told our
parents maybe they could've been more
understanding, or stopped him committing
suicide or something. I feel that it's my fault for
not telling.
Suzy, age 14

Dear Suzy,
We will never know exactly why your brother
committed suicide. I'm sorry this has happened,
and the upset and grief it has caused you and
your family. Being gay may have been part of

the reason. Then again there may have been other things happening too. What we do know for a fact is that Ewan wasn't happy. That in itself is sad. It wasn't your fault, Suzy, so please don't blame yourself. You don't know that if you told your parents he was gay Ewan might have felt betrayed by you or really angry, and then when he committed suicide you'd have been worrying that you shouldn't have told your parents. You can see how tangled up this can all get, thinking 'If only I'd done this or that ...' When a family has a suicide occur in it, everyone can struggle with feelings of guilt. It is important that you do not carry this feeling of guilt with you as you grow up. Do you have someone you can talk to about all of this? Some grief counselling for you and for your parents about what happened with Ewan could be enormously helpful for you all. Maybe Mum and Dad won't go to counselling, but see if you can get some for yourself. Ewan would want you to heal from his suicide and go on to live a good and healthy life.
Dr Claire

For some boys, finding out they are gay causes them enormous heartache, especially if they feel great pressure to be heterosexual from their family, peers, school and so on. And some of these boys are filled with confusion, guilt and self-loathing, and may feel ashamed of their sexual desires and actions. Feeling isolated and alone with their feelings and thoughts can seem overwhelming to them.

Although it is not possible to say in Ewan's case whether this was a factor in his suicide, it does seem that worry and anxiety and guilt about homosexual feelings and actions is a factor in some male suicides in teens and young men. If you think you are gay and that you cannot live life, please remember there is always someone you can talk to who can offer you help. Keep going until you find someone you trust and who you can talk to about all the deepest and most troubling things for you.

Remember, gay people, like heterosexual people, can choose to live great, love-filled and good lives. If you are gay you have the right to get on with your life and enjoy it fully without feeling shame or guilt or any other negative feelings. In our society that can be tricky because of prejudice. If you are gay try to draw strength and support from friends, family and others who you know love and support you. And make use of gay support services like counselling to help you in your journey.

9 Sexual Abuse

Margaret gets a lot of emails from sexually abused teenagers. They are often afraid to talk about what has happened to them and they grow up feeling bad and ashamed of themselves. Our message is there's nothing so bad it can't be talked about and it's okay to tell someone and get help.

Where do most sexual assaults occur?

Research tells us most girls and boys who are sexually assaulted have this happen to them in their own home or the offender's home, usually by a person they know. For example, it may be a relative like their father, uncle or grandfather, or a stepfather, neighbour or friend of the family. Abuse of children and teenagers can also occur by other people who they know such as a teacher, sports coach or youth group leader. Although women can sexually abuse children and teenagers, research indicates the offender is most likely to be a man.

In what sorts of families does sexual assault occur?

Sexual assault can occur in any family of any background, social class and religion.

What sorts of things happen in sexual abuse?

Sexual abuse most commonly involves an adult making a child or teenager engage in sexual activities. The abuser is usually in a position of power over the child or teen. Both boys and girls can be sexually abused. Sexual activities include:

- having your genitals or breasts looked at, touched or fondled or kissed
- someone masturbating you, or forcing you to masturbate them, or being forced to take part in oral sex
- a man raping you or trying to rape you, putting his penis in your vagina, anus or mouth, or putting his fingers, tongue or some other object in your vagina or anus
- being made to look at pornographic films, magazines or photos, or being forced to pose while someone takes photos of you or films you nude or taking part in sex acts
- being made to take part in some other sexual activity.

What are the effects of sexual assault on the victim?

There can be physical effects like injuries, sexually transmitted diseases, pregnancy, and infertility (being unable to have children) later in life. The psychological effects can include:

- feelings of shame and guilt
- loss of self-esteem

- poor body image
- eating disorders
- self-harming behaviour, like cutting at yourself
- using drugs and alcohol to numb out emotional pain
- depression
- panic attacks
- flashbacks and nightmares
- poor personal boundaries, such as finding it hard to be assertive and say no
- anger
- acting out with violence or sexual promiscuity.

Note that having these symptoms does not necessarily mean you have been abused in the past because there can be other causes for these problems. However, these sorts of problems have been found to be common in survivors of childhood and teenage sexual abuse.

People who have been sexually abused as children or teens often grow up feeling very bad about themselves. They can carry the secret of their abuse for years, feeling they cannot tell anyone what has happened. They may blame themselves for what happened, often because the abuser told them they are bad or that they were responsible for what happened. The truth is that the person doing the abusing is a hundred per cent responsible.

Why don't children or teens speak up if they are being abused?

Dear Margaret,
My brother who is now 17, has been sexy to me since I was 10. He says it's what most brothers

and sisters do. But I saw on TV about sex with
family members, and now I think it's wrong.
Isn't this called incense when a family person
does it to another family person? I'm too scared
to tell anyone in case it's abnormal and people
take me away to live in a home, because that's
what Dan said would happen if I told anyone.
Mindi, age 12

Dear Mindi,
Your brother knows full well it's against the law
for him to have sex with you. It's called incest.
He must be made to stop. Tell your parents and
the police. Don't be scared of him. He has
violated his position as your brother and that's
bad. I would go and talk to the school counsellor
about getting some help to feel good about
yourself. If you do this, the school counsellor
will have to report your brother to the
authorities, so think carefully about how you'll
feel about this too. In the short term all hell
will break loose but in the long term, you will
be able to live a fulfilling and guilt-free life.
And remember, if your brother gets into trouble
after you speak up, this is not your fault for
telling but totally his fault for doing this to you
in the first place, okay?
Margaret

Sex abusers may convince the child or teenager that there is nothing wrong going on. They may say, 'This is what all fathers do', or 'I'm only teaching you the facts of life'. Sometimes boys and girls are kept silent by threats of violence or blackmail, like 'It would kill your mum if she found out what we're doing', or 'You don't want to get me into trouble, do you?' Remember that often the abuser is a person who has a lot of power and influence over the child, like a father or a stepfather. This is one of the more damaging things about sexual assault in that the abuser is betraying the child's or teen's trust. Fathers, grandfathers, uncles, stepfathers, teachers and other trusted adults are supposed to protect and care for children, not sexually abuse them.

Dr Claire,
I was abused by the minister at our church when we went away for a youth camp. He is an older man and a father of teen kids himself. He said I couldn't tell anyone because if I did they would never believe me because he is such an important person in the community and in the church. He knows my parents and even comes around to our house for dinner. I am scared he will do it again. Does this mean I will grow up to be gay because this happened to me?
Trevor, age 13

Dear Trevor,
I'm very sorry that you've been abused by this creep. No, you're not bad and not gay because of

this experience. This guy is an adult male in
a position of trust and this is sexual abuse.
He needs to be reported so that he doesn't keep
doing this to other boys, okay? Tell your parents
first, then if they are too scared/shocked/
stunned/angry to act, go to the police. But I
think you'll find that your parents will be very
supportive and will take action. There are other
religious people, including ministers and priests,
who have been convicted of sexually assaulting
boys and girls, so people like your parents and
especially the police will know this is something
that unfortunately does happen. You have
nothing at all to be ashamed about. You were the
victim of a crime called sexual abuse.
Dr Claire

Abusers in prominent positions, like church leaders, can
abuse children and teens and get away with it because
their victims think no one would believe them if they
spoke up. Sometimes what happens when one victim
speaks up is that it is discovered that there have been
other victims too, as sexual abusers usually abuse more
than once. So it is important to speak up.

If you have been abused you need to find someone
who you can talk to. Because your trust has been
betrayed once it can be tough to find someone who
you trust to talk to. But it is important to find someone
to talk to who can help you feel safe again.

Victims of sexual abuse can feel guilty if their body

has responded during the abuse. Our bodies have lots of sensitive nerves in our genital area, and even when we are being touched in situations that are abusive and feel uncomfortable to us sometimes our bodies just respond because of these sensitive nerves. This does not mean you liked or wanted the abuse, even if some parts of the abuse resulted in pleasurable or sexual feelings.

Also, if you are a boy and you were abused by a man it does not mean you will grow up gay. Nor does it mean there is something wrong with you sexually because you were forced to get sexually involved with a man.

Where can I go for help if I have been sexually abused?

Most capital cities and regional towns have Centres Against Sexual Assault or some type of sexual assault help centre or rape crisis centre. The people who work at these centres have special training in how to help victims of sexual assault. Usually you can find these centres by looking in the phone book, often under the Community Services section up the front. If you can't find the number you can ring one of the helplines like the kids helpline or any other helpline. Your family doctor or local community health centre can also help you. You may be able to speak to another trusted family member or friend, but usually it is also best if you can get some professional help in the form of counselling.

If the abuse is currently happening to you then one of the help sources listed above will be able to help you get it stopped. You can also go to the police for help.

10 Being Pregnant

Dear Margaret,
Hi, I hope you can help me out with a bit of a
problem. I am 16 years old and I've been going
out with my boyfriend for six months. The other
night we were in his room and we got a bit
excited. We had all our clothes on and he was
lying on top of me and we were just kissing and
stuff. Well, this mightn't sound so bad, but the
problem is that I missed my period and I usually
am regular. Now I'm having 'oh-crap-I'm-
pregnant' freak-outs. This sounds stupid but it's
not really possible to get pregnant through
clothes, is it? Because I'm usually so regular I'm
pretty worried. So what should I do?
Dana

Dear Dana,
Look, it's not possible to get pregnant through
layers of clothes, however, if your boyfriend was
very excited and some sperm leaked onto his
fingers and he put them inside you, then it is
possible. Or if his penis was rubbing on your
underwear and he came through the side ...
But it's unlikely that you're pregnant. Because
you're worried, it's more likely that your tension
has affected your cycle. Millions of women

through the centuries have waited anxiously for late periods. If you are truly worried, you can always buy a pregnancy testing kit, but I'm sure you'll be okay if you really were pashing on between layers of denim. Sperm are great swimmers but they're not superheroes leaping through zips at a single bound!
Margaret

Dear Margaret,
I've been going out with Daniel from school for nearly five weeks now. Anyway, I was over at his place yesterday and we sort of started messing around up in his room — you know, like touching each other and stuff. It was really nice and everything, then just like at the end before I had to go, he had his penis between my legs and it was pushing up and down on the opening. Don't get me wrong, it wasn't rape or anything, and I wasn't forced, but I'm a bit scared. He didn't actually go inside me, but what if some sperm leaked out or something? Is it possible to get pregnant from that? I think I'm in the middle of my cycle at the moment and I read that girls are most fertile at that time. Do you think I'm pregnant?
Flick

Dear Flick,
I'm afraid I don't know if you're pregnant or not. It's possible that the champion swimmer of

sperms swam up through the opening to your
vagina and kept on swimming and mated with
an eager egg. The boy's penis does not have to
be inside you for you to get pregnant, although
that's how it usually happens. And you know
how you get all wet down there when you get
sexually excited, well this fluid can make a nice
slippery pathway for those little sperms to find
their way inside you even from sperm that's
hanging around close by on the outside. But on
the other hand, maybe this didn't happen. If you
are worried you can buy a pregnancy kit
yourself from the pharmacy or go see your
doctor or local family planning clinic. If you did
turn out to be pregnant, then obviously this is a
whole big new problem you would need help and
support to deal with. It's unfair that it's the girls
who get stuck with the problem, because no boy
is ever going to get pregnant. So it's up to us
girls to protect ourselves. Next time, if you're
going to pash on in your boyfriend's bedroom, be
prepared with a condom. Or make a rule not to
go in his bedroom if you don't want to have sex,
because as sure as eggs are eggs it's going to
happen full-on sooner or later, and I'd guess
sooner. Like a scout, Be Prepared.
Margaret

Worry and tension, illness and changes in routine can
affect the monthly period cycle. You can get pregnant

the first time you have sex, particularly if it's a really fertile time of the month. This fertility time can be unpredictable, especially when you're a teen and your menstrual cycle is still settling down, so rather than work on the hit-or-miss theory (and remembering that old adage, 'hope is not a contraceptive'), it's better to be safe and protected by contraception than sorry and pregnant.

Being Prepared

Being prepared can often be difficult. You're out with a guy, pashing on, and suddenly things get out of hand and next thing you're having full-on sex. Or you've had too much to drink at a party and your guard's down. And, full of good cheer and relaxed morals, you think, 'What the heck?' Or you don't think anything because you're too out of it.

Then again, you could be going with a guy permanently and he wants to have sex and so do you. At least in last situation you can plan together what contraception you should use. It's the unprepared sex that sneaks up on you and can cause so much heartache.

Dear Dr Claire,
I had sex with Andy. It was the first time I'd had sex, and I thought you couldn't get pregnant the first time you did it. Well, I found out the hard way that I was wrong, because I ended up pregnant. I had to tell Mum and I had to go to a clinic and have an abortion. I was really, really upset, especially when I told Andy and he said

that it was my problem, not his. He's got a new
girlfriend now. I don't think I ever want to have
sex again.
Cindy, age 15

Dear Cindy,
I'm sorry you had to go through this trauma.
Can you talk to your mum about your feelings?
If you're really troubled then counselling
would be a good idea. Did they have
counselling at the clinic where you had the
abortion? If you don't want to go back there
then you could find somewhere else, like your
doctor, local community health centre and so
on. Having an abortion can be a difficult time
in your life in terms of the physical effects
on your body and your sense of self as a
potential mother.
   You are not alone, however, throughout time
many women have had to struggle with the
same sort of problem. You may feel hurt that
Andy wasn't supportive. You may feel betrayed
and used. Please remember there are many boys
who would have been supportive and caring of
you in this situation, and not just dumped you
like Andy did. You need time to get over all of
this. I'd suggest giving romance the flick for a
while and trying to get out and about again with
your girl buddies. I'm sure you will trust a male
again one day, but when you decide to have sex,
don't rush into anything. It might suit you better

to first build up a friendship over time with a boy, so you have a sense of trust in him before you decide to have sex. And make sure you have contraception, won't you? Good luck and I hope life gets better for you from now on.
Dr Claire

Sperm talk

Sperm don't care how they get into the girl's vagina: they can be transported there in semen that's got on a boy's or girl's finger when they are being sexual. Also, the little bit of fluid that comes out of a boy's penis when he first gets excited and hard, and long before he ejaculates, contains sperm too, so if that fluid makes its way into the vagina and meets an egg, hello baby. Of course the most usual way sperm gets in there is when the boy ejaculates during intercourse.

Myths about getting pregnant

Myth 1: You can't get pregnant the first time you have sex.
WRONG! Sperm don't care whether this is the first time or the thousandth time you've had sex.

Myth 2: You can't get pregnant standing up.
WRONG! You can get pregnant in any position you can imagine: sideways, upside down, backwards, hanging from the ceiling! Sperm are very strong swimmers and are happy to swim in any direction on their mission to find an egg.

Myth 3: You can't get pregnant if you have sex
during your period.
WRONG! You can, especially when you are
a teenage girl and your menstrual cycle is
just getting established. Eggs can be
released from the ovary at irregular times,
so you're never quite sure that an egg
couldn't be lurking around at any time,
hoping to meet up with a sperm.

How can I avoid getting pregnant?

The only absolute way to ensure you don't get pregnant
is not to have sex! The next best thing, if you are going
to have sex, is to make sure you use contraception.
There are many different types of contraceptives.
You've probably heard of some of them, like the pill and
the condom.

Contraception is best discussed with an
understanding doctor or family planning nurse. You can
go to see your doctor, a local Family Planning Clinic or a
Community Health Centre.

The simplest form of contraception is a condom. You
can buy them at pharmacies, supermarkets (look in the
men's section near the deodorants and the razor blades)
and vending machines in public toilets. But you must
use condoms properly, otherwise you may as well stick
it up your nose for all the good it will do you. (See the
section on condoms on pages 185–87.)

Other contraceptives include the pill, the diaphragm,
and other hormonal methods like the depo-provera

injection for girls. To get a diaphragm, the contraceptive pill or hormonal injections you will need to see a doctor. He or she will want to check that you have no other illnesses that might interact badly with the pill or injections, and will talk to you about the potential side effects. All medicines have side effects, but then you have to remember that being pregnant can have 'side effects' as well. When it comes to side effects, you must weigh up the balance between the risk of the contraceptive against the risk of getting pregnant. Your doctor can help you to choose correctly for you, and can help you change to a different contraceptive if one doesn't suit you.

If you are taking the oral contraceptive pill, remember it won't work unless you take it properly. It is no good forgetting to take the pill, it is best taken at about the same time each day, so link it up with something you do every day at about the same time, like brushing your teeth. Remember too that certain medications such as antibiotics can interfere with the pill, and if you have had vomiting or diarrhoea the pill may not be absorbed properly. Make sure when you get the prescription you know what you should do if you miss a pill or have been sick. Read the information sheet inside the packet. If you have any doubts, use a condom and speak to your doctor or family planning nurse. You can telephone your doctor's office or the clinic to ask for advice.

Remember, only the condom can offer you the advantage of some protection against sexually transmitted diseases. If you are on the pill and having sex your best protection against STD is to use a condom as well.

Most importantly, if it all seems too difficult and you don't know what to do, use a condom. You can buy condoms fairly cheaply, and you don't need to see a doctor.

Dear Dr Claire,
Help! I had sex with my boyfriend last night about 10 pm and didn't use any contraceptives. Is there anything I can do?
Marnie

Dear Marnie,
If you had sex without using contraception then you can see a doctor for the 'morning-after pill'. This is actually medication (usually you take two doses, 12 hours apart) that stops the egg from developing any further, so it won't make a baby even if it has met up with some sperm. So I think you'd better get to your doctor fast!
Dr Claire

Sometimes you do the right thing and use a condom and things go wrong. For example, a condom could break (although condoms that meet Australian standards are very strong and not likely to break when used properly) or maybe you didn't use the condom properly, like making sure it was on the boy's penis before the penis went inside you. Or maybe you'd forgotten to take your contraceptive pills regularly. Or maybe you hadn't used any contraception. Not to panic. You can get the morning after pill from your doctor, a family planning clinic, or you can ring up or go to the emergency department of a women's hospital if you don't know where to go. You have up to 72 hours to take the morning after pill. If you ring your doctor and the receptionist says there are no appointments for three days, say you need the morning after pill and if they can't fit you in for an appointment ask where else you can go. The pill has to be prescribed by a doctor; you cannot just go and buy it from the chemist.

The morning after pill is not something you should use instead of contraception. It is there as a back-up in case things have gone wrong. It is not a drug you should be taking frequently. The medication can make you feel a bit nauseated and not the best for a day, but this is minor compared with the trauma of an unwanted pregnancy.

Dr Claire,
I had sex with my boyfriend and now I think I'm pregnant. I can't tell my parents. My mum will kill me. What should I do?
Cherie, age 14

Dear Cherie,
First of all you need to find out if you *are* pregnant. If you think you are, you can buy a pregnancy test kit at the chemist, which you use

to test your urine with a special plastic test stick. The kits these days are very accurate. If you prefer you can go to your doctor or family planning clinic and get them to test you. This can be a good thing to do because it means if you find out you are pregnant you have somebody with you to talk to and get some support from. But don't just hang on and hope that it will go away. The sooner you find out for sure whether you are or not, the sooner you can stop worrying. Or start making plans about what you're going to do if you are. This means telling your parents. Can you enlist the help of someone in telling your parents? Do you have an older relative or someone you trust who could be there with you when you tell them? Usually most parents, after their initial shock, end up being supportive. If they will not help you, which is hopefully very unlikely, then you will need to tap into the support services that are available in your community. Your doctor, family planning clinic, a supportive teacher or school nurse or school counsellor or maybe a friend's mum can help you to get the support and help you need. Good luck.
Dr Claire

Finding out that you are pregnant

If you are pregnant you will need help and support to get through this. Find someone you can talk to.

Although parents may at first be upset to learn you are pregnant, they will usually settle down pretty quickly because they know you are going to need their help, and they want to help you. If you feel you can't talk to your parents, find another trusted person, like another relative, a friend's parents, a teacher. Don't stick your head in the sand and hope it will all go away.

You will need to decide what your options are. Basically, this will boil down to either having the baby and keeping the baby, or adopting out the baby, or having the pregnancy terminated. In Australia, termination of pregnancy is legal and is done as a medical procedure under anaesthetic.

Of course, you will be aware that in the community there are deeply differing views about termination of pregnancy. There are people who believe strongly that termination of pregnancy is morally wrong, and that no one has the right to terminate a life under any circumstances. There are other people who believe that women should have the right to choose to have a termination, and should not have to go through an unwanted pregnancy. Then there are people in the middle, who don't like the idea of abortion all that much but can see that it can be a way out of a very difficult situation for a young girl. You will have to work out for yourself and with your family what is right for you.

Finding out you are pregnant is no easy thing, and can lead to lots of grief and despair. So please, please use contraception if you are going to have sex. Both girls and boys who think they might have sex should carry condoms with them. You can carry condoms very discreetly. And remember that to use them is to care for yourself and your sexual partner.

Having sex is an adult activity. Like driving a car, it comes with enormous responsibilities. You can't drive a car without first having lessons and passing a test, but there is no test to pass before you have sex. So it is up to you to learn about things like contraception and sexually transmitted diseases.

Try to keep your common sense on when you take your underwear off.

11 Alcohol and Drugs

Caitlin's Story

I went to this party with my friends. We had
it all organised. Victoria was supposed to be
our minder and she wasn't going to drink, so
that she could look after the rest of us.
Lexie got right off early on. She was drinking
subs and doing some dope, and she sort of
disappeared somewhere. I had a few vodkas
— well, I'm not sure how many, because I
was swigging from the bottle. I know I
had a couple of beers because I remember
thinking, 'I don't drink beer'. Abbey was
fairly cool and not drinking much, although
she was smoking. Well, this guy Tim started
pashing with me on the banana lounge. I
tried to look for Victoria but she'd changed
her mind and was drinking with her crush
in the billiard room, like, she was supposed
to be minding me. Then it gets a bit fuzzy but
things happened that I can't remember. But
lots of people were laughing and cheering.
So now I'm the city slut and Tim's the hero,
and worse, I've missed my period. Mum and
Dad'll kill me if I'm pregnant. And I'm so mad

at Victoria, because she was responsible for me.
Some friend!
Caitlin, age 16

Drinking alcohol can get you into all sorts of trouble. But
drinking is also a socially acceptable thing to do. It's
almost a rite of passage into adulthood in our society,
because we don't have any others, except maybe at
sixteen you can legally drive a tractor and have sex and
at eighteen you can get a licence to drive, and you can
vote in this country. And at twenty-one you get the 'key
of the door', which really doesn't mean much nowadays.

When Margaret worked for eleven years as an alcohol
and drug education officer and counsellor for young
people, she found that teenagers were confused about
alcohol. They all knew they could get drunk, but also
they knew that sometimes they didn't drink much and
got pissed quickly, and other times they didn't. Also
sometimes they wanted to get drunk, and other times
they didn't. Some of them had decided not to drink at
all. Some of them had decided to get totally wasted
every time they drank. Here's part of an email from Tom:

Like, there's different ways of drinking. I'll have
a few beers with my dad at a barbecue. I'll get a
bit pissed when I go to a party and try and get
on with a girl, but not smashed out of my brain
because girls don't like it when you spew on
them. Then if I'm out with my mates, I get
totally wasted.
Tom, age 17

Tom had figured out that there were different behaviours for different situations and was making some choices. Getting totally wasted with his mates wasn't such a bright idea, but that's how Tom wanted it.

However, when we look at Caitlin's story, we can see that heaps of things went wrong. First of all, you can't always rely on the minder. That means you always have to rely on yourself! And in fact, Caitlin blamed Victoria, but *Caitlin* was the one drinking recklessly and it was her responsibility to stay in control, not her minder's responsibility. How could one sober girl mind three drunk girls all at one time anyway, even if she did stay sober?

Secondly, if you are necking a bottle of spirits, you've got no idea how much you've had to drink, unless, of course, you've drunk the lot, in which case you've probably passed out or you're in a coma. However, people do this, so it's a good idea to remember that each decent swig is probably equal to about one standard nip. Which means five decent swallows of straight spirit — vodka/bourbon/whisky — equals .05, the legal limit for driving a vehicle in this country.

When you're .05, you're well on the way to being drunk. Your vision's impaired, your speech starts to slur, you can become loud and raucous, and over-confident. Your inhibitions are reduced because the drug is at work on your brain, slowing it down, slowing its thinking processes and reaction times. Why? Because alcohol is a sedative-type drug, even though initially you feel excited and charged up. If you keep drinking it, eventually you'll pass out because the brain just gives up. So Caitlin's inhibitions were almost non-existent, and at that point of drunkenness she didn't care if she degraded herself in front of an audience.

Thirdly, Caitlin and her friends didn't seem to be eating any food, or drinking water in between the alcohol, which meant that they got drunk quicker. If it's your goal for the night to get drunk quickly, then be aware that you can end up having an accident, you can overdose on alcohol and die, you can wreck the linings of your throat and stomach, damage your liver and other organs, and get brain damage *if* you keep up this behaviour. A lot of young people think they're invincible and that this can't happen to them, and anyway, it takes years. Not necessarily. Margaret saw a number of eighteen-year-olds with liver/brain/pancreas damage because they started heavily drinking when they were thirteen or fourteen. Interestingly, when Margaret talked with hundreds of young people, most of them said they didn't want to get drunk, they just wanted to have a good time.

Tips for safer drinking

1 Before you go to the party or barbecue, eat a decent meal. This lines the walls of your stomach. Eating a meal will not prevent you from getting drunk, but it will slow down the absorption rate of alcohol into your bloodstream. It's also healthier on your stomach.

ALCOHOL AND DRUGS

2 Drink alcohol *slowly*. You can chat to friends or walk around with a glass in your hand and just take occasional sips.

3 Drink soft drink or water in between each alcoholic drink, because alcohol actually dehydrates your body, so you get thirstier and drink more of it.

4 Be aware that crackers, nibbles, crisps and stuff like that are very salty so they make you thirstier. Don't quench your thirst with alcohol.

5 Drink light beer instead of heavy.

6 Smoking dope or using other drugs while drinking alcohol can be dangerous because you're mixing drugs in your system. It might seem cool to do it, but it's not hip when you have to go to hospital.

7 Move around, dance, play pool, do something that doesn't involve drinking all the time.

8 Don't leave your drink unattended. Someone might drop a drug into it. Reasons? For a prank, because they're too drunk to be sensible, or to make you pass out so they can rape you.

9 If you're a driver, either don't drink or leave the keys at home.

10 Do not stay at a pub or bar or party on your own if all your friends decide to leave.

11 Never *ever* get in a car with someone who's had too much to drink and who's determined to drive the car.

Dear Margaret,
My sister is dead. I just can't get over it and I
keep wanting to hide and cry in my room. Her
boyfriend wrapped the car around a tree
because he was too drunk to drive. He's escaped
with minor injuries. If I see him, I am going to
kill him. I really am!
Jarrod, age 16

Dear Jarrod,
I'm sorry that this dreadful thing has happened
in your family. Killing the guy might alleviate
some of your pain and rage, but then it won't
solve anything in the long run and you'll end up
in jail. He has his own living hell, and the guilt
of what he's done will haunt him for the rest of
his life, so you don't need to get revenge. Please
get some counselling to deal with your anger
and your grief, Jarrod. With time, your hurt will
be lessened, but not for a while, so allow
yourself to feel sad.
Margaret

The problem with alcohol is that it allows us to do
things we would never normally do, like drive a car
recklessly, beat someone up, smash public property,
belt up a family member, be abusive, have unprotected
sex. Alcohol changes our way of thinking, and our
personality.

ALCOHOL AND DRUGS

Dear Margaret,
I got really drunk at this party and I went
totally psycho, smashing chairs through windows
and punching my friends. I felt so ashamed the
next day. I've decided never to drink again, ever.
Alcohol and I just don't mix.
Sam, age 17

Dear Sam,
You've made a wise decision, because some
people do turn into maniacs every time when
they've had alcohol. Others can be okay when
drinking and then one day they flare up and
smash things and people. A lot of this behaviour
is because they are angry and frustrated inside,
and it all erupts. Anger and alcohol are a
dangerous combination. You should be proud of
yourself for recognising this and deciding not to
drink alcohol. And let me tell you, Sam, you're
not alone in this. More and more young people
are deciding the same thing. Good on you!
Margaret

You see, you can't blame alcohol for turning you into
Mr Hyde, or for allowing someone to have sex with you,
or for causing an accident, or for verballly abusing
someone dear to you. Alcohol is only the catalyst, the
enabler. *You* have to take responsibility for how much
you drink and how you behave. Alcohol doesn't give
you a licence to run amok.

Dr Claire,
My mother is a recovering alcoholic. Like, she
has got help and has been in detox three times.
She hasn't had a drink now for a year. But
I'm really scared that I've inherited her
alcoholic genes or something, because when
I drink, I can't stop. I don't want to end up
like my mother.
Jessie, age 15

Dear Jessie,
I don't know whether you have inherited your
mother's disease or not, but alcoholism does
tend to run in families. An alcoholic is someone
who can't live without drinking alcohol. They
could have a few days or even a few weeks
without drinking, then binge drink, or they could
be a steady drinker. The point is, alcohol takes
over their life. Most recovering alcoholics can
never drink again, because they are 'allergic' to
alcohol. That's the simplest way that I can
explain it. It seems like you're already getting
some warning signs that alcohol is a problem for
you because you've identified the feeling 'I can't
stop'. I think you are wise to take notice of that
feeling, and indeed it may be the best thing for
you not to drink any alcohol.

Growing up in an alcoholic home can
adversely affect your personal development.
There is a good group for relatives and friends
of alcoholics called AlAnon. They also have

special groups for teens called AlAteen. The
phone number should be in the phone book.
These groups are free, they just ask for a small
donation if you can afford it, like a dollar or
two. I'm sure that given your experience with
Mum you would find these groups interesting
and helpful. Also there is AA (Alcoholics
Anonymous, also in the phone book) which is a
recovery group for the alcoholics themselves.
They also have young people's groups. You might
be interested to go along to one of their
meetings just to learn more about alcoholism in
young people. Also your local library or your
school library may have some books about
alcoholism. There are people from alcoholic
homes who choose not to drink alcohol at all
because, like you, they are afraid they could end
up alcoholic, and they don't want to give
themselves the chance to become alcoholic. That
is a perfectly okay choice to make, and it could
save you a lot of future heartache.
Dr Claire

Myths about alcohol

Myth 1: Drinking coffee will sober you up.
WRONG! Coffee is a stimulant so it gives
you the feeling of being alert, but the
alcohol you've consumed is still in your
system and only time will get it out.
Myth 2: Running a few k's will sober you up
because the alcohol is sweated out.

WRONG! You can only sweat out so much, about 10 per cent. Another 10 per cent is peed out, another 10 per cent breathed out, and the rest has to be slowly processed out over time from the bloodstream, where most of it was absorbed in the first place.

Myth 3: Drinking milk will stop you getting drunk.
WRONG! Milk is a food and so it will slow down the absorption rate of alcohol through the stomach walls into the bloodstream, but it won't stop you getting drunk.

Myth 4: If you have a good sleep, then you'll be sober.
WRONG! Often people go to school or work still affected by alcohol. They feel all right apart from a headache, but the alcohol is still present in their bloodstream. If this person was breathalysed they could have a high reading. Many drivers get busted for drink-driving the day after!

Myth 5: If you quickly swill some mouthwash and hold your breath, when you breathe into the breathalyser you can get a low reading.
WRONG! Many mouthwashes contain alcohol and so you'll get a higher reading.

Myth 6: You'd have to be paralytic drunk to get brain damage.
WRONG! Brain damage occurs easily and quickly in some people.

Myth 7: It's okay to drink some alcohol when you are pregnant.

WRONG! Doctors now say that ANY alcohol can be too much for some women. If you're pregnant, don't drink alcohol or do drugs because the foetus can be impaired.

Myth 8: Getting drunk is good for you if you have a cold.

WRONG! Alcohol depletes vitamin C and B in the body, both needed for the immune system to fight a cold.

Myth 9: If you spew up the alcohol regularly during a session, you can't get drunk.

WRONG! Alcohol is absorbed straight into your bloodstream as it passes down your throat into your stomach. You're mainly spewing bile and the watery content from the drink.

Myth 10: I drive better when I'm drunk.

WRONG! You just think you do. Go to a place where they do simulation tests and you'll find out how impaired your driving will be only after two or three drinks.

Alcohol is a drug of addiction. Many people in the community are able to handle alcohol wisely, but there are plenty of other people who go through hell because of their alcohol addiction. Why do some people get addicted and others don't? Well, we know that some people have the propensity to become alcoholics, and some grow dependent on it because they use it a lot.

Some people may have inherited 'alcoholic genes', some people seem to be physically sensitive to alcohol, and there may be psychological reasons that contribute to becoming addicted to alcohol.

Other drugs in the community can also be addictive and we'll discuss them now.

Psychotropic drugs

Here's a list of common psychotropic drugs. Psychotropic means that the drug changes your thinking and behaviour, depending on a number of factors we will discuss later on.

- Stimulants speed up the brain and the body's reactions. They include caffeine, cocaine, amphetamines, nicotine and ecstasy.
- Depressants slow down the brain and the body's reactions. Examples of a depressant are alcohol, marijuana, morphine, heroin, pethidine, tranquillisers and sleeping pills.
- Hallucinogens distort the brain's thinking, which can make the user behave in a bizarre manner. These include MDMA, LSD, PCP (angel dust), ice, GHB, magic mushrooms, trumpet lily, salvia, peyote and mescalin.

Some drugs have both qualities. For example, marijuana (or dope or grass) is a depressant because it mellows the user, but it can also cause fantasies so it's hallucinogenic to a certain extent. People who use more than one drug at a time are called 'poly-drug' users. It's dangerous to mix drugs.

You might have noticed that caffeine is in the stimulant group. It's legal. Heaps of people use it. But if you could actually consume a whole large jar of coffee at one sitting, you'd be very sick.

Often young people are fascinated by what drugs can do. It's all mysterious and somehow exciting, but they forget the insidiousness of drug use and how it can take over your life.

It's dangerous to mix drugs because the drugs can interact badly with each other. Also, you multiply the risk of bad side-effects of the drugs on your body. Let's say you mix heroin (which can interfere with your breathing) with another drug like tranquillisers or another narcotic drug like morphine (which can also interfere with your breathing) and bingo, you could stop breathing! And if you stop breathing, it doesn't take long until you stop living — that is you are dead.

A major cause of death from drug abuse is this effect of drugs on your breathing. And then there is a whole group of people who've ended up brain damaged rather than dead, because their brain was starved of sufficient oxygen during the time their breathing was affected. All of this is not a pretty picture.

Dear Margaret,
I have this problem. You see, my group of friends take drugs. Like at first it was just pot but now they've grown out of that and they're keen to move on to something 'more exciting' like ecstasy and stuff. I'm really against taking drugs and I hate them taking them. I just

finished reading your book *Back on Track —
Diary of a Street Kid* and then I read *Anna's
Story*, and she was, like, a normal girl from
a normal family who took ecstasy and died.
I keep thinking, 'What if it's one of my friends
who react to the drugs like that?' They all tell
me I overreact, but I don't think I do. I don't
want to lose one of them to drugs. If they start
on drugs now and get hooked, what are they
going to be like in the future? That is, if they
are still alive. Do you know what I can do
because I'm really worried?
Emily, age 14

Dear Emily,
You are to be commended on your stance not to
take drugs. Are your friends the same age as
you? And are they drug-raving, that is,
dreaming off in their heads, or really trying
ecstasy? And if so, where are they getting the
money, because ecstasy is not cheap, like
$40–60 for one pill? Unless they have heaps of
cash, or big brothers/sisters/boyfriends, they
can't afford it.

Many teenagers want to experiment with
drugs because they see this as exciting and
rebellious and against the law. Most out-grow
this phase, but some obviously don't. Hopefully
your friends are just full of it and it's all talk.
There's a huge difference between smoking pot
and taking designer drugs or intravenous drugs.

Not that pot isn't harmful if too much is smoked over a long period of time, or if the person has a mental illness which can be exacerbated by marijuana.

You ask, what can you do? First of all, you can lend them *Anna's Story*. But the problem is that most teenagers think, 'That can't possibly happen to me'. Second, you can ask them why they think it's so cool to take drugs, because it's not, it's dumb. Third, you can get a cool older person to try and talk some sense into them. Is there a ringleader who's egging them all on? If so, she needs to be told how irresponsible she is being.

But ... if the group (and how big is this group? Four? Six? Eight?) all decide to do drugs, then you'll find that their activities won't include you, the non drug-taker. My Gran used to say, 'Birds of a feather flock together', meaning friends usually like to do the same things. So if their behaviour continues to spiral downward into the drug world, you might have to find some new friends. Hopefully, they'll forget the idea of drug experimentation and get on with their schoolwork.
Margaret

Rave parties are common, and drug taking at these is rife. But you don't have to take drugs to have a good time. You can learn to kick in your natural endorphins

and adrenaline, and get off on the music. That's what
I do when I go clubbing. And I drink lots of water.

Why do people use drugs?

Basically, people use drugs because drugs make them
feel good. It's hard work trying to convince people not
to do this, because everyone likes to feel good. The
trouble is that all of these psychotropic drugs can be
addictive. And the more you use, the less the effect they
have on you, so you have to increase the doses. Like, a
young heroin user will need to score (buy the drug and
then inject it) about every three to four hours to
maintain their feeling of wellbeing. This habit costs
money, and even though the price of heroin on the
streets has dropped, depending on the quality, it still
costs a lot of money per day, depending on the grading
of heroin and the street price. Driven by the
desperation of their addiction people get into crime, or
they start to sell their bodies to get money to feed their
addiction. All this just begins a spiral downward into
feelings of despair and desperation. The sad part is, the
feeling of wellbeing goes down while the need for
more of the drug goes up.

Some people use drugs like pain-killers and sleeping
tablets, and even morphine or pethidine for extreme
physical pain, like cancer. In this situation, however, the
medicines are properly prescribed by a doctor, and play
a very important role in helping with cancer pain.
Other people start taking these drugs recreationally
simply for the effects they get while on them, and they

end up addicted. But most people use drugs to prop
them up emotionally and give them a false sense of
wellbeing.

How can you stop people using drugs?

Basically, you can't if they don't want to. When I worked
with the street kids, a lot of them were full-on drug
users. There was no way they were going to stop using.
So I tried to get them to use more safely. If a new batch
of drugs or a new dealer was in town, or they were
trying something new, I suggested they use only a
quarter of a tab or a deal until they knew what effect it
had. They learnt to use clean needles and not to share.

To stop people using drugs you have to give them
something better than what they've got. Like a better
job, a better life-style, and if they're white-collar workers
struggling to stay bright and breezy for long hours, then
they need to work fewer hours.

Should some drugs be legal and others illegal?

Cigarettes are an interesting example. Twenty years ago
people smoked in theatres, restaurants, at work in the
office, in buses and in taxis. Now there's a huge push to
ban public cigarette smoking, because of the effects of
passive smoking and also the cost of ill health to
the community. Could cigarettes one day become
illegal? Would people then pay huge sums of money
for one cigarette?

Heroin was a legal drug in the nineteenth century but then was made illegal. When a drug is legalised, like alcohol, people think it's all right to use a lot of it. The consequences can be financial problems, broken marriages, violent relationships, illness, drink driving problems, work-related problems and so on.

When a drug is illegal, there's no quality control. The price goes up. Crime goes up. So there's no easy answer to this question. Many people think heroin should be legalised, because the crime rate would then drop and the quality would be controlled.

But then we'd have to do that with amphetamines, ecstasy, marijuana, cocaine … Where does it stop? And what would be the legal age for buying, say, heroin? Would the drug store or milk bar sell it over the counter? And even then people who were under the legal age would still want to acquire it illegally.

If we educated the community so people didn't need to use drugs to be happy, healthy, pain free and productive, then people wouldn't bother taking drugs.

How can I tell if my friends are using drugs?

You can't, unless of course the person reeks of alcohol and marijuana, or is acting crazy, or is falling over. Someone with red-rimmed eyes might not be smoking dope. They could have an eye-infection or been reading late at night. The only sure way is to test their urine or blood, and that's a bit drastic. The best way is to ask them outright.

ALCOHOL AND DRUGS

Dear Dr Claire,
My friend and I were using speed, just to keep
us awake through the rave, but Mandy suddenly
went all sort of numb and flaked out. We'd all
used the same pills and the same amount from
the same dealer. Why did she react?
Melanie, age 18

Dear Melanie,
There are a number of reasons. Even though the
pills came from the one dealer, the dealer could
have bought them as different batches from
different suppliers, so they may not have been
the same thing. There is enormous variability in
the composition of street drugs. They're not like
prescription drugs where tight controls ensure
that each pill of a particular type of drug is
identical. A lot of speed is cooked up in backyard
laboratories under horrendous, unhygienic
conditions, so you wouldn't really know just
what you were getting. Your friend could have
taken a pharmaceutical drug before she went to
the rave — for example, an antihistamine for
hay fever, or a prescribed drug for anxiety —
which interacted with the speed. How much
alcohol had she been drinking? Is she a smaller
size than you are? Her whole physiology could
be different from yours. People vary in both
their response to drugs and how fast they
metabolise drugs and excrete them from their
bodies. Two people of pretty much the same size

can react differently to the same dose because their underlying body chemistry varies. And what was her frame of mind at the time? All these things have a bearing on what happens when we take a drug.
Dr Claire

Why do people react to drugs in different ways?

1 Different physiology — that is, age, height, weight, whether male or female, metabolism. That's why the anaesthetist in hospital prior to an operation asks you questions about your age, weight, allergies, other medical conditions, other medicines you take, so that the correct dose can be worked out. Even then they have to monitor you carefully under the anaesthetic to make sure you are getting the correct amount, because even people of the same age and weight can vary significantly in how they respond to a drug.

2 Mood of the person taking the drug. Because these are psychotropic or mood-altering drugs, if you're angry and drink alcohol, you'll probably explode. If you're sleepy, you'll get sleepier.

3 The quality of the drug changes and what's in it, if it's an illegal drug. There's no quality control. You might have been fine with the drug before, but now you're not.

4 Hormonal changes can affect the way a female in particular can react to a drug.

5 Other drugs in their system, such as

antihistamines, prescribed drugs for medical conditions, other street drugs or alcohol.

6 The person's immune system is down because they're recovering from an illness.

7 The situation in which the drug is being taken. For example, whether the drug is for physical pain or emotional pain.

8 The environment in which the drug is taken, the people you are with and what's going on around you.

9 How the user is feeling when they take the drug — that is, happy, tired, angry, sad, depressed.

There are so many variables that it is virtually impossible to predict what will happen. So our advice to you is not to do drugs. It is not possible to have respect for your body and yourself and to CARE for yourself and do drugs, they just don't go together. However, we can't stop you from using them, so if you do use drugs there are some things you can do to be a bit safer.

1 Never take anything in a full dose that you haven't tried before. Take only a quarter or a little bit.

2 Never take drugs for the first time when you're alone. If anything happens like you pass out or stop breathing no one will be there to help you, and like you could be on your own and dead.

3 Be aware of the potential risks and complications.

4 Try not to think of drugs as a fun thing without any consequences. Do you really know what this

stuff is doing to your mind and your body?
Also, you could get hooked on this stuff and
wreck your life.

5 If you have a bad reaction, go straight to the
nearest hospital. If you're with a friend who has a
bad reaction, be ready to tell the doctor what
your friend took.

6 If using intravenously, never share a needle. Use
a clean needle each time. Think AIDS, hepatitis B
and hepatitis C — all can kill you and make you
extremely sick before they kill you.

7 Think about why you need this stuff to feel good.
What are the alternatives? Like, go to counselling
to sort out problems and bad feelings, do yoga,
tai chi, take a course that will improve your job
skills, enrol as a volunteer. If you can't stand the
human race work with animals, get a new hobby,
a new set of non-using friends, a new job. In
other words, change your pattern of doing things.

8 Seek help to get off drugs if you get hooked. It's
not easy, but you can do it. Thousands of people
have. So can you.

Dear Dr Claire,
I'm 17 and I have a serious drug habit with
heroin. I have just come out of a private
psychiatric hospital where I did detox, and I'm
seeing a psychiatrist, but I'm terrified I'll start
using again. Do you have any suggestions?
Phoebe

Dear Phoebe,

I believe addictions need to be surrounded on
many fronts. Apart from your individual
counselling, what about some group support?
Have you tried Narcotic Anonymous (NA)
meetings? There you will find support from
other recovering users. Stick with the strength,
especially when you're new. Seek out those who
have good solid lengths of time being clean. Here
you will get phone numbers of recovering
addicts, and when you feel your addiction
speaking to you saying things like 'Just one hit'
or 'You can manage it now', you can ring up one
of the fellow members and get support, even in
the middle of the night. Also, you can't afford to
hang around old friends who are using. It may
sound harsh but you need a new set of friends.
If you hang around with the drug crowd you can
guarantee you'll start using again. Also, think
about things to improve your health and reduce
stress generally. Many people find things like
yoga, tai chi and meditation helpful. Expect that
you will get cravings and stinking thinking
where your addict mind tries to lure you back to
drugs. Say to yourself, 'That's my addiction
speaking, this will pass.' As they'll tell you at
NA, you only have to get through one day at a
time, and those one day at a times can add
up to a lifetime of being clean. Good luck, and
take care.
Dr Claire

12 Stress

Stress is something we all live with every day. Some people handle it better than others, and we can all learn to cope with it better.

Dear Margaret,
I am getting really stressed out at school about exams. I get so freaked out before they start I can't study. I leave the study to the last minute, and then stay up all night. My stomach is constantly churning, I can't sleep for worrying, I think I'm going to fail everything. Help!
Simon, age 15

Dear Simon,
Both Dr Claire and I have done more exams than we want to remember. Doing exams is never going to be a fun experience, but there are things that can be done to help. Talking to someone and getting individual advice and support can be helpful. Do you have a school counsellor or can you talk to your teacher? Some schools are now running classes on dealing with study stress and how to study effectively. There are also courses run in the community on these topics, so look in the Yellow Pages, or maybe your teachers at school may know of some.

Here are our tips:

1 Start early in the year. Find out how you will be assessed, and practise exam questions right from the beginning of the year as you study a topic. This way you get used to doing the questions throughout the year, rather than when the exam is hanging over your head like a big scary thing at the end of the year.

2 Find out what type of exams you will have — short answer, multi-choice, essay — and practise these types of exams for each topic.

3 Talk with your teachers. Seek guidance on how much you need to know about certain topics, so you make sure you cover what is important and don't waste your time studying unimportant stuff.

4 Don't just passively read chapters in books. Make summaries, do problems and practise questions, summarise your summaries, make lists of things you have to remember, like formulae.

5 Use colours in your notes to highlight important points. Consider different-coloured folders for different topic summaries so it's easier to find your stuff. That is, all your chemistry stuff is yellow, your maths is green, English is blue etc. You can buy coloured manilla folders and plastic document folders.

6 Use games and tricks to help you remember stuff. For example, you can put important stuff on index cards with a question on the front and the answer on the back. Practise with yourself or a mate looking at the question on the front, saying or

writing the answer. Then check whether you're right by looking at the back.

7 For stuff like formulae and things you have to know off by heart, make sure you set aside some 'memory time' each day to practise remembering this stuff. Make yourself recall and write down the things you need to know. Correct your work with a red pen, keep it and try again tomorrow. Check to see how you are improving, or if there is something you never seem to be able to remember. After a while you'll remember your corrections with the red pen and it should get easier.

8 Study with a small group of mates. You can present summaries of topics to each other, you can mark each other's practice exam papers, you can ask each other questions out loud or write questions for each other to answer. Not only is this a good way to learn stuff, but it helps to break up the loneliness of studying on your own.

9 Plan your study time and your relaxation time so you know when you are relaxing. You are entitled to that time off, rather than feeling guilty that you should be studying.

10 Find an amount of time that suits you to study, and then take a short break in between study times. For example, two lots of one and a half hour study times with 15 minutes off in between.

11 Plan things to look forward to at the end of your study session, like your favourite hot drink,

listening to your favourite CD. Build in rewards for yourself.

12 Get a good night's sleep before the exam so you'll have a fresh brain. Organise the stuff you need to take with you, like exam number, pens, calculator and watch the day before. Work out how you are going to get yourself to the exam in plenty of time so you are not rushed.

13 If you have a series of exams over several days, leave the exam room and skip the post-mortem where people stand around outside talking about the exam. This will just increase your stress levels and waste your time. That exam is finished, put it out of your mind and go home, have a rest, then start studying for the next one.

14 In the exam, read the instructions and the questions carefully, and answer the question asked. It is sad but true that people write answers to questions they have misread or misinterpreted.

15 Stay healthy, get adequate sleep, take time off for relaxation and exercise, and eat well. Your brain needs to be healthy if it's going to perform for you.

Good luck. Margaret and Dr Claire

What is stress?

Stress means different things to different people. Most people probably use the word to describe either the problems they are facing or their response to those problems. We all have stress. Teenagers, parents,

teachers, everybody suffers from their own type of
stress. Never be ashamed to admit you feel stressed.
Being stressed doesn't mean you are weak or a wimp
— it means you're human.

What sorts of things can cause stress?

Different things will cause stress for different people. As
a teen, things that can stress you include relationships
and family problems, peer pressure and worries about
being accepted, schoolwork (such as, assignments,
deadlines and exams), your teachers' and parents'
expectations of you, worry about choosing a career,
dealing with part-time or full-time work, and all the
changes going on as you grow and change from a child
into a young adult.

- School — there might be too much to get done,
  constantly feeling the pressure of not enough time
  or constant deadlines for assignments. You might
  have difficulty understanding the work. You might
  have a teacher who is a problem.
- Work — you might have a part-time or a full-time job
  that causes you stress. You might have a difficult
  boss, or you might have to face customers who
  complain and demand. You might be worried about
  money.
- Family — you might have trouble at home, such as
  your parents argue a lot, there is violence in the
  home, your parents are divorced, Mum or Dad is an
  alcoholic and you have to deal with that, or you have
  constant fights with your sister or brother.

- Other relationships — maybe you're hassled by having a boyfriend or girlfriend: how serious is the relationship, how often should you see them, especially if you're trying to study. Sex is another potential pressure, whether to do it or not do it, and with whom?
- Career — people ask you, 'What are you going to do when you leave school?' There's a zillion things you could do, how do you choose? Perhaps your mum or dad want you to have a career you don't really want? You might be stressed about getting the marks you need to get you into the course you want to do.
- Modern living — the pace of life is pretty fast these days with computers, faxes, mobile phones … Life can move along in the fast lane, and you can feel that your body and mind are constantly on the go
    A student will have school and studies, but may also have sporting or group activities outside of school, plus a part-time job, plus a social life, plus chores at home …

And some of the things going on inside you can also cause stress:

- Difficult emotions and thoughts — like anger, fear, guilt, and especially lack of self-esteem. All these things can cause you stress as you try to deal with them. For example, if you have really low self-esteem, then just doing the ordinary everyday things like interacting with others can cause you a lot of stress.
- Stressful habits — like procrastination, which means

putting off doing things until the last minute and
then stressing out as you rush to get them done.
Or perfectionism, which means you expect an
unrealistically high standard from yourself and
others all the time. For example, you might re-do an
assignment that is already very good to try to make
it perfect, or you might say that you're no good
because you got a B instead of an A at school, or you
might think that unless you can do something
perfectly you won't do it at all. You might like
painting, but because you think your pictures aren't
perfect, you decide not to paint at all.

Another stressful habit is using substances to
try to cope with stress, like smoking, drinking
alcohol, taking drugs and overeating. All these
things might make you feel temporarily better for a
short period of time, but they don't take away the
stress and you can get an extra problem like
getting addicted.

- Not looking after yourself — like eating lots of junk
  food, not getting enough sleep, not exercising.
- The 'woulda, coulda, shouldas' — giving yourself a
  hard time mentally by going over and over what
  you 'shoulda' done, what you 'coulda' done, what
  you 'woulda' done and so on. 'I shoulda included
  that diagram in my assignment', 'I coulda played
  in the footy team at school if only I'd tried out
  for the team', 'I should never have had sex
  with Peter', and on and on it goes. You can really
  stress yourself out going around and around like

this over things that are in the past. You cannot change what has already happened, no matter how much you think about it. What you can change is your attitude to what has taken place. Try to forgive yourself for past 'mistakes' or things you wish you'd done differently.

How do I know if I'm stressed?

Here are some of the things you might notice happening in your body: feeling tense or nervous, irritable or cranky, tight muscles, churning stomach, trouble sleeping, tiredness, feeling wiped out, lack of concentration, headaches, stomach aches and cramps, overeating, undereating, itchy skin and rashes, frequent illnesses such as colds. It's a long list!

Also, you might have the feeling that you are constantly busy and pushed for time. You might long to say 'stop all this' so your body and mind can have a rest, but you can't stop and just have to push yourself on to the next thing.

Dear Margaret,
I just feel I can't keep going. There's so much pressure — schoolwork (I go to an all-girl private school and the pressure's on to do your best all the time), I have netball practice on Monday, do piano on Tuesday, ballet on Wednesday, extra maths tutorials on Thursday followed by saxophone, and youth club and tai chi on Friday. On Saturday I play netball. And on

Sunday I have to go with the family and visit
my grandparents.

Help! I feel really tense lately.

Findlay, age 14

Dear Findlay,

Obviously you are doing far too much. You
haven't any spare time to daydream, chat to
friends on the phone, do unorganised fun things.
Sometimes we try to do more than humanly
possible. Our bodies and minds need some down
time, where we don't have to do anything. You'll
have to decide what you're going to drop, or else
get up an hour earlier to fit more in. I'd opt for
dropping something!

Margaret

Why is it important to deal with stress?

First of all, because stress can make you feel so darned
miserable, and secondly, because over a period of time
the stress can build up and affect both your emotional
and physical health. If the stress goes on for long
enough either your body or your mind or both can get
worn out, and you can become physically or emotionally unwell. This stage, where your body and mind give
out from too much stress, is sometimes called 'burnout'.

Mandy's Story

I was getting these terrible headaches up the
back of my neck and head. Then I started to feel

dizzy all the time and very tired. Mum took me
to the doctor. He sent me for an X-ray of my
head and to see a specialist. I thought I had a
brain tumour. It turned out I didn't have a brain
tumour, I had stress!
Mandy, age 16

Stress can give us all sorts of strange feelings and
symptoms in our bodies. Many people end up going to
see their doctor, thinking they have a physical illness,
only to find out what they are suffering from is their
body's reaction to stress.

Can there be good stress as well as bad stress?

We all need some challenges to make life interesting
and exciting. If we have nothing at all to do or think
about, after a while we become bored, frustrated and
fed up, and feel stressed from having nothing to do.
Think of the strings on a violin. If they're all loose and
floppy there is no music. When they have just the right
amount of tension and pressure as they are tightened
up, then you can get beautiful music. But keep
tightening the strings until they're so tense and taut and
under so much pressure and twang, they break!

When there is a nice balance in your life between
stress and being relaxed, you will be performing and
feeling your best. As stress piles on you, you'll begin to
suffer the negative effects we've talked about. When
you are feeling stressed-out, it means that you are being

pushed past your optimal level of tension. In the long term, this can lead to burn-out.

Of course we all have times when it seems we just have to put up with stress — for example, during exams there will be stress. However, even then you can help yourself to cope with the stress as best you can by following our suggestions on pages 257–59.

By noticing the unpleasant feelings of stress in both your mind and body, you will recognise when you are going past the optimum level of stress and pressure for you. Use those unpleasant feelings as a barometer or gauge of how stressed you are. You can take action to keep your pressure and stress at a level where you can enjoy your life and perform well.

How come my best friend never seems to get stressed and I am always stressed?

We all know people who seem to be able to run around and do extra things like taking extra subjects at school without getting stressed, and we all know people who get stressed out over what to us looks fairly minor. Just as people come in all different heights and sizes and some people are good at running and some people are good at art or maths or whatever, so there are some people who are 'good at stress'.

They may have inherited genes that mean they are more robust when it comes to the stresses and strains of life. Their bodies might tolerate stress feelings better than the rest of us. Probably the way they think about themselves is good, and they have a good sense of self-esteem. You have to work with what you've got. Some of us are more sensitive than others to the stresses and strains of daily life, but there is a lot you can do to improve how you deal with stress.

Our advice to you is to RELAX: Rest, Enjoyment, Living well, Attitudes, eXercise.

Rest

We can consider that 'rest' covers rest and sleep. Did you know that research reveals that many people in modern-day life simply do not get enough sleep and are what is called 'chronically sleep deprived', which is a fancy way of saying they need more sleep. Guess what? That includes many teens. If you think back in history people tended to get up when the sun rose and went to sleep when it got dark. Nowadays we have electric lights and appliances that mean we can stay up until all hours reading, watching TV, using the computer, and so on.

Try going to bed earlier for a week and see if you notice a difference in how you feel and in your stress levels. The average amount of sleep recommended for an adult is eight hours, but many teens will need more than this. Some experts say we should be getting at least nine hours of sleep a night.

Dr Claire,
Every night I go to bed and can't get to sleep. Then when I finally do, I wake up two hours later. Should I take sleeping pills?
Gabrielle, age 17

Dear Gabrielle,
No, I don't think you should take sleeping pills,
you just need to change your sleep habits. Try to
create a little routine you go through before you
go to bed, so you signal to your body that now is
sleep time. Make sure your bed is comfortable
and the room is quiet and dark. Make sure you
don't drink cola or coffee or eat a lot of
chocolate for at least a few hours before bedtime
as the caffeine can keep you awake. Write down
any worries before you go to sleep, and tell
yourself you'll deal with them tomorrow. And
practise a relaxation technique before you drift
off to sleep. If after all this you still find you are
not sleeping well you may need help from an
expert. There are sleep disorder clinics that have
doctors who specialise in sleep problems. But
often simple measures at home will do the trick.
Dr Claire

Here are some tips for good sleeping:
1 Try to create a routine that you go through before
   you go to sleep. It's hard to suddenly stop in the
   middle of doing something, like studying, and
   then leap into bed and expect to go straight to
   sleep. Your mind is likely to be still whizzing
   around at top speed. So try to establish a routine
   that signals to your mind and body that you are
   shutting off for the day and going to sleep. You
   can try having a shower and imagining all your
   worries and tension being washed away and

flowing down the plughole. Or you can wash your hands and face and imagine your tension draining down the plughole. One of Grandma's favourites was drinking a mug of warm milk before bed. Do a relaxation exercise or listen to a relaxation tape.

Try some aromatherapy — dab some diluted essential oil (maybe lavender or orange) on your neck and wrists, the smell can signal to your brain and body that it's time to go to sleep. Or massage your feet and lower legs. Or write in your diary or journal to mark the end of the day.

Some people like to read before they sleep, but be careful you don't become so engrossed in the book you keep on reading and next thing you know it's midnight. Sleep experts say you shouldn't read in bed, if you want to read sit out of bed to do it. The reasoning is that you should associate your bed just with sleep, not other things like reading.

2 Try to keep to regular sleeping hours, so that you go to bed at about the same time each night and get up at about the same time each day.

3 Avoid drinks that contain caffeine, like coffee, tea or cola, or eating a lot of chocolate in the late afternoon or in the evening. Caffeine can take three to six hours, sometimes longer, to get out of your system. Caffeine is a stimulant — that is it hypes you up — which is not what you need when going to sleep. Try decaf coffee or decaf tea,

or try herbal teas. You'll find there are stacks of different herbal teas that contain no caffeine.

4   Try to make your bedroom quiet and dark. If noise is a problem, get yourself some earplugs. If light is a problem and you can't afford a new blind or curtain, buy yourself some eye shades. You can get them in the travel section of a department store or a travel shop.

Dr Claire,
I get into bed but my head spins around worrying, or sometimes I go off to sleep okay but then I wake up with everything spinning around in my head. What can I do?
Ben, age 17

Dear Ben,
Things always grow out of proportion in the middle of the night. You can wake up thinking, 'What was *that* all about?' Keep a folder or an exercise book with a pen by the bed. If you start spinning things around in your head and worrying, then write down your thoughts and worries. Then tell yourself you'll deal with them tomorrow, whether that will be by yourself or by getting help from someone.
Dr Claire

Imagine sticking all your worries and problems into a box. Now close the lid and lock the box. You can open the box tomorrow when you are awake and prepared to deal with these issues.

Once you've put your worries away in their box, drop the box to the bottom of an imaginary ocean. Let it sit right down on the bottom of the ocean floor while you float up gently through the water to the surface, where it is so warm and peaceful floating on the surface, surrounded by peace and safety …

Okay, so what about rest? You've all heard of the saying, 'Don't just sit there, do something.' Well, the reverse of that saying, 'Don't just do something, sit there', can be a very good saying for your mental health.

We all need a bit of time in our lives where we don't have to do anything. Life can end up just so busy as we rush home from school, rush off to play sport, rush home to do our homework, get up in the morning and rush off to school again. We need some time out to do nothing much … maybe sit out in the backyard and pat the dog, look at the clouds floating past, lie on the bed and read a magazine or just stare at the ceiling and let our minds wander, have a daydream.

If you're used to being frantically busy it can feel weird and kind of scary to stop and do nothing for a while. Regularly practising relaxation exercises can help with that feeling.

Try to have some regular time where you don't have to be anywhere or do anything — time out, just for you. Don't feel guilty because you're not 'doing something useful', because in fact you are doing something very useful for your mind and body by having some down time, some dawdle time.

Also, if your schedule is so tightly packed that you are exhausted from going to school, studying, going to a hobby class, doing music lessons, going to scouts, being on the school debating team, having a boyfriend or girlfriend, having a part-time job … whoa there! Maybe it's time to give something the flick. It's tempting to try to be more than human these days, because let's face it, there are heaps of interesting things to do for hobbies and sports. If you're constantly on the go and feeling worn out, it might be time to give some of your activities the chop, so you can live your life in a more comfortable way.

Enjoyment

A very interesting thing to do is to imagine you've been taken hostage by a group of dangerous terrorists who announce that all the hostages are to be executed tomorrow morning. This gives you less than 24 hours to live. As you look back at your life, what is it that you wish you'd done more of, what is it that you feel sorry you've missed out on, and what is it that you have valued most in your life?

Write down your list. Maybe it looks like this:
I wish I'd gone surfing more often.
I wish I'd spent more time outdoors in nature.
I wish I'd seen more movies.
I wish I'd told my friends how much they mean
    to me.

Whatever you have on your list, when you read over it, you'll see things that you'd wish you'd spent more time doing and the things that you value.

Now, it so happens that a SWAT team conducts a raid and you are rescued from the terrorists. You go home with your list. How can you make sure you start to do more of the things on your list?

Putting activities and things that you enjoy into your life is a good way to help relieve stress. Very few people have lives where they enjoy everything. For most people their studies and/or work is a mixture of things, ranging from parts they really enjoy to things they can't stand but have to do. For example, at school there may be subjects and teachers you really enjoy and others that you really dislike. You might feel fairly neutral about some subjects. And sometimes studying, even the subjects you do like, is just a hard slog.

Try to find some enjoyment every day. Often it's little things that can cheer you up, such as using nice-smelling soap when you have a shower or silky body lotion or talc, eating foods you really enjoy, listening to music you like, taking your dog for a walk, patting your cat, lying on your bed reading a good book, chatting to friends on the internet, writing poetry, drinking a big steaming mug of your favourite tea or cocoa, watching the sky, looking at trees and birds and flowers, going for a run or a swim, watching your favourite TV program, going windowshopping, riding your bike, going out with friends for a cappuccino …

If your life becomes a constant daily grind of things

you have to do with no opportunity to do things you really enjoy, then life becomes simply a burden to endure. Make sure every day there are things that you enjoy, that you value — things that have meaning for you. They don't have to be complicated or expensive things, or time-consuming. Actively seek out things you enjoy and these will become the substance of the life you remember as you grow older.

Living well

Living well means taking care of yourself. It means you don't endanger your health and wellbeing by doing things like smoking, drinking too much alcohol, and shoving illicit drugs into your body and mind. It means eating well, not filling your body full of junk food. Good nutrition helps your body deal with stress. That means plenty of fruit and vegies (at least five to seven servings a day) and cutting down on fatty fried foods and other high fat and sugary foods.

Good nutrition gives your body and mind the good things they need to help you fight stress in your life. Grandma used to say, 'You are what you eat.' This means if you eat lots of junk you're going to feel like junk, but if you eat healthy that's going to help you feel healthy.

Living well means looking after yourself mentally and physically, taking CARE of yourself (caring, acceptance, respect and encouragement). It means you value yourself most of all: you put yourself first. Consequently, you don't have sex with someone unless *you* want to, not because someone else wants you to.

You don't put drugs into your body just because somebody else is doing drugs and says you should too. It means you *value yourself* most of all, and you get the hell out of any situation that is causing danger to your body or mind.

Living well means that your need for acceptance and approval by others does not matter as much to you as *your own* acceptance and approval of yourself. Read that sentence again. This is one of the most difficult things we need to learn as we grow up. Of course we all want to fit in and be accepted by our particular peer group We all have to conform to some extent with society's rules to live comfortably within the society. But if you know that the most valuable thing you have in your life is yourself, then you won't compromise yourself on important issues like sex and drugs just to please your friends. Find yourself a different group of friends who respect themselves and respect you, and wouldn't dream of expecting you to do something harmful to yourself.

Attitudes

Dear Margaret,
I've seen the counsellor at school because I'm really stressed. She said I have an attitude problem and I worry too much about the little things in my life. How can my attitude affect my stress level? And doesn't everyone worry?
Julia, age 17

Dear Julia,
You sound like a person who worries a lot. It
also sounds like you have a case of the 'What
Ifs'. The What Ifs can take on huge proportions
— you worry about something, and then nothing
happens — and you think, 'Why did I worry?'

How you talk to yourself daily can change
your attitude. When you start the What Ifs,
change them to happy, positive ones. 'What if I
meet someone exciting today? What if I do some
fantastic art work? What if the new babe in
Year 11 notices me and asks me out? What if
Mr Brown thinks my assignment is really good?'
I think that's what the counsellor means by
'attitude'. Give it a go. It doesn't cost anything
except some time to reformat your thinking.
And it *does work* because I do it all the time.
Margaret

Your attitude can affect your stress level, but what
about your attitude to worries and problems? Let's look
at that.

Get yourself a folder and several pieces of paper. At
the top of each piece of paper write down the thing
that is worrying you. You might write 'school' on one,
'girlfriend' on another, or 'acne' or 'sex'. Then under
each heading write down all the things you can think of
that are worrying you about that particular problem.
Also, write down anything you have done so far to try
to fix that problem.

Here's an example of what Con, age 16, wrote.

Sex
My worries
Everyone else is having sex.

My girlfriend Jenny says she won't have sex, she says she's not ready and she wants to wait until she's older.

I'm ready for sex. I'm going to go crazy if I don't have sex.

I could dump Jenny and find another girlfriend who'll have sex.

I could keep Jenny and have sex with someone else, and keep it secret from Jenny.

What I have done so far
I've talked to Jenny until I'm blue in the face, I've taken her out for romantic evenings, I've tried to get her worked up.

What else can I do?
Pressure Jenny some more, but I don't want to force myself on her.

Find another girlfriend, but I'll miss Jenny.

Who can I talk to about it?
I wonder if I can talk to Dad about it, or maybe to Uncle Steve?

Getting your worries and problems out on paper can make a big difference. You can 'brainstorm' about your problem, and write down all sorts of possibilities and potential solutions. Then you can sit back and look at all of what you've written for a particular worry or problem, and ask yourself, 'What can I do about this?' 'Who can I talk to?' 'Who and/or what could help?'

Remember, you can get help for worries and problems by talking to people, getting information (your school or local library might have books that could help — for example, on sex and drugs and relationships) and trying to nut out a plan of action to take to sort things out.

Dear Margaret,
I'm stuck with my problem, nothing's going to change it. My Mum died two years ago and my Dad's got this girlfriend called Cindy who's a total witch and she's moving in to live with us.
Mark, age 13

Sometimes there are problems that we can't change. However, what we can change is our attitude to the situation. Sometimes we have to accept that things are the way they are. We don't have to like it, agree with it or approve of it. We can say to ourselves, 'Well, that's the way it is. Now, where do we go from here?'

Mark is probably going to be stuck with Cindy moving in. He has two choices really. One is that he can be totally miserable and be really difficult to get on with and make the whole thing worse, and the other is he can accept that Cindy is moving in and do the best he can to get on with his life. That doesn't mean he should pretend to himself that everything is wonderful when clearly it is not, it just means he does his best not to make the situation any worse. For example, although he can't stand Cindy he can try to be polite and get on with her. It would be good if Mark could talk to his dad about Cindy, and explain his concerns and his feelings. Also, it will help Mark to keep a journal where he writes down his feelings, and to have a friend to talk to about Cindy.

Exercise

Research shows that people who regularly exercise feel better mentally and physically. Their anxiety and stress levels decrease, their self-esteem and confidence increase, they are less tired and have more stamina to get through the day, they have increased immune systems (better germ-fighting ability so they get fewer colds and flu), and generally they feel better. As you grow older, exercise decreases the incidence of heart disease and can also decrease your chance of getting cancer and osteoporosis (thin bones).

There are two main types of physical exercise:

1 Aerobic exercises, which are exercises that increase your heart rate and give your heart and lungs a good work-out. Your lungs take in more oxygen and your heart works harder to pump the increased amount of oxygen around your body to supply the muscles that are working hard too. During the work-out, your body releases

chemicals called 'endorphins' into your bloodstream. These chemicals give your body and mind a natural high. Aerobic exercises include brisk walking, running, cycling, swimming, the treadmill or stepper at gym and aerobics classes.

2 Strengthening exercises are exercises like working out with weights and weight machines. These exercises help you build stronger muscles and also help to produce an inner feeling of personal control and power. Both girls and boys can do strengthening exercises. Learning how to do these exercises properly is important. It is more effective for your muscles to do the exercises using correct technique at a lower weight rather than try to heave heavier weights around using incorrect technique. If you are interested in weights training your local gym should have a qualified instructor who can help you work out a good program for you, or your phys ed teacher at school may help you. Girls can also do weights training. It doesn't mean you're going to grow huge muscles and look ugly, it means your body will look toned and it can certainly help with improving your self-esteem because you will feel better.

To improve your body's fitness and resistance to stress you need to exercise at least three times a week for at least 30 minutes a time.

Here are some tips for successful exercising:

- Try to pick something you like. If you hate jogging, it's probably not realistic to think you will go jogging three times a week. Try some different exercises or sports until you find something you like.
- Make it realistic. If you love swimming but the nearest pool is a 45-minute drive away, unless your parents are prepared to drive you it might not work if you decide you'd like to go swimming three times a week.
- The most important thing is *consistency*. It's no good going to the gym every night for a week and then not going at all for three weeks. You don't have to push yourself to achieve more and more each time you exercise. Better to find a level of exercise that you enjoy and that you can stick with week-in and week-out. The consistency is what will build fitness and stamina.
- Don't forget your local gym. Often they have student memberships that are cheaper than regular membership fees. They might have classes like aerobics, which come in all different types these days but are usually upbeat and held with music. Or you could have a personalised program combining weights training with aerobic training like the treadmill or stepper. If you have a gym at school you may be able to work out there regularly.
- Choose something where the time commitment fits in with the rest of your life — don't pick something that will take up so much of your time it becomes a burden in an already tight schedule.

What about relaxation exercises?

This is the other type of exercise that is very important in relieving stress. Just as physical exercise can help to relieve stress in your body and mind, so relaxation exercises can help to relieve stress. You can learn relaxation exercises at classes or by reading books or listening to tapes. Your local library probably has books and tapes on relaxation. We will show you some simple relaxation exercises that you can do. It's best if you can practise the exercise twice a day for 10 to 15 minutes a time, but even once a day can help.

Lie down somewhere quiet and warm where you won't be disturbed for the next 10 to 15 minutes. Become aware of your breathing. As you breath in you feel your tummy rise up and as you breathe out you feel your tummy fall.

Now start at your feet and in your mind say to yourself 'Feet relax, feet relax'. You can tighten and then relax the muscles in your feet as you say this to yourself. Then you focus on your calves and you say, 'Calves relax, calves relax.' Again you can tighten up your calf muscles and then let them go floppy. You then work your way up your body to your thighs, tummy, chest, back, upper arms, lower arms, wrists and hands, shoulders, neck, face and head.

In this way you move from your feet to your head, focusing on each different part of your body in turn, tightening up the muscles first of all, then letting them go floppy as you tell yourself to relax that part of your body.

Once you have gone all over your body and relaxed each bit, then you can say to yourself, 'My whole body relax'. Imagine that each time you breathe in you are breathing in peace and calm, and each time you breathe out you feel all the tension leaving your body. You can say in your mind the word 'peace' or 'calm' each time you breathe out. You just lie there quietly breathing in and out and feeling all the tension and stress drain out of your body.

If you like you can imagine yourself somewhere nice, like down at the beach or in a forest or in a lovely garden. You can imagine the smell of the ocean or feel the sun on your skin or the smell and colours of the garden or whatever fits your special scene of relaxation. Imagination yourself lying there, maybe feeling a gentle breeze on your body as you breathe in and out saying 'peace' or 'calm' to yourself.

When you first start learning to relax you may find your mind wants to keep whizzing off and thinking about other things. Imagine the thoughts are just clouds in the sky, and let each cloud float past you without you getting caught up in the thoughts. Or you can imagine your thoughts written on a giant blackboard in your mind and you just wipe them off with a duster when they come.

The idea is to lie still, quiet and peaceful, feeling very calm and relaxed. With practice it becomes easier to achieve this state of relaxation. Ten or 15 minutes is usually enough to start with, you might want to use a timer. When you have spent enough time being relaxed

then you can count up to five in your head and open
your eyes and get up from your relaxation session. Once
you get the hang of it you'll find it easier to lie down
and relax without your thoughts or worries intruding or
bugging you.

Relaxation exercises have been shown to be very
beneficial to your emotional and mental health. If you
feel stressed at school and you can't go and lie down
somewhere, just imagine your special scene of
relaxation, like the beach or the garden or the forest,
focus on your breathing in and out and say the word
you use in your relaxation exercise like 'peace' or 'calm'.
Doing this can take just a few seconds and you will feel
your mind and body start to calm down.

13 Depression

Dr Claire,

I feel terrible. I hate everyone, especially at school. Inside I just feel sort of sad and empty, like nothing matters anymore. I don't want to get out of bed in the morning. I've given up going to netball practice, so now I'm chucked off the team and everyone hates my guts for letting them down, not that I really care anymore. I've been writing a lot of poems — this is one of them:

> The sky is black
> I can see the sliver of moon
> But I can't touch it
> I am cold and I bleed
> Tears
> Dripping
> Surrounding me in a pool ...
>
> I will drown in my tears and no one will
> notice me gone ...

I'm not eating much, everything tastes like nothing anyway . On weekends I stay in my room, and often I cry cos I just feel so awful. Mum and Dad keep going spacko because I've been like this for two months. They yell at me to pull myself together. They keep telling me how lucky I am to have everything, and that I should

stop feeling sorry for myself. Their words can't hurt me. Nothing can hurt me anymore because I felt dead inside.
Aimee, age 15

Dear Aimee,
You could have an illness called depression. It can strike anyone at any age, sometimes without much warning, and it makes you feel like crying and you feel sad and low and miserable. You need to see your doctor who will sort out whether you do have depression and will advise you on things that can be done to help you start to feel a whole lot better. You don't have to struggle on by yourself feeling this bad, there is lots that can help you. So either go with your parents or alone to your doctor, and get some help, okay?
Dr Claire

Unfortunately, depression is something that can happen to anyone, and it makes you feel really low, desperate and unhappy. Let's look at some of the things we know about depression in today's world.

What is the difference between 'the blues' and depression?

We all have times when we feel blue or sad, feel down in the dumps, or perhaps we just don't want to go on. Sadness is a normal and healthy human emotion, part

of a normal life. Especially as a teenager you
might be prone to moodiness or feeling blue. As a teen,
your hormones (chemicals in your brain and
bloodstream) are changing and this can affect your
body chemistry. Sometimes you feel moody, negative,
stressed out and emotional. These feelings are normal
for lots of teens and are usually temporary, lasting for
a few hours or days.

Sometimes we don't know why we feel sad or blue,
and other times we know it's because we got a bad
mark for a test, or our team lost the match, or we've had
an argument with our friend. Usually the blues go away
in a few hours or a few days. But if your mood remains
low for several weeks and interferes with your ability to
get pleasure from your life, to go to school or work, get
on with others, and to do the things you used to enjoy,
then you may be suffering from depression.

How do I know if I have depression?

If you have a depressive illness the symptoms may
include feeling really low, experiencing feelings and
thoughts of hopelessness, helplessness, worthlessness,
guilt, pessimism (thinking nothing will work out right)
and sadness. You may feel like there is no pleasure or
joy in your life. These feelings and thoughts may last
throughout most of the day, nearly every day. You might
feel tired and irritable, and have trouble concentrating.
You lose interest in school, work, hobbies and sports.
Your eating patterns may change, you may lose your
appetite or overeat. You may have trouble sleeping,

often waking up early in the morning. Some people oversleep to try to escape how lousy they feel. Although you may sometimes try to put on a brave face, underneath you feel awful.

You may feel withdrawn from other people, and if you are depressed you may want to avoid social situations like going out with friends or going to clubs or group activities, and you may avoid doing things with your family. Other things that can happen with depressed teens include being really, really irritable and having angry outbursts, having trouble at home and at school, getting into trouble with the law and drug abuse. In severe cases of depression teens can become preoccupied with death or harming themselves. This is very serious. We will talk more about this on page 000.

Sometimes it is hard for you, your parents, teachers and other adults in your life to know whether your feelings are just part of the normal ups and downs of being a teen or whether they are symptoms of a more serious problem like depression. But feeling miserable for several weeks without getting any better means it's possible that you have depression.

Have people always got depressed?

'I cry during the day and into the night. I am weary with my groaning. My heart is sore. My strength is dried up. Lighten my eyes, or I may sleep the sleep of death …'

No, this is not part of an email sent by a depressed teen to Margaret. These are the words of King David, written almost three thousand years ago. Depression has been around for thousands of years. There wasn't much that could be done for depression then, but nowadays there is lots that can be done to relieve the suffering of depression.

Why do people get depressed?

No one knows exactly why some people get depressed and others don't. Most doctors and people who do research in the area of depression would agree that there are a number of different factors that together lead to depression.

First, there are the physical factors — that is, your physical body and the chemicals in your brain, which are called neurotransmitters. These chemicals or neurotransmitters help our brains work so that the cells in our brains, called neurons, can communicate with each other in different parts of the brain and with the rest of our body. Now sometimes these chemicals get out of balance, so there isn't as much as there should be of some of the chemicals in our brain, and this can lead to getting depressed. Some of the names of these chemicals include serotonin and noradrenaline.

Second, there are the psychological factors. Now, before you panic this doesn't mean you are psycho or crazy. This means your mind, your emotions or feelings, and your thoughts. There are certain ways you can think and feel about yourself and other people and the world around you that can lead you to get depressed. Sometimes you don't even know that you're thinking in these ways, until someone else points it out to you. For example, you might have learnt to think that nothing you do is any good, that nothing ever works out for you. You might think that you are to blame for bad things that happen to you or to your family or people around you. Sometimes we have learnt to think about ourselves in very negative ways which can make us feel very depressed.

Third, there are environmental factors, like your family, the society you live in, what's happened to you at home and at school. Environmental stresses are things that happen around you. These stresses may be present now or have happened in your past, and may trigger depression. Examples are your parents getting divorced, problems with your friends, sexual and physical or emotional abuse, violence and poverty.

Dear Dr Claire,
My sister has severe depression and has been in hospital and everything with it. I find it a bit hard to understand, because I feel pretty good and am involved in lots of sports and activities, and she hardly leaves the house. Am I likely to get it too?
David, age 15

Dear David,
Sometimes within the one family there can be someone with the illness of depression and their brothers or sisters feel fine. Depression is not something that you 'catch' off somebody. Your

life seems to be going well for you now, so I would try not to worry too much about getting depressed in the future but work on building your self-confidence and your self-esteem because this will help you generally in your life. I hope your sister is getting proper help for her depression. If you are worried about her you should talk to your parents about your worries. Sometimes seeing a different doctor or having different medication can make a big difference. This might be something for your family to consider if she doesn't seem to be getting better. Sometimes too it can be helpful for the whole family to go to counselling for some family therapy, as sometimes the undercurrents that are going on in families can be difficult, and that is also contributing to the depression of a family member. I know it's not easy but try to be supportive of her as much as you can. Hopefully one day soon with the right help she'll start to feel a lot better.
Dr Claire

Here are some facts about depression:
- depression is common. According to research as many as 26 per cent of women and up to 12 per cent of men will experience major depression at some point in their lives.

  Each year about 4 to 8 out of every 100 teenagers will get clinically depressed (i.e. seriously depressed).

- a famous sports star can get depressed
- a beautiful model can get depressed
- someone who gets straight A's at school can get depressed
- teachers can get depressed
- doctors can get depressed
- many famous people have suffered from depression
- people of every race, ethnic background and religion can get depressed
- being depressed does not mean you're weak
- being depressed does not mean you're crazy
- you do not need to be ashamed of depression
- you don't have to feel depressed forever, because depression can be treated.

What can be done to help teens with depression?

There is a whole lot that can be done to help you if you have depression, but first you need to visit your family doctor or general practitioner. There are physical illnesses that can cause you to feel low. These are things like problems with your thyroid gland (which makes thyroid hormones), being anaemic (which means there isn't enough haemoglobin chemical in your blood, making you feel tired and run down), and other illnesses that can leave you feeling low.

When your doctor has ruled out any other illness that might be going on, then treatment for your depression can be worked out. If your depressive illness is a milder form, then going for some counselling or

therapy may help you. If your depression is more
severe you may need to take prescribed medication to
help lift your depression, as well as having counselling
or therapy.

What is counselling or therapy?

Counselling is 'talk therapy'. It means you go to see a
specially trained person and you talk with them about
your feelings and thoughts, how low and miserable
you've been feeling. What they can do is show you how
some of your thoughts and feelings have got out of
balance. They might help you to see that your self-
esteem is really low. They might help you to understand
the things that have been going on in your life that have
triggered off the depression. And they can help you
learn new skills when dealing with your own emotions
and in interacting with other people.

Usually, therapy will help you with both your
thoughts and your feelings. 'Therapy' is a broad term,
because in fact there are many types of therapy.
Traditionally there was psychoanalysis, where you lay
down on a couch and talked and the therapist sat
behind you and didn't say much. Different types of
therapy were developed, ranging from behaviour
therapy, which focused on your actions and how to
change them, to things like primal therapy which has a
focus on helping your body release painful feelings that
may have been buried inside for years. Most therapy
these days involves sitting in a chair while the therapist
sits across from you and listens but has a lot of input,

explaining things, pointing out things, making
suggestions for ways you can change your thinking, and
helping you deal with painful and difficult feelings.

Dr Claire,
I hate school and all the teachers suck. My
parents are morons and my sister's an idiot. My
life's full of crap which is not my fault, because
people keep picking on me. My parents want me
to get some help. No way am I going to go and
see a counsellor. Why should I?
Jay, age 13

Dear Jay,
You say that you hate school, all the teachers
suck, your parents are morons and your sister's
an idiot. Plus people keep picking on you and
you say your life's crap. So if you see a counsellor it can't make life much worse than it is, can
it? That's why I think you should give it a go.
Dr Claire

Years ago, even before people knew about counselling
or therapy, they knew it was a really good idea not to
keep things bottled up inside. They called it 'chewing
the fat' or 'getting it off your chest'. Although talking to
a friend or relative can help, it's often more useful to
talk with someone who has special training in the area
of thoughts and feelings, and in how to help someone
with depression. If you needed your appendix out you'd

go see a surgeon, wouldn't you? You wouldn't expect your best friend (unless she's a surgeon!) to take out your appendix. So in the same way you should go to see a person specially trained deal with depression. Now, you're actually very lucky because there are people specially trained to help you 'get it off your chest'.

Research has shown that talk therapy and learning new skills to teach you to deal with your emotions and thoughts can help you to feel heaps better about yourself. You can learn things that will help you for the rest of your life.

Who do you see for counselling or therapy?

There are different people who do counselling and therapy. These include your family doctor, psychiatrists (medical doctors who do extra training so they specialise in dealing with people's thoughts and feelings), psychologists (people who are trained about the human mind, how it thinks and feels), counsellors and social workers (people specially trained in how to listen to others and help them).

And remember, if things don't seem to be working out with the person you go to see, or you don't feel comfortable or safe with them, then you can try somebody else.

Do you have to pay?

That depends on who you go to see. Your local doctor or psychiatrist will be partly or fully covered by

Medicare. If your family has private medical insurance this can help pay for seeing a psychologist. You (or your family) can pay to go and see a psychologist or counsellor, or use community services that are either free or at reduced cost. Some public hospitals offer free psychiatry and psychology services. Your local doctor or local community health centre or your local council should know about the free services in your area. School counsellors are usually free.

Dear Dr Claire,
My friend Renee has been very depressed so now she sees a psychologist. She told me that she has to write things down about how she feels during the week, or do drawings about what's happened in her life or how she feels about things. It sounds a bit weird. I thought psychologists and people like that just talk to you.
Belinda, age 15

Dear Belinda,
It's a really useful thing to write down how you feel or express yourself by drawing things. Writing and drawing are powerful tools that can help a person express their innermost anxieties and fears and frustrations. That's why Renee is doing this. Hopefully it will help the psychologist help her.
Dr Claire

Writing and drawing are both very good ways to express yourself, your feelings and how you see things in your life, even if you aren't depressed. Many teens keep a journal or diary where they write down what's happening in their life and how they are feeling. Drawing can be really good, especially sometimes when things are hard to put into words. You don't have to draw scenes or people, although you can if you want to. Sometimes it's just good to draw your feelings with colours or shapes or symbols, but whatever you want to draw is fine and can really help get your feelings out, especially when you are upset. You can show your drawings to trusted people or keep them to yourself.

What natural ways are there to help depression?

Dr Claire,

I have been depressed for several months and my doctor has put me on antidepressant medication. I don't like taking pills, like how do I know they won't change my personality? Are there any natural things I could take instead? What else can I do?

Brianna, age 16

Dear Brianna,

I'm sorry to hear you have been depressed. I think what you need to do is go back to your doctor and talk to him or her about your concerns. It could be that your doctor has put you on the antidepressants because he or she is concerned that you have more than just mild depression and thinks the medication will help you. These types of medications won't change your personality, what they are designed to do is to lift your mood so you don't feel so depressed. Are you also having some counselling or therapy?

In terms of 'natural' things you can take, there is a herb that has been used to treat depression called 'St John's wort' (I know, that is a weird name, 'wort' is an Old English word for plant). It comes in tablet form so you don't have to chew leaves or anything. However, you should not just start taking this willy-nilly, because it can interact with some prescription medications including some other antidepressant medications. Even though it is a herb it still has some side effects of its own. You can talk to your doctor about whether this would be suitable for you. St John's wort has been shown to help with mild to moderate depression, but for more severe depression you'll probably need different antidepressant medication.

Exercise has been shown to help with depression. Regular exercise can definitely help to improve the level of your mood. The trouble is that when you are depressed you often don't feel like exercising because you feel low and sluggish. But even if you can get yourself out for a regular brisk walk every day, this may well help, and if you can get into other exercise like swimming or

gym or whatever, this is very likely also going to
help. Other things to help your general wellbeing
include eating well and getting adequate sleep.
Also, you may want to look at ways to help to
reduce stress in your life, maybe by learning
relaxation or some simple meditation techniques.
I hope you are feeling much better soon.
Dr Claire

Antidepressant medicines

If your doctor prescribes antidepressant medication,
then it is likely to help you. Until recently there weren't
the types of antidepressant medications available that
there are now, and the old-fashioned ones didn't seem
to work so well for children and adolescents. Now
we're lucky to have newer antidepressant medications
that can really help to lift your mood and help you feel
a whole heap better about yourself, and can make your
thoughts clearer so when you go for your talk therapy
you get more out of it.

Dr Claire,
I've been very depressed. I'm going for
counselling. My doctor prescribed antidepressant
medicine for me. If I feel really bad should I
take some extra?
Ben, age 17

Dear Ben,
No, it is not a good idea to start taking extra
medication without discussing it with your

doctor. The dose will have been worked out for you by your doctor, so what you need to do if you're not starting to feel better overall is to go back to see him or her and tell them. They can then decide if the dose should be changed, or whether you would be better off changing to a different type of antidepressant medication. So hot-foot it back to your doctor, okay?

Dr Claire

As in any illness, your doctor will work out which medicine is best for you and how much of it you should take. Dosage of medication is worked out based on things like your age, your weight and the type of symptoms you have. Taking too much can make you feel awful and is not good for your body. Only take what your doctor tells you to take. Sometimes the medicine can take a few days to a week or so to start working, as the tablets help the chemicals in your brain build up to the correct amount again. Your doctor will adjust your dose if it needs to be adjusted. Talk to your doctor about what is the best dose for you. Ask about any possible side effects that might occur. Sometimes you will be started off with a small dose and then your doctor will gradually increase the dose. If you have any questions about your medicine don't guess, ring up your doctor's office and say you have a question about your medicine or go back and talk to your doctor.

I hurt my body

Dear Margaret and Dr Claire,

I hope you don't mind me writing to you, I know you must be very busy and everything. My life is a mess. My mum died when I was six. I never knew until this year when I found out from my cousin that my mum had committed suicide. My grandmother has just come back to Australia after living overseas for years. I want to ask her how my mum killed herself but I am too afraid. I have been depressed for as long as I can remember. I am fat and I am ugly. I come from a very well-off family. My dad tells me I have everything. He thinks I'm weak because I am fat. He would get really pissed if he knew I was writing to you. He hates me, as far as he is concerned he just wishes he didn't have me around. He brings home these young glamorous models who he meets through his work. I just stay in my room most of the time. I know I am a bad person, I know I must stay away from other people so I don't upset them. Also, and you'll find this really really gross, I've started cutting myself with little cuts on my arms and legs where no one can see. I don't even know why I do it. I know you probably won't have time to write back to me but anyway I really like your books.

Amber, age 17

Dear Amber,

You've had a lot to cope with in your life. It's
not easy to lose your mum when you are so
little, and then to find out she had committed
suicide must have come as a big shock to you.
It sounds like you have struggled with
depression for a long time, and also it seems you
are very alone with all of this. Sometimes people
start cutting at their bodies when they feel
overwhelmed inside by hurtful and difficult
feelings. When they hurt their bodies they can
shift the focus from the inside emotional hurt
and confusion to the physical sensation of the
cut, and it may give the illusion that you can
control the hurt inside by hurting your body.
However, hurting yourself physically can start to
take on a life of its own, where you can start to
feel compelled to hurt yourself more often and
feel you've lost control over it. Then you not
only have the original problems inside that lay
behind physically hurting yourself, but you have
the whole other problem of trying to stop
hurting your body. You are not the only person
to do this, and psychiatrists and psychologists
know how to help with this.

Amber, you need to get some help with all of
this. You need to see a doctor who will refer you
to a psychiatrist or psychologist for help with
your depression and with hurting yourself. The
shame that you feel about yourself is part of the
problem, somewhere along the line you've learnt

that you are a bad person. You are not a bad person, you are a troubled person. Talk to your father, or what about your grandmother, or else go on your own to your doctor. Be honest about what you've been doing. It might take a while to untangle all of what's been going on in your life, but you can with proper help get out of this lonely dark place that you are currently in. Also some people say that when they are learning not to cut at themselves that holding an ice-cube against their skin instead of cutting can help, as it gives you a sensation on the skin you can focus on. Write back to us and let us know how things go for you.

Margaret and Dr Claire

Friends and depression

Some of us will go through depression in varying forms at one stage or other of our life. But what if your friend has depression and you want to help?

Dr Claire,

My best friend Lachlan has had depression. He even had some time off school. Now he's come back to school I'm not sure what to do. Some of the kids found out he was depressed and they call him names like cry-baby and girl, because he cried in school once before he had the time off. How can I help?

Liam, age 13

Dear Liam,
You can help Lachlan by being a good friend.
Since depressed people often end up very
isolated, you can ask Lachlan if he'd like to join
you in some outings or activities that involve
socialising. Lachlan may want to talk to you
about what happened when he was depressed
and what's going on now. The best thing you can
do is to listen, and maybe you want to share
with him times when you were feeling down too.
The other kids at school are probably ignorant
about depression. If Lachlan had been off school
to have an operation like having his tonsils out,
they wouldn't be calling him names, would they?
You might talk to the others and explain to
them how depression is an illness and they
could be suffering from the same illness
themselves one day.
Dr Claire

Family and depression

When one member of the family suffers from
depression it can be a huge strain on the rest of the
family. Sometimes it's not the teenager or younger
children but one of the parents.

Dear Margaret,
My mother has depression. She cries a lot and
stays in her room. Dad and I have to look after
her when she's really depressed. I worry that
it's my fault that she's depressed. She's told me

she wished I'd never been born. Sometimes she
tells me if she hadn't had me she'd have left my
dad a long time ago and she wouldn't have all
these problems. I feel really bad.
Jessica, age 14

Dear Jessica,
It's very hard for a teenager to deal with an ill
parent in the home. It's not your fault that she's
depressed and you didn't cause it, okay? I
gather that she's getting medical help?
Remember that she is ill and wouldn't be saying
these upsetting things to you otherwise. Try to
find things in your own life that give you
enjoyment, to give you a break away from the
worry with Mum. Work at building your own
self-confidence and self-esteem. Find activities
where you can mix with others away from the
house. Talk to your dad and try to have a good,
supportive relationship with him. If you're still
feeling bad then get some counselling for
yourself, as it can be a big stress on you to have
a very depressed parent. Hang in there and help
look after Mum. She'll thank you for it very
much one day.
Margaret

When children and teenagers have parents with
depression, it can be very hard sometimes for them to
understand that their parent's depression is not their

fault. Adults are responsible for getting themselves help when depressed, which means that the parent needs to be getting help from a professional person like a doctor.

Parents are responsible for bringing you into the world. If you've made it onto planet Earth, then you belong here. So even if they tell you they wish they'd never had you or that you've ruined their life, remind yourself of how you got here in the first place. It sure as heck wasn't your fault you were born! Depressed parents can say all sorts of hurtful things because they are seeing you and their world through the haze of depression, so they're not thinking rationally.

Sometimes the whole family can go to see a counsellor so all the messy things in the family can be brought to the surface and talked about, instead of everyone trying to pretend. If a parent does try to blame you for their depression, remember that depressed people don't think clearly because their brains are often in a fog. You can say, 'I'm sorry to see you depressed and unhappy Mum/Dad, but I know that it's not my fault.' Believe it.

14 Suicide

A lot of people find suicide a very confusing and scary topic, and don't want to talk about it. Sadly, every year in Australia young people commit suicide. Nowadays we think that talking about suicide and educating people about suicide will help to reduce the number of people who commit suicide.

Dear Margaret,
My best friend Sharnia killed herself four months ago. I didn't even know that she was unhappy, which makes me feel awful. I mean, we were so close and I should've known that something was wrong. I really miss her. I don't understand why she took her own life.
Cassie, age 16

Dear Cassie,
I'm sorry you've lost your best friend. Believe me, if she didn't want you to know that things were wrong, that's how she wanted it. I know you probably feel that if she'd confided in you, you could've helped her. But she didn't. So you can't blame yourself. I really think grief counselling would help you, because you're not only dealing with the terrible shock of her death, but also that she was your best friend

and you're missing her. So please seek some help. Your school counsellor or your doctor should be able to put you in touch with someone who specialises in grief counselling. Best of luck for the future.

Margaret

Often we don't really know exactly why a certain person kills themselves. People who are emotionally and mentally healthy and stable don't kill themselves, so usually something has gone haywire in that person's emotional and mental health. These are some of the reasons people kill themselves:

1 Depression — when people have a severe depressive illness (sometimes called major depression or clinical depression), their thoughts and feelings get right out of balance. They feel so sad and miserable and they will be that way forever. They think there is no way out and, sadly, they decide to take their life at a time when their thoughts and feelings are all muddled up. Being seriously depressed is thought to be one of the main reasons why people kill themselves.

2 Other types of mental illness — there are other illnesses that can also muddle up a person's thoughts and feelings so they get seriously disturbed about themselves and their life and commit suicide.

3 To escape from what seems to be an impossible situation in life. In this case, people can see no way out of their problem except to kill

themselves. Again, their thinking is usually out of balance and they are mentally unwell. They can see no other solution to their problems. However, there are always other options than suicide to solve problems, it's just that sometimes people need someone else to help them see that and to help them sort things out.

4 People commit suicide for what may appear to be particular reasons, like they wanted to get back at someone and so on, but research shows us is that the majority of people who commit suicide are suffering from a mental or emotional illness at the time.

Emotionally and mentally healthy people don't commit suicide.

Dr Claire,
I've heard that you shouldn't talk to a depressed person about suicide because it will give them the idea.
Jodie, age 17

Dear Jodie,
It used to be thought that if you mentioned suicide to a depressed person that you might somehow give them the idea. What we now know is that severely depressed people may be thinking about suicide anyway, and they appreciate that someone understands enough

about how awful they are feeling to bring up the topic of suicide. It can be a big relief to a depressed person to be able to talk about suicidal feelings, because this may be something that for them is a very scary part of their depression. Also, by talking about the feelings and bringing it out this can open up ways to get help and deal with suicidal thoughts and feelings. Professional people such as doctors, psychologists and counsellors will ask depressed people who come to see them if they have had thoughts of suicide.

Dr Claire

Myths about suicide

Because suicide can be a pretty scary topic for a lot of people there are a number of myths or untrue sayings about suicide. Let's look at some of these.

Myth 1: **You shouldn't talk about suicide because it will give someone the idea.**

If suicide is on someone's mind it is vital that it is brought out into the open. If someone you know is hinting about suicide, talk about it. Saying the word 'suicide' won't give the person the idea to go through with it. Talking about suicide will help the depressed person know that you understand just how strong depressed feelings can get. Talking about suicide can help the person to see that there are other options, and that help is available.

Myth 2: **People who talk about suicide never do it.**
Talking about suicide is a warning and should be taken seriously. If you have a friend or a relative who talks to you about suicide, you must talk to a responsible adult about it and let them know. Tell your parents if your brother or sister talks to you about suicide. Never keep secrets about suicide. The person needs urgent help and assistance.

Myth 3: **After an unsuccessful suicide attempt the person will be ashamed and embarrassed and won't try it again.**
People who have already tried to kill themselves are likely to try again unless they get help.

Myth 4: **People who attempt suicide want to die.**
Many people who make suicide attempts really don't want to die. They may be crying out for help, and perhaps use a method which leaves room for being saved or rescued. However, there is sometimes a thin line between a suicide method that

will leave you alive and one that will leave you dead. Many die who really didn't plan to. Jemma, age 14, took a small amount of pills in an attempt to show how desperate she was feeling. Unfortunately, Jemma did not realise that these pills were very harmful to the liver in even fairly small doses. They caused major damage to her liver and she died. Stories like this one are very sad and the deaths so unnecessary. Obviously, if you are feeling desperate there are much better ways to let other people know how you feel and that you need help other than by making a suicide attempt. Talk to people and get some help for your hurting feelings and thoughts.

How would I know if someone was planning to suicide?

Any clues or hints of suicide should always be taken seriously. Clues can include:

- making threats of suicide, either directly like saying, 'I'm going to kill myself', or indirectly, 'You'll miss me when I'm not around any more' or 'You don't have to worry about me any more'
- behaviour or statements indicating the person is saying goodbye

- listening to songs about death, drawing or writing about death
- giving away valued possessions
- statements about being a burden to others
- talking about death
- previous suicide attempts.

What should I do if my friend threatens suicide?

Try to stay calm and tell your friend that you are concerned. Tell him or her that you know how to get help so that the bad feelings can be made to feel better. Stay close with that person while you tell a responsible adult.

You can tell a parent (either your friend's parent, your own or a parent of a friend), a teacher or school counsellor or the principal of your school, an adult relative or friend, a coach, a youth worker or youth group leader. If you don't think you can tell any of these people you can help your friend call a suicide helpline listed in your local phone book.

Don't say that your friend should just 'snap out of it'. If they could they would have.

Don't promise your friend you won't tell anyone. Your friend needs to know that you care and will get help.

Don't try to bluff your friend by saying 'Go ahead and do it'.

Don't think your friend is 'just trying to get attention'.

Kylie's Story

I went to visit my best friend Jess and she said
she was going to kill herself that night. Her
boyfriend dumped her a month ago and hooked
up with another girl who used to be a friend of
Jess's. I knew she'd been really upset, but I
didn't realise that she wanted to kill herself. I
didn't know what to do, then I told her we were
going to ring a crisis line and I rang up with
Jess there. The lady on the phone was really
good. She really understood. She spoke to me,
then to Jess, and Jess agreed to go home and
talk to my mum, because her own mum was at
work. That's what we did, we went home to my
mum, who listened to Jess, who was like crying
and really upset. Jess stayed with us until her
mum was home from work. Then we drove her
home and my mum talked to her mum, who took
her to talk to their local doctor.

Kylie, age 13

What if I want to kill myself?

Dear Margaret,

Sometimes I just want to end it all. My dad's in
jail and my mum has a new boyfriend, Dave,
who keeps trying to feel me up. The teachers at
school all think I'm feral, so I can't ask them for
help. I can't tell Mum because her last boyfriend
did the same thing and then she had to choose
between him and me. She chose me. But this

time I think she'll choose Dave. If I really feel
that bad that I want to kill myself, what's wrong
with killing myself? Well, it's my body and my
life, so why can't I? Is it legal?
Ash, age 15

Dear Ash,
Whether it's legal or not isn't really the big
issue here, is it? No one can stop you killing
yourself if you are really determined to do it,
but why waste your life? The point is, you don't
know what's going to happen for the rest of it.
It's like reading half an interesting book then
shutting it and not knowing what happens next.
Once you get over this lousy part of your life at
the moment, things could be heaps better in the
future. Okay, I've never had a dad in jail or a
mum with a boyfriend who's tried to feel me up,
but I know that it must be awful for you. But
not that awful that you can't get some help. Find
someone you can talk to about all this. Look in
the phone book for sexual assault services
(because that's what happened to you) and ring
them up and talk to them. They will understand
what's happened to you and should be able to
offer you a lot of help. I'll bet Mum would
choose you over Dave. Tell this man that if he
touches you, you'll tell your mum *and* you will
also go to the police. That should scare him off.
And if he comes near you, do it!
Margaret

One of the saddest things about people committing suicide is that they think there is no hope, no help for their problems or painful feelings. To commit suicide is to use a permanent solution for what is a temporary situation. People who are feeling desperate, who are in all kinds of mess and trouble in their life, *can* find help. Really bad thoughts and feelings don't have to last forever. You can be helped to feel better about yourself and your life so you no longer feel like you want to die. You can be helped to again find pleasure and joy in your life.

Let's say a tap in your house is leaking. Now, you don't fix the problem by going out into the street and permanently turning off the water supply. You fix the problem with the actual tap. In the same way, you don't fix a problem with yourself by turning off the life source, you get help to fix the problem.

You don't have to kill yourself to fix yourself

How do I tell someone I feel like killing myself?

If you feel like killing yourself it is important you talk to someone about how you feel as soon as possible. You can say, 'I really feel bad — I don't want to go on living', or 'I'm having thoughts of harming myself, I need to get help', or 'I'm having thoughts of dying. Can I talk to you about it?'

Some people mightn't know what to do, or they might brush you aside. Or they might panic. Or they might laugh it off and tell you you're just having a bad hair day. But it's important that you find someone to listen to you.

Dear Margaret,
People think I'm just being a drama queen when I tell them I want to kill myself. In fact, Dad even laughed at me. I don't have a mother, she died when I was four. I tried to talk to my aunty about my problems but she was a total waste of time. She said I had turbulent hormones. How do I know if I try to talk to someone else it won't be the same waste of time? No one seems to care how bad I feel inside.
Sarah, age 14

Dear Sarah,
Unfortunately, some people you try and talk to might not be as much help as you'd like. When you're feeling this bad it's very important you find someone you *can* talk to. Dad and your aunty might have been freaked inside when you talked to them about it, so they dealt with it badly by trying to make a joke. You could try Dad again and tell him it's not a joke, that you seriously feel this way. If he just can't handle it *don't give up!* There's your school counsellor, or maybe a trusted teacher (it can be any teacher at school you trust, even the school principal), a friend's parent, your doctor, a youth worker, or try one of the phone crisis lines or Kids Helpline. These days teachers, counsellors,

doctors and people on the phone services are
trained in how to talk to young people who are
struggling with painful feelings. Keep trying to
find someone until you get the help you need.
Write back to me and let me know that you've
found someone to help.
Margaret

It's too awful to talk about
Some people think they're the only person in the whole
world with a particular problem, or who are feeling so
hurt and confused and angry. Believe us, there are
others out there with the same problems, the same
feelings.

Dr Claire,
You're a doctor so I guess you see and hear all
kinds of things. But I'm even scared even
talking to you. I couldn't talk about my problems
to anyone really. I'd be too embarrassed or
ashamed.
Todd, age 16

Dear Todd,
My grandma used to say, 'There's nothing new
under the sun'. This means that whatever's
happened to you or whatever you're thinking or
feeling, you're not going to be the only one in
the history of human kind to feel that way or
have done that thing or had that thing done to
them. There is *nothing*, and I mean *nothing* that

you can't talk about. Often it's sexual things we've thought or done that cause us a lot of shame, or maybe somebody abused us sexually and we feel we could never talk about what happened to us because we feel so ashamed. Maybe we've been physically or emotionally abused in other ways. Maybe we've hurt others or abused others. Maybe we've been physically hurting ourselves. Maybe we've broken the law.

Anybody who works with people, like a doctor or a psychologist or a counsellor, will have heard all sorts of things you couldn't begin to imagine. The terrible shame you are feeling is part of the problem. Find someone you trust and start talking. You can blurt it all out at once if you like, or it might take you a while to slowly trust someone and you might try them out with a little bit to start with. Anybody you go to see like a doctor or counsellor should treat you with respect, and not put you down or laugh at you or tell you that you are a bad person. And remember, if it doesn't feel safe or right when you are seeing a counsellor or a doctor, you can leave that person and find someone else who you do feel more comfortable with.
Dr Claire

I want to pay-back my parents
Don't trade in your life to get back at your parents. Remember that most people who kill themselves are

mentally or emotionally ill, and will benefit from getting proper help for their problems.

Dear Margaret,
This probably sounds really bad but I hate my parents. I can't tell anyone because my father's the mayor of the town and my mother's got a business. They are high profile. They take no notice of me and most nights I'm home alone with TV dinners while they're out at functions. They don't even try to understand my problems because they've never got time to talk. I've figured that if I kill myself they'll know how much I hate them. The town will be shocked and they'll be exposed for who they really are. They've done other stuff that I don't want to talk about too. So, what's the best way to kill myself? I don't mind pain, but I want to really teach them a lesson they won't forget!
Sam, age 13

Dear Sam,
Please don't kill yourself, because no other human beings are worth killing yourself for. Yes, your parents would be shocked, upset, the town would be horrified, all that stuff. But time would heal their grief and their lives would go on. Whereas yours would be snuffed out like a birthday candle — no more birthdays. Think carefully about this. I really think you'd be better to tell them how you feel and if you can't

do this face to face, then write them a letter and explain how you feel. Or get a trusted relative or friend to act as a mediator. You also need to find someone like your doctor you can talk to about all of this. It's hard when you come from a prominent family, but there are plenty of famous families where behind the scenes there are all sorts of problems. But don't kill yourself, okay? Write again and let me know how you get on.
Margaret

Here are some healthy things you can do to show your parents how angry and hurt you feel. First thing is to try sitting down with your parents and telling them how you feel. Or you can write them a letter and give it to them. Write down your feelings and the things that bug you and how bad you've been feeling. Another thing is to find a trusted adult — another relative, your teacher, your coach, your counsellor — and open your mouth and start talking about everything. Do you know there's even counselling where teenagers and parents go together to talk to a counsellor? This is often called family therapy. Then you can say all the stuff you want to, open and honestly, without having to pretend anymore.

Emma's Story
I used to feel suicidal a lot. When I was seven I remember I wanted to throw myself out of the car. My mum and dad abused me, and I grew up thinking I was a really bad person. Then I got

really depressed when I was 15. I drew lots of pictures of me being dead — skeletons and hanging myself. I really wanted to die, I felt so bad.

I ended up seeing my local doctor and then he sent me to see a psychiatrist. No way was I going to see a psychiatrist, like no way, I wasn't crazy. Anyway, they said if I didn't go to the psychiatrist they'd put me in hospital. She said I was severely depressed and I had to take pills to help and I had to go to see her and talk about how I feel and stuff.

At first I thought, I'm not taking any pills. But Dr Jane was really nice and after a while I felt like I could tell her all sorts of stuff. She never laughed at me or put me down. I decided I'd take the pills. I showed her my drawings of me being dead. She gets me to do drawings at home and I bring them in and I talk to her about them. She helps me a lot.

I haven't drawn a picture of me being dead for about four months now. You know, last week I went bushwalking with three friends and my friend's sister and her boyfriend. We came to the edge of a mountain where there was a waterfall. I stood there looking out at the view, looking out and looking down. Usually, when I was up high I'd get thoughts of how I wanted to throw myself off. You know, now I didn't feel like that. It was sunny and I looked out into the blue sky and I thought, Hey! I don't

feel like I want to jump off anymore! I laughed
to myself.

It hasn't been easy sometimes, but I can tell
you there's no way I'd kill myself now. I've got a
life to lead and I feel so much better than I did.
Emma, age 16

Conclusion

A famous writer named Ernest Hemingway once wrote that 'The world breaks everyone, and after some are strong at the broken places'. Well, it would seem that the world does bash some people about badly, while others get by with hardly a scratch. But if you feel broken by things that have happened to you or continue to happen to you, then we hope that you can find what you need to help yourself heal so you will be strong at those places in yourself that have been hurt.

There is a lot we can do to help ourselves when bad times come, but also it is important to reach out for help sometimes when we need it. This may mean your family and friends. We are also lucky to live in a time when there is a lot more known about how to help people with problems. So make sure you don't try to struggle on with problems alone when you could gain so much by going to have some counselling or seeing your local doctor or calling a phone helpline or going to a support group.

Some problems can be fixed fairly simply, others are going to take longer to sort out and untangle all the emotional hurts and things that are wrong. Never give up. Keep searching for a way to make a bad situation better for yourself.

There is a saying that 'When life gives you lemons, make lemonade'. Which means try to make the best of the lemons or the difficult situations in life. Sometimes it is the difficult times in our lives that can lead us to a greater understanding about who we are, how life works, and to give us empathy for others during their difficult times.

We hope your lives are happy and healthy. We'll be thinking of you.

Other Books about important Teenage Issues by Margaret Clark

Secret Girls' Stuff

You want to ask a boy out on a date but what if he says no? You walk up to a group of girls and they say, 'This is a private conversation, do you mind?'

You wish you could sink through the floor when your teacher embarrasses you. Your best friend suddenly isn't talking to you.

There's this boy who's trying to bully you into going out with him. Your clothes don't fit.

Your family just doesn't understand you. You don't understand yourself either.

One minute you're happy and the next minute you're sobbing into your pillow.

Does this sound like you, or someone you know? Then read on ...

mellissa has not been able to take her eyes off that boy since we got to the movies ...
SECRET GIRLS' STUFF
and that means You!
keep out!
Margaret Clark
Contains material of a sensitive nature, which some readers may find disturbing. Age 15 plus.

More Secret Girls' Stuff

In **More Secret Girls' Stuff**, I deal with issues that are even more compelling than those in the first book **Secret Girls' Stuff.** Girls tell me that their lives are being wrecked by the cruelty of other girls who say bitchy things — sometimes they are forced to move to another school. Some guys say they love girls, have sex with them then dump them.

Some girls dump guys and are then victimised by being called sluts. Some parents throw things. Loved ones die and there is no one to understand.

How do you know if a guy likes you? What if you ask him out and he says no?

And if he says yes, how can you kiss him when your braces keep cutting up his mouth?

Read on and find out what goes on behind closed doors ...

I love acting though I'm very shy. But when I perform I forget about being shy. Why can't I be like this all the time?

more

SECRET GIRLS'
STUFF

keep out!

I'm stuck in the middle of two bitching friends. Help!

Margaret Clark

Contains material of
a sensitive nature,
which some readers
may find disturbing.
Age 15 plus.

Margaret Clark is one of Australia's most popular writers for young people. She has worked as a teacher and university lecturer and at the Geelong Centre for Alcohol and Drug Dependency. Her novels for older readers include *Coolini Beach: The Search*, *Coolini Beach: Cool Bananas*, *The Big Chocolate Bar*, *Fat Chance*, *Hot or What*, *Famous for Five Minutes*, *Kiss and Make Up*, *Hooking Up* and a trilogy about the Studley family: *Hold My Hand or — Else!*, *Living with Leanne* and *Pulling the Moves*. *Back on Track: Diary of a Streetkid*, *Care Factor Zero*, *No Standing Zone*, *Bad Girl*, *Secret Girls' Stuff* and *More Secret Girls' Stuff*, for young adults, have become best-sellers. Margaret lives in Geelong and enjoys reading, sailing and walking with the family dog. She writes full-time.

Claire Fox is a doctor who lives in Victoria. She enjoys yoga, reading, writing, picnics, movies and making time to do nothing. She doesn't enjoy going to gym, but goes anyway to keep fit. She has a long-standing interest in personal growth and development, and a keen interest in helping teens deal with difficult times and develop their potential. For relaxation she likes to go walking in the bush or along the beach with her husband and her dog Ben.

Dr Claire on a trip to Canada.